For you. And you.
And even you...

LEQUIN

Prologue:

Welcome to Bradford County!

Bradford County, Pennsylvania isn't much more than a pit stop on the way to Williamsport, Wilkes-Barre or New York City. But growing up there was undoubtedly interesting.

I was born and raised in Salt Springs, PA, smack dab between the small burghs of Towanda, Canton and Troy. It was really like any other small town. Quiet and peaceful, with the exception of the occasional heroin overdose or hunting accident that required a middle-aged man to hitch a ride to the Troy Hospital via ambulance. (Took on average damn near 30 minutes for it to get there though.)

Not much ever happened but when it did, it was accompanied by a litany of secrets and corruption.

But there some were damn good people at the top of the Salt Springs Totem Pole, like Chief Doug Harris. Man lost his daughter to cancer when she was only 13. His wife just about lost it but he was able to cope, even though it was damn difficult. After he lost his daughter in '98, he lost tabs on the town. Heroin and meth started to take its course and there was nothing he could do with his small budget and lack of resources. He realized that these were important matters, and while he tried to fix it, petty shit started to emerge.

Take the kids of Salt Springs for example. We were bored. Bored as fuck. When you have to drive a goddamn hour to get to civilization, you had to make your own fun. We took up the innocent pranks, the streams of toilet paper that flowed from Mr. McNeil's pine trees gave us a high, but it was an elation that one gets when sniffing a Sharpie. We wanted the full-on snort. The closest to that peak was the Bishop Toilet Papering of '06, it was October 14th to be exact. Police were called, I maneuvered through backyard shrubbery whilst evading the flashlights. No injury, no trouble, no visits from the reporting officers, Pete Wile and Luke Larson. The only commemoration of the annual shit-paper gala was a small trail of mud on some Nike's and clumps of scattered burdock upon the sleeves of my Pittsburgh Steelers hoodie.

Officer Larson was a complete dickhead. While on duty he sought out the parties amongst the young folk. Said extravaganzas normally took place at the O'Sullivan residence. Sara was a damn dime piece with rich parents who didn't give a shit about the parties, hell, they bought the booze. Grey Goose to Molson, whatever the fuck they wanted, it was unreal. While Ron and Angie swung up to Lake Nephawin or skiing in the Poconos, just about every damn student at Salt Springs High School polluted their livers in their family room.

It was only commonplace for Luke Larson to scope out the O'Sullivan estate from up the road; always dining on his Pump-n-Pantry (scaled down Sheetz, or Wawa for those on the East Coast) chicken sandwich and a Coke. He didn't care about the notion of underage drinking, mind you. His concern was following teenage girls to the edge of his jurisdiction, and relay their options; they all lick the Larson Lollipop, or they were headed to the drunk tank in Towanda. The 45-year old cop with a wife and three kids never failed. Rumor has it, his body count was well passed 300.

He was a third generation police officer of Salt Springs. His old man was police chief for 27 years, and Luke was bound to step into those shoes eventually. He twilighted as head basketball coach for Salt Springs High School. He lucked his way into all of that success too. His Spartans finally picked up a winning season in 2006, the first one that Salt Springs High had in 35 years and of course, ole boy felt he was the reason. Of course it had nothing to do with a 6'7 center and 6'5 power forward that came up through the junior high ranks. If it weren't for the Millionaires of Williamsport High, they would have picked up three straight district titles. Well, actually, Wilpo High wasn't the *only* reason, his fear of running a zone defense kind of fucked them too.

Welcome to Small Town, U.S.A! Those with the dough, run the show!

Amongst the most powerful was the aforementioned Ron O'Sullivan. He owned 17 properties in town and while not keeping tabs on his rentals, he was the only dentist in Salt Springs. His wife was the principal of Salt Springs Elementary and lead the "Mothers Athletic Club", a cultish group. Nay, it was borderline autocracy. Angie was the dictator, and two of her cronies, Mira Davidson and Jen Reynolds had a voice, but no others did. They organized and produced all of the sports fundraisers and they all failed miserably each year, except one. A basketball game between students and teachers but there was a catch... everyone rode donkeys... while playing basketball... wild thought, aye?

And then there was me, I even acquired some immunity, at least before Kate Ford kicked me to the curb. 9th through 11th grade I was untouchable. In a town of 2,000 people in Northeast, PA, three straight All-State football honors will make you an absolute God. Everyone knew you already, but that wasn't enough. They wanted to be your family.

It all came to an end though in '08. That was the last call for me as deity of Salt Springs, Pennsylvania. The day of our opener that year, Ryan Wilson and I glued birdseed to the driver's seat of Coach Ward's Dodge pickup. Early September, too, we thought. Fuck it, stink up the joint, let's pour some mayonnaise on the cloth front seat. This all because that bastard made us run five rounds of suicides the day before. Wyalusing was the opener each year, and Coach Ward hated that trip, especially on the bus.

He about came off his rocker when he saw the interior doused with Hellmann's and seed. Coach was in a pinch, though. The bus was his only option and you better damn well believe that son of a bitch hurled all over one Danny McBride, his starting fullback. Wyalusing Mountain took its fair share of casualties, and that Friday afternoon Coach Tom Ward joined the list of its fallen soldiers.

That was only the start of the douchebaggery, my friends. A month later, Todd "Bush" Brown ratted on Dave Ramsey for sneaking liquor into the Homecoming Dance. Bush thought he was slick, like Iago from Othello, or, for the intellectuals, the parrot from "Aladdin". I'd venture to say it was the parrot. Kid's back looked like it was covered with black feathers.

Dave made him write his American History paper, but so it turned out, Dave got a better grade than Bush! At the time, in all of our teenage jockiness, we thought Bush was just being a real jackass about the whole thing. So we went and lit up that hairy fucks house with rotten eggs and Ryan even took a shit on his porch. The Browns knew who the culprits were, or at least who one culprit was.

We had custom wristbands, like those Livestrong bracelets (damn, this story is really showing its age) for football. Somehow mine broke off and it was found on their sidewalk. Officer Wile showed up to the doorstep later that night dangling the green band with black letters transcribing, "SALT SPRINGS SPARTANS| BRISTOL #31". After five minutes of explaining myself, Wile and Chief Harris left only demanding that I apologize. Nothing further.

Then there was the bathroom incident. Mr. Hollinshead caught Kate Ford and I nailing in the men's room the last day before Thanksgiving break. It was the last Thanksgiving that we were together so at least I have one fond memory of our relationship. Her hands gripped the sink in the handicap stall and I was going at it from behind.

Kate and I didn't get a whole ton of chances to do it, our moms were unemployed. Her dad was a psychotic Baptist minister that would expose a crucifix every time I saw him like I was Linda Blair in the mid-70's. *No sex before marriage! No dating until you are in college! You are going to get pregnant by breathing! Get that piece of shit Bristol kid out of my house!*

Anyways, Hollinshead barged in, looked at us for a second and panned to Kate. Hollinshead was a big shot math teacher and he liked Kate a lot. Too much. Kate used to wear low-cut, yet modest tops that barely exposed her cleavage. On those days, he snuck up from behind and looked over her as she sat.

"Quit chewing gum!"... "Put your phone away!"... "Oh, sorry Ms. Ford, my mistake."

It was annoying at first but it ended up being kind of funny. Hollinshead wanted just wanted a glance at my girl's, well... girls. What's wrong with that? Except for the fact that he was twice her age and was her *fucking* math teacher.

After the second of perceived daydreaming in the bathroom, presumably a mental Photoshop of his body rocking the ass of the minister's daughter in lieu of mine, Hollinshead said, "Finish up, Zack."

Silver Spring High, Silver Spring High, You're the fairest school to me.... This motherfucker told me to *finish the job*. Oh boy, oh boy! Where else could you get that reply?!

It down spiraled after Christmas. Mom lost her unemployment, I injured my neck in a baseball game that spring and eventually Kate started seeing a dude from Mansfield. Kid from her church, and of course, his parents were heavy donors to the clergy.

Yes sir, you guessed it, her damn dad approved of him. He goddamn encouraged it!

When I lost Kate, I felt like I lost everything. The scent of "Night Blooming Jasmine" didn't leave the nasal cavity. I got her a bottle of it on our first Valentine's Day together. She loved it and wouldn't wear anything else.

Her green eyes sparkled and bloomed like sunflowers when she smiled. Her right canine was slightly crooked, but it only *posed* as a simple flaw. It really wasn't though. She was self-conscious, but she had no reason. Her smiles weren't visible for long periods of time, she always covered her mouth quickly after but it never hid the high cheekbones of the most beautiful face that I have ever seen.

I couldn't take it. I exaggerated the neck injury and quit football. Toledo, Western Michigan, and Rutgers among many others lost interest in my services at tight end and I lost interest in just about everything. Sadness turned to anger and anger turned to rage, but the final feeling was to do everything imaginable to forget about her. Half-assed suicide attempts, a visit to the school guidance counselor, you know, the works.

Why the long preface? Well, every small town has the dirty cop and every damn village is a product of elitism. But it's most real similarity to larger populations is their youth. All kids rebel. Sara O'Sullivan drank like a fish, Ryan Wilson was a vandal, Kate Ford disobeyed her father at all costs. But me? I didn't. I still don't drink, I love my mom more than anything and I would never wreak havoc on someone else's property. I was a good kid, but I had some sort of venturesome attitude that only a few other people could ever possess. Again, simply put, petty little pranks weren't enough.

We tried the kids' stuff; toilet papering, egging, soaping windows, none of that could pass the time quick enough before getting the fuck out of that deadbeat town forever. We got through September fine, but on October 3rd, 2008, a chosen alternative would quite literally haunt us forever.

It's an almost cliché group, a hedonist, the depressed, a punk, a genius, two hot girls, a jock and the only two minorities in a virtually all-white town. We were a nine-student Psychology class that was taught by Mrs. Paulette Bishop, the victim of the "Shit-paper Gala of 2006."

Alumni weekend is finally here, and now, I'm kicking myself in the ass for not backing out of the class presidential race in '08. Should have just let Emma Green win, even if she was a bitch. Now, I have no excuse to *not* give this speech. Work's slow. Goddamn Red Wings don't give journalists a whole hell of a lot to write about these days.

No hotels in The Spring anymore. Mom moved to Washington, DC. My sister, Beth, lives in Denver, Colorado and the most of my family left with them. So here I am, sipping on my morning coffee in my cousin's guestroom in Williamsport, PA, still about an hour away.

I have been dreading this reunion. But to be frank, meeting up isn't the issue. I loved them. I still do and *always* will. Husbands, wives, children, careers, etc. that's great. I'd love to talk about that. But all of us in Salt Springs together… damn… I really don't know how this is going to go. Nor do I want to find out.

It's been 10 years since I've stepped foot in that town, and I have been thinking a ton lately of the terror that began in October of '08, especially after the article in the Williamsport Review this morning.

Three Dead in Crash on Route 6
Emma Winters, 16, Austin Pettit, 17 and Tyler
Lucas, 17, all of Stoney Corners, died on impact.
Drugs, nor alcohol were a factor.

It was happening again. Someone went in.

It may be a coincidence but I'm sure it had something to do with that motherfucking church. It wasn't even a church, or even just a building, it was...

Hell. No doubt about it. Or at least the closest thing to Hell that a human can endure.

It's Bradford County's deepest, darkest secret. It's not like Camp Crystal Lake from "Friday the 13th" or Woodsboro, California from "Scream." It's darker and much more sinister.

But most of all, it's *real*. Everything about it is *real*.

So here I sit. Just thinking. In about 12 hours, I'll be speaking to the Salt Springs Class of 2019. But before I do that, I must tell you a story. And damn, I have one hell of a story for you.

Evil isn't just a personality trait, or some kind of idea. It's also a physical place, and it stands in Lequin, Pennsylvania.

15

PART 1: WHATEVER YOU LIKE

Stacks on deck

Patrone on ice

And we can pop bottles all night

Baby you can have whatever you like

I said you can have whatever you like

-T.I. (2008)

CHAPTER 1: Psych Class

I began the long walk along the front of the cafeteria to discard the contents on my plastic green lunch tray. It was the typical high school lunch; a chicken patty, side cup of applesauce and two chocolate milks. The minute hand turned from 12:41 to 12:42. A loud bell rang to send us to sixth period.

My heedless jaunt to the dish-washing and waste paper stations wasn't fully due to the irrelevance of Mrs. Bishop's upcoming class. Psychology was a filler for us. We needed a few easy credits to graduate and they were it. For Mrs. Bishop, she was only a stone's throw away from retirement, so she didn't necessarily take it serious either. For the last three weeks, our class lecture focused around the shuffleboard league at the VFW. Sounds boring, in reality though, it was *fucking* great.

Kate was the main reason for the dilly-daddling. After a six-month hiatus, the pastor's daughter was back in my life. Nothing serious, just hanging out in school and an occasional meet-up at Lamb's Lookout for a Horizontal Mambo in the back of her Subaru Outback. To the innocent bystander at Salt Springs High though, it was just ex's being civil.

...Oh, look how nice! Zack and Kate are friends... I couldn't do that with my ex! ...What? Getting back

together? No way. Kate is with that kid from Mansfield and Zack is leaving for Duquesne in the fall!...

She and I dumped the lunch tray's contents into the trash cans by the open dish washing station. We added to the small stack of green trays, and retreated to our classes.

An aroma of no. 2 Dixon Ticonderoga's overwhelmed me as I infiltrated Mrs. Bishop's room. A loud, booming voice hit me quickly after the punch that I received from that stench, "Oh this mothafucka right here!" Laughter erupted from eight occupied chairs in room 216. Each of those scoundrels looking directly at me while doing so.

"Ms. Jacobs, we all know Zack is a buffoon for jumping back in bed with that girl. No need to announce it out loud." Mrs. Bishop said. Her voice turned sarcastic, she continued, "And don't drop F-bombs until the door is closed."

Well, I guess *some* people were suspicious of Kate and I.

Sasha Jacobs was my best friend. She was one of the guys. The night we egged Bush Brown's, she sat in the back of Dave Ramsey's car, sipping on a can of Miller Lite. I'll never forget when she said, "Yo Wilson, bet you won't drop a shit on his doorstep."

"Done, bitch." he said.

When we did any shit-papering or egging, she was always the quickest one out.

Sasha was a big sports fan and an exceptional basketball player. Above and beyond the womens' squad's best player, even through my eyes. Kate was the point guard and the entire offense ran through her, but that team would be 0-25 every year if it weren't for Sasha. Averaged 22 points and 11 rebounds per game during her junior year. She was soon to be named one of Pennsylvania's top 100 high school women's basketball players.

Sasha's life was basketball. Both playing it and watching it, specifically Kobe's Lakers. It was something that linked us together ever since she moved from Pittsburgh in the second grade. Making her the only black kid in Salt Springs.

"Sorry Mrs. B," Sasha said and she turned to me as I pulled the seat out next to her. "But I feel you, Z. If I had a dick, my black ass would be pounding that booty for 9 months 'til the muhfuckin' kid came out."

More laughter exploded through the room, Frankie Perez chuckled "Jesus Christ" as he rubbed his palm on his forehead.

Mrs. Bishop began her reports of the previous night's shuffleboard contests. Her rundowns always lacked the game's x's and o's. It was more of a Deadspin article rather than play-by-play or color commentary. Like how people acted, why they acted like such, who is sleeping with who, etc. Small town gossip.

Turns out September 30th was a doozy. Officer Luke Larson clocked Tina Mitchell going 41 in a 35 down by the bingo hall on Route 14. It's a tough spot, of course. Empty road, speed limit signs are far apart, but everyone in the whole goddamn town knows its 35 through there.

Tina pulled over in the funeral home parking lot down the road, VFW right across the street. She knew what she had to do, Larson was the only one on duty. He got her when she was a senior in high school, seven years ago. She knew from experience.

Urban legend, of course. She had to blow him to get the reckless driving allegation knocked down to a speeding ticket.

Mrs. Bishop and Rob Killings saw the flashing lights and looked out of the VFW's windows. They watched the whole thing.

Larson went up to the window of Tina's Ford Taurus and stood there for five minutes, he got animated but nothing note-worthy. He returned to his police cruiser, panned the scene, got in the driver's seat and drove the car behind the funeral home, out of sight.

Tina cupped her hands over her eyes, just weeping. Probably referring back to her teen years, realizing that seven years later she was set with the same ultimatum. Blow the dirty cop, or get plastered with a fine for a false crime. It was reoccurring, Rob Killings said that Larson threatened Tina numerous times for sex. No alibi this time, unfortunately.

Poor Tina was trapped. After high school she could have moved to Minnesota with her mother, gone to college up there and started a new life. But Salt Springs is almost a curse. If you turned down one opportunity to leave, you were locked in with all of the demons associated with it forever. It had a real Derry, Maine type feel.

"What are you kids' plans this weekend? Anything yet?" She asked.

Mrs. Bishop's plans always revolved around the VFW, or the gossip discussed within. She noted that the first weekend of October would be no different. A big billiards tournament this weekend. Singles, 50/50 pot, Kirk Manson will probably win.

The entire class was close friends. Normally we spent our Friday nights together in some way. Sasha and Frankie, or "Pears" as we called him were the only minorities in the whole damn town. Pears and I played Little League baseball together. All the kids were chosen at "random", and of course, by random, I mean that the kids of the town's elitists were put on the same team while the peasants got the leftovers. Pears and I were on the latter squads, starting at only four years old.

He ran into some trouble with the law in 2003, even if it was for a bullshit reason. Pears started to chum with a group of misfits. They actually called themselves a gang and they fit the description. Spray-painting graffiti on walls, sold a bit of pot, this, that and the other thing. Kids started to make fun of their gangster-like appearance and one day a few of them flipped. Freddy Turner and Cal Thomas wrote up a hit list, and guns were actually found in their lockers. They planned on going full Columbine on Salt Springs High.

Pears was guilty by association, and spent six months in a juvenile detention center.

Matt Knickerbocker (Not those Knickerbocker's) was the nicest person on Earth. Family owned a big dairy farm, but they treated the animals better than family. Craziest thing about Matt K. was that he was a literal genius. Probably ranked 20th in a graduating class of 70, but he knew everything. One night he was over for dinner and my mom had Jeopardy on in the background. Alex Trebek said "Triskaidekaphobia" dryly. He yelled from the kitchen, "What is fear of Friday the 13th?"

On the contrary, Brooke Beckett wasn't all that intelligent. Her grades were fine, but started to falter. She was going through a break-up, her mom had just gone to prison for stealing money from the electric company and her dad was an asshole. It was a rough time for Brooke, but as cheerleading captain, she had to keep a high spirit.

Gordy White sat next to her. Nerdy fellow. Loved video games, anime and Dungeons and Dragons, but he was disguised as a metal head. His long, brown, scraggly hair flowed to the middle of his back and his wardrobe choice consisted of blue jeans with a t-shirt supporting the logo of a heavy metal band. Gordy was one of my first friends that I ever made. Our mothers were friends, plus Ms. Linda was a Boy Scout leader when we were kids. Two weeks after we both started, Matt K. walked through the door to join us.

Then there were Jade Davidson and Kara Murphy. Two of the most "popular" girls in school.

"Popular", what a bizarre adjective for high school chicks. Jade and Kara weren't popular. The lower and middle echelons of Salt Springs High hated them, because truth be told, they were both absolutely beautiful.

Two of the four horsewomen of Salt Springs High. Them and throw Sara O'Sullivan and Ellie Reynolds in the mix.

My God, Jade the Babe though, there were some days when I thought of proposing a hall pass to Kate Ford. Of course, I'm kidding, but Jade was an absolute smokeshow.

Maybe Kate and I could go unicorn hunting? Maybe Jade was a bit of a freak and I could have both at once?

Nah, I doubt it.

The final student in class was Ryan Wilson. My good buddy that I acquired once he and his mom moved down the street from me. Played football and baseball together. We were both damn good, but he had the cocky attitude to accompany it. I didn't. Even though his demeanor was a little hard to manage at times. The kid was the best.

"Well?" Mrs. Bishop asked. "What are you guys doing? You know, you should really get Mr. Hollinshead."

It was a good idea. Nobody liked Mr. Hollinshead. Guys couldn't stand him because he was an asshole, and the girls didn't like him because he was a bit of a pervert. I just wasn't completely feeling this idea though. It wasn't because I was softening up on the guy or anything. It was just that pranks were getting boring. Turns out, the rest of the group felt the same.

"First weekend of October. Scare Yard's open." Matt K. said. "I'll drive us all in the Explorer, if you want."

Scare Yard was a pun for the Ware Yard. Ware Yard was a giant open lot just over the New York state border. It held concerts and other events but in October, they made it into a Halloween-like environment with three levels of fright. The first was easy, the second scared the piss out of you and the third was a terrifying maze through the woods. If you could make it, you got a fourth level for free but there were restrictions. You had to sign a waiver and the actors could basically beat the hell out of you. A lot like Pittsburgh, PA's *Scarehouse Basement.*

"It's packed opening weekend, broseph." Pears said.

"True, true" Matt pondered. "We could shoot for next weekend then."

It was wild that a group of teenagers couldn't come up with plans but that was Salt Springs. It was an hour drive to actual civilization any way you drove. Elmira, New York to the north, Williamsport, PA to the south. Sara O'Sullivan normally threw a party on Friday and Saturday nights but that wasn't *always* appealing. Some didn't enjoy the partying. The others were simply getting sick of it, and they obviously weren't even to college. That's when partying is supposed to happen and eventually get old.

"Ulster Cemetery" Gordy said. "Scary as hell. Not too far. Plus, it's free. Only have to worry about pigs."

"No pigs going all the way up to Ulster, Gord." I said.

Ulster was a mining town about 10 miles east of Salt Springs that was completely wiped out by the plague. The town is now an assembly of dense

forest and tangled vegetation with a few
gravestones that commemorate the fallen.
Somehow they are still there.

Creepiest part about it was the drive up. A long
four-wheeler path led you to a walkway. The whole
thing smelled like shit and the bugs sucked the life
out of you. Not worth the time. White guy Yelp
review here. I give it a 3/10.

Ryan started to crane his arm around Kara's
shoulder. He pulled her in with a hand and said
deviously, "Remember when we went up there?"
His non-verbal cues were an announcement to the
class that they went up there and bumped uglies.
Bizarre place for it, but hey, more power to them.

"Why do I like you?" Kara snickered. "You're such
an ass."

He kissed her on the cheek and winked.

I was partially responsible for their ongoing
"friendship." Way back in the day, Ryan had a crush
on Kara and I played the role of wingman. She liked
him too. They never *actually* started dating but
everyone knew what was going on. They were both
really good people and the romantic in me really
wanted them to make it official.

Others chimed in. "Yeah, I went up there with the team last year." Sasha said. "Aint shit but *GAWTDAMN,* if a muhfucka wanted to kidnap someone's ass, Chris Hansen wouldn't even be able to find a nigga up there. But didn't you have some shit go down, B?"

Brooke went on a tangent about how terrifying her visit to the Ulster Cemetery was. She claimed that she saw eyes in the woods and her boyfriend heard footsteps. Her ex-boyfriend was a bit douchey. We never fully approved of him, one of those toolbag types that wore an off-centered flat brimmed hat of a baseball team he didn't follow.

Just like we didn't tell her how much of a douchebag her boyfriend was, we didn't tell her that the eyes and footsteps were probably a deer.

Ulster Cemetery was one of many urban legends in the town that included a supposedly haunted tunnel on Confederate Avenue. The tunnel used to house trains and years ago a little boy was killed by a passing locomotive. Maybe true, maybe not.

The town of Ulster was a true story, just like Luke Larson threatens felonies on women if they don't fuck him and the O'Sullivan's provide alcohol and drug paraphernalia for every minor in town.

Every small town, or area in this case, has a secret.
It reflects an ugly or shameful past. Erie, PA has the
"Pizza Bomber." It could also be a murder or a rape
committed by a high town official. All of them are
true evil committed by a human being, but it was
different in Bradford County. This might have been
at one-time human, but it wasn't now.

"The Lequin Church" Matt K. said.

Silence struck the classroom. A stray No. 2 pencil
rolled off of a desk and snapped on the floor. We
sat in shock. To most people, there are two things
that you never speak of: religion and politics. For
those in Bradford County, Pennsylvania, you didn't
talk about the Lequin Church. That was off *fucking*
limits.

"You can't even get up there. They have the whole
thing boarded up." Mrs. Bishop said. "No one has
been in there in years. Hank Stonehammer shut the
whole place down and Route 6 is in *terrible* shape."

"Just imagine if we get in there though." Pears said
curiously and dropped his doodling pencil on his
notepad. His fingers laced through the stubble on
his chin. "The shit in there. *Plus* at night. Bro, Matt,
I've never been so fucking in."

"Nope! I've seen pictures of that place and that's
good enough for me!" Jade said with pep as she

stroked her blonde hair behind her ears. She waved a finger in front of her, "Yeah, fuck tha—"

"Ms. Davidson!"

"Sorry, Mrs. B."

"I'd expect that language from some of these neanderthals but not you!" Mrs. Bishop laughed.

Everyone wanted to go, Sasha and Pears were both adamantly in. Kara and Ryan were both stupid kids and hell, maybe the pews are cushioned for her elbows and knees. Brooke followed up in agreement, she just wanted to be involved with something to get all of the heartbreak off of her mind. Jade the Babe was the only one against it but we could all tell that she wasn't going to allow herself to be left out.

I was the final word, the bell was about to ring and demand the departure for seventh period.

"Zack," Jade said sincerely, but with a touch of sarcasm. HeR baby blue eyes glowed in my direction, "I absolutely love you but if you say yes, I *miiiiiight* gouge your eyes out with a plastic spoon." She smiled, exposing her flawless, white teeth.

"Oh man, this is so tough because you're so beautiful," I joked, but deep down I was more than serious about it. Jade rolled her eyes and smiled larger.

"Why not? Let's do it."

Jade bit her lip and let out a sigh. The air through her teeth made an attractive sounding hiss. Mrs. Bishop's head dropped, chin to chest. Her glasses fell to her desk in unison with the bell.

CHAPTER 2: A History Lecture

Most of northeastern Pennsylvania was occupied
with forestry and farmland until after the Industrial
Revolution, but more specifically, post-Civil War.
Bradford County was a checkpoint of the
Underground Railroad, a passageway for slaves
that fled the south for free states and Canada. The
void of humanity and industry made the area
obscure as opposed to the larger, more populous
areas within the region such as Williamsport,
Wilkes-Barre and even Elmira, New York.

Once the Union reigned victorious, the area
thrived. Salt Springs, Canton and Minnequa were
the culture capitals of the county. Awful funny
saying that phrase in 2019. Passing through
Western Bradford County today, you may see some
bars and corn fields. Certainly not an opera house
and theatre that once occupied Route 14, the road
that connected the three villages.

Towanda and Stoney Corners were the haven for
farming. Residents from the entire area
congregated here for nutrients. Milk, meat, eggs
even. Hell, about 300 yards from downtown
Towanda was Bear Run, their market had the best
fish and deer jerky west of the Poconos.

Great years blessed the area that was once without
any resources. Instead of reserving an entire day

for a trip to Williamsport or Elmira, residents had their needs and even wants at their fingertips.

One town that never fully developed was Lequin. Lequin was a pass-through -- a pit-stop if you will along the main drag, now known at Route 6. Route 6 was the main connector of these villages, now the path is barely beaten thanks to the highway installation in 1999, but back then, it was the only way east or west.

One of Lequin's only residents was Isaac McKean, the best woodsman in the area. His shop was about 500 feet off of the main road, but the only way up those 500 feet was to trek Steam Hollow Road, the path was up a gradual hill adjacent to Route 6.

One morning, Isaac had visitors. A legitimate one. Not the theatre in Minnequa or a barn in Towanda, either.

Titus McLaughlin entered with his wife, Ernestine. Each were holding numerous parts for doors, knobs, hinges, etc. Titus was a tall man. Six foot three, perhaps. His hairline was a flawless windows peak, one that would rival Eddie Munster. The difference was the prancing silver along the sides, it looked as though a toddler stabbed his scalp with a grey marker.

Ernestine was lovely, blonde hair and green eyes that favored that of her husbands. Something was off about her, though. Mrs. McLaughlin looked promiscuous, her blouse was tight to her bosom and featured and unhinged button, revealing some of her right breast.

Titus was a minister. He and his wife bought the large plot that separated Isaac's shop and Route 6, they were building a church and were inquiring about some assistance. He was blessed for the opportunity to help them and he looked forward to the clergy. But he was mostly excited to work with Ernestine McLaughlin.

A wooden church stood on the grounds within six months. White painted siding, a rock foundation, and a small porch. A bathroom facility, or more bluntly put, an outhouse, stood five feet from the back of the structure. Nothing on the inside more than 10 pews (five on each side), a raised cylinder-shaped pulpit and a balcony that traced the upper walls. Access to the balcony was inside, the staircase was next to the main entrance.

Titus McLaughlin had a congregation of 100 within a month. He gave off a mysterious vibe, he had the personality of a character at a performance at the Minnequa Theatre. The minister was a showman; his charisma was unparalleled. His electric, and almost contagious personality helped him generate relationships in all of the communities in the area.

The McLaughlin's quickly became area's 'first family'. Ernestine frequented Minnequa Theatre and the Montague Opera House near Canton, she even volunteered and acted on occasion. Titus kept the books for Isaac McKean, and did manual labor on the Jennings Farm. Their kids, Jed and Gabriel, picked eggs for the Jennings's and pressed the jerky for the Bear Run Market.

How did they have the time? All of the community outreach *and* operating the clergy in Lequin. People wondered how (a). they could be so generous and (b). have the time to do so.

They support us, we must support them.

Their second month of operation, April of 1871, was their best. The congregation increased to 250 people and they even originated the first youth choir in the area. 10 children ranging from ages three to 12.

The choir was a success, and doubled in size within two weeks. Titus even implemented subtle choreographies, a simple sway from left to right and hand clapping to the beat of the hymn. They were years ahead of their time, it was strange, yet very enticing.

As choreography increased, the community saw less of the McLaughlin family. Except Isaac McKean, who saw plenty of Ernestine.

Ernestine blamed multiple moments of weakness on the church, Titus had so much on his plate that he couldn't sustain her needs. Isaac and Ernestine participated in weekly fornication. A sin, sure. An emotional attraction? No. A physical attraction? Yes. Isaac wanted Ernestine on that first day that she and her husband brought in door knobs. She developed an attraction once he started helping Titus in the church.

Titus lost touch with his family, the church was an obsession. As he spent more time working, his relationships dwindled and his power in the community faltered as well.

The children's choir only decreased to 15, and the overall congregation dropped to 200 by the first of May. By the second Friday of May, the congregation plummeted to zero.

Titus McLaughlin traveled Steam Hollow Road, passed his parish and entered the confines of Isaac McKean's shop. Beyond the tools and machinery, Titus saw his wife mounted atop the proprietor of "McKean Lumber". Her blonde hair swayed, and her body rocked as Isaac lay beneath her. Isaac's lumber was all of the way in and light moans synchronized with their thrusts. Not screaming, but they were about midway. Titus saw Isaac's paws clamp on his wife's ass. For every 10 thrusts, he gave her cheeks a slap.

...aaaand down the stretch they come...

Titus interrupted the party. According to McKean, their eyes met, husband and wife, one catching the other being unfaithful. That moment wasn't the disturbing part; it was when Titus smiled at them. Titus's smirk curled back, exploiting his pearly whites that quickly transitioned into yellow and crooked. His pink gums turned black, and the lips surrounding them cracked and oozed blood that poured down his paling chin. The once green eyes went beet-red.

Titus's normal façade returned. He did his volunteer work at the Jennings Farm in the afternoon and later that evening, the church held the children's' choir practice.

Only fifteen minutes before children's choir was set to kick off, Abraham Jennings noticed a few missing pigs and buckets.

The children's choir was greeted by two large wooden crosses that flanked the pulpit and one that loomed atop the cylinder. Twenty children showed up that day. Titus lined the children up as always but in a strange turn, he tied their feet to one another, creating three rows of six restrained children. According to legend, it was first presumed to help them practice their choreography in unison. It wasn't the case.

Reverend McLaughlin then tied the children's hands as if they were being incarcerated, a bucket full of blood lay before them. Titus tore the white, button-down shirts of the choir, exposing bare, undeveloped chests.

One-by-one, Titus soaked a stake in the blood and carved an inverted pentagram into their skin. All perfect artwork, despite the jerking and seizing from those trying to escape. Children cried their innocent scream. Blood trickled down their bodies, splashing onto their shoes and the hardwood floor.

Once all three rows were marked, Titus crucified the nineteenth and twentieth members of the choir. The fruit of his loins, Jed and Gabriel.

Titus marked them with the same satanic emblem. According to the legend, both sons were willing, but he took Gabriel first. Titus nailed a stake through each hand, one of the stakes were the weapon to carve the inverted pentagrams on the rest of the choir.

He returned to the middle cross that resided in his own ministerial bearings. In the pulpit, he stood directly in front of the wooden crossed structure and dumped the remaining blood on himself. In that moment, every cross in the church flipped upside down. Even the ones that his own children were nailed to.

Titus McLaughlin torched the Lequin Church that night. All beings in the church that day were killed. Upon investigation of the rubble, by some miracle, the only survivors were the 10 pews.

In a state of guilt, Isaac McKean built another structure on that same lawn. A church, with the exact same layout as Titus McLaughlin and many others' final resting place. Same color, same balcony, same shaped pulpit and literally, the same exact pews. The ones that survived the fire a year prior. There was only one difference, the surrounding yard was marked with 21 burial sites, topped with gravestones. Even one for Titus McLaughlin.

The next minister, Sebastien Adams also set aflame his entire congregation in October of 1874. Yes, the congregation, not the church. All individuals in the church charred, but the structure survived, unscathed.

Isaac McKean told the Minnequa Register that Adams had a personality change as well. Charisma turned to gloom very abruptly and as it did in 1871, Isaac found the church's only two full time pastors burnt to death in the same place: the raised cylinder that the faithful call a pulpit. He excavated sixty-one additional graves for each fallen victim, the perpetrators graves lay next to one another, 20 feet in front of the entrance.

Isaac McKean and Ernestine McLaughlin held church services there once a month for three more years, until they passed away on the second Friday of May in 1877. They were found dead in the pulpit.

The Lequin Church was abandoned for 126 years until local historians took over the property. In 2003 they held monthly services, but by 2004 a congregation met only quarterly. In October of 2005, Hank Stonehammer, of Canton, PA, locked the doors for reasons, and I quote, "Reasons I don't want to get in to."

Stanley Daniels, of the *Towanda Times*, asked Stonehammer, "is the closure because of the building's history?"

Stonehammer replied, "You could say that."

A paid group of paranormal researchers were secretly hired by the Bradford County Historical Society, but their results were unpublished. The paranormal team quit their practice two weeks later.

Since 2006, the Lequin Church is condemned. Any trespasser will be prosecuted to the full extent of the law.

CHAPTER 3: Thursday League

"...and who the fuck is really going to catch us up there?" Pears said.

We were still over a day away from this adventure, or whatever you want to call it. Thursday nights were dedicated to the bowling league but this night was different. I didn't have a good feeling about our idiotic commitment due in about 24 hours, but only two of us involved weren't 100% on it. Everyone can't be wrong, right?

Our Thursday night league was a breeze these days. Pears was getting better, Butch Slocum brought the handicap, but Dave Wilson and I were the pin pushers. They overheard Pears and I from the bar, we had a break between our second and third games.

"Yuh boys got sum pussy lined up fer the week'n?" Butch asked. Butch was a grumpy bastard that you'd associate with an 80-year-old. Got coffee at the Chatterbox and shot the shit with the clientele on the weekends but the man was only in his 60's. Rude, crude, his wife hated him, but he was the best damn handyman in town. Every shirt he ever wore was smothered with grease stains, as well as being a few inches shy of covering his beer gut.

"Yeah, Bitch. Tons. Look at us sexy fuckers." Pears laughed. I joined, not because of the general comment but when Pears called Butch, "Bitch", it struck me hilarious.

"Seriously, wudder y'guys up to? Goin' to the game, tomorrow?" Dave asked. "Ryan would love yuh t'come."

Dave was Ryan's uncle. Much older uncle. He was 15 years the elder of Ryan's mom, Tracy but strangely, the same age as my mother. Dave and my mother grew up on the same street and were the best of friends. Dave walked to her house each morning to walk to school with her, and once the school day was over, he walked right to the doorstep of 48 Second Street to make sure she got home okay. Mom never caught feelings but he did when they were 14. He never lost them.

He was a nice man. Felt like if he got out of Salt Springs when he had the chance, he would have become something special. He always made subtle remarks about social injustices, and was one of the only townspeople that didn't jump down your throat about how Barack Obama was the anti-Christ.

Dave is also a historian of sorts. He's was the proudest of citizens in Salt Springs. Dressed up like Santa Claus for the town's "Light Up Night" to bring in the Christmas season. He was the valedictorian of the last graduating class of West Valley High School, which was later branched into three schools. Salt Springs High, Canton High and the now defunct, Minnequa High. Dave Wilson had the chance to go anywhere. If he had it to do over again, he claims Penn State would be the first trek. Major in history and see from there but truthfully, I think the farm would always be the move. Dave was a Springer, and one of the good ones, that's all there is to it.

I didn't want to go to the football game. In-depth discussions about Coach Ward's play-calling wasn't my idea of a good Friday night, but breaking into the Lequin Church wasn't at the top of the "fun" list either. I loved the guys, I was a liar, and I let them down. I felt guilty, they were 2-2 and I wanted an excuse to get out of this shitstorm that I've put myself in.

"Possibly. Kate and I were going to go down to Williamsport for a movie. They have the new flicks down there." I said. It was realistic, the theatre in town didn't get a chance to run the new stuff until a month after its release.

"You're back with the Ford girl?" Butch asked. "Good 'fer ya. Gotta nice 'lil ass on her. Am I right David?"

I just remembered that we were being discreet, I tried to then shut down the notion that we were back together. "No, Butch. Just friends."

"You're lying." Dave said coldly as he sat back in his chair. Dave always seemed to be smiling, but he wasn't right now. His jowls enhanced with his frown.

He was right. I was lying... again. Kate and I were back together and I trusted my bowling partners to help me keep this secret, I was coming clean.

I sighed, "Yes we are back together, but not officially. We're keeping it a secr—"

"Not about Kate, son." Dave said. "Your plans for tomorrow. Ryan told me. He's going too."

"Kickass right?" Pears included.

Dave's eyes peered between the bill of his ball cap and bifocals. "Boys, you really don't want to go there. You can get in a lot of trouble." Dave said seriously.

We sat in silence. I know that I didn't want to go, but Pears did. Matt did, Sasha did, Gordy did, Ryan did, Kara and Brooke too. Jade and I were the ones hesitant. So yeah, Dave. You're right. I didn't want to go.

"How many of ya's are goin'?" Dave asked.

"Nine." Pears said.

Dave portrayed a look of intrigue. He adjusted his faded Philadelphia Eagles ball cap. In the same motion, he rubbed his eyes with his thumb and index finger. Even his mouth showed a wince.

"Boys, please don't g—"

"Dave, we're taking one car and nobody goes that way anymore to get anywhere." Pears interrupted. He was getting frustrated, and his voice started to slightly fluctuate. "No construction on the highway, plus who the fuck is driving through Lequin on a Friday?"

"I'm not worried about the cops, Frankie." Dave said. "That's not a good place to go."

"Dave, all respect, don't take this the wrong way." Pears asked. He took a sip of Mountain Dew and continued, "But how do you *know* that?"

Dave inhaled strongly. A mannerism that favored Dwayne "The Rock" Johnson before he would presumably yell... *Finallyyyyy The Rock HAS COME BACK TO SALT SPRINGSSSSS...* This topic of conversation was stressing him, but the aroma of musky, old bowling alley cut the sniff abruptly.

"I went to some of those services that Hank Stonehammer put on back a few years ago." Dave paused and faced me, but our eye-contact broke. His eyes traveled over my shoulder, "It just didn't seem right, boys. Something's off about that place."

"What's off about it?" I asked with sincere curiosity. I could tell that he knew more.

He adjusted his hat again. A droplet of sweat trickled down his forehead and onto his rosy cheek. Sweat dropped to his fleece and he looked down to moisture. "Just noises and stuff during the service, Zackary. Even when we were there it was odd."

Dave's eyes looked toward the bowling lanes, "They're ready for us. Let's get goin'."

CHAPTER 4: Mama

Michelle Bristol is the sweetest woman that you'd ever meet. Was 58 years old at the time, and was a mother of a high school senior. She had a youthful personality, but the patience and generosity of a grandmother. It wasn't easy being a parent of a teenager, but especially at a more advanced age.

"Shelly" was used to the difficulty. She raised two kids on her own. Her husband left when her daughter was 7, and her son was only 3 months old.

Her daughter, Beth, always loved Oreo's. To this day, Shelly always takes a pack of them when she goes to visit her.

As for her son, I have always loved Cheetos and I grabbed the sack of cheesy snacks out of the cupboard as soon as I came in the door on that Thursday night after bowling.

My mom has always been my best friend. Sacrifice after sacrifice, under the table jobs to moving us in with her sister for a short time. Everything she did was for my sister and I, never for herself and that's why I felt so terrible. I was a fraud. My own mother didn't have a clue.

I was a liar. I faked my football injury. Football was potentially the thing that could get *her* out of this mess.

I was selfish, I hated it and I was depressed because of a 17-year old girl. And now, said 17-year old girl comes back into my life and she didn't know. Why didn't I say? Well, disappointment, for one. She saw my reaction when Kate left me, and in an instant, she may see it again. Who knows?

"How'd you do, hon?" she asked as she took a bottle of Pepsi out of the fridge.

"Took two of three." As I crunched into another Cheeto. "Rolled a 268, 219 and a 175."

"Oh yikes, 175? Bet you were pissed, eh?" mom's Canadian ties still come out years later.

"Not too much" *crunch.* "We already had two wins, it was the last game."

Mom put the Pepsi on the table and went to the living room. I could hear her shifting pillows on the couch, searching for the television remote.

"What are you doing tomorrow night?" she asked and the television turned on. 11 o'clock news on WNEP. "I have to house-sit for the Wile's. Guess they're going out of town. I won't be around all night."

The Wile's were neighbors with Kate, lived just north of town. A little village named Windfall, really close to the big town called Troy.

There goes that excuse...

Couldn't even sneak in to Kate's to get out of this. I was locked in. I didn't have a choice than to go, but I did have a choice to tell my mother the truth for once, but I passed. My lie was just as natural as Joe Snedeker reporting the weather.

"Crew's going to Williamsport. Movie or something, I don't know."

"Just call when you get back. Be back by morning." She smiled as she kissed my head goodnight. Sleep didn't arrive until six in the morning, the alarm went off at seven.

CHAPTER 5: The Day Of

Sasha picked me up, as she did every morning at quarter of eight. She had a car, I didn't but I had always walked to school before my senior year. The walk was easy; our two-bedroom apartment was only a mere half mile from Salt Springs High.

I actually liked the fact that Sasha picked me up before school. At first I wasn't keen on the idea, maybe people, especially Kate, would think something was up between the two of us. We even admitted that it was bizarre that a 17-year-old boy and girl were so close without something more. But it was true, there was nothing. It was like we were separated at birth, we were family.

Every morning was the same, we went to the Chatterbox Diner. Grabbed coffee and a breakfast sandwich from Tracy Wilson. She told us to keep an eye on Ryan for her each day and Butch Slocum chummed with us for a few minutes afterwards. The dialogue on Friday's always started with bowling talk from the night before but ended with our football picks for the weekend. Sasha and I always picked the Steelers, and for good reason, easily the best defense in the league. Butch's rebuttal was always about how the Bills were "gonna pull one out their ass this week" and he was normally wrong.

After breakfast we went to school, her 2000-something PT Cruiser had one hell of a bass. Lil Wayne's "Tha Carter III" album blared as we entered the school premises. Sasha wasn't a great driver; she didn't pay the slightest attention behind the wheel. Without slowing, we hit the speed bumps that sprinkled the school driveway. A daily occurrence. The events were unbuffered, Sasha kept dancing in the driver's seat and "Lollipop" didn't skip.

12:42, lunch contents were thrown away, Kate and I walked to the staircase at the end of the long first floor hallway. For the first time since in several months, we stopped and talked at the base of the stairs. She wanted me to walk with her to her car after school. Something that also hasn't happened in months, I obliged but was concerned. I was pessimistic, at first. Was she choosing the Baker kid? Was this reunion over? Was I headed down the dark and dreary road to depression again?

I was optimistic once the bell rang to indicate the start of period six. She was always so concerned with getting to class on time but not that day. We stood alone in the hallway, leaned up against the concrete wall. She gripped her binder at the side and smiled as her eyes met mine. Green, sparkling, unbelievably perfect eyes. With her free hand she twirled her blonde hair.

She wasn't ending it, no chance. This was a look that I haven't seen in two years. She wanted me back, and damn, I wanted her.

I leaned in slightly and her neck began to reach up, she placed her hand on my chest. Our lips pressed together for what seemed to be a minute, until her Spanish teacher interrupted.

"I'm going to pretend this didn't happen, okay?" the Spanish teacher, Mrs. Murphy said. Mrs. Murphy didn't care about things like that, she realized we were (almost) adults and especially in that school, there were bigger fish to fry than PDA. Kate followed her into the classroom, I went upstairs.

"Look at this guy," Pears said as I entered Mrs. Bishop's classroom. "what has you so happy?"

The only ones that knew that Kate and I were on the way back to a relationship were Sasha, Pears and Matt K. It was probably only a matter of hours until they were all informed but I decided to refrain from telling them all at that particular juncture.

"Nigga you look like you just took a big ol' shit that you been holdin' in for three days." Sasha exclaimed and the whole class burst out laughing.

Sasha mocked my face, she portrayed a look that someone who make after having vinegar placed under their nose. Or, for me, when someone rubs two pieces of Styrofoam together.

"You're late, Mr. Bristol." Mrs. Bishop said.

"Like you care." I chuckled. Mrs. Bishop gave me a phony scowl. "Just kidding Mrs. B, love you."

"Love you too, Zack."

Mrs. Bishop turned to her computer and brought up Spider Solitaire. She was an expert, played on the hardest difficulty level and succeeded more times than not. When she didn't though, you could tell. She slapped her mouse against her desk.

Matt K. took the lead. He owned a newer Jeep Liberty, one of the only students in school that completely owned the car. He turned 18 on the first of September, he bought the Jeep, got his own insurance, registration, the works. The Jeep wasn't going to be large enough to transport nine teenagers, he had already made the negotiation with his mother to take the family car, a 2001 Ford Explorer. Mrs. Knickerbocker's hoopty held eight passengers. She had additional seating in the back after having their fifth and sixth child in 2004, so one of our nine would have to double up. Ryan made it known that it would be Kara sitting upon his lap, much to the dismay of every guy in the group. Having Jade or Kara double-up on top of them would be any guys' jackpot.

We would convene at Salt Springs Lanes at 11:30, football game would be over at 10 so Ryan would be able to get ready as well as Brooke, the cheer captain. Jade and Kara were headed to the game, also and Sasha was going to make an appearance. Matt had barn chores until dark, but Gordy was going to join Pears and I at the alley at 7 to bowl.

With every extravaganza, a trip to the Pump-n-Pantry was in order. Whether it be to grab a sandwich, a slice of pizza or a drink, these trips were a formality. You ran into the drunks, skanks but most of all, it was a free-for-all. The biggest junkie in town manned the graveyard shift. Anything went, Seth Dunlap was normally too baked to remember to charge you.

That was the plan. Meet at the bowling alley, steal a bunch of food from the Pump, and break in to a condemned church. It was a long way from toilet papering a teachers' trees, this was more exalting. Mission accomplished.

Exit bell rang for seventh period. I gathered my books from the floor next to me and followed my classmates out of the door.

"Zack, wait." It was Mrs. Bishop; her voice was shaken. "Hold up, I'll write you a note if you're late to P7."

I returned to her desk and sat in a seat across from her. Her wrinkled hands trembled and she looked at me with her deep brown eyes.

"Please do me a favor." She said, "Convince them not to go. If anyone of you can do it, it's you."

In less than a day, two true Springers pleaded that we stay home. We knew the stories, Titus McLaughlin really was an evil man, that was true. He lit the place up. No doubt. The Satanic rituals, though? Awful specific and far-fetched. Plus, why would some, McLourie or whatever build another one if that was true.

But it doesn't burn. That's true... no, it can't be.

"Hank closed it for a reason, Zack. It's off limits. Forever." She said. "You got the girl back, hon. Why are you doing this?"

"I don't know Mrs. B." I added reluctantly. "What else is there to do?"

Mrs. Bishop sat up erectly, shocked at the question. Her gray hair shuffled on her shoulders and her eyebrows formed a perfect 'V'. "A ton!

Christ! Go sneak out with your girl. I know you don't drink but I imagine the O'Sullivan's left the house to Sara. Your mother's housekeeping for the Wile's this weekend... they have a *goddamn* pool table! I know you want to be a kid, but be a *fucking* smart one!"

Mrs. Bishop shed a tear that disappeared into the wrinkle on the side of her mouth. The nine of us in our entirety were her favorite class, many thought it was because she didn't work while teaching us. We took the class over on day one, but in that moment I realized that we were her favorite class because she loves us, every one of us individually. She didn't have children of her own and those days had passed, she was 68 and we were the closest thing she had to her own. She was terrified.

"I'll see what I can do" I said, knowing full-well that I was not even going to attempt to alter the minds of my daring colleagues.

"If you go, I guess I'll have to hear about it on Monday." She said and she slipped me an orange Post-It note with a phone number written in blue pen. "Don't give this to *anyone*, Zack. I will be awake. Call me as soon as all of you are home tonight. I need to know you are okay."

CHAPTER 6: Kate Ford

It rained that afternoon. The first of the heavy downpours were during the final period of school until around four. A two-hour break until another front around six but after nine the forecast was clear. No rain. No wind. Nothing.

The first of the showers pelted Kate and I as we left the school. She donned a blue waterproof American Eagle jacket, but her hair didn't compel the rain. Her hair soaked within moments and surprisingly, her mascara only smudged around her long eye lashes.

I, being anything but a scholar, did not wear a waterproof overcoat. The Pittsburgh Penguins hooded sweatshirt that she got me for my 17th birthday was a proverbial sponge that day and the bill of my Steelers cap dripped like a leaking faucet.

"So," Kate said as we took cover underneath the canopy of the football field box office. It was on the far side of the student parking lot. She was an underclassman, only a junior, so she didn't have the seniority but today the spot was convenient. The entire back row was reserved for the underclassmen, that is except the one the held a PT Cruiser only three spots away. I could see Sasha in her car through the rain covered window, waiting for me, of course.

"My *father* has to go to some conference this weekend." She took a step closer to me, her tongue pressed against the inside of her lower lip as she smiled. "My mom," her hands entered the front pocket of my sweatshirt, "is taking Tommy and Anna to our grandparents, soooo--"

"You have the house to yourself." I said and smirked.

"Zackary Bristol: Jeopardy Champ." She said smiling and moved herself closer. I could feel her chest softly rest against my abdomen. I removed my hands from the front pocket and placed them on her waist.

"When they coming back?"

"Sunday."

A honk from a car a few spots up, it was Sasha losing patience. I was almost done talking though, my plan was set. A 48-hour sexual rendezvous would have been ideal, but mom was house-sitting their neighbors. No fucking chance would she have approved of it. But the Wile's were only concerned about Friday night; Saturday was optional for her. Similar to my commitments.

"Shit, babe. I'm tied down tonight but tomorrow I am all yours."

She raised her chin and whispered sexually, "I want you tonight though."

I sighed in disgust. Not for her but for me, going to Lequin was a bad idea. At first I felt alone, but after talking with two of Salt Springs's elder states(wo)men, Dave Wilson and Mrs. Bishop, this notion of fun was becoming a farce.

Kate perked up, "Well, I'll want you tomorrow, too. You win. What are you doing tonight though?"

"I don't know if I should tell you," I said. "Dave and Mrs. B jumped up my ass about it."

"Why the hell would they do that?" and for the first time in that conversation, Kate didn't look flirtatious or happy, only confused. Dave Wilson and Mrs. Bishop weren't the type to persuade out of adventures, they talked you IN to them.

"You ever hear of the Lequin Church?" I asked, and Kate followed up with a nod. "Well, we're going to, ya know, break into it tonight."

In disbelief, Kate offered a sarcastic chuckle, "Seriously, Zack. Where are you guys going tonight?"

Neither spoke, she could tell this was serious and she spilled the most common phrase of the past 24 hours, "Please don't do it."

"Oh Jesus, babe not you t—."

"Seriously! Mr. Stonehammer locked it up, you probably can't even go in there." Kate proclaimed. "Like a million people were killed in there! The man was the devil!"

"It was 84 I think and how do you know any of that even happened?" I asked and saw her reveal a taken-back façade. An *excuuuuuussseeee me* look. I immediately regretted it. "I didn't mean it that way, I'm sorry. But really, how does anyone know? Urban legend."

"Except there is actual stuff about it. It's not like Ulster where the plague killed a whole town. Evil-ass people killed innocent ones in there, Zack. It's true. I don't believe it's haunted or anything but still..."

I apologized, but reinforced that I felt like I didn't have a choice. It was a group decision amongst eight of my closest friends. She started to understand, although it still wasn't a popular move.

Another honk. "The whole class is going?" she asked. "Even Jade?"

"Jesus, *yeeessss*." I groaned.

"She gonna get scared and run into your arms? You gonna be her hero?" she said sarcastically, yet flirtatiously.

"Well we aren't *officially* back together yet, so you can't be mad when that happens." I posed the same flirtatious tone and her only rebuttal was a smile. Our lips began to move closer, with two inches to go until paradise, our eyes closed and hear--

"Hurry up, nigga! Fuck weekend 'bout to be over soon." Sasha went from honking to unleashing her inner city roots. The N-word was never used (as slang, of course) in Salt Springs until the Jacobs family adopted her. She brought the vocabulary from Pittsburgh's Hill District, the place she called home until she was 7.

"Gotta go." I said and courage was at the forefront. We publicly kissed earlier in the day and almost did a second time. Might as well go ahead and say "Kate, I love you."

Her eyes glistened, "I love you too, Zack" and we kissed. She turned to her car door and I walked towards Sasha's PT Cruiser. The door handle was drenched and it took two slippery attempts to open the door.

The PT departed. It was only a matter of time now.

CHAPTER 7: Knickerbocker Dairy

He knew that the rain would present a challenge to the work he needed done that afternoon. Matt Knickerbocker had lived his entire life in Stoney Corners, only about eight miles east from school in Salt Springs. Stoney Corners always got the worst of any weather front in the area. Just two years before, the village suffered the wrath of two tornados. One per year is a rarity for northeast Pennsylvania, but two is almost paranormal and Knickerbocker Dairy was the poster child for the aftermath of both.

In June, three heifers were slain by the F2 cyclone that traveled a mile from the barn. Their demise wasn't like the famous scene in the movie "Twister", but much more sinister. Steel panels ripped from the side of a neighboring silo and sliced the girth of two of the cows, the other was struck by a stray cinderblock in the head, she died from internal bleeding.

Two months later, steel siding was ripped from the barn. Thankfully, no animal or person was hurt, but the damages were of a large expense for the struggling farmers. The Knickerbockers didn't hire somebody to fix the mutilation, just a father and son rebuilding what their ancestors created over 100 years ago.

As it normally did on stormy days, the Towanda Creek flooded and doused Route 414. It was the only path for Matt's destination, Knickerbocker Road was a dead-end dirt trail that turns right off of the main road. The large Knickerbocker farmhouse and barn marked the end of the way.

Matt pulled the Jeep in to the driveway between the house and barn. Rain continued to fall, and thunder rumbled in the background. He could remember a lesson taught years ago about how far away the storm was, but the details were fuzzy. All he could remember was that when there is thunder, there is lightning. Adding large hunks of steel to the barren end of the barn was a bad idea for the day, it would have to wait until tomorrow.

Not being able to side the barn freed up a lot of time in the afternoon. Friday's were mostly milking days and the heifers needed their afternoon feeding. Matt did most of the chores in the mornings, he developed it as a habit accidentally earlier that year. It was a warm spring, and by afternoon it was too hot to bale. That continued into the summer and although it was cooler now, Matt liked to have the afternoon and evenings for friends and school.

Much to his father's dismay, Matt wanted out. Out of Stoney Corners, out of the barn, out of the entire area. Matt had a passion for environmental reform, the natural gas industry had entered the northeast and was polluting the soil. The population has never been so cruel to its environment and Matt had the solution already. He would attend a large university, Penn State was at the top of the list and he would make a difference. If anyone could do it, it was Matt.

He waited for the rain to cease before he departed his car, but after 15 minutes, he lost patience. His boots sank into his car's neighboring puddle, mud splashed on his blue jeans and rain soaked his green Carhart t-shirt. Mud squished under him despite the evolving puddles. By the time he reached the steps to the side door, his boots were caked with mud and rain leaked in to drench his socks. He removed both once he entered the house.

Randall greeted him and the afternoon ritual had begun. A big bowl of IAMS for the big Irish Setter, and a turkey and swiss for Matt. ESPN played on the living room television, and this time of year, Matt was glued to it. He loved football and was yet another product of a long line of Philadelphia Eagles fans, as were many families in Salt Springs. The Knickerbockers were top three though. Matt's father, Robert taught the family dog to bark when the Eagles scored a touchdown but Matt was the one who named him after Randall Cunningham.

Matt washed the sandwich down with a glass of milk, the drink of choice amongst the Knickerbockers since it was completely free of charge. He placed scraps of crust from the rye bread into Randall's bowl, covering just a few loose kibbles.

After Matt and Randall finished their afternoon snack, Matt headed to do the barn chores. The family was particular, almost obsessed about the doors being completely shut. During the tornado in June, Matt's younger sister, Dana left the side door unlatched and the wind dismantled the entire kitchen. Although there was no wind this afternoon, Matt still pulled and pushed the doorknob. Rest assured that door was sealed tight.

Rain slowed to a drizzle and over the hill passed the pasture, a beam of blue peeked over a grey cloud. He pulled out his Samsung flip-phone, the clock read 4:02 pm. *Two-hour break, startin' back up at 6, endin' at 9.* The mud was still prominent, the muck made a sucking sound around his boots on the walk to the barn. It isn't the most appealing sound, but Knickbockers were taught from a young age that it was *"the sound of money."* Hard work when the others weren't working at all is what brought in the most dough. Sounds crazy, but they were extremely successful until factory farming began its reign.

Much of the surrounding towns still utilized the Knickerbocker farm's resources. They said it was to support good people and a local business but truth be told, the flavor of the eggs and milk were supreme. There was no competition.

But when the Walmart was built in Salt Springs, the Knickerbockers began to struggle. It was easier to grab milk and eggs during a weekly shopping trip. Plus, Knickerbocker Dairy didn't take cards. Oh yes, the classic "First World Problem", you *had* to go to the ATM to get cash and you *had* to drive all the way out there. Driving was only an excuse, Matt often dropped off contents at doorsteps before school. When it came down to it, the corporate America grocery store was more convenient and a touch more affordable. As a result of those trying to save money, the Knickerbockers lost it. Robert and Anne had to get jobs to compliment the farm which left their daughter, Dana in charge of the chicken coop and Matt with control of the 84 heifers that called the barn home.

In the back of the barn were ten milking stalls equipped with state-of-the-art milking technology. The feat was easy. Herd them 10 at a time, have each enter the cubby and *kazam!*

It wasn't a long process, but Matt was getting overwhelmed. He knew he was a damn good farmer, but the early morning runs to deliver milk and eggs were starting fuck him. Up at four in the morning, ate a granola bar, loaded the jeep and shot over to Towanda by 4:30. Come back, grab a second load, and the deliveries to Canton are on their way. Repeat, repeat, repeat. Every single day and once that's over, it was time for school.

Next 10.

He thought about the money he made. Matt Knickerbocker was his only employee, and made good money despite the gradual fall of the barn's revenue. He had the brand new Jeep, and had plenty saved for college already.

Next 10.

Penn State wasn't going to happen, he had the grades but he couldn't get up and leave with the barn in this condition. Half the goddamn siding was still off of it from the tornado. Who was going to take care of it? His father couldn't, it wasn't enough money to support both he and his mother. Murphy Contracting paid Robert well, 20 dollars an hour to run the bulldozer. Anne only made eight dollars an hour at Ron O'Sullivan Dentistry and she wasn't in good health. 20 years of smoking was starting to take its toll on her.

Next 10.

He wanted to get away. Matt Knickerbocker wasn't the stereotypical farmer and he wasn't just passionate about environmental reform. He was passionate about social justice issues. Gay and racial equality were atop his docket, and those were not priorities of the small conservative area. Above all else was his love for his family and he realized it, he couldn't leave his family and all of their hard work.

Next 10.

Lycoming College has environmental studies and it's only 30 minutes away. It'll be an easy commute, it's a straight stretch on Route 414 until you hit the highway. Come back in between classes and take care of business at the farm.

Next 10.

Never mind, in between classes may not work. He didn't even know his schedule. Matt remembered a conversation with an admissions counselor at Penn State, he would have to take 12-18 credits to be a full-time student. That's the only way he could get federal financial aid. 12-18 credits came to about four to six classes, each with mandatory homework. Which was "much more than high school", the admissions counselor said.

Next 10.

Matt came to the conclusion that he would need help. Who in the town will need a part-time job? Tommy Ford? Not a chance, Tom Sr. wouldn't have his boy work for a coconspirator of his daughter's relationship. Duncan Lee? No, kid's too far south. Ralston is halfway to Williamsport. He won't come all the way up here. Most of these kids aren't willing to work anyways, he thought. Matt felt like one of those old Springers down at the Chatterbox that slandered the millennials. If only he could get someone that was willing, not even a volunteer, just willing. Like when Titus McLaughlin helped the Jennings Farm.

Last 10.

Matt cringed at the thought of old Titus McLaughlin helping out the community. One-hundred and twenty-six fucking years ago, that bastard was manipulating hardworking folk right up the road from Stoney Corners. Of course they'd go to his church, it was his pay and the sacrifice of children was simply cashing the check.

Final 4.

He attached the machinery to utters once Bertha, Betty, Didi and Lola entered the milking sites. The Knickerbockers treated all of their animals with dignity, which was both noted and respected by the community. When you got the eggs from Walmart, you knew of the mass production. With milk, you knew about the hormones. At Knickerbocker Dairy it was all natural, and in a bizarre way of thinking, you felt like a friend of the chicken or cow.

Those closest to Matt got Lola's milk. Of all the heifers at Knickerbocker Dairy, Lola was the queen. Matt referred to her as his sister and even made a Myspace page for the cow. She was a sweetheart and she was always the last to milk.

Matt counted as he unattached the milking mechanism. *Eighty-one... eighty-two... eighty-three... and Lola-Girl, the best for last... eighty-four...*

The heifers returned to their congregation, a large open space in the barn where all of them could roam. Matt, nor Robert believed in placing each in a specific stall, although it was hard to do the final count. He counted the heifers to ensure all were present, their ear tags made the task simpler.

All accounted for. All eighty-four. Matt felt he needed to remember that number for some reason. Was it something for school? No, it couldn't have been. No math classes and it wouldn't be relevant in any other class. A grade? No, he hadn't marked a grade that low since---

The door creaked open. It wasn't one of the front doors what was machine operated, but a screen door in the direction of the office. Lola stood next to him, he wasn't concerned, it was sure to be his father coming home from work early. Matt checked the time, hoping his phone wouldn't be dead. It was running low when he was eating his sandwich.

It wasn't time for Robert to be home from work. According to his phone, Matt saw that it wasn't even six o'clock yet. He wasn't surprised, it didn't take him long to do the barn chores, but his phone's battery percentage did shock him. It read: 84%.

Impossible. It was almost dead when he came home. Matt Knickerbocker then reconciled the Minnequa Register article that he read in study hall. *Eighty-four graves surround the Lequin Church, each representing those slain within the structure.*

Matt heard the door finally slam. After the thud he called out a "hello", but didn't get a response. Lola retreated towards her mooing compadres and her master grabbed a pitchfork from the barn wall.

He creeped through the barn sanctuary towards the office. Shuffling continued to emerge from the concrete, sounding like sandpaper on plywood.

Matt inched closer, "Hello...?" he asked. Nothing. Just continuous shuffling. His heartrate increased, sweat trickled down his sideburn. Hay laid under his feet and he kicked the straw out of his path involuntarily.

Matt raised the pitchfork and entered the office, he couldn't believe that it was only Randall.

Randall stood with his tongue exposed and his tail wagging. Unharmed, unintimidated and his owner now felt unthreatened. Matt was confused about how the side door could have been left open. He thought that the push and pulls did the trick, but apparently not. He led Randall back to the house.

They reached the side door. Shut and latched. No one came home and he didn't sneak out with the door open. The only logical explanation was that another door was ajar.

There wasn't. Matt investigated each door. They weren't just shut and latched, but locked. Sealed. Two locks to be exact, the doorknob and the deadbolt. There was *no way* that he got out on his own.

Randall, how'd you get out buddy?

CHAPTER 8: Salt Springs Spartans vs. Muncy
Bulldogs

In the Northern Tier League, schools got hyped for
Week One, Week 10 and whenever their team
played Cowanesque Valley, the easiest win of the
campaign. Week Five still brought the town to
Ralph Ward Memorial Field in Salt Springs on
October 3rd, 2008, but only the visitors' *families*
made their way in to occupy the opposite
bleachers.

Muncy, a small school south of Williamsport, came
to town that night. They were tough, solid players
all around and sat one game ahead of the 2-2 Salt
Springs Spartans in the standings. Muncy's
schedule wasn't all that difficult. Cowanesque and
Bucktail had been slain by the Bulldogs over the
last two weeks, the worst two teams in the league.
Their weak schedule led all of the newspapers to
pick Salt Springs by a touchdown, but as the
Towanda Times said, "Xavier Richardson could
change all of that."

Xavier Richardson was easily Muncy's best player.
Stood about 6'4, 210 pounds, he was 17 and the
size of Randy Moss. A three-year starter for the
Milton Mountaineers, but his father got a job
closer to Williamsport and thus, the big wide
receiver had to go from a state championship,

Quad-A school to Single-A mediocrity. College scouts didn't hold it against him.

Ryan Wilson was the most hyped man in the town for the Week Five contest. Scouts from Temple, Rutgers and Syracuse were on their way to watch the Friday night matchup but if he could shut down Xavier Richardson on the perimeter, he might get a visit from Penn State.

Being one of the "Springing Three", (used to be the "Springing Four", but, you know, 'neck injuries') he was always one of the three players that the team, school and town counted on each Friday night. He played cornerback and wide receiver, but preferred the corner. His hands weren't anything special and his route running sucked. But if you needed speed and physicality, Ryan Wilson was your guy.

Muncy got the ball first. Rain sprinkled just hard enough that the drops were seen through the shine of the beaming field lights. The grass field was soft, but didn't resemble the sludge that Matt Knickerbocker had to fight at his farm. All in all, the night wasn't terrible. No wind, light rain and about 50 degrees, some would call it perfect football weather. Salt Springs High School Marching Band began the alma mater and those in attendance, including Sasha Jacobs, Jade Davidson and Kara Murphy, sang along.

Salt Springs High, Salt Springs High, you're the fairest school to me!

Ryan panned the crowd, and finally found the group. He stood on the bench and flailed his arms to get their attention. Kara was the first to see him. She tapped the shoulders of Jade and Sasha, the group waved at Ryan.

Fight on! Salt Springs!

Lyrics and the pompous chants concluded, it was game time. Ryan, still looking up at his friends, yelled, "Yo K! Watch this shit!" He grabbed his helmet by the green facemask, slammed it on and slapped the Spartans logo on each side.

Muncy liked to test the defense on the first play and throw up a bomb to Xavier Richardson. Coach Ralph Ward Jr. knew it; Ryan was responsible for covering Richardson but he'd have safety help over the top. Essentially a double team.

Shotgun formation, the center snapped the ball back to the quarterback. They were doing it. They were throwing a bomb to the "X-Factor". *Good call for once, Coach.* Richardson had a step on Ryan. He looked towards the middle of the field for the safety but no dice, Adam Branch biffed it on his first step. Ryan read the pass, it was on the way down but he could tell it was a bit underthrown.

Xavier began to leap and snatched the ball at the top of the jump. On his way back down, Ryan smacked a shoulder pad into the number 10 on his jersey and speared him down to the turf. Xavier's lower back was the first thing to hit the ground and his head was second. Ryan saw the ball next to Richardson, out of his possession, incomplete pass.

Ryan celebrated. He pounded the Adidas logo on the left side of his chest but he stopped abruptly when he saw blood gushing out of Xavier Richardson's mouth. His once greenish-grey eyes rolled into the back of his head, revealing what looked like white discs in his eye sockets. His chest started to pulse and blood spewed even more like a geyser.

Ryan waved both arms like a man possessed, signaling for the medical staff from both sidelines. For a moment, he heard gurgling. Blood bubbled in Richardson's mouth like boiling water for what felt like a minute before it stopped. Xavier Richardson was unresponsive, the trainers came out and eventually the ambulance. Richardson was later diagnosed with a concussion, broken ribs with a punctured lung and a ruptured spleen, his once promising football career was over at the hands of Ryan Wilson.

Ryan was shaken for the remainder of the first half, but the other two of the "Springing Three" talked him down. The old, "the hit was clean" speech, "You didn't mean to hurt him." Coach Ward wasn't going to coddle them at the break, they had to figure out a way to slow down the backup. It's terrible when backups come in and dominate, but especially this one. He talked a lot of trash, much of which was violent and extremely unsportsmanlike. Coach Ward wanted to say something to his opposing coach about this number 84 kid.

Sasha loved football, and understood it. Of course she did, football is lodged in your brain at infancy when you grow up in Pittsburgh, and her love for the sport continued after her adoption. At halftime, she took Jade's program, Brooke gave the group one for free before the game. She turned the roster section, but there wasn't even an "84" on the team according the program.

The group went to meet Sara O'Sullivan and Ellie Reynolds. That was a good time to meet up with friends, despite the crowds. It was halftime and Salt Springs was getting the ball at the beginning of the third quarter. Normally, people would think the opposite but now the ideology of the Spartan faithful was, "nothin' to watch without the Bristol kid at tight end." *Why, thank you.*

Sara and Ellie were going to be late, Ron and Angie left for Lake Nephawin after work. Some of the alcohol they left had to be chilled, jello shots had to be made and Jonas Crasno, Ron O'Sullivans' lawyer, wouldn't deliver the weed. There was just too much to do before the weekly, immoral extravaganza. Sasha, Jade and Kara didn't want to go. Sure the "party goes all night", as Sara says, and they would probably be back from the Lequin Church at about 1:00 am. Plenty of time to do both, but the three friends weren't like that. Jade enjoyed a drunken evening every now and then, hell, throw in a regretful hookup once a month.

This would be three weeks in a row that she was dragged up to her best friends', nay, former best friend's estate to just...drink. Jade was a good kid, a little wild, but she had her priorities. Sure, she was sexy, she knew it and she dressed like it, but she was a really solid student. Unfortunately, consistent honors weren't good enough for her father. Mark Davidson was the mayor of Salt Springs, was for 10 years, each term he was unopposed. Many thought he had his hand in the town's drug problem, but he did know about Luke Larson's methods. That was a fact.

Jade could never please her family, so she always felt the need to please her friends. Even when she dreaded the thought of doing so.

Kara was an eerily similar situation; her father was a power-whore also. Jim Murphy owned a contracting business with 10 employees, including

Robert Knickerbocker. Jim always treated his employees terribly, he fired workers for one mishap and even pushed his 15-year-old ditch-digger, Quinn Baxter for not being quick enough. Murphy Contracting paid well, so it was easy to forget about the abuse.

Kara and her mother, Anna weren't paid by Jim, so the abuse wasn't forgotten. Until she was 12, Kara didn't even speak to a boy. Jade actually approached her about it in 8th grade when Ryan started to like her. Kara only said, "Dad is the only one I can talk to." Even at 18, quite often Kara comes to school with bruises on her arms and over the summer she was at the bowling alley with a few friends, donning a black eye.

Anna was the same, the school's only Spanish teacher missed 25 out of 180 days last year. The entire town knew what was truly happening, but Dave Wilson actually came in and fixed their staircase for free. "Anna, you've fallen down these too many times." he told her.

Kara and Anna compared schedules so they wouldn't be alone with Jim. On the weekends and on weekday evenings, Anna went to her parents' and Kara went to the Davidson's or the Wilson's. She drank to help ease the pain of emotional bruising.

Sara and Ellie though, the other half of the "Four Horsewomen" of Salt Springs High, just liked to party. Smoking, drinking, fucking, they did it all weekly. They were the easiest slam dunk for the horny teenage male and they embraced it. Most of the time, the class bicycle (*everyone's had a ride!*) is halfway up the sexiness totem pole, but not at Salt Springs. Sara and Ellie were two of the top dogs.

Sasha, Jade and Kara regretfully accepted the party invite. Kara was hoping that Ryan would come, she loved him, although she didn't want to admit it. Three of the nine that were going to the church were definitely going to the party after, it would definitely, at least, come up in conversation at the church or something, she thought.

The five girls went back to the bleachers. The third quarter was almost finished and the score was still 14-7. Their seats were taken, and there weren't five seats open, so they stood at the fence behind the cheerleaders.

Brooke Beckett lead the cheerleading crew in a synchronized chant. *Let's go! Let's go! L-E-T-S-G---*

"Brooke watch out!" One of the girls' screamed. Brooke was blindsided by number 84. He was pushed out of bounds ten yards back but kept

running and barreled into the Salt Springs cheerleading captain.

"You like getting hit from behind, don't you bitch?" number 84 said to Brooke as she lay on the ground. Everybody behind the fence on the sideline heard it, and he suffered serious verbal abuse from the Salt Springs fans.

"You fucking cock sucker!" Sasha screamed, and Jade followed that up by throwing a glass bottle of Fanta at the wide receiver.

Number 84 approached the fence, pushing Spartan cheerleaders out of his way. Referees tried to stop him, but he pushed them out of the way also. He unfastened his chinstrap, spit out his mouthguard and lifted his helmet slightly, exposing his sneering mouth.

"Go hang in a tree, you fucking nigger!"

Sasha began climbing the fence, but Jade hauled her down and they both fell to the concrete behind them. Kara chucked her nachos into the chest of Number 84, cheese dripped around the embroidered number.

The three girls were escorted out. Despite the ejection, they were able to find Sara and Ellie, who walked away after the racial climax to find out who this Number 84 was. They did find out that Alex Giroux, a supposedly kind sophomore, had to change his number before the game and the only extra jersey that the Muncy Bulldogs had was number "84".

That explains it....

Giroux tied the game with a 20-yard touchdown, but the Ryan turned on the burners with a 76-yard touchdown reception a minute later. The Salt Springs Spartans were victorious, 20-14. Alex Giroux met Ryan Wilson in the handshake line and said, "this ain't over. It's never over."

Before the Muncy Bulldogs got on their team bus to depart home, Giroux ran to Ryan and apologized for his behavior during the game. Giroux claimed that he didn't know what got into him, and wondered how he could apologize to 'the African-American' girl. Ryan accepted the apology, he knew how competitors got and they talked for 10 minutes. Muncy Bulldogs dropped their football pads into large vans and filed into the bus, still wearing their jerseys. Most schools in the area did it that way after a loss, you still wear your jersey after a loss as a sign of commitment and unity.

Ryan began to walk back to his mother's Chevy Impala. "That didn't seem right..." he thought, thinking back to his recent conversation with the shit-talking receiver. Ryan turned around, his eyes glared toward Muncy's bus. He confirmed that the thought was true. His mind wasn't playing tricks, he wasn't dehydrated and he sure as hell wasn't hallucinating.

Alex Giroux was wearing number 20 after the game, not 84.

CHAPTER 9: Salt Springs Lanes

Pears got to the alley first, about 10 minutes before Gordy and I. Salt Springs Lanes' proprietor, Dennis Kelly, normally opened the bowling alley at 6:30 for the regulars. Especially Pears though, Mr. Kelly originated Pears' secondary nickname, "Frankie P". Fridays at 7:00 pm was the opening time for the casual crowd even though nobody came in until after the game during football season.

Dennis had Lane 5 ready for us upon our arrival. It was the best lane, was the dead center aisle and had a large gap between its neighbor to the right. We had a little bit more room.

Gordy put his backpack down and walked to the back toward the shoe rental. Dennis stood behind the glass counter. Dirty, multi-colored shoes rested in the display case. We could see Gordy point through the glass at a pair of size 12's.

Pears and I had our own equipment, so I began jotting down our names on the score sheet. It was an old bowling alley, and didn't have the automated scorecards. We liked it though, drawing a big "X" in the frame after you rolled a strike was insanely satisfying.

I wrote my name first, Pears' second and as I wrote Gordy's name, I asked Pears, "How much do you know about this place?"

"About what place, Lequin?" he asked. I nodded in reply.

"Crazy pastor turned on the church. Guess it was Satanic, that's what I heard." He said. "He carved some shit on to these kids' chests and set the whole fuckin place on fire."

"Yeah, I know that." I said and looked down, "Another minister did the same thing pretty much. Evil motherfuckers. I was talking about what happens now. Like what did Hank see? That ghost hunting crew too?"

"Now, I don't know for sure bro, but I heard that Stonehammer went in one day to tidy the place up before one of the monthly services." He said seriously, a rarity for Frankie P, "Old bastard left for five minutes. Had to get something out of his truck and when he came back, every damn bible was open to the same page."

It was the first time that I heard that, my stomach dropped but I didn't physically show my tension. I just set the pencil back into the tray, turned to Pears and furrowed my brow, not as in a scowl, but as in intrigue.

"Heard those ghost hunters saw a green mist or something. I don't know though, bro." he said, "you know how Butch bullshits."

Butch Slocum was indeed the town bullshitter, hence why my conversations with him are limited to football and bowling. He tries pry sex stories from me but I ignore it. There were five high school girls that all men (even the old ones) liked, the "Four Horsewomen" and my girl, Kate Ford. Old "Bitch" Slocum asked everything from how tight her pussy was to the color of her nipples. He was an old pervert, and I really didn't like to talk to him about too much.

First game ended. Gordy rolled an 84, Pears tallied a 179 and I knocked a 205. Solid games all around based on our experience levels. In between games we grabbed some food from the bowling alley's attached bar. Dennis made the burgers out of ground bison and they were the best fucking meal in town. Cameron Creekside sucked, "The Holy Grail" was overpriced, and the Chatterbox was great for breakfast but other than that, didn't have a great variety. The best restaurant in town was a *fucking* bowling alley. Imagine that.

Pears and I grabbed a burger and fries. Gordy got a large pizza, all for himself. The kid could eat a ton, but he never gained a pound. Typical rock star, but he could do this without the help of cocaine and acid. Gordy played lead guitar in "Magnum 5", a heavy metal band that was starting to get some clout. Canton and Troy Fair in July, bar gigs on the weekend, they were growing.

We ate our food at the bar and watched a few minutes of the Florida State-Clemson football game on the television.

Touchdoooooowwwwwn Seminoles! blared through the television speakers. The game caught our attention much more than the usual Friday college football broadcast. Tigers, Seminoles was a hell of a lot better than Central Florida and Tulsa.

Bells jingled on the side door, we were no longer had the alley to ourselves. We just hoped it wasn't some family with three youngsters kickin' and screamin'. *I want a milkshake! I want French fries! No, shut the fuck up. Damn children take three hours to roll one fucking frame!*

We turned around and it was Matt K. Matt yelled, "Dennis, burger and fries please!" and he walked toward the bar. Dried mud broke off from his boots, littering the carpet. Matt tossed the keys on the bar and he mounted a stool. Confirmed. He brought the family vehicle, the eight seat Ford Explorer. We had it planned all along, but damn. A part of me was hoping *something* in this plan would fall through. If he had to drive his own vehicle, I would have gladly volunteered to stay back.

"Oh shit. I got to show guys this." Gordy said and grabbed his backpack from the table behind us. He pulled tangled contents from the bag and we couldn't tell what it was until he placed two voice recorders and a camcorder next to Matt's keys.

"We can't use your sh—"

"All good, brother." Gordy said, "all extras, just backups. Plus, Kirby Lewis bought all new recording stuff so really, we won't ever use this."

"Fucking sick!" Pears exalted, "Bro if we get shit on camera… Holy shit, let's gooooo!"

"We're going to record the trip? You guys sure you want to do that? I mean, it's proof that we're trespassing. I don't want that on me." Matt said, thinking about this certain educational and financial pickle that he was in.

"Matt, you realize who we're with tonight. Mark Davidson's kid? Come on, bro. Even if a cop shows up Kara and Jade can show their titties or something." Pears joked and we all laughed, "But seriously, man. Route 6 is dead, all of Lequin is. Cops aren't out there."

Matt K. didn't bowl, but Gordy, Pears and I rolled a second game. Another 84 for Gordy, 152 for Pears, and I choked in the tenth frame to tally a 287.

A drink was then in order in between our final games. Dave Wilson came in about halfway through our second game and told me about the game's highlights. Ryan scored the game winner and laid a big hit on Muncy's star receiver, ended his night. A kid from Muncy came off the bench and played like Hines fuckin' Ward. Dave described him as a scrappy son of a bitch, talked a lot of shit too. Had a run-in with Sasha, Jade and Kara during the game. "Girls got kicked the fuck out for his bullshit." He said.

"Wait, had a run in with... how?" I asked.

"Bastard got pushed out of bounds but never stopped!" Dave exclaimed, his jowls jiggled with the shake of his head. "Ran right over your friend, Brooke."

"Like on purpose?" Pears asked.

"No doubt, Franklin. Looked right at her and said something. Everyone down on the field started yellin' and you know Sasha and the Davidson girl, they were right there in the middle of it. Son of a bitch called Sasha the 'n-word'." Dave took a sip of coffee, "that little fucker is lucky she didn't get over that fence."

On cue, the bells rang and in came Sasha, Kara, Jade and Brooke. None looked all that happy, but you could tell they were in the refreshing stage, the girls were calming down. Like a married couple that is an hour removed from a bad fight.

"Hi Dave!" Kara yelled and she jogged over towards her love interests' uncle.

"How ya doin', sweetie?" Dave extended an arm around her and kissed her on the top of her head. "Beautiful ladies, how are you all? Cleaned up, eh?"

Everyone in town, including the girls loved Dave. He was the kindest man, and really knew everybody. Dave Wilson might have been Ryan's uncle by blood, but spiritually, he was everyone's family.

The girls gladly confirmed his inquiry. Of course, fucking teenage girls have to redo their make-up and change their outfit after a football game to go to a possessed church.

"There's a party later." Jade said shyly. *That explains the yoga pants and exposed cleavage.* She was almost ashamed to admit it in front of Dave.

"Hon, don't be shy about it. You're kids!" he said, "It's what you should be doing. Just be very careful. Please."

"Always are Mr. Wilson." Sasha said, "We have our bags packed and everything out in the car. No driving for us tonight."

"Oh, be careful with that too." Dave chuckled momentarily, but the stern expression returned to his face as he said, "I was talking about the church. Bristol didn't talk you out of it, so... I just want you kids to be careful, that's all."

Brooke replied, "We'll all be in Matt's car and I gotta tell you, Dave. No cars go out there anym—"

"I'm not worried about that, hon." Dave said. "That church is a bad place. A very bad place."

Bells jingled, Ryan took two steps in the door and yelled, "Let's go motherfuckers!"

"Jesus Christ, Ryan. You're in public!" Dave said.

Ryan looked like a deer in headlights. "Sorry, Uncle Dave." Ryan replied.

We tidied up the lane, gathered the recording devices and the half full bottles of Pepsi. Kara followed Ryan out of the door. Sasha and Brooke were only a few steps behind them. Jade put her coat on, and she flipped her blonde hair over the hood of her jacket. Pears and I elbowed each other and smiled when she turned around and left. Jade's jacket was just short enough that her ass was uncovered. Black yoga pants hugged her perfect round ass cheeks, complete with an indentation in the middle. *G-string? Phew. Commando? Even better.* Pears offered a grunt, "Holy fuck, what I would do…"

I closed my eyes and whispered, "Remember Kate, remember Kate, remember Kate." Pears choked on his laugh and spit a small stream of soda. It dribbled down the front of his shirt.

Matt K. grabbed his keys, a trail of mud tracked behind him and Gordy carried the backpack by the top handle. Pears slapped me on the back and said, "It's time, Zackary. Let's fucking do this" and he left in front of me.

I followed my friends out of the door. One by one the door opened and rebounded shut. During its final closing attempt, I grabbed the handle and looked back at the bowling alley bar. Dave Wilson turned around on the swiveling barstool, slowly shaking his head. I shrugged and he mouthed a phrase that I didn't comprehend until I was in the bowling alley's parking lot:

Don't go.

CHAPTER 10: Pump Run

Gravel crunched under the Knickerbocker SUV when we pulled into the parking lot of the Leroy Pump-n-Pantry. Leaning on the large gas station entrance was Seth Dunlap, one of the many meth dealers in town. Seth lived in Salt Springs, did his business there by day. In Salt Springs he got the west crowd, clients from Minnequa and Canton came to him for the goods. When he got the job at "The Pump" in Leroy, his network expanded to Troy and Towanda.

Seth pushed his long, "Paul McCartney with longer bangs"-style haircut to the side and crushed his cigarette out on the wall as we pulled into the parking spot next to him. He grinned, black teeth spread across his ungroomed face. "What's up, guys?" he said excitedly.

We were regulars, well, at least Gordy, Sasha, Matt, Pears and I. Us five always went to the Made-to-Order stop when Seth was working. Mostly because he had good stories of junkies coming in to masturbate in the chip aisle, but he also hooked us up with free grub...whether he knew it or not.

On this night we had to pay for our sandwiches, but the shelves were fair game. There was more than just tobacco and nicotine in that cig. He wasn't all aware of the snack ransacking that included, but not limited to, my infamous 'seal back on the Pringles can' trick.

We took advantage of Seth for sure, but we had enough respect for him to tell him our plans for the evening when he asked.

"You fuckers are crazy," Seth laughed. I didn't know how I felt about being called 'crazy' by a meth dealer, but fuck it, I've been called worse.

"I was just in there three weeks ago. Went right in." He said.

We were shocked, Hank Stonehammer locked that place up. There wasn't supposed to be any possible way that someone could actually get inside. We were all under the impression that it was padlocked shut, Matt K. had bolt cutters because we sure as hell weren't going to break a window.

"You just… 'went right in'?" Pears asked.

"Yeah, dude. Fuckin' door was just tied to this metal thing… fuckin baler twine or something." He replied. "We were there for a couple minutes, or hours… I can't remember we were all so fucked. But I swear something grabbed my leg and something choked Graham Lowry."

Jade put her hand on her chest and swallowed hard, unfortunately, it was a nice view sitting across from her. Covering up that chest should have been a crime. She was uneasy at the thought of someone getting choked, but Sasha broke the anxiety.

"You motherfuckas were high as hell though, come on son..." she said.

"I know what I felt, man." Seth replied.

Pears suggested that we should get going, and most of us began to pack up. Kara, Ryan and Sasha placed their chairs back at their original table and Jade bent slightly over the table as she stood, giving a nice avenue to see the clasp that connected the cups of her bra. She caught me, actually, she caught us. Matt K., Pears and I all sat in awe of the sight of her D-cups. Jade smiled, no big deal, she was used to it and was almost always flattered. As a matter of fact, we had ongoing "what we wanted to do to her" jokes that she was included on, even if the guys were relatively serious.

Brooke was the only one left seated, she yelled to the group that congregated by the exit, "I think we should just stay here." She laughed, jokingly but serious. We urged her, and finally after the coaxing, she slid out from the booth.

We left the gas station and loaded in to the car. Brooke, Pears, Kara and Ryan got in first, filling the back of the SUV, the back windows were tinted so a passersby wouldn't be able to see the human stacking. In hindsight, it was the middle of the night in Bradford County, Pennsylvania. No one would see that. I followed Sasha and Jade to the middle row. I was on the end, hoping for a few bumps in the road with Jade to my left. As Gordy was opening the passenger's side door, he said, "hey Matt, do we know where we're going?"

"Route 6!" We heard from the gas station. It was Seth, he jogged to the vehicle. "If you get on by the Taxidermist's in Troy, it's only a few miles. Once you hit the woods, it's a mile to a really fucked up looking barn. Steam Hollow Road is the next road on the left after it."

Matt K. was grateful for the information, none of us had a real idea of where we were going. It was Route 6; it couldn't be that hard. There were no houses or anything on that road anymore, we were going to just use the handy 'process of elimination'.

We thanked Seth, and he was appreciative. No one has thanked Seth for anything other than meth in years. Beneath the surface, I was confused. Seth Dunlap was the biggest junkie in town, how did he remember that so clearly?

To paraphrase Wayne's World, *for a meth dealer, he had a lot of information, don't you think?*

CHAPTER 11: Route 6

Machmer Taxidermy stood beside us. The closed
sign was on the door, but a single light dangled in a
front window. Doug must have been doing some
work before the Saturday morning demands from
the local hunters. Doug's taxidermy shop was the
last business left on Route 6 in all of Bradford
County and we were of course the only ones
traveling at that time of night. Matt proceeded
through the stop sign and turned right on Route 6
towards Lequin.

Empty fields quickly evolved to plains of dead corn
stalks and eventually to rows of pine trees.
Headlights shined on the paved road and the
surrounding forestry. It was eerie. All of our
dancing, flirting and joking halted. The engine
hummed just loud enough to hear over T.I.'s
"Whatever You Like" that quietly came through the
speakers.

There was a slight bend in the road. A deer stared
at us as we passed, his eyes illuminated by the
piercing headlight like two large bicycle reflectors.
He stood still on the road's shoulder. Calm and
stoic.

Abruptly, the road became rough. Like dried gravel
on a washboard and it no longer donned center
lines. Gordy cracked the passenger's-side window

to spit out a sliver of fingernail. The air entering the window sounded like a typhoon in the midst of the silent vehicle.

Matt drove by the abandoned barn. It looked like a leper. A black barn was scabbed with erosion, and its wooden siding dangled like large hangnails. We were silent, the tension in the car was thick, like the air on a humid day.

"Should be right up here." Matt lurched over the steering wheel to get a better view of the potentially hidden side road.

"There." Sasha said dryly as we passed Steam Hollow Road. He pointed a long dark finger to her left.

Matt stopped the car, reversed 25 feet and entered the adjacent avenue. No chance of any traffic from behind. Matt turned the wheel, and the rear of the Explorer fishtailed through the loose gravel.

The waning gibbous moon became more obstructed as we trekked the steady incline of Steam Hollow Road. 50 feet ahead of us, a white steeple topped with shingles, peeked over the trees.

Steam Hollow Road flattened, and the forestry opened. Next to the road was a graveyard. Old white stones with curved tops lined evenly up the road, only disturbed by three trees. Miniature American Flags scattered the yard, poking out next to randomized gravestones. The soil raised around many of the burial sites, as if someone pressed from underneath the grass.

Beyond the graveyard was the large, wooden church. White paint began to chip on the outside and six windows evenly distributed the side walls. An unpainted, wooden porch held up by stones complimented its entrance. The porch was bare, with the exception of one closed door. Directly in front of the porch were two tall, monument-like gravestones.

Behind the church was a gravel driveway and Matt pulled in. The filthy track turned to grass 100 feet off of Steam Hollow Road. Matt K. parked his mother's Ford Explorer where McKean Lumber once stood.

He turned the ignition off and we admired the sight. It was a flawless night, constellations were viewable in the black sky. A slight smell of rain and pine lingered, but the air was dry and had been for a few hours. Coyotes howl in the distance. Staring at us though was the demoniacal denomination. The graveyard was still, but the structure looked hungry. It was its time to feast. A stream of shingles drooled off of its roof like Pavlov's dog. The rear façade winked, only five windows bore the back wall of the church. Three at the bottom, two at the top. The top left was covered with plywood from the outside.

The Lequin Church always had a craving for humanity, and we all came to this realization. No one said it, but we knew. We were all in the same situation, we didn't want to go in. Eighty-four people died in this goddamn place, all in terrible ways and if it weren't for Hank Stonehammer shutting the place down, there would probably be more. So here we are, a bunch of teenagers without a clue of the world, barging in on a cursed building. If the stories were true, this wasn't coincidental. One pastor might have gone crazy, but not two. There is no way.

A car door opened. Brooke's jump was simultaneous with a scream. But it was only Sasha, "Let's get this shit over with." She said and exited the vehicle. We all followed suit. Nine teenagers began to trudge through the final resting place of those slain in the Lequin Church.

CHAPTER 12: The Cemetery

Pears and Sasha were the first to enter the graveyard and pass the *NO TRESSPASSING* sign with large red letters.

"Jesus Christ you guys in a hurry?" Brooke asked.

"Bitch! When my people got white folk behind us we gotta be safe! We runnin'!" Sasha said.

"And I've been running since I crossed the border." Pears added immediately.

Our laughter calmed Kara and Ryan enough to be the next penetrators of the church grounds. Ground squished below their feet. The air was dry but the ground certainly wasn't, mud started to sprinkle across Ryan's American Eagle blue jeans. Kara began to slip on the evening dew, but her "Knight in a Shining Polo" wrapped his arm around her waist to haul her erect. She straightened her long brown hair and smiled to the rest of the group. Blushing, of course.

Jade, Gordy and Matt were the next ones in, Matt made the sly, sarcastic remark, "You need help, Jade?" and he began to crane her arm towards her. "I'm fine, Matthew!" she snickered.

"Don't mind me. Just wanted to make sure."

That left Brooke Beckett and I. Brooke was just terrified, but she agreed to do it. The difference was that Brooke had no pride left since her boyfriend left her. She needed all the help to get her mind off of it and if it were dangerous or life-threatening, so be it. If she met her demise, she didn't care. I, on the other hand, had too much pride. After being the top dog at Salt Springs High for so long, I had to do something monumental, heroic or something to keep my reputation high. I was ready to get out of Salt Springs, but I'd be damned if they forgot about me.

Truthfully, in hindsight, I loved this group and I just wanted to be with them. We all had our own unique friendship story. Pears and I played Little League together. Gordy, Matt and I were in Boy Scouts starting that age 4. We've all been friends ever since. We were actually the first to welcome Sasha when she moved to town. Our classmates were unsure of her at first, none of us had ever seen a Black person before Day 1 of second grade.

Ryan moved into town from Stoney Corners in Junior High. We hung out every day and one day I went to their house to sleep over and I had my own room. Tracy put a mattress and television in their storage room. She was even sweet enough to tack up a Michael Jordan poster on the back of the door.

Ryan started to like Kara in 9th grade, the same year I started to flirt with Jade, so he befriended Jade and I befriended Kara. A valiant attempt of wingmanship, but Kate Ford ended any developments between Jade and I. Hey though, here we are, three years later and although they never officially became a couple, Kara and Ryan were still going strong.

Growing up in a town of 2,000, *everyone* knows *everyone* from *day one,* and our time together was limited. They say that you meet your lifelong friends in college and adulthood. I strongly disagree. The people you become an adult with are the ones you love and cherish the most. *They are who make you*, just like your mother or father. We were family and we could fully comprehend that when all of us stood together in the middle of the mass of 84 gravestones outside of the Lequin Church.

CHAPTER 13: Jed McLaughlin and Old Glory

There was a discolored gravestone near the porch. All other stones were white, but this one had a greyish tint.

As we walked closer, the grey stone was cracked at the top. Its fissure traveled three quarters to the bottom and the text had mostly faded.

Sasha was the first to notice the marker. She crossed in front of Pears, and she bent over to get a closer look.

We huddled around the stone. Sasha and Matt knelt before it, and the remaining seven stood behind them. Moss grew on the sides but only a quarter of the way up, its face was freckled with black permanent blotches, like moles on a witch.

Matt felt the grave marker, trying to decipher its possessor's name but it was difficult. Letters ran together and others felt too similar with just a feel. He asked if anyone had a marker or pen.

Brooke had a collection of Sharpie's. An awful random thing to have, but she never removed them after creating signs for the Salt Springs football game. She was annoyed that she had to make the goddamn things, that was a job for the freshmen. Brooke, in her infinite wisdom, asked what color Matt wanted.

"Ummm... black?" he said as he stood and hiked up his Wrangler's.

She handed him a black marker and Jade shined her phone's flashlight upon the stone. She had one of the brand new iPhone 3G's, and her battery life was at an optimal 84%.

"Gord, get this on camera." Matt demanded and Gordy obliged, he fished out the camcorder and started recording.

The air chilled, but there was no breeze when Matt began to trace the stone's indentation. With every traced letter the temperature seemed to drop five degrees. Hair on the back of my neck spiked and blood began to curdle in my chest. My entire body began to quake when Matt began saying, "Jedidiah McLaughlin, 1866-1871. Five fucking years old."

"Jed McLaughlin? The ministers kid?" Pears asked.

"Well, that lines up, doesn't it?" Matt answered rhetorically. "Of *all* the graves to do this to... it was this one. Of *fucking* course..."

Ryan and Kara looked puzzled. They made subtle eye contact and scowled. Ryan had to know about

Jed and Gabriel McLaughlin, his uncle knew everything about the area's history. But Ryan clearly didn't. They were along for the thrill of breaking into a creepy building but they were both unaware of the history of this sinister urban legend.

"Wait... what are you guys talking about?" Ryan asked as he tugged on his shirt collar.

"The original minister burned the church down with a bunch of kids in it." Matt said and Ryan nodded in agreement. That much he knew. Matt continued, "Well, he carved inverted pentagrams on the choir and he crucified his own kids before he did it."

"Inverted pentagram?" Ryan followed up.

"Satanic emblem." Matt replied.

Kara gasped and Ryan groaned, "Why the fuck are we here then?"

It was a hell of a question, and we wanted to turn back. Go to the Leroy Pump-n-Pantry and fuck with the meth head some more, that was a better idea than this. I could have been knocking boots with Kate. Brooke would be sure to join Jade, Sasha, Kara and Ryan at the O'Sullivan's. Matt, Gordy and Pears could have been back at the White's playing the new Halo video game. Instead, we were all staring at the gravestone of a five-year-old that was killed by his father... on Satanic fucking grounds.

Something caught my attention in a side window. Staring back at me through the glass was a child. A little boy, probably around six. Despite his innocence he looked strong in his collared, white button down. A loose bowtie wrapped around his neck, as if the young man had been tugging on it for an entire sermon.

He wasn't threatening, but it wasn't my imagination. It was all too real. There was a boy staring directly as us, although I was the only one aware. My jaw dropped but my body wouldn't move. I wanted to scream but my vocal cords froze. My hand extended in an attempt to get Jade's attention, but it failed. I was paralyzed.

The little boy's stoic face began to dissipate. His eyes turned to a pair of solid white discs. Green slime started to pour from their inner corners. Trickling around his scabbing nose.

He flashed a sinister sneer, blood began to pour from his cracking lips, exposing rotting teeth that extracted by the second. Moss crawled up his scalp. Jet black eye brows raised as he began waving his fleshy, clawed hand.

I managed to make a muddled sound and in that instant, the little boy vanished. "Umm guys," I continued. "I think we should get out of here."

Matt stood and without speaking, we all began to retrace our footsteps back towards the SUV. Sasha led the way, I followed in the middle of the pack with my head facing the ground. I recognized a tree root in my peripheral, indicating that we were close. We were only a mere 20 feet away from the *No Trespassing* sign when I smacked in to Gordy's back. I looked up, and the entire group halted before me.

Two graves with small American Flags separated us from the Knickerbocker Explorer. The flag by the entrance waved in the still air.

We stood about 15 feet from the flag. This wasn't momentum from fast-paced walking or from any kind of air current that could have been streaming through. Something was moving it, something was waving this flag.

The flag's staggered flow accelerated until it resembled boat sails in the midst of a tempest. Its force frayed the end of the cloth, but the twig protruding the ground was unaltered. In seconds, it refrained. Stopped. Dead in its tracks. The stick

remained perfectly vertical, but the flag was
tattered and torn.

The closer flag started to beckon but this one was
stronger and evolved faster. It flapped loudly in the
midst of our silence. Unlike its neighbor, this one's
pole began to flex. Mud started to rise behind the
twig during the constant rush. The surrounding
ungroomed grass started to tear away from the
Earth from the flag's shifting power. The ground
could no longer support its force and the flag
catapulted into the air and pelted Sasha in the
forehead.

Sasha plummeted to the ground and tumbled back
down the path. Head over heels. A Nike flew off of
her foot and knocked into the side of the church.
She continued to toss and turn down the hill. Pears
ran after her but couldn't catch up. Her momentum
was finally stopped when her back cracked against
the rock foundation that held the church's front
porch. Blood leaked from her left brow.

"Sasha! Sasha!" I screamed. She didn't answer but
she was conscious, she dabbed her brow with two
forefingers.

Pears was the first one to her, his voice trembled,
hiding his tears, "Fuck, fuck, fuck are you okay,
Sasha?" He gently touched her shoulder. Gordy and
Matt joined him, Matt used the sleeve of his

sweatshirt to wipe the blood. Gordy held the camcorder to his side, he didn't film.

I vomited on the grave of Jedidiah McLaughlin. *Those teeth, those eyes.* More of the bile/chicken speedie cocktail painted the soil. Kara fell to her knees and sobbed. Jade and Brooke remained standing but also broke out in tears.

Ryan grabbed ahold of Kara and buried his face into the top of his head, his torso began to seize and a small droplet of water ran down his cheek.

Sasha looked up and nodded to Gordy, Pears and Matt. An inaudible way of communication that she was okay. Sasha had that attitude. Regardless of her pain, she would fight through it. Maybe it was growing up in the hood. Maybe it was because she was adopted. Whatever it was, we admired it.

She stood up and brushed off her purple Nike sweatshirt. Matt and Pears began to reach around her, offering assistance back up the hill. Sasha refused. She lifted and slapped her left boot onto the stone porch step.

Then the right.

Sasha took two more steps back and stood alone on the porch of the church. She loomed over us, looking angry, blood still oozed from the wound but much was caked on her face. Her nose scrunched and she sniffed.

We were terrified at the sight but I knew it was still Sasha, even if the others weren't sure. Brooke and Kara looked as if they were staring at the Lequin Church's 85th victim. Her eyes met mine. I knew what she was thinking, I've known her for too long. We were best friends. This is the same girl, no, woman that played the final 10 basketball games of her junior year with a broken ankle. She averaged 15 points and 9 rebounds in those games. She was physically tough, but she was even stronger emotionally. I was the only one who knew the true story about her parents. City police responded to an anonymous tip about a drug deal and her father matched the description.

Well, he was black. That was about it.

He did nothing wrong, and continued to deny any knowledge of the matter. The police took a nightstick to his head and beat him to an oblivion. Her mother tried to stop it but she was shot in the temple. Sasha entered the apartment and placed her Rugrats backpack on the hook by their front door. She entered their kitchen in time to see one final crack to the skull of her father. His blood splattered on her pink Angelica Pickles t-shirt.

The woman that witnessed all of that didn't fear a goddamn thing. She stood tall on the wooden porch and demanded sternly, "Zack, let's go."

I joined her on the porch.

Kara, Ryan, Brooke and Jade were astonished. Their looks resembled one if they saw, well... a ghost. Tears dried to Ryan's face and the girls all sported running mascara.

I could tell that Gordy, Matt and Pears were going to follow us, but I didn't have that feeling about the rest. If we continued into that church, they were going to leave and God only knows where they would have ended up. That's why I began to persuade.

"Ryan...Kara..." I said, "Do you guys remember that weekend at the lake two years ago?" They nodded.

"Remember when my aunt caught you two fucking in the bathroom?" They nodded again.

"I covered for you two. I begged my aunt for *hours* to not tell your parents." My voice elevated to a weak yell. Ryan bit his lip.

"You two owe me one" and I cocked my head towards Sasha, "she should be the one scared. Not us. Let's go."

The group hesitated. Gordy began filming again and he joined us on the porch. Sasha and I waited in the doorway of the main entrance to give the entire crew room. Matt and Pears came next. Jade grabbed Brooke's hand and climbed the steps.

Kara and Ryan still stood in the muddy graveyard. Her hands covered her face, she wiped outwards. Smearing her makeup even more. I maneuvered through the group to the top step of the porch. Ryan looked over his shoulder momentarily but then put his hand on the small of Kara's back, guiding up the stairs.

Physically, of course, we were all together but even more so we were all there together emotionally. Sasha and I stood in the doorway. The only thing separating us with the inside was a white, wooden door that was tied to a metal stake.

We looked back at our friends. Nobody needed to say anything. We were all in this together.

"Zack. Together." Sasha said and she grabbed the rope that was loosely tied to the stake.

Together, Sasha and I said, "Three… two… one…"

She released the rope. The door of the church swung open and knocked on the wall behind it. Dust particles fainted in the entryway.

We went in.

CHAPTER 14: The Church

Its interior design was unlike any church we had been in before. It was one giant room. Thirty feet wide and fifty feet long. Small walk ways separated the cement walls from the pews but the seating arrangement lined straight across, facing a large cylinder pulpit. Next to the door was a staircase that led to a U-shaped balcony.

There wasn't much to it. Walls were cement on the inside, wooden on the outside. That would explain how the rickety building didn't blow away in a simple thunderstorm. It was just an old building that reeked of a musky attic.

We wandered through the sanctuary, observing the surroundings in an awe-inspired trance. All of those stories. All of the rumors. All of the people slain. We were standing in the exact spot as they.

We didn't pay attention to one specific thing, as if we were in the Lycoming Mall, looking for no product nor store, in particular. Window shopping, if you will. Sections of pews were blemished with what looked to be black dye. Bibles and hymnals were stacked on top of one another at the end of each row, and throughout the balcony's barrier. Floorboards sobbed obnoxiously under our feet, breaking the hypnosis.

A few of us penetrated deeply into the sanctuary but Jade was the only one to reach the final row of pews. There was a series of carvings into the center of the last bench. She walked towards them, able to make out three large crosses dug into the lumber, splinters outlined the sketch. A stick figure was etched onto each crucifix. More stick figures scattered before them, each aligned perfectly in three rows.

Jade counted them aloud, *one... two... three... four... fi—*

Her flashlight flickered twice before the darkness stayed.

She pressed the power button but her phone was dead, it drained 84% of its battery in less than 15 minutes.

Brooke, Kara and Ryan remained close to the entrance. Their flashlights illuminated a snow shovel and a broom that leaned up in the corner.

Pears and Matt traveled the walkways beside the pews. Gordy joined Matt until the fifth row, but peeled off into the seating area to pan the camera in each direction to record the church.

Gordy spun around slowly. He recorded the bottom floor's dull blue shade from the moon's illumination. He held a small flashlight next to the camcorder to shine across the recording path. Nothing of note on the first floor, as expected. After his first full turn, he directed the camera upwards to film the balcony.

Still nothing special. Old bibles and hymnals stacked atop the bannister and a lightning bolt of cracks decorated the concrete on the left wall. Gordy started to lower the cameras view when a speck of liquid dropped onto the camcorders screen. It was dark and thick. Gordy looked up to check the origin of the residue. Natural discoloration spotted the ceiling, but no leaks were active. He was intrigued. Gordy fled his index finger through the dew, the stroke created a long maroon smudge before the camcorder died.

The dark streak of fluid smeared Gordy's finger. He rubbed his thumb against it, and he raised his hand to take a whiff.

Sticky. Coppery. It was blood. No doubt about it.

Gordy stared into his hand, the blood was fresh. He admired the smudge of maroon as it caked into the divots of his fingerprints. Crust cracked as he rubbed his thumb and index together. The flakes floated to the ground.

A voice startled Gordy, but it was only Sasha. "Hey guys..." he said.

Fear struck all of us, but I was especially afraid. It was a similar phrase that I uttered after seeing the boy. "Everything okay?" Pears asked.

"Yeah, all good." she replied. Air released from our balloons of fear. "I have an idea."

Sasha called for us to reconvene. We huddled between the pulpit and the staircase to the balcony. Gordy and Jade didn't speak of their findings at the time, but their once tanned faces were paled. Jade's showed a hint of motion sickness green.

They turned to each other and flashed a certain look. Their eyes met and their lips curled inward. Jade's released back to regular form with force, like the over exaggeration of a *pop* sound. They know something that we don't. They've seen something we haven't. They were two Vietnam Vets that saw too much.

"Who wants to go upstairs with me?" Sasha asked us.

None of us *wanted* to but after the flag incident, we all felt like we were somewhat obligated. Sasha took the biggest blow; her experience was physical.

Every one of us saw those flags wave but Sasha was the only one hit.

A little boy with rotten flesh and teeth waved at me, but he didn't touch me. Blood dropped to Gordy's camera, not him. Jade saw the carvings, nothing was carved into her. But then there was Sasha, standing there with a giant gash on her forehead.

We all agreed to, but she refused. Sasha wanted the old *Scooby-Doo* adage. *Let's split up, gang! Let's all isolate ourselves to the monster can pick us apart one-by-one!*

"By threes. Zack, go to the pulpit." She said. I could feel more vomit creep to my throat but was able to hold back. A small winding staircase lead into the cylinder, atop the pulpit were two books. One was open.

"Gord-O, Matt K., come with me." She said and they followed her up the stairs.

"Who wants to come with me?" I asked the remaining crew. Pears and Jade volunteered.

Brooke snapped, "Wait, where the fuck are we going then?" Ryan and Kara looked on blankly.

"Guys, just chill in the pews." I said empathetically, "I know you guys don't want any part of the other shit so just stay there."

They took a seat in the first row. Kara rested her head on Ryan's shoulder, and he nestled his chin on the top of it. Brooke stared at the floor, elbows on knees, and her chin resting on her hands. Ryan's eyes fixed in our direction as we climbed the pulpit staircase.

Ryan's face started to animate in discomfort. "You feel that?" Ryan asked the girls around him. They nodded in agreement. Heat rose from the pew. It began to feel like the heated seat in his Dodge pickup, but elevated to a scald that was much worse than the initial touch of a leather car seat in July. They were on a theoretical frying pan.

The sensation worsened, forcing the group to their feet. *Rrrrrrriiiiiiiipppppp!* The stitching on his back pockets had disintegrated and two petrified squares of denim fastened to the bench. Steam rose from the patches in long streams.

They didn't say a word about the pew, but Sasha's group and saw their reaction. Nothing needed to be said, we didn't know what happened specifically at the time, but we knew something was off. Their balloons overinflated, but surprisingly didn't pop. If we weren't watching them, the burst would have been extravagant.

Pears, Jade and I were surprised at the size of the pulpit. It looked huge from the sanctuary, like one of the large tanks at the Park Street Brewery in Canton. Benches flanked the ends on the inside. Very similar to the pews in the sanctuary but lacked back support. Jade took a seat on one and Pears parked across from her. I remained standing to watch Sasha, Gordy and Matt begin their investigation of the balcony.

Sasha led the way. Without hesitation, she walked to the back of the rounded balcony. Clunking followed with each step, but the expedition was quick. She bent over, planted her elbows on the wooden barrier and watched Gordy approach her. A floorboard screeched in the silence.

Matt was the last one up the stairs. He looked down the way to Sasha and Gordy, he took a deep breath and began to penetrate the opening of the upper deck. His boots knocked on impact with the hardwood floor, specs of mud retraced his trail. A window appeared in his peripheral vision, he was only halfway to the rest of his group.

He turned his head towards the window and stared at his reflection, but it wasn't an exact replica. It was more of a diabolical mirage. Milky cataracts replaced his dark brown eyes, patches of hair fell from his scalp into the nothingness. Shards of flesh emancipated from his skeleton. Matt remained still but his reflection started to inch towards him, looking zombified. It smiled at him. With each step it took, a tooth fell into the abyss. It reached toward him, both hands straight out. Skin melted from its bony fingers until they were bare.

The reflection looked to Matt's face and inhaled. What was left of its bust raised and its mouth gaped. It released and Matt's body shot backwards, tumbling into the barrier.

He rubbed his head to ensure connected skin and hair. Sasha and Gordy ran to him, but the window began to quake rapidly. Its glass began to crack and the wooden frame splintered. Shards of glass showered the floor.

"Shit, what's going on up there?" I asked.

"Everything's good." Matt choked. "Window broke." There was no more movement or sound. They were paralyzed from scalp to toenail.

Except for the broken window, everything seemed fine from the pulpit. Pears was sitting down, he had one of Gordy's voice recorders and was asking questions in the silence. He had a love of the show "Ghost Hunters", and hoped to pick up some

Electronic Voice Phenomena, or the abbreviation, EVP.

I stepped towards Jade and glanced at the two books on the pulpit's ledge. A bible and a hymnal. The bible was closed but coincidentally, the hymnal was open to the chapter "Hymns for Children."

"Well, that's a little fuckin' spooky." I said.

"What is?" Jade said. She stood up and peered around me. Her cleavage nestled my arm. The smell of her perfume caught my attention, it was fruity, but not cheap. It was like walking into a Bath and Body store at the Lycoming Mall. Blonde locks rested on my arm.

"Oh…" she said as she looked at the hymnal. Her voice was low, an alto in a choir but certainly not manly. It was sexy, could make a lesser man climax just on the audio. I was envious of anyone that heard that voice at a moan.

Kate hated Jade and for no great reason. Jade and I had a *flirting thing* long ago but all of that ended once I met Kate. She had beautiful green eyes that would sparkle on the darkest, most ominous day. Her long, dirty blonde hair always laid perfectly in place. *And* that butt, firm and impeccably shaped. Her personality was suspect, a little dry at times but she was a good person despite the pair of cheating fiasco's. We made it work the first... *and second* time, but apparently Colby Baker did something to really 'wow' her.

Jade was a great person, too. Even in terrible moments, she could make you laugh. We lost to Southern Columbia in the District Championship last year. The whole team was depressed after the game; it was the closest we ever got to the State Championship. Jade came up to Ryan and I after that game and told us that it was okay, because "you two had the nicest asses on the field."

I just never felt like there was an emotional connection between Jade and I. But was there? That night in the pulpit, I started to think of moments that she and I shared. Jade and I had a lot of good times. *A hell of a lot more than Kate and I.* We never fought. *A hell of a lot less than Kate and I.*

Regardless, I was more physically attracted to Kate. I knew it was more than that but I loved her green eyes over Jade's baby blues, her darker tones over Jade's lighter hair, and of course, I was an "ass guy". But Jesus, there was something about Jade Davidson that night. I don't know if it was the way she smelled, or the way she flirtatiously angled herself toward me to look at the eerie hymnal. Either way, I wanted her badly...

I turned toward her, clasped her buttocks and kissed her. She was into it, Jade lodged her waist into my groin and her hips began to thrust. I pushed her bleach blonde hair aside and started to kiss her neck. She moaned a deep, seductive moan. She dug her nails into my back with one hand and caressed my erection with another. She tightened on the root, but eased on the head. Up and down, up and down. My hands ripped open her pink blouse, exposing her bra. I dismantled the cups and started sucking on her breasts. My jeans began to unfasten, I heard unzipping. Oh yes, a cold hand pulled back on the waistband of my boxers and...

"What the fuck was that?!" Jade screamed and she broke my trance. I was upset, the damn alarm clock in the middle of a wet dream. The thought went away when I looked down.

A green powder smeared the crotch of my jeans.

"What was what?" Pears yelled as he stood up.

"Something *fucking* grabbed my tit!" Jade looked down and held her arms straight out. She gasped. "Zack, look at me!! *FUCKING LOOK AT ME!*" she screamed.

Green painted the front of her blouse. It was the shape of a handprint with eight inch fingers.

I quivered, "Uhhh guys, I think we better g—. "

We heard three large thumps. A stack of books fell from the balcony. The other group's paralysis broke. We looked in the direction of the fallen pile.

Across from Sasha, Gordy and Matt were two boys and a man. Bowties hung loosely on their maroon splattered dress shirts. Moss grew on the boys' scabbed faces. The man had a jet black widow's peak with periodic streaks of grey. They smiled at us. As their lips spread across their face, their blue lips cracked. Their eyes were pits of black.

"Get them." The man said. His voice husky and sinister.

The boys sang as they jumped off the balcony. Pews broke their fall, the one's head crushed against the wood. Blood squirted out of his ears like a Super Soaker.

Jesus loves me… he sang.

The other landed on one knee between two rows. His patella dislocated to the outer side of his right leg. Neither was phased and they started towards the groups. Bones cracked as they hurdled the pews like track stars. Sounding like old arthritics, but had the athleticism of a guard in the NBA. Their master was fixed upon Sasha, Gordy and Matt, he stared at them and began his jaunt.

Ryan, Kara and Brooke sprinted toward the exit but the door slammed shut in their face. No wind, no person. They looked back and saw the boy, holding out his hand.

He reached them, licking his lips. The boy taunted them, pounding his feet like a sumo wrestler. Blood splattered the floor beneath him on impact. Kara and Brooke wailed as they hugged Ryan's arms. Their backs were pasted to the door.

My eyes met the boy en route for the pulpit and he stopped dead in his tracks. It was the same little boy that I saw from the cemetery. His head cocked to the right, his fleshy claw raised once again.

Jade and Pears began to run but I grabbed their hands. We were trapped. The entrance was blocked and I didn't want to test our luck with any of the family. But strangely, I didn't feel threatened by the boy. When I first saw him staring at me from the window, I was. Not now, though and he knew it.

The man was only 10 feet from Sasha, Gordy and Matt. Both Gordy and Sasha tripped over their own feet as they retreated toward the steps. His jog turned to a trot. They skootched on the hands and rear-ends. Brooke and Kara began to scream even louder downstairs.

Ryan braced himself against the door and used the leverage to deliver hard kicks to the boy's chin. Blood flew to the walls, but he was unaffected. The boy got stronger with each kick, and seemed to enjoy it. His grin exposed teeth. The rotting enamel started to accompany the blood splatter on the floor.

Ryan started to tire. His kicking frequency started to fall but the power was stronger. He yelled out a determined groan and ruptured the boy's nose with a punt. Splinters of bone sprinkled like candy from a piñata. The only affect was a snort with the boys laugh. His hunger for human flesh strengthened with each blow.

"Fuck this." Sasha yelled. She told Matt and Gordy, "Run downstairs"

Matt and Gordy turned towards the staircase. Sasha pulled her sweatshirt sleeve over her fist, creating a cloth protected club out of her hand. She started to punch remaining glass fragments from the window frame.

The shards littered the space below, but Sasha didn't care. She leaped out of the broken window, plunging twenty feet to the muddy soil of the graveyard.

Sasha landed on her feet but the momentum took her to her knees. A dull ache traveled from the knee around to the middle of her back. She wiped her muddy hands on her thighs, creating a solid brown coat from waist to ankle. Through her own pain-filled grunt, she heard screaming intensify from inside the church.

The boy caught one of Ryan's kicks and held it under his arm like luggage. Ryan saw the boy's sinister look. He opened his mouth and ran his tongue over what was left his decayed smile. His free hand started to rub his belly.

"*MMMMMM IM HUNGRY, RYANNNNNN!*" the boy said, his voice pre-pubescent but strong.

Ryan reached out and shook his hand at the boy. Knowing what was on his mind. "Please don't." Ryan cried.

The boy released a low, Regan MacNeil-esque laugh. A slimy nude-shaded worm started to wriggle through his deserted eye socket. He rocked his head back with laughter and violently sunk his black, rotten teeth into Ryan's ankle. Blood erupted like a geyser from the eight punctures.

Ryan screamed and fell to the floor, bringing the girls with him.

"TASTES LIKE YOUR MOTHER'S DIRTY SNATCH!" the child screamed. *"MMMMMMM TRACYYYYY!!!!"* he started to feast more aggressively.

Matt and Gordy ran down the stairs. They saw some of the boy's bites into Ryan's leg. Chunks of Ryan's calf splat on the hardwood. Gordy vomited on the staircase, splattering onto Matt's boots and into the hair of the feasting child.

The door swung open. "Come on!" Sasha screamed.

Kara and Brooke pulled Ryan out of the church. The little boy turned to Gordy and Matt. He licked the blood from his lips and sneered. Strands of skin parked between the teeth he had left like he just gnawed corn on the cob. They turned to go back up the stairs, but the man stood in the top doorway. They were cornered.

"Go." I said. Pears and Jade ran down the steps of the pulpit. I followed but my side crashed into the wooden railing. I heard something fall to the floor but there was no time. We ran to the porch, passing the little boy who craved the skin of our friends.

We didn't realize it when we passed, but the little boy was beginning to climb the steps to the balcony. One black shoe slammed the wooden steps. He bent over and hissed. The worm crawled out of his empty eye socket and his other boot slammed down to the wood.

"ZACK! JADE! *GUUUUUYYYYYYYYSSSSSSSSS!*" we heard as we started to run off of the porch. Jade quickly turned around and reentered the church. She lunged toward the boy. Her arms extended toward him as he stomped up another step. Blonde hair flew back from her speed; her black-polished fingernails were only six inches away from the evil child when the other little boy turned the corner and appeared from beyond the pulpit. He raised his own claw, streaks of blue decorated his flesh. His face wasn't sinister, it was content. Blood began to leak from his lips, but he was speaking, not sneering.

"Oh-Aye" he said. *Go away? No way? ...okay...* He walked towards us, Jade turned her attention to the lesser of the two evils. She raised fists but I held her back. *This* little boy at least, wasn't a threat.

He began to climb the steps and touched the shoulder of his hungry brother. The hissing suddenly stopped. Boots slammed the lower steps and both boys ran back into the sanctuary, disappearing into thin air. Gordy's shoulder slammed against the door casing as he and Matt ran out of the door. All of us sprinted through the graveyard and leaped into the Knickerbocker SUV.

It was a clown car. No specific seating except Matt in the driver's seat.

We managed some organization as Matt turned onto Route 6. Kara grabbed a roll of paper towels from under the driver's seat and rolled up Ryan's blood-soaked pant leg.

No marks. No bruises. No blood. Nothing.

CHAPTER 15: Truth Be Told

I couldn't go home alone. The idea of going to Sara O'Sullivan's party never crossed my mind, nor did the thought of joining Pears, Matt and Gordy at the White residence. Only one person could ease my mind at this time. My mother.

Pete Wile's house was only five miles from the church. It was the closest drop-off and Matt drove there first.

Calmly, I told my friends goodbye and started walking the paved driveway. My walk escalated to a jog once the SUV was out of sight. I could see Kate's house over Pete's hilly yard. A light in her bedroom was on. Probably her desk lamp, shining on a Nicholas Sparks paperback.

Halfway up the driveway I heard leaves begin to rustle and felt warm breath on the back of my neck. The sound inched closer, but the Wile's yard was well groomed. No leaves. The breath was now audible, sounding like an asthmatic in gym class.

I reached the Wile's front door.

"Mom! Mom! It's me! Let me in!" I screamed as I pounded on the metal entrance.

"Zack?" I heard her say from the inside. The sound of utensils clanked from beyond her voice, followed by a slam. Light shined through the window curtain.

"Yes, mom! Pleeeeeeeeeaaaaassssseeeee!" I cried.

She pulled the curtain back and started to unlock the door. In her hand was a large cutting knife. Even holding a knife, she was the least intimidating human alive.

The door swung open and I embraced her, the knife fell to the floor and clanked on the marble. My tears drenched her reddish-brown hair. My mom released a gentle, drawn-out "shhhh". It was something that she always did when comforting my sister and I. The sound calmed us, but in reality, it was her that eased our emotions. Her warmth, her demeanor, her love.

"Honey, what happened?" she asked as she took a seat at the kitchen table. "You smell like a goddamn cellar."

"Mom, please don't think I'm crazy." I sniffed snot back into my nostrils. "I lied to you. We didn't go to Williamsport."

"Where did you go?" my mother asked earnestly.

"Okay, so there's this place out passed Stoney Corners." I said strenuously, "It's like... in the middle of nowhere... and... it's supposed to be... ummm... haunted."

"You talking about the Lequin Church?" she asked.

I was surprised. I didn't think she would guess it but I should have. Everyone knew about it, just maybe not the specifics.

"Yeah." I sat up.

"Jesus Christ, Zackary." She rubbed her forehead and took a sip of Pepsi. She wasn't angry or sad, but her voice was frustrated. "You didn't go in there, did you?"

"Yeah, we did." and I slumped back into the chair.

My mother collected herself. She never got angry, but you could tell when she was on the cusp. This was one of those times. She always shot subtle clues, like calling me "Zackary", instead of "Zack". My favorite was when my sister came home drunk when she was a junior in high school. Beth snuck in at about 3:00 am and woke up in time for breakfast. My mom sat at the table with one leg crossed over another. She flipped a page of the Salt Springs Sentinel, staring over the top of her glasses and stated clearly, "Elizabeth Patricia, you have some explaining to do."

This look rivaled that but she also looked concerned. "What happened, Zack?"

I exhaled, "Okay, so we got there and there's a cemetery around i--."

"I know there's a cemetery, Zack."

"Okay, well, we were in it. And I looked in the window and there was a boy looking at me. But... but... he changed. His teeth turned black and his eyes went white. Then he just disappeared."

My mom grabbed my hand, "What else?"

"We went to leave and one of those little American flags flew and smacked Sasha in the head." The pace of my speech increased and I continued telling her how we ended up inside.

"Something happened to Matt in the balcony and something happened in the... the... main part..." I started to stagger. Mom nodded and patted my hand.

"But something grabbed Jade and I. Then there were *THESE FUCKING PEOPLE THAT CHASED US OUT OF THE GOD DAMN PLACE, MOM!*" I started to weep. I didn't intend to tell my mom the final part because there was no possible way that she would believe it.

"Zack, honey. It's oka—"

"IT'S NOT OKAY, MOM! THE ONE BIT RIGHT THROUGH RYAN'S FUCKING LEG! HE WAS GOING TO DO THE SAME MATT AND GORDY!"

"What stopped him?" she asked.

I started to calm. I sniffed more snot back into my nasal cavity.

"It was the other little boy. Mom, he was the one I saw earlier. The one that looked at me through the window."

"Do you think they were real?" she asked.

"No, mom... They weren't... I think they were..."

"Ghosts?"

"Something like that." I said. "There was blood everywhere when that kid bit Ryan. But when we got back to the car he didn't even have a damn scratch!"

She looked at me blankly. Her hand released mine and she grabbed another Pepsi from the refrigerator. I held my head in my hands and started at the table.

"I know you don't believe me, but I am telling the truth." I said. She pulled out the seat next to me and flopped down into it. Her left hand rubbed my back.

"I believe you." She said.

I released the grip on my scalp and turned to her. Snot and tears poured down my face. My eyes were so bloodshot that the room appeared dark. My mom's aged face appeared through the droplets of water that parked on my eye lashes.

"What? You beli—"

"I believe every goddamn word you just said, Zack."

My mom insisted that I stay the night. She claimed that Pete wouldn't care and it was true. Pete Wile was a great man. Not a great police officer, but he really good person. His house was huge and he paid my mom well to look over it on the weekends. I had no interest in the pool table in the basement, just the couch and reruns of "It's Always Sunny in Philadelphia".

"I'm going to bed, honey. If you need anything, just yell." she said. "I'll be in the guest room."

She offered me the guest room but I declined, I wanted open space. I had had enough confinement for the night.

I emptied my pockets and placed the contents onto the coffee table. My wallet was missing.

I remembered the thump from when we sprinted out of the pulpit.

My wallet was still in the church.

CHAPTER 16: Party At Sara's

Jade Davidson paid no mind to the crowd that welcomed her into the party at the O'Sullivan's. She flashed a smile to those who she cared about but several were pushed aside on her way to the kitchen. She immediately poured orange juice and vodka into a red Solo. The screwdriver was a bit heavy on the vodka this time around.

She leaned against the marble island and chugged her first drink. She felt the short-term memories of the church begin to fade. The second drink lasted longer but her buzz approached quickly.

Kara and Ryan then pummeled in. Kara branched off to the living room couch but requested that Ryan get her a rum and coke. She was tired, mentally and physically. Her arms ached from squeezing Ryan's in the church doorway and bruises on her neck pulsed. Two days ago, her father clubbed her in the back with a barstool from their kitchen. He heard about his daughter's outfit at school. She left the house that day in her usual t-shirt and jeans but she changed before the opening bell into a pink sundress. It wasn't extremely revealing, but the dress exposed more of his daughter's legs than he wanted.

On his way to the kitchen, Ryan was cornered by a few of his teammates. They drunkenly congratulated him on the game winning touchdown.

His teammates followed him to the kitchen. He and Dave Ramsey shotgunned some Miller Lite's before he made Kara's drink. Ryan returned to Kara with her drink and a pair of beers for himself. They sucked the alcohol quickly, and Ryan made a second trip to the kitchen less than five minutes later.

Sasha and Brooke remained outside while the others entered the party. They took a seat on the porch step. The O'Sullivan's house overlooked Salt Springs. Streetlights shined over the empty roads. The smell of pine released the hillside's evergreens and traveled up the slope. The only obstruction of the beautiful view was Luke Larson's police cruiser that sat still 100 feet down the road.

Brooke removed a pack of cigarettes from her purse. She didn't smoke often, but when stressful times arrived, she treated herself.

She popped a Misty in her mouth and lit the end. The first drag was long and then released a cloud of smoke. She offered one to Sasha, and she accepted.

After Sasha finished her second cigarette, she crushed it on the concrete step. They agreed to go in. The living room was littered with beer cans and plastic cups. Their classmates danced on the tan carpet. In the midst of the mass they saw Kara and Ryan making out on the couch and Dave Ramsey was snorting a white powder off of the glass coffee table.

They reached the kitchen. Jade Davidson still stood there, sipping on the vodka-heavy screwdriver.

None of them were having a great time. Jade was drowning her thoughts in vodka and orange juice. Sasha's forehead started to burn. Her wound disappeared after they left the Lequin Church but the pain never eased. Beer cans served as an icepack on the vacated puncture.

Brooke felt numb. She was no longer depressed or fearful. Of course, Shawn had left her but her string of bad luck continued beyond that. Drexel denied her because of low SAT scores. She had another opportunity to take them but the final football game of the season was at noon on the same day. Cheerleaders had to be at the field at 9:00 am, the same time that the testing started.

Robin Beckett, Brooke's mother, was arrested and sentenced to a year in prison for stealing money from the electric company. Her father was nothing more than a drunken bastard who blamed the whole thing on his daughter. He said that she should have gotten a job to help around the house instead of that goddamn cheerleading. *Fuckin' sluts just get in the way of the game anyways!*

But now the memories of her visit to the Lequin Church haunted her. She could only think of the little boy's teeth sinking into Ryan's leg. Over and over, bite after bite, and the blood squirting into the air. *How did he know Ryan's mom's name?* The hissing and the screams seemed to play over the speakers in the living room. She tried everything, she reached around Jade and began drinking Grey Goose straight from the bottle.

A boy approached the group. For once, it wasn't a carnivorous one. Well, really, with the look he cast at Jade, he might have been. He walked closer and Brooke continued to swig on the bottle. Brooke saw

his sharp blue eyes. Crisp, with a slight sparkle from the kitchen chandelier. His t-shirt was tight, his round, muscular pecs hugged his shirt and his abs jabbed the inside of his shirt. He rubbed his hands together and his biceps flexed to a bulge with a decorative vein.

"Get 'em Jade, get 'em! Pleeeeassseee fuck him." she thought. *"He could do whatever he wanted to me."*

His face started to transform. Eyeballs and teeth fell to the floor, his nose rotted to a simple hole in the center of his head. It was rebuilding itself, though. The boy transformed into Shawn. Yes, Shawn Pratt, her ex-boyfriend. He was an exact replica, but he wasn't coming for her. He was coming for one of her best friends, Jade Davidson. *He reached around and clapped his hands to her buttocks for leverage. He kissed her passionately.*

"Hi Mike." Jade said.

Brooke woke up from her trance. It was the attractive boy that she saw from the beginning. Not a sinister one and certainly not Shawn Pratt.

"Jade Davidson. What's happening?" the boy said slyly.

The boy was Mike Wilde, a kid from the neighboring town of Troy. Mike was the male equivalent of Jade Davidson, a straight up dime. A perfect 10. A bombshell. You name the idiom.

Mike played basketball for the Trojans. Point guard. Salt Springs was better at basketball now, but hoops weren't exactly popular. Springers didn't feel like the games were interesting. Except the one against Troy. Females summoned to each gym that Mike Wilde entered. The only problem was that he knew it. He was a narcissistic, egotistical maniac.

"Nothing much." Jade replied. She was friendly, but not overtly.

"How you been?" he asked, offering a crooked smile and he inched closer to Jade.

"Been good. You?"

"I didn't know you'd be here so, I couldn't be better." he said.

Mike was only inches from Jade. He leaned up against the island and faced her. Jade remained forward.

"You look... so..." Mike stammered. "So... beautiful... So sexy."

He leaned in to smell her hair but she cocked her head back. Sasha started to intervene until her heard Jade start speaking.

"How's Kaysie, Mike?" Jade asked.

"Kaysie? She's good. She's not here." He replied.

"Yeah, no shit." she sneered. Her disgust was audible. "I didn't think you'd be that much of a pig with your girlfriend here."

"Okay, bitch liste—"

Jade grabbed the bottle of Grey Goose out of Brooke's hand and said, "I'll shove this whole fuckin' bottle up your ass if you don't get out of this kitchen." she said. "Will probably fit with all the cock you take in it, get the fuck out of here." Mike mumbled and retreated to the living room. Sasha cheered, but Brooke only flashed a smile.

"Ooooooh gaht damn girl!" Sasha said. "Tell that nigga!"

"Creepy son of a bitch, isn't he?" Jade laughed and rattled the bottle of liquor. The vodka splashed around at the bottom. She pointed the top of it towards Brooke, "Finish it up, girl. Let's go try to have fun."

Jade could feel Brooke's pain. Her arm wrapped around Brooke's shoulder and they returned to the living room. It was a T.I. kind of night. "Whatever You Like" blasted over the living room speakers, just like the Knickerbocker SUV on the way to the Lequin Church.

They joined the crowd. Some danced, many were grinding, and a few looked as though they were seizing. Colt Lewis passed out during the third verse, he crashed through the glass coffee table. Cocaine flew onto Ryan, Kara and Dave Ramsey.

Brooke swayed to the beat. She watched Kara and Ryan rise and brush off the powder. Admittedly, Brooke was jealous. Certainly not of Ryan or Kara, but of their situation. They were happy. But most importantly, they were together.

Stacks on deck

She turned to Jade and Sasha. It looked like they were starting to have fun. They faced one another, screaming the tune. Brooke admired Jade's beauty. Jade always said her eyes were light blue, but that wasn't the case. They were periwinkle. She stood a perfect 5'6 with an ass and chest that could make the Earth stop on its axis. Brooke didn't have any of that, especially after her recent weight gain. She hated those extra 20 pounds, but she hated herself even more so.

Patrone on ice

And Jade was so strong. Mentally and physically. First and foremost, she had the confidence to take on the little boy that attacked Ryan and she probably would have stopped him. And just literally

five minutes ago, she told the biggest asshole on
the planet to basically, fuck off. Brooke knew that
she could never do that.

And we can pop bottles all night

Brooke then watched Sasha, impressed by her
dancing ability. She danced like her personality.
Eccentric and charismatic were only two of the
many words to describe it. Brooke used to laugh at
everything that Sasha said, but not anymore. It
wasn't to the fault of Sasha; her material was
unchanged. Brooke couldn't really laugh at
anything anymore.

And baby you could have whatever you like

Sasha had different strength than Jade. Only a few
knew the real story of what happened to her
parents, but regardless, they both passed away.
Brooke supposed that Sasha saw her parents' last
moments just based off of things that she
mentioned in passing. And now she's with a brand
new family and helps them pay the bills. Brooke
was ashamed that she couldn't keep up with her
studies and cheerleading, let alone get a job on top
of it. She felt if only she were better, maybe her
mom wouldn't be in prison.

I said you could have whatever you like... yeah...

Brooke looked towards the stairs and saw someone signaling for her to follow. She couldn't believe her eyes. It was Shawn, wearing the same shorts and polo combination that he did on their first date two years ago.

Shawn winked at her and continued the "come hither" motion with his fingers. Brooke pushed through Sasha and Jade. The living room crowd parted like the Red Sea. She was at the foot of the stairs. Shawn reached a hand out toward her and she grabbed it. They jogged up the stairs.

He led her to the upstairs bathroom and he started to undress. He placed his shirt in the sink and started to kiss Brooke's neck. Brooke placed her hand on his back, but she jerked back quickly after the initial feel. He was scalding. Just like the church pew.

Shawn's skin began to boil, and patches of flesh started to erupt like a volcano. Fire released from his ears and he began to melt in Brooke's arms.

Brooke screamed at the sight. Flesh dripped onto the linoleum and he fell to her knees in an attempt to gather Shawn's liquefied body.

She scooped him into her hands. Her palms started to absorb the flesh. She kept scooping. Handful after handful until Shawn's melted carcass dissolved in her.

Her bottle of Grey Goose shot across the bathroom floor as the bathroom door swung open. It was Jade.

"Brooke, are you okay?" she asked.

Brooke sobbed on the bathroom floor.

"It was Shawn! It was Shawn! He's gone! He's dead!" she screamed as she pounded the floor.

"Brooke... Shawn isn't here."

"I fucking know that! He isn't now! But he was! He was just here..." Brooke wailed.

"Brooke, babe..." Jade said calmly and she handed Brooke her phone. "He's visiting his sister at Lycoming College. She just texted me. He's been in Williamsport all day."

Brooke didn't believe it but it was true. The text messages were right in front of her. Shawn went down to spend the afternoon and evening with his older sister who was a freshman at Lycoming College. His sister was taking him to a few college parties and Saturday morning she planned to show him around the school.

"Just come back downstairs, okay?" Jade pleaded.

"Just give me a minute." Brooke said and Jade nodded. She shut the door and went back down to the party.

Brooke looked to the ground. Her tears flooded the place of her hallucination.

But was it?

Brooke looked back toward the bathroom window and what she saw next was real. It was the little boy from the church, swinging the bottle of Grey Goose. Grass fell from his hair and scattered on the floor. A worm crawled out of his eye and onto the bottle.

Blood trickled down his chin and he wiped it with his rotting forearm. His purple lips smiled as he cracked the bottle over the porcelain sink like a scene from an old western.

Shards shattered over the pool of blood, tears and grass. The boy walked towards her, crunching glass beneath his feet on the way.

A clear shard punctured the bottom of his black shoe and poked through the top. Blood gushed from the hole in his foot. He was unaffected by it.

His face was only inches from hers and be bent over to pick up a hunk of glass. The boy shoved it in front of Brooke's face and said, "Do it."

"No." Brooke started crying harder.

"It's all your fault! You failed your mother!"

"STOP IT!" Brooke wept.

"The overnight guard raped your mother last night because of you! She's in prison because of you!"

"NO! NO!"

"Shawn didn't want your fat sloppy clam anymore! You disgusting whore!"

"SHUT UP! SHUT UP!" she screamed.

"Shawn doesn't want you! Your father doesn't want you! Your friends don't want you!"

"WHY ARE YOU DOING THIS?!?!?! WHAT DO YOU WANT?!?!?!"

"DO IT! KILL YOURSELF!" the boy screamed in her face. Blood from his lips sprayed Brooke's blonde hair. The worm started crawling up her arm.

Brooke snatched the glass from the boy and dug it deep into her wrist. Blood flew to the wall and she began to fade.

"MORE!" the boy screamed.

She used her remaining energy to stab her arm again. Chunks of meat fell to the floor, creating an audible splat.

"AAAHHH YES! YOU FAT FUCKING WHORE! DIG BITCH!"

The boy laughed as Brooke stabbed herself again.

"MORE!!!"

And again.

And again.

CHAPTER 17: Gordy's Studio

Pears and Matt joined Gordy at his house to play the new Halo video game. Linda White always kept the refrigerator and cupboards stocked with the best snacks and sodas. She was accustomed to having teenage boys around since she gave birth to five of them. Gordy was the second oldest and although all of the boys were popular, Gordy brought the most friends over.

Linda was sitting on the couch when Gordy, Matt and Pears came in. She thumbed through a National Geographic to peruse the nature photos that was lit by a lamp on the end table. Linda claimed that once the boys were out of school she and her husband would move to a forest in northwestern Canada.

"Evenin', oops, I meant mornin', boys!" Linda joked. She was quirky like that and unlike most boys his age, Gordy didn't mind the wittiness of his mother. In order to raise five boys, you had to have a special personality and everyone appreciated its uniqueness. Of all the mother's in our group, Ms. Linda was one of the two favorite's. The other, was my own, Ms. Shelly.

"Mom, what are you doing awake?" Gordy asked.

"Well, I was waiting for you boys! Didn't know if I'd have to bail ya's out." she said. "Had to keep right by the phone." She nudged a thumb towards the old rotary.

After they dropped off the rest of the group, Gordy, Matt and Pears were fine. They were certainly a little jumpy still, but they didn't feel any threat. Sure, they saw the flag shoot out of the ground, but it felt like an eternity ago. Matt started to feel like the window was a simple figment of his imagination. It was an old window, probably just a distortion. Plus, he was a big dude. The window probably broke from the vibration after he fell.

Nothing happened to Pears, specifically. He was the only one in the pulpit that wasn't grabbed, and of course he heard a few floorboards crack when he was asking questions. *Ghost Hunters* always tried to debunk activity first, and Pears had the same idea.

Gordy's camera started to work again but he lost all of the footage. He thought the syrupy liquid was eerie and it sure as hell smelled like blood. The building was old though. It rained all day and the roof probably leaked. It was nothing more than tar or something that seeped through with the rain.

They all agreed that the man and two boys were creepy but there had to be some explanation. One of the others must have told people their plans for the night. It was the first weekend of October, a prankster's Christmas, or at least Easter. In the morning they would probably discover that they were Jade's cousins playing a prank.

Gordy, Matt and Pears went into the studio. Gordy's studio was designed for audio production, but the back had a few couches that faced the gaming systems and television.

Pears turned on the Xbox and passed out the controllers. Matt threw the potato chips and Mountain Dews on the floor. Gordy sat on the end of the couch, tossing Totino's Pizza Rolls into his gullet.

The boys killed the sodas and obliterated the potato chips. Grease from their fingers lubed the controllers. The analog sticks completely lost their grip. Finally, after three hours of gaming, they all fell asleep.

Dawn began to break and the rising sun awoke Gordy. He looked to his left and saw Pears and Matt, still asleep on the sectional. Matt had actually slouched to a sitting position on the floor, and his back leaned to the couch.

His backpack perched against the stand that supported his Xbox. The two voice recorders peeked out of the side pocket like cigarettes in an open carton. Gordy pushed his long brown hair behind his ears and slowly stood up. He walked towards the backpack.

Gordy tried to remember the questions that Pears asked in the church. One thing he could remember was that he asked a question right as men appeared. He concentrated but couldn't think of it. Was it something that Pears asked that provoked them? No, it couldn't be. They were a bunch of pranksters anyways.

Regardless, he thought that it couldn't hurt to know for sure. Gordy picked up the backpack and went to the computer by the soundboard.

He removed the memory card and downloaded the files onto the laptop. After 15 minutes, the process was complete. Gordy put on the headphones and began to listen.

"Jesus Christ you guys in a hurry?"

"Bitch! When my people got white folk behind us we gotta be safe! We runnin'!"

"And I've been running since I crossed the border."

He clicked the fast-forward button.

"Ummm... black?"

"Gord, get this on camera."

sound of marker on stone

*"Jedidiah McLaughlin, 1866-1871. Ohhh-ayeeee.
Five fucking years old."*

"What... the... fuck...?" Gordy whispered and he
pressed rewind.

"Mornin' Gord-O." Pears said.

"Morning, brother." Gordy replied and hung up the
headphones. He'd finish listening in the afternoon.

CHAPTER 18: Rejoice!

The fall's first frost struck overnight. It wasn't a strong one, but significant. I had promised my mother that after the thaw, I would mow Pete Wile's lawn and do some other small landscaping chores. She left the key to their garage on the counter when she left for Saturday morning book club.

It was annoying weather. The sky was blue and air was warm, but the breeze created a chill that forced one to bundle up.

I went to the garage and mounted the John Deere. Its leather seat was ice cold, and vibrated as I turned the key in the ignition. Sending freezing waves through my body.

Sun glared in my eyes as I departed the garage and its warmth beamed on my face. I lowered the mower deck as the John Deere reached the yard. The aroma of freshly cut grass began to infiltrate the enovirnment.

A blue car pulled out of the Ford's driveway next door. The car turned left but then reversed back into the driveway. It peeled in the opposite direction. Tires spun in the dirt, creating a large brown cloud. Through the dust, I could see a magnet on the rear fender. A big yellow 'M'. *Mansfield Tigers. Colby Baker. Son of a BITCH!*

I raised the mower deck and rode the John Deere to the Ford's garage. A sidewalk connected the garage to the front door. Concrete seemed to crunch under my stomping feet. My brain and gut were boiling with rage. *She fucking lied! She told me she was FUCKING LEAVING HIM!*

Kate was looking out of the window. She looked guilty as she turned towards the front door and opened it. I stormed in.

"What the fuck was he doing here!?" I screamed.

"Zack, I broke up with him last night. He was picking up some things I had of his." she said softly.

I remembered that he turned in the opposite direction of me, going towards Windfall Road rather than the main drag. *Who goes the back way? He was avoiding me, that's what! Fucking coward couldn't face me!*

"Is that why he went the other way?" I yelled and Kate looked confused. "He turned around when he saw me."

Kate inhaled and shook her head. It's a mannerism that my sister does when somebody says something stupid so I always took offense to the trait.

My blood curdled and my scalp coiled. Steam began to build in my ears but the fire extinguished abruptly when she said, "I told him I wanted you back, okay?"

I was relieved at first and then I turned ecstatic. We had a few hurdles but this was just another one cleared.

A year and a half ago, I caught Kate cheating on me with Carter Winthrop. Carter was an acquaintance of mine but we developed a friendship. His cousin, Courtney was Kate's best friend and lived down the street.

One day, Kate's father caught us kissing in their garage and that concluded my visitation rights to their house. She was only allowed to go two places after that: church and Courtney Winthrop's.

Courtney filled me in on this tip, and I started to visit Carter's when she was at Courtney's. The four of us hung out every single weekend, even if it was just for an afternoon. It was a strange coalition, but it worked. I got to see Kate and Courtney did, as well. During the process, hell, I felt like I made a couple of friends.

That was until the afternoon that I overheard a conversation from Carter's kitchen. I paused a game of Madden 06 and heard Carter say, "I'm hopping in the shower. Want to join?"

Kate replied, "Give me a minute."

I approached both of them about it and eventually Carter told me that there was something between them. He was a little shit. The kid stood about 5'3, weighed about 110. I was shocked that Kate would cheat on me at all, let alone with some rat-faced looking twat.

Carter got three punches to the face that day. His nose and orbital bone crushed. His life was at stake if he told anyone the true story.

Kate simply told me that it was a mistake. She felt that we were moving so fast and she was scared. But now that she was intimate with someone other than I, she knew that I was the one she wanted to be with forever. I believed her and not a soul knew that she and Carter Winthrop had a fling.

She and I rekindled our fire and ultimately, my visitation rights were granted once again. I started going to church with her, and was active in their youth group. For once, Pastor Tom Ford was content with me. He still didn't think I was good enough for his daughter but, he didn't detest the idea of our relationship.

Tom was the pastor at *Rejoice!,* a church just beyond Troy Borough. It was a huge congregation and people traveled over an hour for Sunday service. It was unique. No one in the area had been to a modern Evangelical church before.

There was no dress code. People could wear their Steelers or Eagles jerseys and no one would bat an eye. They had an actual band that led worship and they let Tom Ford have the easiest job in history. All Kate's father did was deliver a five-minute message.

I wasn't keen on the hand flailing and bowing but it was a lot more exciting than the standard sermons and hymns.

Colby Baker was in the youth group. Seemed like an okay kid, but he was one of those cheesy church goers. Always in a good mood, had a soft voice and constantly thanked the *Lord and Savior.* Anyone that had a brain, or wasn't brainwashed by *Rejoice!,* knew that this kid was a snake in the grass. He blended in with the rest of the congregation with his *holier than thou* attitude.

Tom Ford loved Colby and always paired his daughter with him for tasks around the church.

They worked in everything from sound production to landscaping, all to the demands of Kate's father. Naturally, they got close and I started to pick up on subtleties.

Kate finally admitted that they had acted out on their urges for a few months and she liked him. So she kicked me to the curb and started in with Colby full-time. Finally, we started seeing each other once school started and after these miserable few months, I was about to get her back full-time.

Sweat soaked her turquoise bedsheets. I maneuvered around a darker patch of fluid as I dismounted her naked body. We laid on our backs side-by-side, panting uncontrollably.

I didn't even recall how or when we got to her bedroom. Neither did she. It didn't matter, after last night and my fit of rage about Colby, I needed it. And, by the looks of my back and arms, she needed it too.

She threw her arm over me and laid her head on my chest. Her fingers caressed my upper arm.

Kate sighed, "Nice work, Bristol."

We both laughed. "I really needed that." I said.

"Oh please," she said sarcastically. "You weren't the one who was just accused of being a liar!"

"Yeah, sorry about that." I chuckled. "Last night wasn't all that great. It was... umm... Actually, it was pretty fucking awful.

"What happened?" she asked.

I told her. Every last detail. The boy appearing in the church window when Matt was tracing on the gravestone. Flags waving without wind and one springing out of the ground to pop Sasha in the head.

She started to laugh at the part involving the man and two boys. Her laughter turned to a hysteric level when I explained the attack. The only part that I left out was my trance in the pulpit. She didn't need to know about my sexually explicit daydream about Jade Davidson. Plus, I didn't feel that way about her. Kate was the only person that I wanted, so the temporary possession was irrelevant.

Kate was starting to convulse from her laughter. Tears began to dwell in her eyes. "Zack... Stop it..." she shrieked and a cough followed. "Oh wait, I know what happened." she sobered and propped herself on an elbow. Her comforter slumped due to the movement and her chest was temporarily exposed, gaining my attention.

She covered up, "Up here, Bristol." she said, pointing at her face. "You went over to the O'Sullivan's before, didn't you? Were you all drunk?" she asked.

"Holy shit, babe." I replied. The question irked me. "You know I don't do that."

"Well," she said with exaggerated animosity. "If your old buddy, Jade Davidson was like, *ohhhh Zack, there's this party at Sar—*"

"Oh, shut up" I laughed. "But really, babe. I need a favor."

Kate let out an embellished grunt. Like the sarcasm that one would reply after being granted the simplest of tasks.

"What do you want?!?!?!" she exaggerated and started laughing.

"I think my wallet is still there." I mumbled. "Can you take me there?"

"Well, where did you get the condom from?" she asked. "You always keep one in your wallet."

"Jesus Christ, it was in your dresser." I grumbled, "can you please take me?"

Without speaking, she got up and began to dress herself. She traveled across the floor, picking up her outfit. Kate was able to find her bra and panties, as well as her Salt Spring High School t-shirt that she wore upon my arrival. Her pants were missing, though. Welts still decorated her ass cheeks, *Nice work, Bristol.* She grabbed a hair tie off of her nightstand as she spotted her leggings.

"You coming?" she said. "Let's go."

CHAPTER 19: Morning Sickness

Part A:

Sasha Jacobs woke up with a splitting headache
and a terrible case of vertigo. Her temples pounded
like a drummer on a snare. Outlines of her
surroundings blended together like old television
screen powering off. Shapes slowly took form, her
vision improved enough to see her friend Jade lying
beside her.

She sat up, shocked to see the mass of passed out
teenagers around her. A broken coffee table and
some friends to her left. Ryan and Kara cuddled on
the living room couch, passed out next to them was
Dave Ramsey. White powder and chunks of vomit
covered his green Salt Springs High School t-shirt.

At her right, a sea of strangers flooded the living
room carpet. Just a mass of drunken teenagers that
didn't remain conscious through the night.

All of the awaking fuzz cleared and she could see
the living room chandelier above her. Two t-shirts
hung from the faux candles.

Sunlight entered the living room windows. Sasha's
head began to thump even harder and nausea was
becoming a tenant. She raised a hand to block the

brightness and became disgusted by her ashy forearm.

There was only one thing that Sasha didn't like about being Black and that was how ashy her skin could get. Elbows and knees were the normal areas; it was an easy fix with some cocoa butter but it was very annoying. Forearms and hands were hotspots when she was hungover though. She thought it was from dehydration, but she wasn't entirely sure.

The need to urinate quickly overshadowed her headache. Sasha raised to a knee and rubbed her face. Her skin made a coarse sound, she hoped there would be some lotion in the medicine cabinet.

Her initial balance was off and almost landed a foot on Jade's head. She succeeded her evasion attempts until a stray beer can appeared before it was too late. The can let out a loud crush, but nobody was awakened.

The only bathroom that she was aware of was the one upstairs and she followed the same path that Brooke did only a few hours before. Her feet felt like cinderblocks underneath her but she managed to clear the flight after two minutes of labor. White carpet continued in the upstairs hallway.

Sasha turned toward the bathroom, but an
ominous shadow loomed from the bottom of its
door. It was bizarre, there was no light entering the
hall. Each door was sealed shut. The shadow
darkened and she sobered with each step. Her dry
hands scraped over her eyes, assuring that the
shadow wasn't from a loose eyelash. It wasn't. She
became so intent on the space below the
bathroom door that she accidentally shouldered a
family portrait that hung from the wall. It fell to the
shag carpeting. An odor started to rise as the
pressure of her bladder disappeared.

This wasn't a shadow. Sasha was within reaching
distance from the bathroom's entryway when she
bent over to look at the large spot. Moist maroon
spread across the width of the doorframe and the
odor was at its strongest level of fumigation.
Copper and corpse.

Sasha kicked the door open.

CHAPTER 19: Morning Sickness

Part B:

Jade Davidson awoke to a blood curdling scream. Her surroundings were familiar, but foggy. A chandelier above her, the shattered coffee table that scattered before Ryan and Kara. Jade took the black hairband from her wrist and tied back her blonde locks.

Ryan and Kara woke up to the scream, as well. But neither of their eyes opened and they fell right back into their slumber on the living room couch.

Lying on the floor in front of her was a bracelet snapped in half. A yellow rubber one with black text. *HERE WE GO STEELERS HERE WE GO* wrapped around it. Jade thought it could only be from two people, Zack Bristol or Sasha Jacobs. She took the latter. Sasha was nowhere to be seen.

Jade heard a loud thump and frantic sobbing from the upstairs. It was Sasha. She sprinted up the stairs, kicking the crushed beer can across the way. The top of her foot crushed against the top step. Her ponytail flew over her shoulder as her arms extended to the upstairs carpet as she broke her own fall.

Down the hallway, she saw Sasha sitting on her knees leaning on the bathroom door casing. Jade arose quickly and ran towards her, but she vomited once she hit the foul odor. The large orange blot wasn't complimentary to the white shag, but there was no time to be concerned with that.

She recovered, wiped her chin clean of the bile and vodka. Sasha wrapped her arms around Jade's legs at the knees at the furthest point of reach. Jade looked down at Sasha. Her face was buried in between Jade's knees.

Jade looked into the bathroom and couldn't believe her eyes. There before her was the remains of Brooke Beckett. Her forearm looked as if it were chewed on by a shark. Gashes and deep craters donned her arm from wrist to elbow. Some of the marks looked as though she was digging with the glass that littered the flood like a landfill. Bloody meat and rotten skin plastered the linoleum in globs. Blood splatter reached the toilet, sink and bathroom entrance.

They held each other tight and wept. Their faces buried into each other's neck. Sasha had a mouthful of her hooded sweatshirt.

A door swung open from behind them. The welling of their tears obstructed the view, it was a girl in her bra and panties and a boy in his boxers. Tears wiped. It was Sara O'Sullivan and Mike Wilde coming out of a bedroom. Sara looked at Brooke's carcass.

"Motherfucker." Sara sighed. "Go get everyone out of here, Mike."

Mike ran downstairs and started screaming for everyone to get out. The downstairs' reaction sounded lax at first but ended up sounding like Knickerbocker Dairy at milking time.

"What do we do!?" Jade bawled.

Sasha started to rise, "I'm going to call the poli—"

"Not yet," Sara said. "Wait until everyone's gone."

"Sara... *Do you not FUCKING see what's going on here?"* Jade yelled.

"Ummm... yeah... I obviously see she's not alive but were all fucked if the cops show up and the place looks like it is."

Sasha stood up straight, her joints cracked as she rose. Her eyes met Sara's as they stood nose to nose. Sara was intimidated, but it was the look of a photo-op before a big boxing match. Sasha broke the stare, cocked her head and said, "Fuck off, bitch." She pushed Sara across the hall, crashing into an end table with a litany of family photos atop it. The shag carpeting saved the frames from shattering.

"If you try and stop me, I'll knock your fucking teeth in."

Sasha grabbed the house phone and dialed 9-1-1.

CHAPTER 19: Morning Sickness

Part C:

Luke Larson showed up alone an hour later. Turns out, Mike Wilde and Sara O'Sullivan had plenty of time to evacuate the house. Probably could have brought the housekeeper in to clean the damn place too.

Sara greeted Luke at the door and she was thankful it was him. They had a history. Sara faced an underage drinking charge when she was only 14. She was with some friends coming home from a party and Luke Larson pulled them over on Confederate Avenue. Larson gave all four girls in the car the same ultimatum. Suck his dick or get an underage, their choice. Well, Sara one upped him. She didn't just blow him. He took her behind the Chatterbox Diner and fucked her on the hood of the police cruiser. They had an ongoing deal, she'd fuck him for immunity but any DUI's from others at her parties were fair game, ever since she was 14 fucking years old.

If it was any other police officer in Salt Springs, they would have been *fucked.*

She escorted him to the upstairs. Sasha and Jade leaned up against the opposite wall further up the hallway.

"You have something to do with this?" Larson asked in a low, intimidating tone.

"Who?" Sara asked.

"You." and he pointed at Sasha.

"Wait, what?" Sasha replied. Her eyes offered a confused squint.

"You're the one that found her, right?" he asked rudely and put his hand on his gun. "Did you do this?"

Sasha started to yell, "What the *fuck* are you talking about you *fucking cock sucker!?* That's my *best fucking friend* down there!" she stood and wiped tears from her eyes. "Why the *fuck* would you think I did something?"

"Well..." he pointed to her dark skin. "That..."

"Oh you *fucking bi—*" Sasha leaped toward him, but Jade wrapped her arms around Sasha's waist and held her back from attacking.

Larson laughed and looked in the bathroom. "Holy shit." he said. Larson clicked his radio and continued, "This is Officer Larson. Call units to the O'Sullivan's. The girl is dead."

Thomas Carney, the County Coroner joined Salt
Springs Police and State Police to analyze the scene
but there was no point. All it was, was simply
protocol. Brooke committed suicide.

Gordy, Pears and Matt heard the call over the
police scanner that Clifford White had in their
kitchen. They heard, "*129 South Avenue, Salt
Springs... O'Sullivan residence... Female...
Deceased...*" Each one of them had a terrible
feeling and their inclination was spot on. Pears
called Sasha on the way to town.

"Sasha! Sasha! Thank God! What's going on over
there?"

"*Fraaaaaank*" she cried over the phone. Sasha, nor
anyone, ever called Pears by his first name.
"*Fraaaaaankkkkk*"

"Sasha! Relax! Tell me what's wrong." he pleaded.

"Brooke." she sniffed. "She—"

"Save it. We're coming over."

Gordy, Pears and Matt sat in the O'Sullivan's
driveway just beyond the yellow caution tape.
Sasha and Jade received approval to leave the

scene and sit with them. Sasha went out to them, but Jade needed a minute.

The hatchback was ajar. Sasha, Gordy, Pears and Matt sat in the void. She explained what she saw and they all embraced in the back of the Explorer.

Jade needed a moment to regroup, or at least try to regroup. She was an emotional person, but she never wanted to grieve in public. Maybe it was because of her Dad. He wanted boys and he got the girliest of girls, a beautiful, blonde-haired, blue-eyed, Prom Queen that wasn't even remotely manly. She was strong, though. Damn strong. But seeing her friends' corpse rot on a bathroom floor was a challenge that she wasn't prepared to face. Not crying or showing sadness is an example of hegemonic masculinity, it was the best she could do. But somehow, it was never good enough for her father.

She stood in the bedroom that Sara O'Sullivan and Mike Wilde departed from a few hours ago. It was Sara's room. Ignored the poster of a shirtless Hugh Jackman, Jade's eyes were fixed to the decoration beside it. A calendar with pink markings jotted throughout. The lines of pink were only a distraction from the focal point above, a picture of a puppy.

Jade couldn't decipher the breed but the pup was white with a long steak of gold on her back. She sat in front of a fire hydrant and her piercing blue eyes conquered all other elements of the photo. Bright green grass stood in the background. Jade always wanted a dog, but her father would never allow her to have one. This dog in the calendar wasn't just any other dog, she was perfect.

"Ms. Davidson." she heard from behind her.

It was Luke Larson. "You okay?"

She nodded and turned back towards the calendar, staring into the puppy's blue eyes. Larson walked up to her and placed his hand on her back. Jade knew it wasn't out of the goodness of his heart, but out of his hunger for young women. She moved her shoulder to shed his hand.

"Ms. Davidson, everything will be okay." he said and lurked a step closer to her. "I hate to see beautiful women upset."

Jade turned towards him with a scowl. "I don't really give a fuck, Luke." she said stoically.

Larson jerked back. "That's actually Officer Larson to you, Ms. Davidson."

"No... It's not. I'm going to keep calling you Luke."
she stated.

Larson was disgusted and retreated to the
bathroom. Over the rattling gurney she heard
someone yell, "load her up" from the hallway.

Jade went to the bedroom doorway and watched
the group carry Brooke away in a body bag. She
had never seen anything like it before. Brooke
looked like she was about to be dry cleaned. Jade
was shocked at how she was carried out.

Two officers stayed put in the hallway. They were
staring down at the linoleum bathroom floor. Jade
tiptoed towards them and she recognized the one.
It was Lou Jennings, retired Salt Springs Police
Officer and a damn nice man. Lou and Jade's
grandmother dated in high school. It didn't work,
but they remained friends throughout the years.

He was still able to come to important matters like
this. Small town loyalty and his sanity played a part
in it.

Lou saw her, and waved a wrinkled hand. He forced
a half-smile through his grey beard but his mouth
quivered the longer he looked at her. Lou felt bad,
but his voice was optimistic.

"Hi Ms. Davidson."

Jade waved as mascara began to run down her face. Her wavy blonde hair was tangled and she bit her lip to hold in her cry.

"Come here, sweetheart." he said sincerely and Jade started to weep while running into his arms. Lou's arms embraced her and she exploded built-up tears into his chest. The other officer comforted her also.

"You have a ride home sweetheart?" Lou asked after a few minutes of consoling.

"Yeah," Jade inhaled. "Some friends are outside."

"Okay, Jade. Say 'hi' to Mimi for me. Will yuh?"

Jade nodded in agreement.

"Say Lou," the other officer said, pointing down to leftover chunks of Brooke's arm. "Little strange, isn't it?"

"Hmm" Lou grunted. "Lil bit, eh?"

Jade turned away from Lou's chest and stared at the linoleum. Blood still soaked the floor but there were distinct wipe marks, it was a piss poor cleaning attempt. *Just like when Zack Bristol spills his chocolate milk at lunch*, she thought. A shard of glass remained and quaked slowly. Back and forth, clinking and clacking until something appeared from underneath it. Jade's jaw dropped and her stomach started to boil. She felt her skin curl at the sight.

A worm crawled toward them from under the glass.

CHAPTER 19: Morning Sickness

Part D:

Warmth from the sun's rays beamed down on the four grieving souls in the O'Sullivan driveway. Through the tears, Sasha paced as she relayed the events of the evening to her friends. Matt and Gordy stood up with her, but Pears remained still with his feet hanging from the open hatchback. Officers started to pour out of the O'Sullivan's main entrance, kicking Sasha and Brooke's cigarette stubs out of the way.

Sasha started to cry harder and Gordy swung his arms around her. "Come on, Sasha. Let's go. Let's go home." Tears soaked his Army green t-shirt, Sasha spit out a piece of his long brown hair.

"Let's go do something. Let's get breakfast or something." Matt said glumly. "Let's go."

"Jade's still in there" Sasha murmured. "Wait for her."

"She's coming." Gordy declared positively. "She's coming out the door now."

Jade walked out onto the O'Sullivan's front porch with two police officers. She stood close to the older one. Gordy thought he looked to be about

75. Being 75 and still on the force would be impressive elsewhere, but not in Salt Springs. Most illegal activity came from the elites, and nothing could be done to them or the whole town would combust. Petty drug stuff came from the lower class, there was no point in disciplining them. They'd all eliminate themselves anyways.

The younger officer halted in the yard. He placed his foot on the brick flowerbed trim. Jade and the older officer stopped beside him as a larger group filed out of the main entrance. The group scattered, revealing the metal gurney.

Sasha fell to her knees as they carried Brooke off the porch. Gordy collapsed with her for support. Pears got up off the Explorer's bumper and put his arm around Matt.

Thomas Carney slammed the back doors of the van and drove toward town. Crowds of officers and investigators detached to their respective vehicles. The older officer and Jade began to walk towards the Explorer. As they got closer, Pears could make out "J-E-N-N-I-N-G-S" on the rectangular name plate. *Oh, old man Jennings,* he thought.

"How yuh kids holdin' up?" Lou Jennings asked compassionately.

"We're okay, Officer Jennings." Sasha said.

They weren't and Lou could tell. He offered a sympathetic smile. "Lou. Call me Lou." he said. Lou placed a hand on Jade's shoulder and said, "Lil Jader here knows where to find me, so if yuh kids need uh thing. Yas know where to go. Got me?"

"Thanks, Lou." Gordy replied.

"Ahhhh, ya son of uh bitch its Officer, to you!" he laughed and the group joined him with a chuckle. "I'm just kiddin', son. Tell your ol' man I said hello, Gord."

Gordy offered a nod, and the group continued to softly chuckle.

"Take care, kids." Lou said sympathetically and he walked away to his car.

Jade's lips quivered before she burst into tears once again. They all embraced in the empty driveway.

Brooke was gone. Up until a few months ago, Brooke was so full of life. But it seemed once Shawn left her, all life drained out. Grades started to fall from A's to C's and it translated to her SAT scores. Her quirky personality became barren. There were no more jokes or blatant disregard for common sense.

She became self-conscious of her weight gain, but truthfully, she didn't need to be. 120 to 140 wasn't awful but Shawn always harped on her when she ate. *You're gonna explode* is what he always told her. Mr. Beckett said the same thing.

Jade started to think during their embrace about Brooke's lasting legacy. She could relate to her issues with her father. Although Mark Davidson never portrayed the verbal abuse, neither one of them were 'good' enough for their fathers. *But that was fucking wrong* Jade thought. *They aren't good enough for us!*

Even through her depression, Brooke loved her friends. She went and testified against her old cheerleading coach at a school board meeting. Coach Shoemaker said something about, "the nigger girl" at practice one day. Brooke approached her about it, and her coach told her that nobody would believe her. The coach blackmailed Brooke, but she didn't care. She turned Coach Shoemaker in. The coach was fired.

Brooke loved her nephews, too. She would take them to bowl and to the park every weekend. Hell, she spent more time with those boys than their parents did.

And she was so excited for her mother to come back home. She had a countdown in her binder. On the day of her death, Jade saw Brooke cross off "316" on her countdown. Robin only had another 315 days in prison.

She loved her friends and her family so much, how could she leave them all behind?

The worm

Jade turned to the house and looked at the upstairs bathroom window. She envisioned the wiped trails of blood and the shattered glass.

She could hear the glass start to rattle in her mind, clinking and clacking. She remembered the worm, crawling from underneath.

"Umm guys," she said and turned back toward the group. "I have to tell you something."

CHAPTER 20: The Wallet

Kate pulled into the gravel lane behind the Lequin Church, the same patch that Matt K. parked in only 10 hours prior.

The church peered over the hillside. Its white paint complimented the bright blue sky like an additional cumulonimbus, watching the pastures and forestry of the valley. Leaves had completely turned and started to fall periodically to the ground. A fawn pranced amongst the graveyard.

Not intimidating, chilling and certainly not sinister. The church looked vintage, almost antique and the sight was picturesque. I lost all account of the night before, except my wallet.

That was the plan all along, get the wallet and get the hell out. But the view was so serene.

"You coming?" Kate said.

I was hypnotized by the beauty and she broke it.

I jumped, "Yeah… umm… yeah…"

The smell of autumn blew in the light breeze. Dew still moistened the cemetery grass, but the soil was firm.

We walked passed the NO TRESSPASSING sign and the atmosphere remained calm. Sunlight beamed through the church windows making the inside visible. I glanced to the windows from afar.

Nothing. No boys. No man. It was empty.

The fields below were still visible as we walked through the graveyard. Leaves rustled in the surrounding woods and the whiff of pine began to emerge through the autumn air.

A leaf crunched under my foot, but I heard a coinciding snap from beneath. I kicked the leaf out of the way, revealing an American Flag with a severed wooden dowel.

At first glance, I felt bad. Growing up in a small conservative town, anything that could be interpreted as disrespect to the American Flag was criminal. Destruction was a goddamn death sentence. Even if it was a $3.00 craft from Bi-Lo Grocery.

There was a stain at the end of the dowel. A reddish-brown tint covered the bottom.

No wind at all. We just stood there, watching the flag flutter emphatically. Mud slowly surfaced as the flag climaxed to the pace of a typhoon. WHACK!

Oh my God, Sasha! Sash—

"Zack!" I awoke from another trance. "Zack, what are you doing? Come on." Kate said from the porch step.

I approached her, dried vomit still speckled the grave of Jedidiah McLaughlin.

Pupils turned back into his head, his eyes turned to two white discs. Blood oozed from his lips. His tongue was puke green, licking his black teeth.

Kate wasn't there and I ran to the porch. The church door was wide open and I entered. She was nowhere to be seen.

"Kate! Kate! Kate this isn't funny!" I screamed and sprinted up the stairs to the balcony. I was surprised to see the lack of seating there; patrons must have stood. My feet slammed the creaking floor boards, the ruckus was sure to collapse the entire damn church. Books dropped to the floor from the impact.

"Babe, seriously!" a wooden step broke as I ran back down to the main sanctuary. One pew, and two. Row nine and ten, nothing again. Just a lonely carving of what looked like a group of stick figures.

A hand raised from the pulpit. I froze, sweat streamed down my face and my heart began to flutter.

"Got it!" Kate yelled and smiled. She flashed the wallet in front of her.

"You fucking asshole." I sighed.

"Sorry," she laughed. "I had to."

She walked down the pulpit steps and waited for me. Kate smiled at me, but I jokingly ignored her. She grabbed the back of my shirt and pulled me back. In the same motion, she wrapped her arms around my waist.

"Round 2?" she asked seductively.

Her large green eyes were inviting. They flashed voluptuously. She flipped her hair back and spread her shoulders to emphasize her bust on my chest. Her torso nudged and swayed slightly against my groin. One of her hands started to stroke the middle of my chest.

I looked around at the empty church. It was an enticing offer. No one would hear or see us. And, quite frankly, I didn't have a *fun* sex story. Sure, we had the Hollinshead incident, but this was different than getting caught in the high school bathroom.

Kara and Ryan had "Lake Nephawin Debacle", Aunt Jodi caught them nailing in the bathroom. But the story of them having sex in the shoe section at Walmart took the cake. It was 2:00 a.m. and there wasn't anyone there but st—

A floorboard creaked in the balcony. We both turned our heads abruptly to the noise, but there was nothing to be seen. Just the emptiness of the upstairs.

"There's got to be a good spot up the road, right?" I asked.

Kate offered a sexy half smile and said, "We can certainly check." Two and a half years into our relationship, that look still made me melt.

Her butt softly wiggled in her leggings and I took a grab as we embarked toward the door.

She took three more steps and then she stopped abruptly in front of me.

"*Uggghhh*" she looked down and groaned. "Disgusting."

Kate eluded a spot on the floor in the doorway and walked out on the porch.

Creeping in to presumably praise Lord Jesus was a long, pale and slimy earthworm.

CHAPTER 21: Chatterbox Diner

"*The fuck you mean there was a worm?*" Pears asked, slamming a bite of pancakes down his throat.

The smell of Marlboros and Maxwell House polluted the diner. Only the older and middle-class crowds frequented the Chatterbox, even if it was maybe the best place to get food in Salt Springs. It was dirty, and it was the only place left in town that someone could have a smoke with their meal. Smoke from the cigs stained the once yellow walls to a shade of brown. But the food was damn good, and only $4.00 for a western omelet.

Tracy Wilson was the cook, waitress, janitor, everything. She worked hard. Got up at 3:30 a.m. to open the diner at 4:00. Truckers were sure to be passing by from all over. New York City, Syracuse, Philly, Pittsburgh, you name it. They all passed through Bradford County and Salt Springs was on the main drag.

"I don't know" Jade said. "I'm just saying that it looked a lot like... that boy..."

"How does a boy look like a worm?" Gordy asked.

"No, Jesus!" Jade snickered. "Like the one that came out of his eye."

Tracy refilled their coffees. Only Jade and Matt actually liked the taste. Pears, Gordy and Sasha drank it merely for caffeine rush.

"I'm so sorry about Brooke, guys." Tracy said wistfully. "The bill is on me."

"Thanks Trace," Sasha said. "How's Ryan taking it?"

"Haven't talked to him." she muttered. "He's probably still out with Kara or something."

Tracy and Ryan's relationship began to falter when he was in 6th grade after his father left. Scott had an affair and ran off with a woman that he met at Murphy Contracting. The woman kept the books and Scott worked on gas lines. Scott's reports turned into something more, and in 2002 they ran off, never to be heard of again.

It shook both Ryan and Tracy. Scott always seemed like a good man, but he did have an occasional outburst of anger. He was a Little League coach, both football and baseball. His son was gifted, but no prodigy. Scott had a blatant disregard for Little League pitching rules, he threw Ryan out on the mound for every game.

When Ryan was 10, Scott taught Ryan how to throw a curveball and he'd be damned if he didn't chuck it against the Ralston Rattlers. One day in April, Ryan's curve didn't break. Scott pulled Ryan from the game and eventually, the season. At 10 years old, Ryan's undeveloped elbow was riddled with tendinitis.

Tracy had to sell their house in Stoney Corners on the cheap. It isn't necessarily a "buyers" or "sellers" market in Stoney Corners, the demand isn't there, nor were surrounding opportunities. Nothing brings people to Stoney Corners.

They rented a small apartment in Salt Springs, and Tracy started working 16 hour days at the Chatterbox. Doses of Ritalin got her through the day and an occasional glass of red wine transitioned to a nightly bottle of liquor. By the time her son came home from football practice, Tracy was already passed out drunk or high on their living room couch. Leaving her teenage son to fend for himself.

Financial difficulties started to emerge as her substance abuse worsened and she started to date Norm Slocum, Butch Slocum's brother. If there was ever a person more crude than Butch, it was his younger brother. He smoked, he drank, and even popped painkillers.

Their relationship was never healthy, or even normal. Norm didn't work, guys like him ruined the reputation of welfare and food stamps. He fed off of the system.

Norm woke up at 11 a.m. each morning to make his gin and tonic. Maury came on Fox 56 at 11:30, so he grabbed a couple Vicodin like M&M's and went to the couch. One by one he washed the painkillers down. He came off of his high the same time that Tracy walked in the door each night.

Norm's ways started to agitate her. Tracy gave Norm an ultimatum: get a job or get out.

He refused, and he started to become violent. Norm was a large and strong man. Each time that Tracy mentioned that he should get a job, he forced himself upon her. Some nights he raped her, other nights he unloaded beatings that crippled her for days. On the worst of nights, he turned his attention towards her sleeping son.

If she left him, he would kill them. They even knew how he'd do it. With each threat, Norm would wield his 9mm in front of them, clicking the safety on and off.

Tracy Wilson's life turned into an episode of Jerry Springer and her son started to spend every day with his friends. Ryan felt bad about it, but he felt that his mother stooped to his level. Norm Slocum was just an old piece of trash. Not a dealer and not one of the elites. If she turned *him* in, the Salt Springs Police Department would actually do something about it.

"Tracy!" a voice said from the dinerbar. "Top me off? Be a friend."

It was old Butch Slocum. One dirt-covered hand wagged his white coffee cup and the other held the sports section of the Towanda Times. Mud caked his fingernails and grease plastered his white Penn State Nittany Lions ballcap.

"Be right there, Butch!" she yelled with her nasal screech.

"Thank yuh!" Butch yelled. "*Heeeeyyyyy Franklin! What's goin' on yuh fuckin' spick?!*"

"What's up, Butch?" Pears replied. Pears was neutral about racial slurs. It was just the norm in Salt Springs, he was used to it. What Pears really hated was his first name. We shared that. For me, it was the pronunciation "Brist-ole." My name isn't a goddamn racetrack, it's "Briss-tahl." "Frank", "Frankie", or "Frankie P" were all fine but "Fraaaaaaaanklin", he used to emphasize a Long-A, was his biggest pet peeve.

"And *Miss Daaavidson…*" Butch said as he panned her from head to foot, offering a provocative grunt to confirm his lust. He closed his newspaper and continued, "Good to see *you* this morning."

With a touch of gall, Jade answered him. "Ya see Canton beat Towanda last night? Clayton Elliott threw for 300."

"Oh you just get more beautiful by the minute," he said. Chewing tobacco dripped onto his grease stained shirt. Naked beer gut started to poke from underneath. "Nawthin' better than a bitch that knows football, am I right?"

Jade cocked her head to the side, like Jim from "The Office" and whispered, "Jesus Christ."

They had enough. If you couldn't get Butch Slocum distracted with some football talk, you were out of luck. He'd just keep talking and harp on the matter at hand. A lot of times it was the upcoming presidential election, *remember to vote McCain! No fuckin' Muslims in the White House!* Other times he started about attractive women, just like this occasion.

Jade led the way out and kicked the swinging door open. They needed to get going anyways. Matt had barn chores, the day was beautiful so he could get started on the siding. Penn State played at noon so if he got a head start, he'd catch the second half.

"Magnum 5" had practice in Canton today so Gordy had to tune up his Les Paul and get ready. Pears and Sasha had to work at Bi-Lo Grocery from 12-8. And Jade didn't quite know what was on tap for her day. Everything that she thought of came back to the worm. It's slow, sloshing crawl over the blood splattered floor. The wriggling through the boy's eye socket and the plop to the floor.

Whatever it was, it came home with them and it killed one of their best friends. Jade knew it, and deep down the rest of her friends knew it.
She didn't fear the worm or the Lequin Church. She *hated* them.

Jade Davidson: innocent beauty on the outside, but completely enraged on the inside. She didn't know when, but it was only a matter of time. Jade Davidson was going back to Lequin.

CHAPTER 22: Your Betrayal

Cell phone service only covered as far out as Stoney Corners, Grover, LeRoy and quite specifically, the Ford's driveway in Windfall.

Kate turned into her driveway and clicked the button on her sun visor. The garage door opened, and each of our phones buzzed.

Her iPhone sat on her lap. She picked it up, clicked the side button and offered it a blank stare.

I watched her out of my peripheral, she smirked at the phone and placed it face-down back on her lap. It was suspicious, but the morning was great. The sex was passionate and meaningful; it didn't lack fervor like it did during the cheating escapades of yore. I couldn't lose her again.

My phone was left unchecked. I was more concerned with Kate. Her phone jingled again, but this time she didn't check it. She pulled into the garage and closed the door.

Kate tossed her purse on the kitchen table. Tampons, a money clip and many more contents flew out of the Coach purse as she ran to the bathroom. Her phone faced up on the veneer, and the screen illuminated once again.

I grabbed the phone and watched the screen as the phone buzzed once again.

This fucking bi—

The phone flew out of my hand and crashed through the kitchen window above the sink. My body went numb, but the rage boiled from within. I grabbed the pots and pans that hung above the meal preparation island. A frying pan obliterated a glass vase on the table. Pots hurled to the open family room, striking the ceiling fan and the large living room window.

Kate stormed out of the bathroom, "Zack! What are you doi—"

I launched a cutting board in her direction and her jaw dropped. It cracked into the family portrait that hung on the wall. The frame shattered to the floor.

"Zack, I'm sor—"

Fire ignited in my eyes. Steam rolled out of my ears like a locomotive's engine. The kitchen table soared to the living room.

"You did this to me! You!" I screamed and ran out of the front door.

My mind wandered about the first time I ever laid eyes on Kate. I had crushes, but nothing like her. She was everything.

I met Kate on her first day at Salt Springs in 2005. She was adorable. Unlike anything that I have ever seen and I stumbled upon her by complete accident.

Salt Springs had combined their middle and high schools into one large building after a steady decline in enrollment. 9th through 12th graders had classes throughout the entire school, but 7th and 8th only had a hallway.

One morning in early September, I went through the middle school entrance to wait for the morning bell. Students were able to linger in the lobby from 8:00 a.m. until 8:30, and in that half hour, I fell madly in love.

Kate, in her 8th grade innocence, stood in front of the large window panes that spread from wall to wall, floor to ceiling. Sunlight glistened through her long hair like an aura and her naturally tanned arms hugged a blue binder. A paper slid in the clear sleeve that had, "Kate" scripted in large cursive letters. Her outfit was modest, a light blue t-shirt under a navy cardigan. Jeans on the bottom and navy toenail polish showed under her flip-flops. She was unlike anything I've ever seen before.

Her sparkling green eyes were traced with the most miniscule amount of eyeliner and mascara. She batted them towards me. Dimples imprinted her cheeks, and her smile flashed brighter than the sun that rose behind her.

She was everything. She was FUCKING everything.

Evergreens flanked both sides of Route 414, and Windfall was the mecca for roadkill. It was impossible for a passing car to see through the pine. Deer only had to jump three feet to meet their demise.

I stood in the midst of the needles, waiting for a tractor trailer heading north. Elmira or Syracuse, it didn't matter. All I knew is where I wanted to go. Mom had Beth, she didn't *need* me. I just caused her heartache anymore anyways, she hated to see me like this. At least it would be over for both of us.

My friends all had each other but in less than a year, most of us were leaving each other anyways. We had fun but there comes a time for us to realize who we are, and I was nothing without Kate.

A big rig's engine roared from up the hill and I started to brace myself. I stood up straight and approached the edge of the pine.

Even Flow! Thoughts arrive like butterflies

When Eddie Vedder was singing, my mom was calling. I ignored the ringing and started to think.

Honey, Mrs. White is leading your scout group. She has a son exactly your age!
Mama! Me and Gordy and Matt made a wooden racecar!
...
Honey, this is Brooke! She going to bowl with you today.
...
Okay boys, if you behave during the game we'll go for ice cream... Zack, you're at 3rd. Frankie, you're going to play second.
...
Hi... umm... I'm Zack. What's your name?
Sasha!
....
Hey Ryan! The Eagles suck! GO Steelers!
Jade's kind of hot, don't you think Ryan?
I'll help you with her if you help me with Kara.
...
Fuck this...

I watched the truck pass.

"Hi, mom." I answered the phone.

"Honey, where are you?"

"I'm... ummm... still at Pete's..."

"Have you heard anything?" she asked.

"Uhhh... no..."

"I'm coming to get you. Stay put."

PART 2: DEAD AND GONE

I've been travelin' on this road too long

Just tryin' to find my way back home

The old me is Dead & Gone, Dead & Gone

I've been travelin' on this road too long

Just tryin' to find my way back home

The old me is Dead & Gone, Dead & Gone

-T.I. & Justin Timberlake (2008)

Ever had one of them days you wish you would've stayed home?

-T.I. (2008)

CHAPTER 23: Brooke Beckett

Part A:

Brooke's death shook the entire town. It is always upsetting when you see a news story about the death of a teenager. Salt Springs saw too much of it. In 2002, a total of seven Salt Springs High School students died in car accidents. Three separate instances, at that. So young, so much life that they were unable to see. But the grief is different in small towns. Everyone knew Brooke, her family, this, that and the other thing.

Salt Springs was saddened by the loss, especially due to the circumstances. It was a rough year for the Beckett family. Robin ended up in jail, Brooke's sister Sierra ended up in drug rehab and Clayton, Brooke's grandfather, died of cancer in June.

We knew that Brooke was struggling, but we were the ones closest to her. Others weren't aware of the depression. They all thought that she seemed so happy on the sidelines rooting on the Salt Springs Spartans with the rest of the cheerleading squad. The only time that she didn't look thrilled was when Alex Giroux from Muncy ran her over.

Which was what, six hours before she killed herself?

I suppose that is why it came across as such a shock. Word got around quick that Thomas Carney ruled it a suicide, and her approximate time of death was at 2:14 a.m. on Saturday, October 4, 2008.

Her funeral was that Wednesday, October 8th.

Her viewing was at 5:00p.m. (Yes, the girl that butchered her arm off had a viewing) and the funeral was at 6. Folks from Salt Springs, Canton, Troy and hell, even Towanda filed in Paul Pepper's funeral home. Many of whom turned away after max capacity was reached in the small parlor.

Sadly, the first ones there were my mother and I, we were a half hour early. Brooke loved punctuality, and I wouldn't disappoint. I'd only exaggerate the characteristic for our final meeting on Earth.

Mom and I stayed in the car for a mere three minutes before we trekked into Paul Pepper's chapel of rest. She claimed it was because Matchbox Twenty's "3AM" was playing on 106.1. I wasn't a huge fan, but she was. Mom was more of a fan of the band's lead singer than the song but give credit where credit is due, the song was 12 years old and still on the radio. Pretty impressive.

We sat idle in the family Buick Regal, facing the side entrance of the funeral home. Rain pelted the windshield, making the building look like a Vincent Van Gogh painting. The smell of October dampness crept through the slightly cracked windows. The AC didn't work so the choice was yours: roast or let a few droplets of rain travel in. We always took the latter. Rob Thomas's voice faded on the radio in lieu of the DJ.

That was Matchbox Twenty's 3AM right here on 106.1, Elmira, New York's home for today's top hits... Now time for a new release! It's T.I. and Justin Timberlake....

Mom grabbed her umbrella from the backseat.

Ohh, hey!. I've been travelin' on this road too long... Just tryna find my wa—

She turned off the ignition and we went in.

CHAPTER 23: Brooke Beckett

Part B:

Paul Pepper wasn't the stereotypical mortician. He wasn't old, he didn't resemble a skeleton with skin and he didn't have a personality that would rival a fabric softener sheet. Paul was well-known throughout the community and well put-together. Certainly no GQ model but it was tough to imagine him embalming dead bodies. Never married, nor had kids. He was close, but he was fonder of the drink than he was of the girl. It would be tough to not have an alcohol problem in that line of work but it never effected his duty. He was damn good at his job. Probably the best.

He greeted us when we reached the parlor.

"Hi, Zack. I am so sorry for your loss." His voice was warm and soft. Almost feminine. It was much different than it sounded on Poker Night at Salt Springs Lanes. His right hand shook mine, and he placed his left on my shoulder.

"Hi, Aunt Shell." His head turned to my mom. Paul played high school football with my cousin Brett. They were buddies and all of Brett's friends called my mom, "Aunt Shell". The nickname has stuck since. "Good to see you." he continued softly.

"It's always great to see you, sweetheart." mom said, "Just not always the best circumstances."

They continued talking but my attention wandered. I perused the parlor. Collages of Brooke propped up on easels, and a display of flowers flanked each side of her open casket. The Beckett's released a statement that in lieu of flowers, Brooke would have wanted funds toward supporting her nephews. People obviously didn't listen and maybe rightfully so, the family had issues. Cooper and Colton probably would have never seen a dime of it.

Chairs sat in rows of 10. Just like the halftime dance routines at Ralph Ward Memorial Field, all the seats would face Brooke one final time.

"Hi Ms. Shelly." I hear. Sasha, Matt, Gordy and Pears walked through the door. Together, we walked toward Brooke in silence.

CHAPTER 23: Brooke Beckett

Part C:

Brooke's hair draped over her shoulders in two long parts. A sheet covered most of her torso, but not enough to hide a lime green t-shirt with the text "HOLLISTER" over it. Not the ideal burial outfit, but the shirt was from her nephews. Not *bought*, but from. Cooper and Colton were no older than six, they picked it out as Brooke's birthday gift and their mother bought it.

Sasha poked her pinky finger toward the sheet and drew in back slightly. She was the first to see Brooke after she passed. She saw her arm then and she saw it now. A simple amputation from the elbow down. Brooke would be buried with a stub.

She pulled a folded up note from the pocket of her black slacks and stared at it. A stray tear moistened a circle on the composition paper. Her lower lip protruded and she began to weep. Sasha felt guilty. She was there that night, literally *the entire night*. The football game, the church, the party, all of it. All of the tell-tale signs surfaced in her mind once it was too late. Brooke didn't get up immediately after Giroux bowled her over, she just rested on her hands and knees. She didn't get up. She didn't defend herself. Nothing.

There was no rebuttal at the party when Jade told off Mike Wilde and she didn't dance either. *And I didn't even ask if something was wrong…*

Sasha thought about the church. Brooke was all for it the day before, but when the time came she was adamantly against it. *I think we should just stay here* at the Pump. *Where the fuck are we going then? —Just stay here… I know you don't want any of this shit…--*

Her head started to thump in pain. *That goddamn flag. Been a week and my fuckin head still hurts. The mark gone? Fuck if I know… Wonder if Ryan's leg hurts? Kid was chompin' harder than the flag hit me. Oh God, that kid… Fuckin nasty ass shit… Empty-ass eye socket other than that worm…*

The worm…

Jade's never talked out her ass before. Might have downplayed her feelings for Zack… man, she fuckin' HATES Kate Ford… Why the fuck would she just say that? Old man Jennings was even there… Wonder if he saw it… No, fuck that. He saw it.

Sasha believed Jade.

Brooke didn't do this…

CHAPTER 23: Brooke Beckett

Part D:

Gordy untied his hair and tightened the bun. It was rare for the time, but he was an aspiring rock star that didn't give a fuck about the norms. In about eight years it would be the style, but at the time it was the subject of judgement.

He also pulled a small note from the inside of his suit jacket. The jacket was large, definitely his father's. His note was more of a small card in an unsealed envelope. He tucked it under the sheet.

Gordy didn't share the guilt, but he did have an uneasy feeling about being with Brooke during her final hours of life. The terror of the church faded quickly for him. As a matter of fact, once they hit Windfall and saw the lights to the gas station, he was completely at ease. He thought the man and kids were some pranksters, but they never came forward. The whole thing was real, not a dream. Not a hallucination. Although he was skeptical of the threat. It was weird to him, and the fact that Brooke killed herself only a few hours later was odd.

That blood was odd too. Ehhhh... it probably wasn't blood... Sure smelled like it. Looked like it... Could it have been blood?... No... No way. Where'd it come

from? The damn ceiling? A leak? No... Hmm...
Raining Blood... Slayer.

I guess it could have come from the boys or the
man... probably that one kid with the worm...

CHAPTER 23: Brooke Beckett

Part E:

Matt K. didn't have a note, card or any sort of memento. He wasn't that kind of guy. His sadness was enough and he didn't feel like he needed to prove it. He knew that he was sad, his friends shared his suffering and although he didn't know where, he knew that Brooke knew of his grief.

Matt didn't own a suit or any dress attire, nor did his father. His formal boots squeaked on the polyurethane from the floor. Nice blue jeans were his most appropriate bottoms and a light blue button-down. Long line of farmers; the attire was acceptable. Probably a quarter of the attendants would be wearing something similar. In suburbia, it would be a death sentence. In Salt Springs, it would be no more than the norm.

He favored a slight smell of aftershave and musky cologne, like an old, blue-collar gentleman at a formal event. It was the best he could do, and he knew that Brooke would realize it. Sure, there was the possibility that he could have gone out and got a suit, or at least more appropriate attire. But he didn't. He didn't go above and beyond; Brooke would have done that. Like that time last year...

She took HER time to help me get the milk and eggs out to Williamsport. She didn't have time for that... the delivery was set for 9am and she had to be at the football field at 11. ...did Troy even score on us that day?... Man, she really got back to her house at 10:30 and somehow made it... All for her friend. Nothing more... Just. Her. Friend.

No... friends hang out. Talk to each other in the hallways and all of that. They wouldn't travel 40 miles to drop off two gallons of milk and six dozen eggs for just a friend. Might do that for a brother or sister if they really needed it... or a boyfriend...

He turned his head toward Sasha and Gordy. *Sasha's done the same thing... Gordy too... Man, I cried like a baby when he gave me that check from his concert at the Warrior Lounge that night.*

And to Pears... *He would have never let anything happen to us. Those new goddamn friends of his a few years ago might have tried, but they wouldn't be able to.*

Damn, I didn't realize how much we've been through... or, well, supported each other through... Pears' problems... Sasha being—whatever you want to call it. Bullshit, is what I call it. But minusculed? Probably a better term. Zack getting screwed over by Kate... Kara's dad... Jade's parents... Brooke's mom and now Brooke's death... Jesus Christ...

The church never came to his mind.

CHAPTER 23: Brooke Beckett

Part F:

Pears' personality was unique. It could say things that were so inappropriate but they would be excused because of his large goofy smile. His eyes would squench together like a sandwich in a panini presser and his crooked teeth would make up half of his face.

And he didn't fear anything. He never thought of death. He was 18, why should he? The only death he ever experienced was long drawn out suffering from his grandparents, and at that point, it was a relief that they were out of their misery.

This was different. It was a feeling that he never experienced before. Brooke wasn't supposed to die.

Pears' suit was tight. It was the same suit that he wore to his grandfather's funeral when he was only 14. He didn't gain that much size, maybe 10 pounds, if that. Pears wasn't ever the biggest guy.

If Brooke would have made it through, he probably would have faced her and made a joke about "giving her a hand" followed by a golf clap. He didn't do that now, but instead his chin rested on the knot of his tie. The hair from his chin made a coarse sound as it dragged from side to side while he shook his head. A tear dropped to the side of Brooke's casket.

His face showed anguish. Certain pain and suffering from within. Strangely, Pears didn't look sad. He looked angry. It was a lot like the day he faced Freddy Turner and Cal Thomas after the two made the hit list.

I might have had a little to do with it... I was their friend...

Pears used to take some of the blame for what happened in 2003 with Freddy and Cal but it was only a correlation from their relationship. He knew nothing of the hit list or their intentions to open fire on Salt Springs High.

He started to breath heavily, the top button on his suit dug into his sternum and he unfastened.

I didn't have anything to do with that shit... Brooke didn't either...

"I love you, Brooke." he said and retreated towards his spot at the front to greet the guests that started to pour through the doors. The first ones in were Jade, Kara and Ryan. Jade was the first of the three to reach us.

"Phew..." Jade said. "Road is flooded by the fairgrounds. Had to take a different way."

I stumbled, "It... i--... it's okay, Ja--, Jade."

I played it off like I was emotional, but Jade looked stunning in her black dress. It wasn't the kind someone would wear to the club... *Black dress... with the tights underneath... 3OH!3 reference, sorry.* But her beauty was so natural. It flared out at the waist and ended just above the knee. Her blonde hair was wavy as opposed to the normal straightening. Probably too hard to fight it with the rain and humidity.

Jade hugged Sasha, Gordy and Pears, but when she reached me, she started to bawl. She saw Brooke's lifeless face behind me.

She lodged her face into my chest and wept. Her hands grasped my sleeves. Dabs of mascara painted the front of my charcoal button-down.

More people filed in. One of them was Brooke's mother, Robin, being escorted by two police officers.

CHAPTER 24: The Service

14 of us stood at the front at the viewing. Her eight best friends, her parents, her sisters and her nephews. Folks that I never met or even saw before offered their condolences. Most of us were grateful for them, actually, to be precise, 11 of us were. Her scrubby ass sisters and her piece of shit father seemed like they were forced to be there. Like an old man with his wife at JCPenney.

Paul Pepper directed us to our seats a quarter after 6, giving the late stragglers enough time to pay their respects. Every seat filled and many stood at the back and sides.

The service was beautiful and elegant, yet glum. Flowers and bouquets spread across the room in shades of yellow, pink and baby blue. Three of Brooke's favorite colors.

Reverend David Morris started it out with a prayer, followed by Robin's address and eventual eulogy. The first of three speeches.

At the end, Paul Pepper announced a dinner at the Church of Christ, Disciples of Christ's assembly hall, concluded the service and called on the pall bearers.

They were, of course Pears, Matt, Sasha, Jade, Kara, Ryan and myself. Gordy played "Every Move You Make" by The Police on the electric guitar while folks departed. Brooke loved to listen to Gordy play and he shredded on that guitar as we carried her out.

Jade, Sasha, Kara and Pears on one side. Ryan, Matt and I on the other. We walked, carrying the casket through the tunnel of people and we hauled it into the back of Paul Pepper's Hearse.

"You going to the church, Zack?" Matt asked.

"Yeah... yeah, I'm going." I replied, rubbing my forehead. "How 'bout you's?"

My friends nodded.

"Okay, brother." Pears said as he placed his hand on my shoulder. "Meet you up there."

They walked towards their cars. Ryan and Kara kept their heads down, but Sasha and Gordy looked stoic.

Jade walked toward me through the sprinkles. She wrapped her arms around my neck and rested her head on my chest. My heart started to beat a little faster, and my hands caressed the small of her back.

She lifted her head, but still clutched my body. The end of her long hair tickled my hands on her back. Her soft blue

Periwinkle

eyes looked into mine and her makeup smeared only a little from the light drizzle and tears. Smooth hands cradled my neck, thumbs placed just under my earlobes. She gave a half smile that I would have thought was sexy given different circumstances. Her gaze broke to the left and she started to chuckle.

"What?" I asked.

"Oh... Kate just walked by us..." Jade bit her lip.

"Really?" I said with concern.

"Yeah..."

"She look pissed?"

Jade sighed. "Very." She continued, "Serves her right though. She missed out on the best."

"Stop it." I said as I looked away.

Jade broke her embrace. I could have kept hanging on, but it was time to go.

"Meet you up there. I'll save a seat for you and your mom." She said as she turned toward her car.

Speaking of mom, where the hell is she?

I saw Paul Pepper fumble his keys by the driver's side of his hearse. He was just about to get into the vehicle to take Brooke up to the Teaberry Hill Cemetery when I asked, "Hey Paul, you see my mom?"

"Yeah buddy, she's inside talking to Dave Wilson."

I retraced the steps back into the funeral parlor. Through the open door casing, I could see my mother and Dave having a conversation by one of the large bouquets. It wasn't heated, but it was certainly animated. I eaves dropped.

CHAPTER 25: Animated Dialogue

"Why the *fuck* would you let him go in there, Shell?"

My mom's head drew back with offense, she was appalled by the audacity. "First of all, don't speak to me like that. And second of all, what the hell are you talking about, David?"

Dave started to pace, his fingers ran backward through his hair. After a single stroke over his scalp, he wiped his mouth and said, "Zackary. Why'd yuh let him go in there?"

Mom started to chomp on her gum with more velocity. I could hear the smack from behind the wall, 25 feet away. "Go in *where*?!"

"That goddamn church, Shell!"

My mother sat in one of the chairs that faced the front of the parlor. Her feet crossed in front of her and she looked down into her lap. "I had no idea, Dave." she sniffled. "Pete needed me to watch the house and the dogs..."

She started to whimper, "I knew he was talking out of his ass when he told me what he was doing... No way was he going to Williamsport, not on a Friday. He can't stand the people..."

Dave sat down next to her and grabbed her hand.

"I thought he would have ended up the road, sneaking into the Ford's house or something." Her tears started to flow stronger. "Lequin didn't even come up in my mind. I had no ide—"

"Honey, it's okay. So sorry I yelled." Whatever my mom had over on Dave, it showed in that moment. He felt her pain, but her pain hurt him even more so. "Forgive me?"

She nodded.

"It's just... that the place ain't good, Shell. You know it's never been good... it still isn't... you know?"

"Really?"

His lips puckered and released, ready to portray bad news.

"It's worse." He placed his other hand on my mom's knee. "I saw it. Recently. More than once when I was helpin' Hankie."

"What happened?" my mother looked up and asked.

"Only tell yuh this one thing, sweetie." Dave's jowls enhanced. He looked over his glasses. "Don't want to scare the beautiful lady."

"Jesus, David. 50 years and you still don't realize that nothing scares me… and men don't come onto me, I come on to them." She chuckled slightly, accompanied by a sniffle. She wiped the snot from her nose with a Kleenex and tucked her hair behind her ears.

"Not comin' on, Shell… Gave up on that when we were kids." He smiled at her and she smirked back.

"What did you see, Dave?"

"Told yuh, I can't tell yuh, hun." He sat back and the chair creaked behind him. It wasn't in severe danger of breaking, but a few more hard, sudden moves might have ended its days as a support. "Only thing that I'll say is that if you heard a story about the bibles in there, that's true."

"The one about Hank going out to his car and the bibles opened to the same page?"

"Yessum." Dave said, "Enough 'bout that. Meetya at the church?"

"Yeah, give me a few."

Dave stood up stiffly, his joints creaked like floorboards and he let out a grunt. He patted my mother on the back and started walking toward the exit.

"I'll make sure he doesn't go back." She said.

Dave turned around and looked at her with concern. His eyes drooped and his mouth started to stutter. He was about to say something that the love of his life wouldn't react well to, and he knew it. He was hesitant, but she deserved the honest to God's truth.

"Doesn't matter now, hun. They let 'em out."

Reddish-brown hair fell from the crevice behind my mom's ear as her head turned toward Dave, her eyes squinted with intrigue.

"Let who out?"

"The McLaughlin's."

CHAPTER 26: A Brief Interlude

Macro-grief turned micro quickly. As it normally seems, life just goes on after the funeral of an acquaintance. The influx of bouquets halted suddenly, and those already received had started to wilt. Mass amount of untouched dinners spoiled in the Beckett's refrigerator.

Grief counselors no longer loomed the halls and guidance offices of Salt Springs High. Brooke's locker was emptied and all forms of her identification at school were deleted. No "Brooke Beckett" on class rosters and the cheerleading captaincy void was filled. The only memoriam given was text at the bottom of every football game's program. In 12-point, Times New Roman font, the text read:

Rest in peace
Brooke Beckett
March 31, 1991-October 4, 2008

Our grief truly never left, but the acceptance of Brooke's passing started to set in. Daily tears dwindled to weekly, but the memories of her never died. Like the way that she would make outrageous claims like, "deer hear out of their antlers." Or her natural elation when leading massive chants at Ralph Ward Memorial Field on Friday nights and the occasional Saturday afternoon.

...or the blood curdling scream when the McLaughlin boy sunk his teeth into Ryan's leg... or when she dug the shard of glass from a broken bottle of Grey Goose into her wrist over, and over again...

I'd be lying if I said that we didn't feel guilty. We saw the blatant signs of suffering, but never went out of our way to help fix it. Guilt continued to heighten, because somehow, word got around the we infiltrated the Lequin Church that night. As crazy as it sounds, the feat gave us borderline celebrity status amongst Bradford County.

Adults, professional paranormal researchers, ministers, you name it... they were forced away by but we went in willingly. A bunch of teenagers stayed the night at the Lequin Church.

Even though it was 15 minutes...

They saw a ghost.

More like three. If that is what they really were.

And something grabbed a few of them!

Or bit right through Ryan's goddamn leg.

The story we told was different than the truth. We all agreed to it. Figured the watered down version would be at least somewhat more believable than the actual transcript. Plus, we thought it would be safer somehow. Maybe people wouldn't find it all that interesting.

We were wrong.

The Lequin Church became a one-stop shop for an adrenaline rush. And, in this part of the state, what else was there to do. The feeling was contagious. It started with us, and infected so many more.

Ironically enough, no one had even close to the same experience that we did.

It was the typical stuff. Hearing whispers, footsteps, the works. No family, no crazy-ass reflection or assault by American Flag. Jimmy Ellsworth said something grabbed his leg when he was in the pulpit, but that was the most vile of the acts against any visitors.

We were invited to go with a couple of groups but passed. The time wasn't right. Deep down we shared the connection. Eventually we would go back, but not sooner.

In the meantime, we listened to the stories. Many of which were tuned out. People were so frightened, yet excited to tell us their "terrifying" experience.

Oh my God, it was crazy, Zack. I heard footsteps in the balcony... there was someone up there but I couldn't see them!

Yeah... reeeeeeeeeaaaaaaaal terrifying... For fuck's sake...

Anyways, post-graduation plans were starting to come-to. Kara got accepted to her first choice, Keuka College, a small school in upstate New York. Ryan didn't like the idea, he wasn't headed to college and certainly not New York. The Natural Gas industry was paying well at the time, he'd end up getting a job at Newpark Drilling or something of that nature.

Matt's plan panned out. He'd be able to run the farm and go to school. Lycoming College in Williamsport gave him one hell of a scholarship for their Environmental Science program.

Of all places, Jade put down her deposit and committed to the University of Wyoming to study Middle Level Education with a concentration in Special Education. Literally, one of the most beautiful girls on Earth was headed to college in *Wyoming*. Florida? Cali? Nope. She looked like a bonafide UCLA Bruin or Miami Hurricane. But no, her love of the Pacific Northwest and dismay for her parents took her to Laramie to be a Cowboy.

Pears and Sasha still weren't sure, but the Army was at the top of Pears' list. Sasha just wasn't ready to think of it.

Gordy was pursuing Animation at The Art Institute of Pittsburgh and I was going to be up the road from him. Right up the Boulevard of the Allies was Duquesne University. Although I hadn't heard from them yet, that was the move. Carlow University, further up the Boulevard, was the backup plan. The Pittsburgh market alone would be enough build my network as a sports journalist, the college in particular didn't matter.

It continues to amaze me how October of 2008 changed all of our lives so much. Just turned seniors in high school, lost one of our best friends and at least most of us had the next four years of our lives locked in. Signed, sealed and delivered.

November came. Salt Springs almost flipped upside down on the first Tuesday of that month, because a black guy won the presidential election. Almost everyone was outraged, but of course, it wasn't because he was black.

Oh, no... I have nothing against black people! My cousin's, step-son has a black friend and he's a nice kid... I'm not a racist or anything...

Yeah, sure thing, Bob. Keep fucking telling yourself that...

NO GODDAMN MUSLIMS IN THE WHITE HOUSE

It *was* because he was black and you know what? I voted for him. My mom voted for him. Matt voted for him. Jade voted for him and *of course* Sasha voted for him. All of us would have if each of us were adults in the eyes of the law. Barack Obama winning the presidential election was *fucking* awesome.

Salt Springs was quiet after the election. Just like we grieved a month earlier, they cried over the GOP's loss until Thanksgiving. Snowed like a motherfucker that year. Flakes came down in small, but constant waves throughout the morning. The soil was at a temperature that allowed it to stick and by dinner time, six inches of powder packed to Aunt Georgia's lawn.

Barack's victory set in with the residents of this small conservative town, in particular. They didn't like it; they hated it. They hated him. But hatred can be tiring, and the entire town was unconscious by it.

Except for us. Come December, our lives were coming into shape. Post-gradation plans were settling in. Pears announced his enlistment to the

Army on December 1st, Sasha was headed to the police academy, unless she got some basketball offers and Ryan got a part-time job that would go full-time after he graduated.

Duquesne finally gave me the nod on December 3rd and I was ecstatic. I was going to be a Duke. Plus, the Steelers were 9-3 and just came off of a New England Patriot ass whooping, 33-10. Brady wasn't playing but fuck it. I loved watching Belichick's face when we lit their defense up over and over again. Old fuck looked like grandma from " The Goonies".

For the first time in a long time, I was content. I started to see that Kate Ford wasn't everything, but I'd be lying if I said that I didn't miss her. She was still beautiful and she still occasionally batted her long eyelashes at me when I passed her in the hall. Courtney Winthrop even tried to reunite us a few times, but I wasn't quite ready yet. I turned down each of the three proposals.

There would eventually be a time that I accepted. I still loved her, but this brief interlude of life was allowing me to find myself. And damn, the search was difficult.

I was going to play the Kate situation by ear, and the rest of my friends would ride out this last leg of our senior year together. I guess maybe that was a reason of why I was hesitant to reunite with the pastor's daughter.

All of that was put on the back burner though on the following Monday, December 8th, 2008. It was my mother's 59th birthday and it was a day that I will never forget.

242

CHAPTER 27: Mom's 59th

My mom was in no way Salt Springs' first lady, but
those who knew her absolutely adored her. She
would make outrageous uncensored claims on
Myspace about how Monday's were the *fucking*
worst and praise Rob Thomas's ass publicly.

But if someone needed something, especially her
kids, she was there with the most sincere,
generous kindness that one would ever fathom. If
there was a death of someone she didn't even
know, she would be at each of their loved one's
house with a baked lasagna and if the church
needed a babysitter for their nursery, she would
volunteer. Even if she didn't regularly attend
service.

December 8, 2008 was her 59th birthday and the
whole crew were surprising her with pizza, cake
and ice cream during Monday Night Football.
Football, pizza and ice cream, in no particular
order, are top the power rankings of "Shelly's
Favorite Things."

.....

The 3:16p.m. bell rang, thank God the day was
over. Hollinshead's final exam was in two weeks,
and he decides that he wants to cover *everything* in
it. I'm talking the shit we learned in September.

What's the point in the fucking mid-term then? Most teachers' final exams were from mid-term to present. This fucker wanted to do the whole thing!

Courtney Winthrop came up to me at lunch and wondered if I was ready to talk to Kate. Of course I *wanted* to, but I couldn't. She burnt the holy shit out of me. Plus, I couldn't accept with Jade and Sasha staring me down from the other side of the table. They looked at my fiercely, eyes fixed directly at mine. I could hear one of Sasha's Nike's tapping the floor, and Jade's fingernails clicked on the plastic tray.

Together, the eight of us fled the confines of Salt Springs High School that afternoon. Trees were barren on the mountainside beyond the football field, and snow parked underneath them. The landscape of our elevation didn't don any precipitation, but the weekend was set to deliver about eight to 10 inches. Joe Snedeker on WNEP is normally right, but it was still far out. Supposed to be the most accumulation of the year so far.

We reached the back row of cars in the school parking lot. Sasha's PT, Ryan's Dodge Ram, Gordy's Park Avenue and Matt's Jeep all parked side-by-side that day. It broke the unwritten rule of Salt Springs High that underclassmen had the back row, but we didn't care. After Brooke's death, we didn't really give a fuck about any stupid ass rule.

Jade stood beside Sasha and I. She was riding home with us. After Sasha dropped me off, the two of them were going to go to Williamsport to pick up a Yankee Candle for my mom as a birthday gift. Only of those $40 jawns. They were going to split it $20/$20. Well over two hours of part-time employment for the two of them gone for Ma's date of birth.

Damn, I wish Kate treated my mom like they did. Kate had the tendency to be rude and standoff-ish, but Jade and Sasha *loved* "Ms. Shelly." Sasha actually started calling her "Mama" recently.

They figured by the time they got home from Williamsport, the pizza would be ready. They put the order in for 7:00pm, so it should give them plenty of time. Sasha started getting discounts on the pies from "The Holy Grail" when she started seeing one of their cooks. Marco Martucci was his name. A little older. Only 22, though. Used to work at his uncle's pizza joint over in Troy. There was a falling out. Money, I believe. So Marco turned heel and joined his uncle's biggest competitor.

Sasha stood by her PT Cruiser that cold afternoon and ordered two plain cheese pizzas, along with a veggie lovers that probably only my mother would eat.

Sasha clapped her cell phone shut and exclaimed, "Three pizzas. Five dollars. Marco hookin' me up."

"Un-fucking-believable." I said in amazement and leaned against the PT.

"Believe it, nigga." she said, and then she turned to the group, "any of you mothafuckas need lessons suckin' dick let me know. I want all you niggas getting' cheap ass pizza."

"Oh, *Jesus Christ!*" Ryan started screaming with laughter. Kara rested her head against his arms and joined his uncontrollable laughter.

The entire group howled until I saw Kate approaching out of the corner of my eye. Her car was parked in its usual spot, three cars down from Sasha's PT.

"So what time should I expect you guys?" I said with a sense of hidden anxiety.

"I get off work at 7 so I'm just going to grab the ice cream and come right over." Pears said.

"Yeah, we'll be there a little after 7, too" Kara spoke for both her and Ryan.

"You already know that mothafuckin' pizza comin' at 7, chief!" Sasha added with excitement.

"Oh Zack, shit. I almost forgot." Jade said quickly. A sudden sense of disappointment came over me. Was Jade not going to make it? How would this be a surprise from the crew without Jade? I felt like if a crush cancelled plans last minute, but Jade wasn't a crush. She was a friend.

"What's you mom's favorite scent?" she said. Freezing wind blustered on the back of her neck, she continued with a shiver, "We're getting her a candle."

Fuck if I know...

"Cucumber melon." I said with confidence. But truthfully, I had no clue.

Kate was getting into her car and she glanced over at me momentarily, but I ignored it. She looked disgusted as she tossed her Coach purse into the front seat.

It was the same purse that spilled on her kitchen counter two months ago.

"See you guys at 7 then." I said and I hopped in the passenger's seat of Sasha's PT.

CHAPTER 28: Murphy's Law

The leather seating in Ryan's truck was frigid, but the heated seats started to thaw Kara's buttocks.

The Murphy household was about two miles up Lower Mountain Road, which branched off of Troy Street just north of the borough.

Ryan had been there before, but was chased out by Kara's father. It was a beautiful home. Nothing extravagant like the O'Sullivan's but it was nice. Plus it was secluded. The Murphy's house was the only one in a mile radius. Probably how nobody ever heard Jim beating his wife and daughter.

Jim was a motherfucker. Ryan hated him, but not because how Jim treated him. How Jim treated Kara was unacceptable, and the fact that people knew about it, made the whole situation worse.

Ryan was anxious, but excited. Jim was meeting with an investor in Syracuse for the weekend. Some rich bastard in upstate New York wanted to buy the contracting business. He wasn't opposed to the idea but he already had in mind that he wasn't going to bite. Murphy Contracting was the only thing that he knew he could control, unlike his daughter's school attire.

Jim had a finished basement that he kept as a "man cave" filled with his own accolades. Everything from old Salt Springs Letterman Jackets to wrestling trophies from the early '80's. It was a shrine of a successful past, both personally and professionally. When he wasn't clubbing his wife for overcooking the chicken, he was in his study observing what was.

He was going to do it. He was going to plow the holy hell out of Kara in Jim's temple. His testosterone was boiling. Ryan hadn't fucked Kara in a week. His balls felt like two tubs of pudding and erections commenced at the sight of the small freckle above her cleavage.

Ryan cranked the steering wheel of his pickup as it rounded the 45 degree angle that was "The Devil's Elbow", a sharp curve a mile up Lower Mountain Road. The smell of the truck's heating unit accompanied the warmth that traveled through the vents. Ryan and Kara's ears popped simultaneously as the truck made its way up the steady incline into a higher elevation.

"Country Fried" by the Zac Brown Band faded out over the speakers and a new tune started its blare.

Oh! Hey! I've been travelin' on this road too long...

...Forgot I put this one on...

"Thank God this seat's getting warm. Holy shit." Kara said as her arms finally uncrossed. She no longer needed to embrace herself for warmth. Her hands rested on her thighs.

"Right? I got to get them fixed. Takes 15 minutes for them to warm up anymore." He replied. "Sorry 'bout that, babe." He placed his hand on her upper thigh, stroking her outer leg with his thumb.

Kara sighed sarcastically, "You're fine...". She looked toward him with her chocolate brown eyes enlarged. It was a puppy dog-like look and Ryan caught it in his peripheral. There was a straight stretch ahead, so he could afford to be distracted by the look. Lines of snow-sprinkled pines flanked each side of the gravel covered road. The house was just beyond this stretch, they were close so he turned to her.

Her eyes seemed to take over her entire façade. An elegant centerpiece of a formal dinner table. But her skin, so smooth and tanned despite the late fall's frigid, dry air. She offered a half smile at him. Lip gloss shined as she revealed most of her flawless pearly whites.

Ryan could feel a swell in his loins and a tingle in the pit of his stomach. His hand squeezed her thigh.

She let out a low pleasure filled groan. Ryan's libido didn't rest, yet it heightened. His hand moved up and started to massage the crease of her leg. With each rotation of the truck's tires, Ryan's hand got deeper and deeper between Kara's wickets.

They reached the "Chitty Chitty Bang Bang" mailbox and Ryan turned the truck with his spare hand into the Murphy's driveway, crunching the untraveled powder. He had managed to unbutton Kara's jeans in the process. Her zipper was only halfway down, but that's all he needed. Her head was pinned to the back of the passengers' seat as Ryan was running his index and middle fingers through her. Moans turned to light yelps with each stroke. With his middle and forefinger, he caressed the outer lips. She was soaked. Kara bit her lip and clutched his wrist, leading him to where she wanted him. Her legs started to quake in an attempt to hold her orgasm.

She didn't notice the now sweltering heat coming from inside the leather.

Ryan released his hand and pulled Kara on top of him in the driver's seat. She leaned against the steering wheel as he unzipped her coat and lifted her shirt. Kara's back pressed against the horn, an occasional honk rang through the cold air like an avalanche's warning siren. Ryan pulled the lever to move the seat back while Kara was unfastening her bra.

Ryan grabbed a breast with each hand, caressing over her nipples with his thumbs. He leaned in and started to suck. His tongue circled the areola's, and occasionally a small mole in her cleavage.

Kara unbuttoned Ryan's pants and started to stroke, she lead him into her and she started to ride.

It was a full-on, hardcore fuck by the fifth stroke. Ryan's fingernails had already busted long bloody scratches into Kara's back. His hands moved down to cradle her buttocks. He offered a good, firm spank. Making her ass jiggle beneath his fingers. He moved his mouth from her tits and started to suck on her neck.

But he saw something through the windshield.

The front door of the Murphy household opened, but he continued to thrust. No one came out of the house. Kara turned around and grasped the steering wheel. Ryan railed from behind.

Three strokes in, Jim Murphy walked out of the door and stood on the front porch. He watched his daughter and her *fuck buddy* have sex in *HIS* driveway.

Ryan gave Kara's ass a hard smack and then they saw him, looking right back at them.

Impossible. He's on business... in fucking Syracuse...

He looked strange. For once, he didn't look all that angry. Actually, he looked pleased. Jim always resembled a lumberjack, but never this much. His bright orange knit cap warmed his completely bald head, and a large grin peeked from behind a long black beard that complimented his checkered flannel.

He lumbered down the steps and walked toward the woodpile next to the house. He started to search through the heap. Wood spewed from the neatly stacked pile and littered the snow around it. Jim was looking for something. Twigs, logs and everything in between flew in all directions, like Scooby and Shaggy raiding a refrigerator, looking for ingredients for a sandwich.

Alas, finally, laying in the midst of the saw dust, Jim Murphy found his axe.

Ryan clutched the gear shift and yanked it in reverse, but the truck would go nowhere. Kara hopped off of him and he tried again. This time it worked.

Jim had reached the driveway. He continued to walk leisurely toward them, twirling his axe like a baton.

The truck sped backwards until tires burst from an object unforeseen. Ryan took a look in the rearview mirror. Fear struck in his gut at what he saw in it.

At the end of the Murphy's driveway were two young boys.

Jim's beard had started to thin, and hair started to grow on his head.

Ryan squinted at the rearview mirror for a clearer image. One of the boys sneered. The boy licked his cracked lips clean of its blood. A worm wriggled in his vacated eye socket.

Jim Murphy reached the front fender of Ryan's truck. He tapped the axe against the metal frame. His beard completely vanished, and streaks of silver hair shined from below the orange beanie.

"Ryan... Kara... it's good to see you again..." Jim said in a low, sinister voice. Only this wasn't Jim Murphy, it was never Jim Murphy. It was the Titus McLaughlin.

"Wha... what... do you want... from us?" Ryan choked. Spit gurgled in his throat. Kara looked down and sobbed toward her bare chest.

He flashed a seductive look at his axe and wielded it into the snow. The man looked directly to Kara, and he began to speak, "Put your fucking tits away, whore!"

Coming from the mouth of Titus McLaughlin, was the voice of her father.

"Fuck off! Leave us alone!" Kara wailed.

Titus moved his eyes to Ryan. They locked glances, but Titus's face was much more familiar. His eyes were a light brown. Potent crow's feet neighbored both eyes. Somehow, his face grew a bit wider too with significant dimples indented to his cheeks.

Mom.

"Ry... why do you leave me alone with him?" Titus blurted out, but that voice... It was Tracy Wilson's.

"Ry... he's killing me. He beats me. Every night! And you aren't there! Why, Ryan?! Wh—"

His voice lowered, crow's feet disappeared, facial structure began to change and his eyes turned blueish-green, with a goatee speckled with grey.

"Yeah, that's right, Ryan." He laughed, sounding just like Ryan's mother's abusive boyfriend, Norm Slocum. "Thanks for the easy pussy every night. No one there to hear her scream. No one there to see me fuck the shit out of your mother's sloppy pussy!"

Ryan started to cry. He wiped his tears with the palm of his hand, "Shut the fuck up. I'll fucking kill you!" Ryan yelled.

"Awww... you cry just like your mommy." Titus said in Norm Slocum's voice. "Should I stick my cock in your mouth like I do your mother's to make her stop? Huh? YOU LITTLE FUCKING FAGGOT."

Titus signaled for the two boys. The one-eyed lad walked toward the passenger's side door. As he got closer, Kara's seat returned to a scald. More heat released from the leather with each step he took. The boy arrived at the passenger's side door and started to pound on it frantically. Just like a kid with a severe mental disorder. He laughed and his tongue swayed at his chin from side to side like a dog preparing for his meal.

The white leather looked like a heated iron getting ready to brand a frat boy. It glared red, and she jumped back onto Ryan's lap. Internal temperature arose well into the hundreds, sweat dripped from their scalps in fluid streams despite the winter chill outside.

"Ry?! Are you warm?!" the Crow's feet returned. "Turn on the A/C."

Ryan's vision was starting to fade. A black border surrounded his line of sight.

"What's the matter you little pussy?" a new voice emerged from McLaughlin. One he hadn't heard in years. "That's why I left you little bitch! You can't fucking take it."

Pain pierced through Ryan's elbows and forearms, just like in Little League. The voice came back to him. It was his father's.

"Little fucking fag! You fucking crying to your mother all the time." He sneered. "She didn't even have a good pussy either! Fucking sloppy ass box! I was doing you a favor you little fucking cock sucker!"

"FUCK YOU!" Ryan screamed.

Ryan gave the truck one final attempt to reverse. The deflated tires spun and sprayed snow through a 15-foot radius but the truck remained still.

"You know, Ryan…" the man grumbled in his own voice. "You ever have one of them days you wish you would've stayed home?"

The speakers in the truck turned back on. It was low, but clear.

I've been travelin' on this road too long… just tryna find my way back home…

"You *all* should've stayed home." The man's voice started to raise and he walked closer toward the truck, "Now you're going to have to *obey!*"

His voice was now a scream. He stood, staring into the driver's side window. A blue vein protruded out of his forehead by an entire inch. His paled skin offered a shade of blue. Gray, pointed teeth gnashed into his gums. A shade of black and blue surrounded his eyes like a raccoon.

The old me is…

"YOU DIDN'T OBEY RYAN!" he screamed, *"YOU DIDN'T OBEY KARA!"*

"No, no, no, no, no, no…" Ryan stuttered. "Please…"

The man stepped back from the car. His vein receded, but the blood still poured from his purple gums. The man's eyebrows raised even with the streaks of gray on his temples.

Dead and Gone, Dead and Gone...

The passenger's seat exploded in a burst of flames. Ryan grabbed for the door handle but it wouldn't open. Kara's hair was the first to ignite. Her hairspray was still potent enough to attract the flame.

Ryan started to choke on the smoke, but quickly, embers from Kara's shirt landed on his pants. He skootched back to wipe them off, but Kara's burning body grabbed him in an attempt to save herself.

He grasped her, flame and all. Ryan lunged their bodies toward the door.

Flames leaked into the fuel line and fragments of Ryan's pride and joy polluted the winter air like an atomic bomb. The only thing that remained in the Murphy's driveway was the front fender...

...and the worm...

CHAPTER 29: Williamsport

Snowflakes started to pelt the PT Cruiser's windshield harder on the way down Lycoming Mall Road. Must have been a bit of ice involved, the precipitation sounded like tacks falling onto glass when they rounded the turn by a Toys 'R Us. Dusk was starting to settle, it was late in the year. Almost to 2008's shortest day of light, the mall was just at the bottom of this slope. The time read 4:47 p.m., Sasha and Jade had plenty of time.

"Let's go in through Dick's..."

Sasha started to laugh sarcastically. People thought the name "Dick's Sporting Goods" was so funny. The store finally opened in the Lycoming Mall after years of negotiation. It's location wasn't ideal, just outside of Williamsport, it would have made more sense to put it in the Golden Strip or at least in downtown, not halfway to Muncy.

"I'm serious..." Jade smiled back at Sasha. "I have a few things I need to pick up."

"Like what, girl?" Sasha asked with high-pitched sarcasm. She yanked the wheel and turned into the Dick's parking lot, on the way in the car elevated over the curb and the quarter panel scraped on the concrete. Sasha was unphased, the car had been through worse.

"Jaderade, we only have an hour…"

Jade rolled her eyes toward Sasha, "It's not going to take us an hour to get a fucking candle, Sash…"

"*DAAAAAAAAAAAMMMMMNNNN* woman! The gaht-damn hostility!"

Jade smiled again, this time larger, holding in a laugh. "I'm serious, Sash! I need to pick up Christmas stuff!"

Sasha's rebuttal was sarcastic, "Well them muhfuckin' gifts 'n shit gonna have to wait…"

"Sasha! Jesus!"

"Bitch! I'm kiddin'!" Sasha laughed, "Where we goin'? I have to pick some shit up too."

"Just a few places."

Sasha pulled into a parking spot and crashed the tires into the small concrete barrier at the head of the space. Both Sasha and Jade's heads whipped back and forth. Sasha's hair didn't wave but Jade's did. She lowered the sun visor and opened its mirror. Jade stroked through her long blonde hair with her black-painted fingernails like a brush. She put her coat on and got out of the car.

Dick's smelled like balls. *Bad sentence. Let me restart.*

Jade and Sasha passed through the Dick's Sporting Goods entrance to the Lycoming Mall. The musky smell of rubber overcame them. It was the combination of footballs, basketballs and bicycle tires that let off such a strong aroma that would make many quiver, but to an athlete it smelled heavenly.

Sasha wanted to grab some new laces for her basketball kicks. She had this superstition of wearing off colored shoe laces during games, none that even came close to resembling her home school's green, white and black. Sometimes she wore yellow, other times it would be pink. Sasha was feeling some baby blue's for an upcoming game against Northeast Bradford.

Jade had no intention of buying anything in Dick's. She just followed along as Sasha speed-walked to the basketball section. Sasha perused the sweatbands momentarily, they had all colors on the shelf including a rare forest green, the primary color of Salt Springs High School. She was tempted to buy, but declined. She went for the laces and found her match for a cheap price.

Immediately after they left Dick's, the smell of rubber was replaced by Auntie Anne's pretzels. A much more pleasing smell, they walked passed a large garden showcase that replaced a kiosk. Vines hung down in long streams like Rapunzel's locks, flowers even bloomed despite the time of year. Just beyond the display was a sports merchandise store that caught Jade's attention.

"There." Jade grabbed Sasha's arm and pulled it in the direction of the store. Flanking the sides of the entrance were two large windows with three mannequins modeling jerseys from Pennsylvania's NFL teams on each side.

The left donned Ben Roethlisberger, Hines Ward and Troy Polamalu. The right displayed Donovan McNabb, Brian Westbrook and Brian Dawkins.

They went inside. Jerseys aligned the back wall representing at least one player from each NFL team with the exception of the Steelers and Eagles, who were represented by six players. Jade walked toward the Steelers players with no hesitation.

"Oh shit…" Sasha said, "They have Santonio Holmes. Never saw that shit before…"

"Okay, Sash," Jade said seriously, "I know Zack has a Stewart jersey… but he doesn't play anymore…"

"Jade… you aren't…."

"...and I know he has Pettis? Dennis? Lettuce?"

"Bettis." Sasha said dryly. "He has a Jerome Bettis jersey. That's his favorite player ever. He's retired."

"So he probably wants a player that is playing now, right?" Jade asked, holding up a Ben Roethlisberger jersey.

"Jader..." Sasha's voice was still dry, but it was becoming increasingly curious. "Those things are like 100 dollars, you don't want to get him something like that. Get him a fucking hat."

"Finding everything okay, ma'am?" a worker came over, only speaking in Jade's direction. He ignored Sasha.

"Yes, sir. Thank you." Jade said. "Quick question, though. How much are these?"

"Steelers and Eagles jerseys are all 125." He said, "I think we have a Plaxico Burress on clearance though."

"He doesn't play for them anymore, right?" she asked him and he shook his head.

"So, who is the best player out of all of these guys?" she asked him. He walked toward her and grabbed the jersey from her. He placed his hand on her shoulder and said with a touch of flirtatiousness, "If you want the best player, you'll want this guy" and he unracked a small Troy Polamalu jersey. "I'll check you out." and he smiled.

"That won't fit Zack." Sasha claimed.

"Who's Zack?" the worker asked.

"Our fr—"

"My dad." Jade said sternly. Her blue eyes never left the worker. She batted them three times and puffed out her chest. Jade twirled a lock of her blonde hair with a finger as she started to gnaw on her gum.

"What size does he wear?" the worker's eyes started to wander over Jade even more. She caught him glancing at her chest and she panned over to Sasha.

"ONE. X." Sasha mouthed. *"EXXXX ELLLLL"*

"Extra-large." Jade said softly, but yet sexy. The worker released an extra-large Troy Polamalu jersey from the rack. They followed him to the counter. During the walk to the checkout line, Jade unfastened a button from her blouse, just exposing enough of her chest to mesmerize any man. She pulled her cami down, giving a clear path to her cleavage.

They got to the checkout line, and Jade immediately leaned over the glass counter. The counter worked as a display of autographed memorabilia. From baseball cards to helmets, Jade acted as if she were impressed. Truthfully, she didn't know the difference between a signed Sandy Koufax rookie card and a Deshea Townsend autographed coffee mug. What she did know was her way with men, and it was working to perfection. She could see his eyes staring down her shirt out of her peripheral.

"Call it 50 dollars." The worker said and Jade handed him two 20's and a ten. "Make up the other 75 by calling me." And he wrote his phone number on the back of the receipt.

"Thanks." Jade read over the receipt, making sure of an *employee discount*. "Jack?"

"That's me." He said, "and you are?"

Jade turned to Sasha and smiled, "Sara. Sara O'Sullivan. From up in Salt Springs."

"Talk to you soon, Sara." The worker smiled and winked. Jade winked back but when she turned in the other direction toward Sasha, she rolled her eyes in disgust.

They found a trashcan just outside of the sports merchandise store. Jade looked at it curiously and hollered, "Hey Jack!"

He looked out of the storefront, his eyes met Jade's. She crumpled the receipt and tossed it in the trash. The worker's jaw dropped halfway to the floor. Jade and Sasha turned their backs and started their walk toward the Yankee Candle store for Miss Shelly's birthday gift.

They took longer than expected inside of Dick's and the sports merchandise stores, so their time was dwindling. With only 20 minutes until they had to head back up Route 14 to Salt Springs, Sasha and Jade walked with intensive force toward the candle shop.

They passed kiosks on the way, ignoring their aggressive lotion and makeup salesmen. They hit the stretch of scents, a Bath and Body Works store, Hollister and Yankee Candle. Both Jade and Sasha remembered that Kara wanted lotion and perfume for Christmas. Bath and Body was her temple, a religious customer of the scented domain. The specific scents were only available there.

Kara's gift was a concern two weeks in the making, what they needed now was a birthday present for Miss Shelly. They passed the large Hollister storefront and reached the final shop of the hallway: Yankee Candle.

Sasha and Jade entered side-by-side. Much different than Jade's dragging of Sasha into the merchandise shop. The hallway was dark, but inside the store was golden. Lights shined on the wooden shelves of candles. The first display were all Christmas themed scents. The aroma of sugar cookie dominated the first steps of the shop. Sasha removed the cap and whiffed around the wick. Her eyes closed at the pleasure from the smell. Jade enjoyed the scent of a gingerbread candle.

They walked deeper into the store and the air shifted to a fruity smell. It didn't match the season like the front, but this was Miss Shelly's bread and butter. Sasha and Jade sampled candles like two middle-aged women at a wine-tasting. Scents started to merge together in their nasal cavity, and the offerings had no definitive smell. They burned their sniffers out, until Sasha pulled a cucumber melon jar off of the top shelf. She looked at the bottom to see the price.

35 dollars for a fuckin' candle? The fuck????

Jade saw the price tag, "Worth it." She said.

"She is." Sasha replied. "Mama Shell deserves it."

They checked out and Sasha started to think of the Troy Polamalu jersey. She had been suspicious a few years ago, but it was all coming back.

You don't get 'just a friend' a 100 dollar Christmas gift...

"Jade, babe." Sasha said with sincerity as they entered the dim of the Lycoming Mall walkway. "I don't want no bullshit either. I want to know..."

"What's up, Sash?"

"What's your deal with Zack?" Sasha asked.

"What about him?" Jade's face became serious. Her eyes narrowed and her mouth was still. She offered no look in Sasha's direction, only straight in front. She couldn't get to the car quick enough.

"You like him." Sasha rebuked, "It's okay if you do Ja—"

"Yeah," Jade's faced remained forward, "as a frie—"

"No, fuck that Jade." Sasha started to scold and Jade cocked her head toward her. She didn't look angry, more confused but not because she didn't understand her. Her look favored a child's once mom catches them in the cookie jar.

"I did, yes." Jade was reluctant but admitted anyways.

"When?"

"Like 8th fuckin' grade, why?" Jade was getting defensive. A salesman from a kiosk approached them, "I *fucking* said no already!" Jade snapped at him and he cowered back to his stand like a puppy.

"I saw you guys at Brooke's funeral." Sasha's tone returned to passionate. It was impossible to be hostile when approaching the Auntie Anne's, the smell of the frying dough was relaxing, "You guys looked... like... I don't know..."

Jade stopped in the middle of the barren path. She calmed from her formerly pissed-off state, "Sash, he's still in love with Kate... There's nothing with him. He's not over her and it fucking kills me..."

"So you admit it."

"No!"

"Then why the fuck are you so pissed about Kate?"

"Because Zack's my best *fucking* friend." Jade was getting animated again, her arms flailed to the side and her neck craned forward. "He's yours too! Why aren't you pissed about it?"

"Why did you get him that then?" Sasha pointed to the bag that held the Troy Polamalu jersey.

"Because he wanted it….?" Jade replied sarcastically. As if Sasha had asked for the answer to 2+2.

"From all of us… we would all put in 10 dollars for it…" Sasha muttered with condescending clarity. "Not from just you…"

"Well I got it for 50…"

"I'll tell you what, Jade…" Sasha snapped. "Do you know what Gordy wants for Christmas? Or Matt? Fuck… Even Pears… what do they want?"

Jade stared back at Sasha blankly. Her eyes didn't move. Tears started to well, shining her soft blue eyes even more. She bit her lower lip, but didn't expose any of her teeth until she developed a frustrated grin. Her tongue groped the inside of her cheek.

"That's what I thought…" Sasha murmured pridefully. But she continued with great sass, "Gord wants picks and strings. Matt needs new boots. Pears wants an new pair of Dexter Bowling Shoes. Just so you know."

Sasha started to continued her stride toward the exit when she heard a phone ringing. One of those default tones that sort of resembled a tune, but an overtly annoying one. Something that you would hear while on hold with the cable company.

She looked back and saw Jade hypnotized by her cell phone. Jade used to be often, but not so much anymore. She was maturing, and was growing out of the 'phone obsessed teenage girl' phase.

This was different, though. She wasn't offering a blank stare into the technology, but it was a gaze of despair. Confusion mixed with anguish. Like the look a cancer patient would give a doctor before hearing the test results.

Jade's thumb hovered over the green accept button. Just as Sasha started to walk back to her, Jade answered the phone.

It was Matt.

CHAPTER 30: Special Delivery

Anna Murphy sent a text to Robert Knickerbocker at around 4:30, still an hour left to moderate after-school detention.

Hi Bob, Kara drank the last of the milk this morning with her breakfast. Got any in store?

Matt will be up this afternoon. Got the usual two quarts for you. Kara can pay Matt the next time she sees him. I know y'all are good for it.

The cold didn't bother Matt K. He actually preferred it. Folks didn't want to go out and run to town in sub-freezing temperatures for just milk and eggs, so good ol' Knickerbocker Dairy profited well from late-November to around early-April.

Dry, northeastern air chilled Matt's neck in that sensitive spot where his hair nor Carhart jacket covered, as he blazed the trail that was the house's driveway. It wasn't his most comfortable trek but just like manure smelled like money in the summer, the freeze felt like quite literally, cold, hard cash.

He tugged on the door handle until he heard the *click*, so he was at least confident that the door was sealed. This obsession had just started to ease for the first time since the first week of October. Randall wasn't getting out, and Matt knew that he

might not ever see the light of day again if his
mother came home to an ice-chest of a house.

Click!

He heard that baby shut, although it could have
easily been some settling ice that cracked under his
feet on the wooden side-porch. It was slick, a size
10 slipped from under him, but he managed. He
grasped the railing a little firmer and walked across
the frozen tundra of their driveway.

Matt didn't get much traction, Stoney Corners got
only a little bit of rain earlier in the day before the
temperature dropped to the mid-20's, but it was
enough. The driveway was a hockey rink and his
skating ability was like Doug Glatt's from the
movie, "Goon." He moved from sheer momentum,
not raising his feet once. Staggering glides led him
to the screen door that led to the barn's office. He
leaned his hand on the door frame with one hand
for support while he jerked on the door handle
with another. Feet continued to slip with each
attempt to pry the frozen door open, but finally it
gave way. Ice busted in the doorframe, and Matt
sighed with relief. Carefully, he raised one foot to
the concrete floor inside the barn and the other
joined quickly after.

84 heifers huddled together in the large farm for
much of the winter, but this was a little early. Matt

completed the chores in which consisted of only milking during this time of season. Bailing was done for a while, but they were plenty prepared for the cow's feed until April.

Matt walked through the crowd like he was at a much quieter and less eccentric nightclub. Compare it to a Tuesday night at the Cell Block in Williamsport. He grabbed drinks and was trying to find his crew. Only there were no drinks, and his crew was Lola.

He shifted through, turned to the side and squeezed in his belly. Evading the large black and white girths. Betty dropped some dung on his boot, but all he felt was a small pat on the top of his foot. He realized it once the smell hit.

Lola was at the back of the barn.

Smart girl, Matt thought. All of the warmth was on her. She was set.

Matt stood beside her, rubbing the top of her head. His middle and ring fingers dug in to her scalp and moved between her eyes. It was Lola's biggest weakness, her eyes became heavy and she swayed on her foundation.

"Got another winter in ya, girl?" Matt asked. He knew there would be no response, but it didn't matter. Humans develop thousands of

relationships over the course of their life. Whether
it be their spouse, child, mother, father, doctor and
a barrage of friends and acquaintances that come
and go. But how many of those relationships have
zero dialogue? None. Except for the relationship
between human and pet. Somehow you never
share a word, but the love is eternal.

Lola cocked her head toward Matt's torso and her
breaths started to become deeper. She was getting
the best of head scratches, until her master heard a
loud electronic *bloop!* breaking his attention and
even hers.

It was his cell phone and normally, he would push
it off until later. It was probably Pears offering him
some asinine trade in fantasy football but he had a
feeling it was something that couldn't wait.

He was right.

2 quarts to the Murphy's if u can. Love u bud.

Got it. Love you too.

"Alrighty girl, I'll be back tonight." Matt whispered
and gave Lola's head a peck. He shimmied back
through the moshing herd of cows and returned to
the office.

They probably didn't need it during this time of
year, but behind the office desk was a large walk in
freezer. Inside the 64 square foot ice box were
crates of milk and eggs, stacked from floor to
ceiling. Each crate held four quarts of milk or 10
dozen eggs. Matt grabbed two quarts and returned
to the office as quickly as he could. It was freezing
outside, and damn, it felt like Antarctica's asshole
in there.

Matt almost forgot about the Mellon Arena-like
driveway and his walking pace halted abruptly once
he opened the screen door. The glass quarts of milk
provided him with at least some center of gravity
during his conservative prance to his Jeep. He
shifted the milk to one hand, clanking together. His
free mitt grabbed the steering wheel for leverage
as he reached over the console to drop the milk
jugs in the front seat.

He got in and cranked the ignition. With the same
force, he yanked the heating unit to his highest
level. Matt sat in the drivers' seat, fighting the urge
to scream *"FUUUUUUUUUUCCCCCCKKKKKKKKKK"*
from the cold.

The Jeep started to warm, but his bare hands
didn't. They were still fire engine red from carrying
the jugs across the driveway.

"They'll warm.." he thought, and he moved the gearshift to reverse.

"14 miles away for two quarts?" Matt thought. *"Old man better expense my gas..."*

Matt figured that the trip would crescendo/decrescendo. The weather in Stoney Corners was frightful, but Salt Springs would have certainly be closer to delightful. And once he hit Lower Mountain Road... fuck the Christmas clichés, that road was going to be a son of a bitch.

Matt was right. The exterior temperature gauge on his dashboard improved by four degrees and ice was minimized to barren by the time he reached Salt Springs. He hung a left at the red light on Main Street and ventured up Troy Street. About a mile up the road, he reached the old Feed Mill, turned on his four-wheel drive and swung onto Lower Mountain Road.

The Jeep's engine hummed and the familiar smell of heat doused the interior. It was a dull smell, but somehow so potent. Matt cracked a window, the aroma was creeping into his cranium. His ears popped from the elevation change and the jeep finally reached the peak of the steady incline.

No time to relax at the wheel, though. Matt steered around "The Devil's Elbow" at a sobering five miles per hour and he was pleasantly surprised at the road conditions once the path turned to gravel.

A light dusting covered the road, only interrupted by one car's tracks. Nay, it was a truck. Width was much large but still, the simplest of Honda Accords could make this trek. The straight rows of pines carried the weight of three inches of snow, creating the most beautiful of Christmas scenery.

Evergreens lined the road for about another half mile until the Murphy's house. Some trees were large, others small. Perfect size for an illustrious living area. Matt envisioned silver garland wrapped around furthest tree. White lights supplementing the open spacing. Throw on a few red bulbs, for good measure. Nothing tacky, just the red globed ornaments. A stream of smoke floated to the sky behind it like it released from a fireplace through a chimney.

Probably the Murphy's coal stove, actually.

The tree was barren once again. Matt snapped back to reality.

Oh wait... Jim's in Syracuse... Kara?... No, Kara wouldn't do the coal stove... Ryan must be up here...

He reached the end of the pine trees. The Murphy's house looked unattended. Just an empty log cabin-looking house. Lights were out, no cars in the drivewa—

Matt's Jeep rolled even with the "Chitty-Chitty Bang-Bang" mailbox. Something was off and somebody had been there. The tracks on the road from a mile back turned into the Murphy's driveway and stopped. That wasn't the eerie part, though. The tracks unevenly retraced. As if the truck reversed slightly to the left and then evaporated into thin air.

"What the fff—" Matt mumbled. He saw some more steaming piles of black in front of the Murphy's living room window, only these ones were bigger and looked like shapes instead of unformed blubber.

Matt parked the Jeep at the curb and started to lumber toward the steaming piles. Silence overcame him with the exception of the clinking milk jugs in his left hand and the snow crunching under his feet.

His intrigue turned to a form of fear. He felt an anxious sensation creep into his neck, just below the chin. Flesh rippled up his spine but it extinguished once he reached a piles and saw what it was.

A heap of melted rubber.

Matt looked back at his car only about 30 feet back. He debated on dropping the jugs at the base of the nearest pile and heading back home.

"Are these all rubber?" he thought as he rummaged to each pile. *"Yep... they are... And what the hell are those?"*

Matt walked toward the burning shapes by the living room window but as he got closer, the smell started to turn his gut. So much unlike the heating element in his Jeep, that smelled like the most pristine of Yankee Candles compared to this.

He bent over and gagged. His hands dropped to his knees but still clung to the jugs of milk that hung by their handles in the grip of his index and middle fingers.

Matt coughed, hoping that he wouldn't regurgitate his after-school turkey and swiss. His head turned involuntarily toward the shapes, but he finally recognized what he pondered deep down all along.

They weren't shapes. They were letters.

Nausea went to the backburner and curiosity barged in. He crept through the snowy yard like

Indiana Jones in the Temple of Doom. The sound of crunching snow elevated as it got deeper in the Murphy's front yard and the furniture through the living room window became a clearer image.

Matt paced from left to right in front of the letters.

"O": a smoldering blend of cloth. Some looked to be clothes, others looked like... *furniture?*

"B": *Denim? More clothes? Hair?*

"E": *Holy shit... that's two car seats...*

"Y": *"That's a fucking arm!"* Matt screamed and his voice raised even more when he saw something start to crawl over the burning Y, *"What the fuck is that?"*

It was a worm.

The television snapped on in the living room window. It held Matt's attention, but he was paralyzed with fear. Matt couldn't believe what he was seeing, the 50" Visio was showing him tracing a gravestone with black Sharpie. "J"-"E"-"D"-"I"-"D"-"I"-"A"-"H"...

That's the fucking tape from Lequin...

The tape cut to the flag waving in the air like ship sails in the midst of a tempest and springing out of the ground, knocking Sasha down to the church's front porch. Then it changed to when Gordy panned the ceiling.

Gord said he lost all the footage

Matt continued to look at the television in a hypnotized state. He saw himself, walking across the balcony. He stopped and stared through the nothingness of the flanking window. The video cut abruptly. Green handprints covered my jock and Jade's chest.

The television went black and Matt started to turn around. But that was only the beginning. It turned on again, the television screen showed a bathroom, smothered with blood and glass. On the floor was an arm. It cut to a white Dodge Ram in the middle of the Murphy's driveway, only something in the truck had exploded. Fire started to erupt from its broken windows until the entire truck blew to pieces and the television turned off.

Matt could see something flying in the window toward him and his paralysis broke. He shuffled back just in time before something crashed through and shattered the living room window. No glass struck him, but laying at his feet was one of the Murphy's doormat's. This one read, "Come Back."

Matt dropped the jugs of milk at his feet and sprinted back to his Jeep. He had the vehicle on and was driving back down Lower Mountain Road within 45 seconds. Still about 20 feet from "The Devil's Elbow", Matt looked behind him, through the window of his hatchback. He was shocked that nobody was chasing after. Only the line of snow glittered pines.

He slammed on the breaks and maneuvered around "The Devil's Elbow". Matt knew where most of his friends were. Safe and sound in their house with their families or at work. Nothing could go wrong there. Except for Jade and Sasha. Matt pulled his cell phone out from his pocket and dialed for the highest alphabetically in his contacts.

Matt K. never answered, nor called anyone. He was always a guy who thought "if it isn't important, it can wait." Whatever he needed right now, couldn't wait.

"Matt?"

"Jade. Where are you?"

Sasha mouthed to her, *"who is it?"*

"Matt"

"Sash and I are still at the mall. Why?" Jade said. Matt could tell that she was inaudibly communicating with Sasha. "What's going on, Matt?"

"Just get back home now." Matt demanded, which was beyond rare. Matt was about as *"whatever"* of a person as you'd meet. Jade's concern elevated once he continued, "and just stay on 414. Don't take any back ways. Just get home."

"Ummmm... okay...." Jade was befuddled, "We just going to meet you at Zack's?"

"No..." Matt stuttered, "No... not at Zack's... yet..."

"We gotta pick up the foo—"

"Can Sash call Marco?" Matt said. "The food might have to wait a minute..."

"Matt, what the fuck is going on...?"

"You'll see. Meet me and Zack up at Kara's."

By the time his conversation was over, he was pulling in front of my house. Matt rushed to the back door, or, as my mother put it, "the front door", because the apartment was at the back of a house.

I heard the pounding, and could see his snow-white face through the window on the door.

"Matt, what's going on?"

"Zack..." Matt stuttered. "You... you... just... can you come with me f... for a second?"

We walked out onto the back... sorry Mom... *front* porch. I stood still just outside of the doorway, but he paced frantically.

"Yo... Broseph Stalin... Chill out. What's going on?" I asked.

"Man... you won't believe it unless you see it..." he rubbed his forehead.

"Matt, we've been friends since we were four..." I said with sheer sincerity. "I'll believe whatever you say."

He lost his frantic demeanor, and started to look somber until he eventually started to cry, "Zack... Ryan and Kara are dead..."

"WHAT?!?!" I was shocked. I felt the tug on my stomach and my jaw felt like it dropped to the porch. "How…? How do you know this…?"

"They got 'em, Zack…" He snorted in the mucus and tears, "They… they got them…"

"Who got them!?"

"Lequin." He said seriously. A sniff was followed by a determined face, *"Fucking* Lequin."

He told the story, from petting Lola to calling Jade and Sasha and I believed him. I didn't want to, but I did. It wasn't over after Brooke, and as much as I wanted to forget the conversation between my mom and Dave, I couldn't. The Lequin Church is a house. A project of an evil man from long ago. And we went in, we *broke* in without anyone's permission. So now they were returning the favor. First the O'Sullivan's house and now the Murphy's.

"Jade and Sasha are meeting us up there." His face remained determined, but started to scowl. "They have to see it."

I was surprised that he automatically assumed that I would be joining him. Maybe he thought that he would have a need to prove this to me too. Again, I really didn't want to believe this, but I did. Just like the fact that I didn't want to *see* this, but I did.

Kara's mom would be home soon, and I prayed to God that we wouldn't be there when she was.

CHAPTER 31: The Yard

The path that was Lower Mountain Road was virtually unbeaten. It looked as though only two cars made their way up the slope, around "The Devil's Elbow" and through the evergreens since the dusting earlier that afternoon. Dusk had settled, and the stars began to twinkle in the indigo-shaded sky. There was still just enough light to navigate, but if it weren't for the white powder of the Murphy's front yard, piles of black blotches would have been difficult to see.

Matt pulled even with the Murphy's mailbox. Actually, the tracks under his Jeep's tires were almost even with the ones it made an hour before.

The air was cold, significantly colder than it was in town, probably by about 15 degrees. Matt even noticed a difference in the property's temperature, it cooled down by about 10 degrees within that last hour at the peak of Lower Mountain.

Matt walked in line with the prints he made earlier but my feet created new tracks. Powder packed together under my feet. Its accumulation lessened as we walked into their driveway

He waved his hand with the ol' "follow me" order. I obliged. But I stayed a few feet back, doing my best to trace his steps. Water was starting to seep through my boots and soak my socks. In the dead silence of the evening, I could hear the putrid squishing of moisture between my toes and the sucking of the soles of my feet.

An odor started to pollute the air as we walked further in to the front yard. This wasn't burning, it favored decomposition. Something dead to the world. It got stronger with each step and by the time we reached the first shape, it was nauseating. Matt was uncomfortable, but he was prepared. He was just there. I wasn't. I was a virgin to the whole situation, and my cherry popped, so to speak. Vomit sprayed out of my mouth and splashed upon the first shape: A giant 'O'.

I limped behind Matt, we both observed the remaining letters: "B"... "E"... "Y"...

"...and look at this..." Matt stated with disappointment as he craned his index finger toward the doormat that rested on the snow.

"Come back..." I whispered reluctantly. A hum emerged from down the road and headlights gradually beamed through the pines.

Please be Jade and Sasha... Please be Jade and Sasha...

Wishes come true. A PT Cruiser pulled out from behind the long line of evergreens and the bass was still bumping when she pulled over on the curb, behind Matt's Jeep.

The old me is dead and gone... dead and go—

"Matt, the fuck is going on?!" Sasha hollered from the road before the slammed the car door shut. She wasn't angry at all, but she was anxious.

A light shined on Jade in the front seat. It was the light from the visor, Jade was checking her face in the make-up mirror. She opened the passenger's side door and pulled on her grey wool beanie. She flipped her blonde hair from out of her coat, spreading it across her back. Jade always looked amazing, and I had a weakness for beautiful women in winter garb. Normally, for men, it's the opposite. I wasn't opposed to that either, but man, this chick could rock a winter jacket, leggings and a beanie like she could a bikini.

"Yeah guys, what's the deal?" Jade added.

"Come here." Matt demanded and they followed the order. They took a similar path as we did. Both looked as if they were preparing for the worst. After all, they had about 45 minutes to ponder about Matt's need to meet them at the Murphy's.

They had a pretty good idea that something went terribly awry.

Sasha was the first to the "O", but Jade was close behind. Their curiosity overwhelmed the foul aroma, but Jade wasn't surprised at all when she passed the spew-covered first letter.

"Weakest stomach of all time strikes again, huh?" her eyes somehow glistened in the dark.

"As always..." I confirmed. She returned with a cocked smile, as if she was trying not to but couldn't help it.

God damn she's so seck—

"The fuck does this mean?" Sasha asked disgruntled.

Seeeee...

"Obey. I don't know." Matt said.

"Oh my God..." Jade gasped. "That's Kara's." She pointed to a bracelet that wrapped around a charred log that helped shape the "Y". Jade looked closer, and saw five frayed streaks just above the bracelet. The worst of thoughts overcame her, and although it isn't ideal. The worst of thoughts can be true, and this was one of those instances.

Kara's severed arm helped shape the "Y".

"I got her that when we were 13…" Jade continued.

Sasha quickly chimed in after. Matt and I couldn't believe that we didn't notice the subject of her claim, "23" she said.

"Huh?"

"23… on that hat in the 'B'" Sasha mumbled sadly, "Ryan's baseball number. He wore that hat to school today."

Both Sasha and Jade stared at us stoically for a moment, but Jade turned back to the letters and read the word aloud, "Obey…"

It came to me…

He raised his own claw, streaks of blue decorated his flesh. His face wasn't sinister, it was content. Blood began to leak from his lips, but he was speaking, not sneering. "Oh-Aye" he said. Go away? No way? …okay…

Jade read my mind, she heard what the boy said that night too. *Okay… Away… O-FUCKING-BEY…* "Guys, what the fuck is happening?" she asked.

"Lequin." Matt stated and he pointed at the doormat. His gut tugged from within when he saw the unbroken pane of the living room window.

"What do we do?" Sasha asked. Snow started to fall gingerly to the ground. Flakes decorated Jade's dark eyelashes. Powder stuck firmly on the fur rim hood of Sasha's jacket.

I began, "We g—"

"We go back." Jade interrupted.

"What about Gord and Pears?" Sasha asked.

"They'll go." Matt said confidently. "Trust me, they'll go."

Wind started to howl and the snow started to fall rapidly. If we waited much longer, we'd have one hell of a time getting back into town.

"When?" I asked.

We looked around, all of our eyes met at least once before Jade finally said, "Friday."

CHAPTER 32: Party on, Shell

"Maaaaaahhhhhhhmmmmm," I called as I barged
in the door to the kitchen. "Look who I found!"

We could hear her recliner creak in the living room.
"Who is it?!" she yelled, as if she wasn't coming to
find out anyways. Our cat, Ms. Olly sprinted from
the living room and into the kitchen. Immediately
rubbing her face on Matt's leg.

Mom reached the doorway that separated the
living room and kitchen. Her smile was electric
when she first laid her eyes on us standing at the
front door. I held the pizza, Sasha had the bag of
complimentary garlic knots from Marco, Matt had
the drinks and Jade clutched onto her gift, wrapped
elegantly with purple wrapping paper. Mom
trotted to us, giving each of us a hug and invited us
to the living room.

The living room was puny. Just big enough to hold
its two recliners, a couch and a television. I
grabbed a seat in my recliner, while Matt, Sasha
and Jade sat evenly on the three couch cushions.

Mom sat in her seat, and immediately perked up,
like a child on Christmas morning. "Can I open my
present?" she smiled largely. Glasses sloped down
the arc of her nose. With an index finger she

pushed them back. As she released, I said, "Wait until the rest get here."

"Who's the rest?"

"Gord-o and Pears will be here in a few."

"Oh!" mom yipped, "That's great! Aunt Eva will be here at 8, and Aunt Georgia might come down too." Mom's excitement turned frantic. "Hopefully we have the room." She pondered for a moment and stood up. "We will... we will..." and she brought a few chairs in the living room from the kitchen.

A knock emerged from the kitchen and the door creaked open, "Ms. Shelly?!" I heard Pears call out.

"Frankfort!" my mom hollered with excitement. "Frankfort" was a nickname that my mom gave Pears years back. "Gordon! Your hair looks lovely!"

"Thanks, Ms. Shelly." Gordy said while flipping his hair back like a model on the runway, or at least for a magazine shoot.

The three of them returned to the living room. Pears and Gordy mounted the kitchen chairs that now sat by the television stand. They turned them back toward us, "Happy Birthday, Mama." I said. I got up from my seat and kissed her on the forehead. Each of my friends followed suit.

"Thank you so much, kids." Mom rubbed her eyes, "This just means so much..."

"No," Sasha said, "Thank *you.*"

"Love you Miss Shelly." Jade said and all of the other chimed in with their terms of endearment.

"Now let me open this bitch..." Mom joked and grabbed the purple package. She sat in her recliner with it on her lap, "This is from me and Jade." Sasha said.

"Oh wow!" Mom said with some mild excitement. "A gift from two of the most beautiful ladies on Earth? For what do I owe this honor?!"

"Mom," I laughed, "Just open the damn thing."

"I've have enough of that language, Zackary George..."

"*Baaaaahhhh!*" Pears mocked, "Zackary George..." he pointed and laughed.

"Alright, I didn't realize we were three again..."

Mom tore the paper and flung it across the living room. She acted like a 10 year old boy that expected that Xbox 360 on Christmas morning, and his parents said, "this is your big gift." She longed for this gift, but she knew that it wasn't extravagant. It was from two 18 year-old girls. That didn't matter. It was the thought but mostly, the love that she had for both Sasha and Jade.

The exposed candle sat in her lap, "A Yankee Candle!... It's a jar!" she was surprised, "Jesus Christ, girls... these things are 40 bucks!"

"I've had enough of you using the Lord's name in vein, Michelle Jane..." I snapped with sarcasm.

"Boooooo...." Pears jeered and Gordy showed two thumbs down.

"Ha... ha... ha..." Mom uttered sarcastically. She read the label, "Cucumber melon? Never had this kind..."

Jade glared in my direction. If looks could kill, my ass would be embalmed by Paul Pepper by now. I shrugged. That was my suggestion and truth be told, Jade's anger amused me a bit. For some reason, she wanted to impress my mother that night. Little did she know, Jade did more than that. Mom's admiration for my friends grew so strong that night.

Mom finally unmuted ESPN's Monday Night Football pregame show. Steelers just beat the

Cowboys the day before, so she could manage listening into "the talking heads."
"They been saying anything good?" Gordy asked.

"Bunch of jargon so far." Mom replied, "Berman said that the Steelers got lucky yesterday... I just couldn't... I had to turn that shit down. Eagles pulled one out of their ass yesterday. Eh, Matt?"

"Sure did!" Matt exclaimed, "Needed that one... can't be .500 this late in the year..."

"Okay, guys..." Pears said glumly, "You can stop talking about it now..."

"Pears!" I yelped, "You're 11-2! Giants got the best record in the NFC!"

"Yeah, I know..." Pears sighed, "I'm just glad Ryan isn't here. Matt's the nice Eagles fan..."

"Speaking of which, where is Ryan?" Mom asked.

The room went silent. You could hear a pin drop on the *fucking* carpet, it was that quiet. Sasha turned to Jade and Jade turned to Matt.

"Yeah, where is he?" Gordy asked, "Wasn't him and Kara supposed to come over?"

Tension in the room increased so much that you could feel it. I did my best to ease it, "They aren't feeling well…"

"Oh no…" Mom said sadly.

"Yeah, Kara had this stomach thing yesterday…" it wasn't a lie, "and when you're doing the things those kids are doing, you know the other is gonna catch it."

"Thanks for that mental picture, hun." Mom replied.

I shrugged again.

"Well, I'm gonna grab a slice before the game starts." Pears said, "Anyone need anything?"

"I'm coming too." Gordy said.

Both Gordy and Pears pranced to the kitchen. It was a chance to tell them the truth. To tell them exactly what happened to Ryan and Kara. To tell them what our intentions were: go back to the Lequin Church and stop the bleeding. Stop this suffering. I followed them through the doorway and into the kitchen.

"Umm, guys…" I whispered. "Ryan and Kara aren't sick."

Gordy stuffed a slice of cheese pizza into his gaping mouth and mumbled, "What? Where are they?"

Pears turned to Gordy with confidence, "Where do you think?" He began thrusting his pelvis.

"You won't believe this guys, but it's true." I said, "Matt saw all of this first hand. Me, Jade and Sash saw it too..."

"*Saw what?*" Gordy grumbled through a mouthful of cheese and crust.

I was reluctant to tell them at all, let alone at my mother's birthday celebration. I had to, though. This might be my only opportunity before we returned later that week.

"Okay guys, you aren't going to believe this but that's okay..." I said, "It might be better that way, anyway. Matt had to deliver milk at the Murphy's this afternoon—"...

CHAPTER 33: The Day Thereafter

Anna Murphy didn't think much when she arrived
to a Kara-less home that Monday evening, but the
phone dialed abundantly after the sight of an
empty breakfast nook the following morning.

Tracy Wilson came off of her high and drunken
stupor when she arrived at work on Tuesday
morning. She hardly ever saw her son these days
and another morning didn't mean too much to her.
The panic would possess her later that afternoon.

The crew though. We accepted it, for what it's
worth. We continued with our lives. Maybe we'd
find them on Friday, under the floorboards of the
Lequin Church or possibly trapped in the outhouse
just behind the building.

But why? We knew they were gone. Lequin got
them. *The fucking McLaughlin's* got them.

...but why?...

Why us? Why didn't they go after Hank
Stonehammer? Dave Wilson? Jimmy Ellsworth?
Fucking Seth Dunlap? All of the kids that have been
in there since we were? Why *fucking* us? Whatever
superhero notion of avenging Ryan, Kara and
Brooke's deaths were just a front. They weren't

coming back and we didn't want revenge. We didn't want war.

We wanted answers.

Pregame planning wasn't necessary this time. It wasn't a maiden voyage and we didn't keep it a secret. Matt was driving, we were stealing food right in front of Dunlap and we were going in. Not much more needed to be said. Psychology class was different the next day.

Remember way back in the intro? When I told you that *everything* was *real?* What I am about to tell you is proof.

We had a substitute teacher that day. In most stories, that means one of two things. First, a sexy female teacher or second, someone without any control. When the cat is out the mice play.

Nope. Neither. Not this time. You can't make this shit up.

Mr. Joseph Estrada was the sub. A dude. A young, very handsome dude. Looked like a jacked rockstar. A sleeve of tattoos inked his left arm. He always wore a tight long-sleeve button-down, but always a light color so the ink below was visible. His well-groomed beard complimented his short black hair.

Rings wrapped around each of his fingers, none of which were that of a grooms.

He mostly substituted at Canton or Troy, but when Mr. Estrada was in Spartanville, the girls of Salt Springs High flocked to whatever room he was in.

Jade and Sasha were no exception.

The guys of Salt Springs High wanted so badly to hate Estrada. He comes in with his cut-ass biceps and his fitted button-downs knowing damn well that he has all of the clitter's twittering. Just like how Jade knows ex-fucking-actly what she's doing every goddamn day.

But then Mr. Estrada says the word, "shit", "hell", or "damn". I even heard him sigh "fuck" once. The beauty of it was that he didn't gave a damn if we said it too. When he caught Jimmy Ellsworth with a wad of Skoal in his lower lip, he just made Jimbo spit it out. No detention, no demerits, not even a report to Ms. Segur about some misbehavior.

You just couldn't hate the guy. He respected us and we respected him. Plus, he was literally the coolest cat in town.

Matt, Gordy, Pears and I entered the classroom. Same set-up, but the projector screen was down. Ms. Bishop had to have something on the itinerary for period 6, so watching a movie was probably the move. *What About Bob?* was our guess.

As we took our seats, I saw Jade peek through the door. She looked in the direction of the teacher's desk and saw Mr. Estrada. Jade turned to her left and started to fan herself with a hand, like she was in a house without A/C in the middle of August. Her jaw dropped dramatically, and Sasha appeared in the doorway.

They remained still momentarily, gaining enough courage to enter the room. Upon a dramatic (and almost pathetic) inhale, they infiltrated the room. Without any recognition to us, Jade and Sasha turned to Mrs. Bishop's desk just inside the door. Their eyes craved for Mr. Estrada. Sasha's look was filled with lust.

"Heyyyyy Mr. Estradaaaa" Sasha's voice was clearly provocative, despite the phrase working its way out through the biting of her lower lip.

Jade's voice was soft, but not weak. A sexy schoolgirl sort of vibe, "Good to see you, Mr. Estrada..."

Wouldn't mind if she said that to me, if we're being honest...

"Hello ladies." Mr. Estrada said in his deep, yet slightly nasal tone. His voice was unique, but that might be the cause of the attraction.

Sasha sat down next to me in her usual spot. "Need to change, sis?" I whispered. A dark backhand slapped me in the chest, like a Ric Flair "Knife Edge Chop."

"Why don't you sound like that when you're talking to me?" Matt asked Jade as she took a seat next to him. "Shut up, Matthew..." she chuckled in reply.

"What's the move today, Mr. E?" Pears asked.

"She said you have a choice of what you want to do." He said.

"*You...*" I heard Sasha mumble under her voice. I had to reply to her...

"*Slut...*"

"What're the choices?" Gordy asked.

"Study hall or—"

"*you...*"

"*slut...*"

"What About Bob." he finished.

"Every. Damn. Time!" Pears laughed. We all thought that Mrs. Bishop's fondness of *What About Bob?* was strangely funny, but Pears more than the rest of us. "What the hell is it with her and the movie?"

"Study hall then?" He asked, twiddling his fingers. Rings clanked on the desk as we agreed with the proposal.

--Study hall--... more like a Fuck Off 101. Of course every class had one overachiever, the one that actually wanted to get their work done then and there rather than procrastinate. But *most* of the time, especially with only two weeks until the final winter break of your high school career, not many used the study hall for its worth.

We didn't. Estrada assumed it in advance, and his assumption didn't make an ass out of you and me. But it wasn't for the reason you'd think.

There was little conversation, but we weren't necessarily productive either. Behind Mr. Estrada was a large window, we could see it was another gloomy, cold, December day but that only added to our emotional fatigue.

Only three minutes of the "study hall" passed before Gordy glanced up from his Beowulf SparkNotes and mumbled "W'time on Friday?"

We all heard him, including Mr. Estrada. His five classmates turned to him in unison, but the look wasn't fond. The girls' wet-daydreams of Mr. E dried up. Our half-assed study habits and doodles halted. Our thoughts of Kara and Ryan's absence returned to the truth. The heaps of boiling rubber and the decomposing aroma of the letters in the snow.

Chunks of flesh on the O'Sullivan's bathroom floor....

Grey Goose...

Blood oozing from his cracked lips...

Those eyes...

The worm...

We were overcome by the heinous thought of returning to Lequin, where the hell of the last two months begun.

Truthfully, the thought was in our minds regardless. It was simply implemented into our brains. The Lequin Church was a part of us now. A formality, if you will. We were the victims in an abusive relationship, but we stayed true. Because we had to.

"Was thinking 11..." Matt said lowly, also fixed on his Beowulf cheat sheet. Ms. Segur's upcoming final was going to be a brute. Good thing she was a sweetheart. Mr. Hollinshead would have never gotten away with this shit.

"Works for me." Sasha glanced away from Mrs. Murphy's Spanish handout momentarily. Tears were welling in her eyes as she filled in the vacated clauses. The recurring theme about "mi hermosa hija" tortured her, knowing that Mrs. Murphy would never see *her beautiful daughter* ever again.

Typing ceased from Jade's ThinkPad. "Same." her voice cracked, as if she had been crying or just getting over a case of strep throat.

Pears and I offered subtle nods in Gordy's direction.

"Should I bring the camera an—"

"No." Pears snapped and glanced over at Matt. Matt's skin was grey, and his lips favored a shade of purple. He thought of the television through the window.

*Gordy's goddamn tapes... What color? Uhhh...
Black? Why difference did the color make? Oh,
Brooke... Ever in her infinite wisdom... The time in
the Jeep... oh Jesus, Brooke... Ha! And be a
SIMPLLLLLLLLEEEEEEEE KIND OF MANNNNNN...
won't you put this... on a bun... in a pan... Who the
hell could really think those are the words?!*

Matt's skin tone returned to its normal winter pale.
"No, it's cool. Bring them."

"Whuddya talkin' bout over there?" Mr. Estrada
called out. He wasn't angry at the additional
conversation, he was only intrigued.

"Ummmm... uhhhh..."

"We're going to the Lequin Church on Friday." Matt
blurted out with an eerily similar jive. It sounded
like we were going there for the first time. "You,
know? That place that supposed to be haunted out
on Route 6?"

"Oh..." Mr. Estrada said with a jovial nod, "I
definitely do." He tilted his head and stroked his
beard. The cuff of his button-down pulled down,
exposing an inch of his tattoo sleeve.

"...Oh my God..." I heard Jade whisper behind me.

"...I'm thinking the same thing..." Matt mumbled to her with a touch of sarcasm. All of us except for Mr. E heard this dialogue and chuckled.

He looked at us with a puzzled smirk, and he returned to his normal, laid back posture. The chair clanked from under him, "You guys been there before?"

"Yes." My reply sounded appropriate, given the scenario.

"Oh..." Mr. Estrada said. "Sweet."

And that was all. Twenty minutes later the bell rang. Pears, Matt and Gordy fled the scene quickly, but naturally the girls lollygagged. Sasha went out first but I waited for Jade.

I put my hand on her back and led her out of the classroom before me. I dropped my hand quickly after but it felt fuzzy, as if I had been touching some magical creature for only a split second.

"Jesus, Davidson..." I joked, weaving through the students in the hall, "Need an AED after that?"

She started to walk closer to me. She cradled her books in front of her loosely and she stared me down in dramatic disgust, "Shut up, Zack..." It was like a baby brother egging on his older sister because of a boy that she thinks is cute.

"He's very handsome," she said calmly. "I bet you think so too…"

"*Gaaaaaaaaaaaayyyyyyy*" I jeered, "No, you're right. He's hot." We laughed as we approached my locker, but it died when we saw who was standing there. It was Kate. Her books pressed against her, and her face offered a fuming scowl. It was evident from 50 feet away.

"*Jesus Christ, here we go…*" Jade whispered. "You don't still want this bitch do you?"

"Honestly…." I pondered and for the first time in almost three years, I could admit it. "No. I don't."

Jade exhaled, "Good." but it didn't seem as she was a friend looking out for my well-being. It didn't sound only relieved, but it sounded jubilant as well. Her eyes widened when I told her, and she perked up. Jade even smiled. Her face was always pleasant.

We were a mere 15 steps from my locker, and Kate looked even more angry than before. Her snarl wasn't directed at me, though. It was pointed and locked-in on Jade. I started to veer away from Jade and toward my locker.

"Later, Bristol." Jade's voice was soft and innocent, yet seductive as she continued down the hall. The smile she flashed at Kate revealed added theater. A taunt toward the enemy.

"You and Jade seem to be getting along well." Kate's voice was so cold it would give an Eskimo hypothermia.

"Always have, Kate." I was exhausted. And my animosity toward Kate was too. I was neutral. The hate was no longer there, nor was the love. The attraction, sure. If she would have asked for me back then and there, I might have said yes.

But her green eyes didn't glisten in the well-lit hall. She didn't seem to have an aura of light shining behind her. I looked at her with no different feeling than Ja—Sara O'Sullivan. Just somebody that I was impartial to emotionally, but not physically.

"Can we… can we talk?" she asked. "I just really want to talk to you." Her eyes looked up at me like a puppy. She knew it was one of my weaknesses. That and the half-smile, but the setting wasn't appropriate for that. Her aura started to illuminate, but not as bright as it once did.

"Sure…" I sighed. "After school today, I guess."

"Great." She said calmly, but she revealed that half-smile. That aura was getting a little bit brighter.

"I really have to go, though…"

"Same"

We separated. No hug. No kiss. Just the driest of "good-byes"

We didn't see each other until 3:16.

CHAPTER 34: More Animated Dialogue

Salt Springs women's hoops had a big time match-up with the Sayre Redskins later that evening. So I knew where to find the Spartans' point guard right after school.

Branching off from the school's main lobby was a L-shaped hallway that led to the gym and locker rooms. I walked alone between the brick walls, knowing that as soon as I turned the corner, Kate would be looming in front of the women's locker room.

The deeper into the hallway, the musky smell of old sweat strengthened. I forgot how putrid that smell was. Dave Ramsey shot around the corner in a hurry, the men's team had practice just before the women's game. Ol' Davey jogged around the corner, "*someone's* waiting for you, Bristol." He slapped me on the back of the shoulder and continued his jaunt back toward the lobby. I wrapped around the elbow of the "L", and there she was. Kate Ford leaned up against the brick with her Nike duffel bag draping over her shoulder like a satchel.

"Howdy." Her voice was dry, but not negatively. She was neutral.

"Sup???" I grunted emphatically.

She turned her head toward me, but it was still fastened to the brick. Kate looked strangely relaxed, "going to my game tonight?"

"*You're game?*" I sneered, "You taking Sayre on 1-on-5?"

She rocked herself from the brick wall. "You know what I meant, Bristol."

"I mean, most of the time it looks like you guys are playing 1-on-5 anyways." my scoffing continued, "Like seriously, help Sasha out. She averaging 31 points a game..."

Kate was slowly walking toward me. I didn't retreat, but I didn't magnetize either. "My 10 assists every game help her out a lot, you know?" she was flashing that damn half-smile.

I snickered, "Kate, you don't average 10 dimes a game." She was close and I was paralyzed. Completely struck by her. Mom told me so many times that Kate was poison to me and I never believed it more than I did now. After everything she put me through. All of the lying, the cheating, the goddamn agony and I still couldn't turn away from her. We stood in the musky hall, chest to chest. Well, her face to my chest. Only a piece of paper could fit between. Her gleaming green eyes gawked into mine. Wavy, dirty blonde hair draped over her bosom that pressed against my stomach.

I had that urge. To forget about the past. Forget all about Carter Winthrop and Colby Baker. I just wanted... no, I needed to do it. I needed to wrap my arms around her, clasp that perfect, firm ass and let whatever happens... happen.
I didn't though. Instead I let out a long drawn out sigh and asked, "What do you need to talk to me about?"

"Zack... I know I've really messed things up between u—"

"Ya think?"

She glanced down, fixed on the quarter of a centimeter space between our bodies. Her voice was low, "Yeah, I do."

"Well, I'm glad you can admit i—" I cut myself off. "Why are you telling me this?"

"Because I want to try..." Kate looked up, but she was hesitant.

I was getting angry. How many times would this proposal come up? She fucks up, I blame myself, she asks for me back, I accept. It's never-ending.

My tone was cold, "Try what?"

"Hear me out," Kate said reluctantly, she inhaled deeply and continued, "I... I..."

"You what, Kate?" I started to scold.

"I... I don't know if I want you or Colby." She finally spit it out, "I can't decide."

My eyes squinted, and I let out a low, breathy, "Excuse me?"

Kate retreated back toward the brick wall, "I know it sounds bad, Za—"

"Yeah, you're *goddamn* right it sounds bad!"

She started to get defensive, "Well, Colb always puts me first and you... you never did... You have *your* friends. Matt, Sasha, Frank, *Jade*... Like when you have something with them, I ought to just forget about even speaking to you. I should be before th—"

"Wait, wait, wait, wait, *WAIT*... Do you know how many times I brushed them off for *you*?! *You* were always first, until *you* started fucking up!"

"Look, Zack, I get it..." she pulled back from her pedestal of rage and sighed.

"See, I don't fucking think you do…" I snapped, "I'm not going to throw them out for you. That's not how it's supposed to be. You don't have to like them, but you do have to *fucking* deal with them."

She cocked her head to the side and scowled, "You can't tell me what the fuck to do…"

"YOU'RE TELLING ME WHAT THE FUCK TO DO!"

"Fine. Forget it… I'm done." She flailed her hands in front of her and shook her head. As she opened the locker room door she turned to me and said, "Never speak to me again…"

"Happily." I said, "And oh, Kate… one thing."

She glared from behind the open door.

"You know if you say that you want me and Colby. You really don't want either of us… all you want is the fucking attention…"

She continued her stare. If looks could kill, I would have been impaled by the daggers in her eyes.

"Don't ruin his life like you did mine."

Without saying a word, she closed the door. I turned back, turned the "L" corner and pulled out my cell phone. My thumb flipped it open and I sent a text to Jade.

Going to Sasha's game tonight?

Yep! You?

Ya. See you then.

CHAPTER 35: Salt Springs Spartans vs. Sayre Redskins

The two best women's basketball teams in the NTL squared off that night. Sayre came in at 10-0 and Salt Springs got out to a surprising 9-1 start. All thanks to Sasha Jacobs, the 5'11 forward who dominated the paint. Sasha was having an excellent season. 31 points per game was the highest mark in the state, regardless of school size. Her 15 rebounds per averaged third in Pennsylvania.

Yet somehow, her biggest college offer was Lock Haven University.

Jade and I marched in together as they were introducing the players. All the way at the end of the gym, we could see Gordy, Pears and Matt, parked in the first row on the bleachers.

AAAAAAAAAANNNNNNNNDDDDDD NOOOWWWWWW FOR YOUR SALT SPRINGS SPARTANSSSSSS

Linda Anderson cried it over the PA. She did the player introductions for years, even after her daughters graduated. People loved her enthusiasm. She had a deep voice that was suited for the largest of arenas.

AT POINT GUARD. NUMBER 2... KATE FOOOOOOOOOOOOORD!!!!!

"That's about right..." Jade murmured and I laughed. Number two... shit joke. Classic. Kate flashed a scowling face at us as she ran on to the court during her introduction. We reached Matt, Gordy and Pears just in time for Linda to announce...

AND THE STATE'S LEADING SCORER.... AT POWER FORWARD. NUMBER 34... SASHAAAAAAAAAAAAAAAAAAAAAAAAAAAAAAAAAAAAAA JACOBSSSSSSSSSSSSSSSSSSSSSSSS

The crowd went ballistic, but us five were particularly rowdy. Hoops in general were not at the forefront of the town's interest, but especially women's hoops. People thought it was like watching paint dry, but damn... *that black girl could play!*

Sasha was fun to watch. She pushed the uniform limits to their brink. Her favorite basketball player ever was Allen Iverson, and she took note of everything that he did. As far as playing style, it was impossible to mimic. They played two completely different positions. But the sleeves, headbands and Sasha's touch of the shoelaces made them both impossible to miss on the court.

Those baby blue shoelaces were for next Monday in Northeast, tonight's were orange. Sasha wore them well. There was absolutely nothing that Sayre could do to stop her. The 'skins doubled her on the post and even tripled her at times. They moved to a 2-3 zone for the second quarter, it didn't matter.

Sasha lit up the scoreboard, and became the first women's basketball player in PIAA history to score 50 points in a game. 51, to be exact, and the rest of the Spartans scored a combined 16 points. It was enough to upset the previously unbeaten Redskins, 67-61.

That was the game. After that night, Sasha finally got her big time look and the Temple Owls would start to pull out all of the stop for her services over her four-year college career.

The crowd left the gymnasium and polluted the lobby. It was a large meeting area. No one wanted to wait outside in the frigid December air and wait for their daughter. Luckily, Salt Springs high school designed it that way, knowing that no soul would desire that.

The five of us found an empty space next to a large trophy case that displayed Salt Springs's most recent football accolades. The shining gold sat on the glass shelf with elegance, it's backlight illuminated the metal that I remember raising so fondly.

2007 NTL Champs... QB: Colt O'Brien... Half-back: Ryan Wilson... Tight End: Zack Bristol...

2007 Old Boot Winners: Salt Springs Spartans 28, Troy Trojans 17

"Miss it?" Pears asked.

"Meh." I forced, "I didn't *think* I did..."

"Miss watching you, bro..." He replied. "You were damn good."

"No..." I said, "*She's* damn good." Sasha was making her way toward us through the crowd. She had the game ball tucked to her side. There was also an envelope tucked into her unzipped coat pocket. It was a ticket for professional decorating to commemorate her state record.

People patted her on the back. She thanked them passively as she walked through the mass of people. Her Adidas flip-flops clapped against the floor under her, other than that and her coat, she still donned her uniform. Headband, knee socks and all.

Sasha took the time to hug each one of us. She reached me last and while unbreaking our embrace, I asked, "Damn, what the hell got into you tonight?"

"You know, mothafucka, I was locked in." She laughed arrogantly. We joined. "Naw, man. I don't know. Just played well. I guess."

"Dude..." Pears said forcefully, "You had 51 of our 67 points and you say you just played good. Fuck outta here." He looked at her stupidly. He had a condescending look, but it was loving. Like the look you give a friend when they say something intrinsically stupid.

"Welllllll....." Sasha started, "if you noticed..." She turned to me, "Ol' girl wasn't passing me the rock. Ash was setting me up a lot better..."

She didn't recognize Tom and Sally Ford standing five feet behind her. Kate was on her way to join them, too. Over Sasha's shoulder, I could see her finessing through the mosh. There were considerably less people congratulating her, and had much less pizazz than Sasha had during her waltz through the crowd.

Kate and I's eyes met from afar. The moment was uncomfortable. It was so different, yet similar to the first day I met her. *Packs of teenagers*

*separated me from the most beautiful girl I had
ever seen. I didn't even know her name yet, but I
was in love. That binder with the cursive letters, the
sun beaming through the window. This girl glowed
like an eclipse. She walked in my direction, but it
wasn't to me. She was on her way to class, and I
just happened to be on the way. Our eyes met for
the first time. They were emeralds on cotton. A fine
jewel that nestled on the pillow that protects it.*

That night though, she didn't glow. Sweat plastered
her hair to her temples. I wasn't sure if the sweat
was from the game or her rage directed toward
me. She was getting closer. Her eyes were daggers,
so similar to what they were earlier that afternoon.
She had no intention on stopping at her parents.
Kate looked like she was headed straight toward
me, and hell hath no fury like a woman's scorn. I
could see it. I knew my future. Kate was coming so
smash my head through this trophy case.

I was shocked when she broke her glare. Her eyes
shot to the left and I followed their direction. We
were now both staring down Jimmy Ellsworth, who
was walking toward the six of us at the trophy case.

"Bro!" he shouted, "I heard you crazy fucks are
going back to Lequin on Friday!"

"That's right, Jimbo!" Pears howled excitedly. I still
wasn't quite sure if he believed Matt's story.

"Dude..." Jimmy caught flakes of chewing tobacco from his lip, "You couldn't fuckin' *pay* me to go back there."

I saw Kate's eyes return to me, but now she was close enough to her parents that they noticed her steaming eyes as well. They tracked the path of her eyes and turned to me. Sally's eyes were soft, she had always been an advocate of mine. Aunt Eva always thought Sally had the hots for me, but I didn't believe it.

Tom struck the daggers toward me, but he quickly turned back to his daughter, who's eyes never left mine.

"Guys, can we go?" I interrupted, I didn't even recognize their conversation.

Jade noticed my trance, and followed my stare. She joined my stare at Kate, but she quickly said, "Sure."

"Pump?" Sasha asked.

"Hell yes." Gordy replied

CHAPTER 36: The 10th and 11th

The next two days were... smooth, in fact. Normality was something that we weren't accustomed to these days. Even the police search for Ryan and Kara was normal. They searched up and down Lower Mountain. Every square inch from Troy to Ward Township was covered by search parties on Wednesday, but they found nothing. Not even as much as a sliver of evidence. We knew they wouldn't, because we were the only ones who knew the truth. But damn, if a bunch of 17 and 18 year-olds went to the police and told them what we knew... we'd be in Sayre Hospital's Psych Ward faster than Chris Hansen can say, "take a seat."

Salt Springs High noticed the unexpected absence and the questions we were asked stemmed from, "where were they the last time you say them?" to "do you think they're dead?" Mrs. Murphy was out, and Mr. Estrada substituted all week for her. Teaching was her only avenue out of the house and away from her husband, but she paid no mind this week. Every officer in Bradford County was out searching, so Jim knew his wife was fair game. Emotional and physical abuse doubled because naturally, it was her fault that their daughter went missing.

We played a damn good part, though. Everyone thought we were clueless, but we knew the answers were, "parking lot out back" and "Yes. They're dead. No thinking, I know."

Two people steered clear of the subject. The first was no surprise. It was Kate Ford. Of course, she didn't talk to us, but her glares didn't soften. She had no remorse. There was no feeling sorry or giving us a break.

But the one that did surprise us was Ryan's own uncle, Dave Wilson. That Thursday night, Pears and I did not expect to see him at the bowling alley for league. Of course, his nephew was missing but his very own sister was a complete mess. Tracy had been rushed to the hospital that Wednesday for an overdose. He visited her during the day on Thursday but he'd be damned if he missed league.

The bells that hung from the bowling alley's entrance jingled. They were the same bells as usual, but Dennis added a touch of holly to them for the Christmas season. Pears and I turned from the bar, our jaws dropped when it was Dave lumbering through the door. He knocked the slush off of his boots by tapping the wooden doorframe.

Dave looked tired, but that was all. No sadness or anger. Just exhausted. He limped slowly toward us and dropped his bowling bag on the seat next to us.

"Y'alright, Dave?" Pears asked.

"Yeah, son... Backs killin' me."

"There yuh are ya old fuck!" Butch Slocum yelled as he slammed the bathroom door behind him. His shirt was getting tighter by the day and unfortunately, his gut was more revealing by the hour. "Better not go in there for a while, boys!" he yelled, "Left a hot n' steamy. Had sum tacos for dinner... and not the ones that have that fishy smell. Wish I did... Need a good bit of pussy. It's been a while."

"I can't imagine why." I said.

"Yeah..." he grunted, rubbing his grease-stained belly. "Gotta lose sum of this. Not all us can be trim like you, Bristol. You got the cute little Ford girl and Ms. Davidson after yuh... lucky motherfucker. I'd take 'em both. Let one ride the dick and the other ride yuh face. Whaddya say, boy?"

"I don't have either of them after me, Butch..." I said, "We bowlin' or what?"

"Yup..." Dave growled.

That was it, though. Dave certainly wasn't his normal self but he made no mention of Ryan or Kara. He was an optimistic guy, so we thought that maybe he was on the downslide of his cautious positivity. It would probably set in this weekend.

I went to bed that Thursday night dreading the following day. All we were was a group of stupid kids looking for some fun. We wanted something to do in the most deadbeat village on the east coast.

Ever had one of them days you wish you would've stayed home? Oh hell yes, TI. I do.

Just the way that it stands there, overseeing the forest of evergreens atop the hill. So rustic and vintage on the outside, a hidden gem in the beauty of northeast PA's scenery during the day. But at night the moon illuminates the graveyard and shines through its windows, awakening the demons within.

150 years of Hell brewing, and a bunch of kids think it's a good idea to go in. Sure, others have gone in but never for the amount of time that we did. Or the time of day that we did.

Did we deserve jump scares from footsteps or a ghostly figure? Hell yes, we did. Did we deserve this, though? Three friends mutilated and intimidating frights so spine-chilling that we can't sleep without light and noise.

I don't think we did.

Pears, Gordy, Matt, Sasha and Jade all thought that this was as bad as it could get, barring any more deaths. But for me, I knew it could get worse.

And it did.

CHAPTER 37: Plans

The school day went much quicker than I had hoped. It was a blur, as is the case whenever you *don't* want to do something. The events leading up to it take no time at all.

Mrs. Bishop asked what our plans were for the weekend and we told the truth. She wasn't a fan, but she dealt with it. Mrs. Bishop didn't think that the church had anything to do with this. Sure there was a correlation, but kids passed away in bad ways in the area. She's been teaching for 40 years. She saw it all too often. Car accidents, illness, and even that time Kelly Kitchen drown in the Towanda Creek. It sucked, but it happened. She took it hard, but the kids took it worse. Any coping mechanism would do, she thought. They've been through a lot, don't harp on them.

We left school that day in usual order. Sasha drove me home (just because) before she had basketball practice, Matt was going to milk, Gordy had a powwow with his band, Pears had to work and Jade, well, Jade was going home to do nothing. Maybe she'd drive to Ellie Reynold's after a while, but she didn't know. Just as long as she'd be out of dodge once her parents started their nightly fight. Weekdays were Monday Night Raw, Friday's were Wrestlemania. All of the bullshit from the week poured over into one casserole of animosity.

Most of those evening plans went to order. Sasha went home and took a quick nap after basketball practice. Gordy, Matt and Pears met me at the bowling alley at 8, while Jade ran to the Lycoming Mall with Ellie Reynolds for most of the evening. Needless to say, it was a Friday night, so Ellie had to be back in time for the party at Sara O'Sullivan's. This déjà vu was all too clear.

A front was set to come in at 10pm, just as Sasha and Jade jingled the bells on the bowling alley's doors. Snow blew in the alley from behind them, and Sasha had to put a little extra mustard on when she pulled the door shut behind her. We were the only ones in the bowling alley. Poor Dennis wanted to close up shop for the night but he couldn't, not until 11.

They looked frozen during their walk toward our lane, but they defrosted on the way. It was like watching meat thaw in the microwave (not recommended), it starts as a solid but its range of motion slowly enhances.

Sasha was dressed for the occasion. Two pairs of sweatpants, winter boots, a hooded sweatshirt and a North Face jacket to top it all off.

Nothing hotter than a chick dressed for winter

Jade, per usual, looked amazing in her leggings, blue Columbia jacket and a wool winter hat. She removed her jacket and hat and placed them over one of the chairs around the scoring desk.

She wore two pairs of leggings, making her look a little thicker than normal. It was a good thick... a *damn* good thick. She parted her locks around her neck, draping them over each shoulder as she sat down next to me. She stared toward the down the alley and at the pins, but I certainly didn't. I was struck by her, even that night. A black American Eagle sweatshirt with their giant logo spread across the front of her filled chest. It was nothing special. Her make-up was minimal. A stripe of eye liner with a dusting of mascara did the trick. The black paint on her fingernails was starting to chip. She picked off drying flakes and stretched her legs out, one crossing over the other.

Jade raised her eyes from her fingernails and peeked at the scorecard. "What's the score?" she said while chomping her gum. The hot cinnamon aroma of Big Red was potent. It was a fresh stick.

"I'm at a 205." I said deeply.

Sasha leaned between us and loomed her head over the scorecard, "Damn cuz.. 205 in the 8th?"

"You know… just playing well." I turned to her and smiled.

"Psssshhhhtttt…" Sasha grunted and returned to an erect stance. "Yooo Matt K… you're gonna need like 150 pins to catch up to this nigga!"

"I know, Sash…" Matt turned around mid-roll with a disgusted glare. He was just about to release the ball, but he backed up and started his sequence from scratch.

"Ya know…" I said. My head was down but my eyes were fixed on Jade's legs. So long, but not lanky. They had shape. Her calves were visibly toned even though they were covered up by two pairs of yoga pants. My eyes continued up, her thighs were equally fit and her bubble butt pressed against the seat behind her. I could feel my stomach start to bottom out and I felt a tingle in my throat. I wonder how she'd feel if…

I took my hand and started to rub her thigh. She didn't mind it. As a matter of fact, it gained her undivided attention. She quit picking at her nails and moved her hands behind her neck, cradling her head. Her head leaned back and her eyes closed as I continued to rub. I firmed my grip, before it was just the length of my fingers that caressed her. Now the palm and thumb were involved.

*She liked it and I knew that she would like THIS...
my hand moved to her inner thigh. Strokes inched
closer to the crease of her legs. I could feel the
warmth from her crevice. Jade let out a soft grunt
as she separated her legs slightly, letting me into
the crease. I rubbed up and down until a could feel
slight dampness that seeped through her
underwear and leggings. Her back arched in the
folding chair and she started to moan...*

"Know what?" Jade asked.

Fuck, not this shit again...

"Oh um..." I stuttered. "The weather is going to get
worse... It'll be a bitch out there. Even worse than
here."

"...and?" Sasha asked.

"I'm saying, I'd be cool if we left right after this
game if you want."

"As long as we're still getting shit from the Pump,
I'm in" Pears laughed. "Dunlap's working tonight."

"Yeah, I'm cool if we head out now." Matt said on
his way back to the chairs. His roll wasn't great.
Split the uprights on an 8/10 split. He plopped in a
chair with disgust, it skootched back from his
weight and let out a screech.

We all cringed from the metal chair scraping the marble floor. "Ahh Jesus..." Pears cowered. He perked up quickly thereafter, "We're still going to the Pump, though. Right?"

"Is the Pope Catholic?" Matt asked rhetorically.

"Yeah, bro. Come on..." I uttered, "Does the Tinman have a sheet metal cock?"

Gordy, Matt and Pears howled with laughter, but the girls let out groans of disgust.

Tears rolled down Pears' face, "Just imagine..." He snorted, "The fuckin' Tinman, running down the road with his dick hanging... and it's clinking back and forth." Pears started to act it out, using his arm as the Tinman's dick. "Clink! Clank!" he yelled.

We started to laugh harder and the "uuuuuggggghhhhhhh's" from Jade and Sasha grew louder. They both moved to the bar and got a drink, while we finished the next few frames. Once we were done, Gordy and Matt went to the bar to meet Jade and Sasha. Pears and I stayed behind to pack up our bowling bags for a minute. I was untying my black and bronze Dexter's when Pears asked, "Hey brother... I wanna tell you something."

"What's up?" I loosened the strings and took off my left shoe. My foot slipped into my work boots quickly after.

"It sounds weird," he placed his ball into his bag. "You should ask out Jade."

"Huh?" I grunted emphatically with confusion. "Why?"

"The way you look at her man," he zipped the bag closed. "She looks at you the same... Whaddya got to lose? Kate's not around anymore and YOU told HER to get fucked this time..."

"Jade and I, bro..." I took off the other shoe, "It's not like that. We've been friends forever... she's like my sister..."

"No..." Pears stated clearly as he grasped the handles of his bowling bag. "You've been friends for a few years. You and I have been friends forever. Salt Springs t-ball, bitch. *That's* forever." We shared a chuckle.

I looked back toward the bar. Of course Jade's back was turned, her hoodie only covered to her waistline and her yoga pants hugged her perfect bulging ass cheeks with grace. Matt started waving his finger, demanding that we hurry up.

"Dude…" Pears whispered, "Look at that ass… That could be *YOURS.*"

"I mean, I'd be lying if I said that I wouldn't fuck her."

"Wouldn't we all…" Pears sighed pensively. His voice returned to its normal tone, "Anyways. Something to think about, brother."

"Yeah, I know." I picked my bag up and followed him toward the rest of the crew.

He brought up a good point. Kate was out of the picture (or was she?) and I really didn't have anything holding me back. But he was wrong, Jade *was* like a sister to me. I couldn't. Plus, she was Jade *fucking* Davidson. Literally the hottest chick around and she was a *damn* good kid to boot.

Even if I did take a chance, and of course by chance, I mean a lob from three quarters of the court in Game 7 of the NBA Finals or a Hail Mary in the Superbowl, it was too early. This was only the first weekend of *this* particular post-Kate era. Maybe in a few weeks. After Christmas, possibly.

The bells chimed and I felt the frigid breeze as the bowling alley door slammed behind me.

But would Kate be back by then? Do I even want her to be? Not now, at least... Maybe in time. I did wonder what she was doing though...

CHAPTER 38: Kate and Colby

Wind howled through the brisk, nighttime air, making the window casing creak. A tree in the front yard scraped against the siding of Windfall's most elegant house.

Snow fell frantically to the ground, accumulating more and more by the minute. Plow trucks didn't go out that far. Anyone coming to or leaving Windfall was out of luck until morning. The hill was covered.

Luckily, for them, Tom had another conference in Allentown and Sally had already left for her parents' house, taking her two youngest kids with her. The Ford estate was vacant and dark, except one room that was occupied by Kate Ford and Colby Baker. A desk light shined brightly at her blue school binder underneath it, but the room was dim. They laid in her bed side-by-side.

"Gotta admit," Colby mentioned frankly and rolled over to his side to face her, "this is kind of romantic."

Kate's rage had mellowed to a steam instead of a boil, she was still angry about Tuesday but she was starting to think more about the conversation outside of the locker room, "Eh..." she continued her glare at the wooden ceiling, "If you say so."

"Come on…" he caressed her shoulder and upper arm with his fingertips. His soft voice trembled, "It's snowing out… we're up here all alone. No one for miles…"

I… I don't know if I want you or Colby… I can't decide…
Excuse me?

"Pete Wile lives a fucking acre away, Colby."

Colby grimaced, "Jeez… Sorry…"

"It's okay…" Kate hesitated, "*I'm* sorry. Haven't had a great week."

Colby perked up, "Well, what's wrong sweetheart?"

Look, Zack I get it…
See, I don't fucking think you do…

"Basketball." She grunted. "Basketball."

"What about it?" he propped up to an elbow.

You can't tell me what to do…
YOU'RE TELLING ME WHAT THE FUCK TO DO!!!

"Ball hogs..." her face remained on the ceiling, tracing the patterns with her eyes.

"Who are the ball hogs?" his brows furrowed with intrigue.

Fine, forget it... I'm done. And never speak to me again.
Happily. And oh, Kate. One other thing...

"Sasha Jacobs." Her pupils reached their breaking point. She couldn't move them and more to the right.

"Baby..." Colby said hesitantly. "She's really good."

Like seriously, help Sasha out. She's averaging 31 points a game

"You sound like everyone else..." Kate said, grinding her teeth together. She relaxed instantaneously thereafter, and continued, "I mean... she is good..."

Her rage returned immediately after.

You have your friends. Matt, Sasha, Frank, Jade... Like when you have something with them, I ought to just forget about even speaking to you. I should be before th—

Wait, wait, wait, wait, WAIT... Do you know how many times I brushed them off for you?! You were always first, until you started fucking up!

I'm not going to throw them out for you. That's not how it's supposed to be. You don't have to like them, but you do have to fucking deal with them.

"*Very* good." Colby reiterated noticing the emerging scowl on Kate's face. He continued to rub her arm, this time tracing further down to her forearm. "She's pretty nice too, if you gave her a chance... I don't know her, but my cousin's one friend knows her very well..."

Kate's eyes remained fully cornered, "Who's that?"

"Jimmy Ellsworth." He said contently, "You might know him. He goes to Salt Springs."

Bro! I heard you crazy fucks are going back to Lequin on Friday!
That's right, Jimbo!
Dude... You couldn't fuckin' pay me to go back there.

"Oh, I definitely know him." he face started to gain its resting form, her intense glare was more of a moderate stare, "My ex is kind of friends with him."

"Zack?"

"That's my only ex, so yes." Kate said condescendingly. She glanced toward the window, snow still fell rapidly. Her facial expression changed quickly, as if she was now pondering something.

She rolled off the bed and stood up. Colby admired the small crease that revealed from under her shorts when she arose. Her shorts were short, barely covering her ass but the XL Salt Springs hooded sweatshirt that she never returned to her ex-boyfriend hung off of her and dangled as she walked to the window.

Colby rolled over to his other side, never taking his eyes off of Kate, "What you doing babe?"

"Bored." She said and looked at the small digital clock on her nightstand, "Wanna do something?"

"Umm..." Colby uttered in a confused tone, "It's almost 11 at night."

"I know," Kate turned back to the window and glared into the night sky. Flakes dropped like ashes in a meteor shower. She focused on the moon, gleaming and full. It illuminated the pasty yard, a gray cloud started to hover in front of it when she said, "Let's do something."

"Bab—"

Fucking Zack..

"Don't call me that."

"Sorry, sweetheart." Colby corrected on demand, "The weather is terrible…"

"We can do something around here." Her gaze at the moon continued.

Colby wondered what had gotten into Kate but after a moment, he paid no mind. The sight of her long, dirty blonde hair in the dim light eliminated any ill thought. Somehow, someway, Kate had a way of making guys fall into deepest of feelings for her.

"Sweetheart…" he said, "There's not much to go out and do here… there isn't anything for like—five miles."

Kate's head began to turn toward Colby. Her eyes were sunken into their sockets deeply as if she hadn't slept for a week. She was still blessed with simple beauty in her large sweatshirt and short-shorts, but she looked different. Not evil or sinister, but she looked like a woman that meant business or, more specifically, ill will. One of her eyebrows scrunched and the other raised. She offered a partially sneering grin and stated confidently, "You ever hear of the Lequin Church?

CHAPTER 39: The Ride

Roads in Salt Springs were plowed and cindered. It was a clear path within the town limits but once we hit the sign just beyond Bi-Lo Grocery that said "Salt Springs Township," powder started to lightly dust the road. But the further east we traveled, the more the road ahead of us looked like Vincent Van Gogh's "A Starry Night."

Wind started to roar through the trees, blowing the snow across the road in streaks. The covered roads made the SUV tough to handle. Matt's grip on the wheel was tight, so much that his knuckles were as white as the precipitation. He leaned over the wheel with his eyes squinted, trying to see the road ahead of him.

A tower of illuminated red and green shapes emerged on the side of the road. The glow was imminent in the midst of black, gray and white. We started to detect the shapes while we approached them. They were numbers, depicting the price per gallon. A "Citgo" logo appeared atop the tower.

It was the Pump 'n Pantry, only about a half mile away.

"Oh, thank Jesus..." Matt sighed.

"Need me to take it the rest of the way?" Sasha asked from behind him. Spitting her words between the door and the driver's seat.

"NO!" Matt screamed. He sat back and lightened his grip momentarily.

"Yeah, I'd rather fuck a porcupine than have you drive in this shit..." I added.

Sasha peered across the back seat and scowled at me. Her lips stuck out like a duck and her eyes squinted into two white slits, "Nigga..." she mumbled.

Matt slowed the SUV as he turned into the Pump n' Pantry parking lot. He braked to a halt, but the vehicle kept moving on the sheet of snow and ice. We shifted back and forth with little to no control. Both the front and the back fishtailed until the tires gained traction on the gravel that covered the vacated lot.

Not a soul to be seen on the Pump n' Pantry's property, except for the graveyard shift employee, Seth Dunlap. Seth was in his usual perch. Leaning on the wall next to the entrance, smoking a cigarette.

Seth flipped his hair to the side. His rotten teeth spread across his smile as he stood upright. He brushed the butt of his cigarette on the concrete exterior and walked toward us.

His windbreaker pants swiped together, sounding like two pieces of Styrofoam rubbing together. "What's going on, guys?" he said through his blackened enamel.

"Grabbin' some grub!" Gordy said while climbing out of the passenger's side door. He almost biffed it. His Etnies had no traction beneath him on the icy gravel.

Gordy caught himself by grasping the side mirror on the SUV. Jade tried to help by clutching his loose sleeve, but she served as no true support. She patted his shoulder and he looked to her. Gordy brushed aside his hair and nodded, confirming his control.

"All the way out here?" Seth was surprised, "And it's snowing…"

I held my palms out, catching the flakes that rushed to the surface, "Really?" I asked sarcastically, "Never would have guessed?"

"Fuckin' A, Bristol." Seth chuckled, "Come in, guys."

Seth led the way through the entrance of the Pump 'n Pantry. The warm air inside was welcoming. No need to keep on the hats and gloves. We each removed our respective layers at the rubber mud mat just inside the door.

The door shut behind me, and the cold air at my back disappeared immediately. As I listened to the large door latch, I watched the crew take a seat at the usual table. A booth, only enough for six. Behind it was a table with four chairs surrounding it. Only two months ago, three of those chairs pulled up to the booth's edge.

I felt my esophagus tie into a knot and tears welled in the inner corner of my eyes... those chairs weren't needed now.

I dabbed my face with my black Pittsburgh Penguins ski cap and all was well.

Actually, it wasn't. Reality is hardly ever ideal, but we live with it.

I watched Matt and Gordy file into one side of the booth while Sasha, Jade and Pears entered the other. Pears started to squat in his seat, but halted. He remained in the position until I noticed him. His ass touched the back of the seat and his hands grasped the table for support. He leaned in like a boss reprimanding an employee.

The group paid no attention to him. "Seth! Chicken Speedie!" Matt yelled and Gordy concurred. "A slice of cheese pizza!" Jade hollered toward Seth, who was preparing our food from behind the counter. "Spicy chicken sub!" Sasha finished off the demands.

Pears remained still and flashed a subtle grin in my direction. I countered with a perplexed stare. He raised erect. His back arched as if he was stretching and he moved to the other side of the table. Pears plopped down next to Matt, leaving an empty spot next to Jade.

Smooth move, Frankfort...

I went and sat down. There wasn't much room for me. One of my legs hung off the ledge but the other perched up against Jade's. My heart started to flutter and I felt warm, like I was sitting next to a furnace.

I was anxious. The thought of asking Jade out never crossed my mind before Pears mentioned it at the bowling alley. She was beautiful, but she was a lot more than that...

She was literally the best. Jade had it all and I never fully understood it before that night. She was smart. Her sense of humor was unparalleled but mostly, she had goals. Jade wasn't out here living a life of "whatever's", she had a plan and she'd be damned if it didn't go through.

I couldn't believe it... but I think that I liked her. It wasn't supposed to be like that, though. Of course, I thought she was hot. Always did. But when I saw Kate for the first time, that was it. There would be no one else. Ever. But now... I wasn't quite sure.

The way you look at her, man... She looks at you the same...

Yeah, you know, she did. *Does.* My fingers started to tap my knee. They were only an inch or two from her leg. Would it be *that* out of the ordinary if they just happened to move over to her leg? No funny business, just a light caress to prove my interest. I felt the strong tingle in my gut and my heart started to beat frantically like the intro to "Hot for Teacher." I could feel the coarse material of her yoga pants on the side of my pinky but I needed more. My entire pinky finger made its way onto her knee and she didn't refrain. As a matter of fact, her leg relaxed. It leaned on mine with all of its weight.

It was time for the ring finger. The outer side started to feel the fabric before the entire finger di-
-

"Jesus Christ..." Sasha said while pointing out of the window. "Look at this shit..."

Snow started to pick up even more. A quarter inch had accumulated on the hood of the SUV and the powder was blowing around the atmosphere like a drunken uncle. Snow fell in no particular sequence. The Citgo logo atop the tower in front was impossible to see.

It was a white-out. A steady snowfall was turning into blizzard-like conditions.

"Think we should get going?" Jade asked. She looked hypnotized by the weather. I removed my fingers from her leg and she stiffened.

"Not yet," Matt demanded. "I'm eating."

We laughed, but in reality, nothing should have been humorous. No one (except for me) had any interest of turning back to Salt Springs and even then, there was no promise that we wouldn't slide on ice and end up in a ditch. I didn't think there was any chance that we would make it another five miles to Lequin. 414 was going to be a bastard, and Route 6 was sure to be a bitch.

I couldn't even imagine how bad the back way was.

CHAPTER 40: Kate and Colby (Again)

The tires of Kate's Subaru Outback spun uncontrollably up the driveway. Snow sprayed from underneath them, scattering the path already traveled.

Kate pressed the gas pedal to its brink and the engine roared. The RPM needle flirted with the red line as the car weaved back and forth up the driveway.

It wasn't a fishtail. That would imply that only the back end fluttered. The car was a caught trout that fell to the dock before release. Flipping and flopping to the point of no control.

She was making very little progress and her anger was arose as fast as the RPM's, the sporty station wagon was only inching closer to the road.

"Bab—"

"I said don't fucking call me that!"

Colby fell silent. Kate's edge tonight was sharp and even the slightest of pokes would draw blood. He felt the queasiness of her stab, but she was too perfect. He would bleed for her and if that meant he had to suffer this metaphorical butchering, that was fine.

His hands gripped his thighs, bracing himself in the midst of this roller coaster ride up the Ford's driveway.

"Sorry, Colb..." Kate mumbled as she cranked the wheel to the left... and then to the right.

"Why do you want to go to this place anyways, sweetheart?" he asked softly.

"Because..." Kate gnashed her teeth and grunted. "I heard it's... cool..." she lifted her foot and stomped on the gas with three hard kicks. That made a difference. The RPM needle hit five and the car started to breeze up the driveway. Dashboard lights illuminated her sneer, "Plus, in this weather... no one will be there."

"Okay than." He agreed. "Looks like it was meant to be." He was optimistic once the car jaunted easily up the driveway, passed the large pine in her front yard and even with their mailbox where the path met Windfall Road.

"Guess it was." Kate cranked the wheel and this time, the Outback fishtailed into Windfall Road. The rear end almost deposited into a ditch, but Kate was able to save it.

Windfall Road was in surprisingly decent condition. It was only about two miles to Route 6 and that trek didn't take any more than five minutes. Even Route 6 wasn't terrible for the first mile but the conditions were dicey once the farmland turned to forestry. The digital thermometer on the dashboard dropped from 29 degrees to 21. Wind started to gush like a tidal wave, jolting the car from side to side. Powder thickened on the road and there were no tracks to trace.

Snow packed onto the branches of the evergreens that flanked each side of the road. The limbs were strong but they started to fail. They wilted to the point that snow spewed off of their sides and dumped onto the road's shoulder.

Kate, nor Colby ever traveled this far out onto Route 6. There was no reason to. Sure, they could have gone this way to Troy Borough to get to *Rejoice!* but going this direction would make as much sense as driving a speed boat to Mars. As a matter of fact, that's where they felt like they were going.

The more trees they passed, the quieter it got. They didn't mind the silence. Actually, Kate preferred it. Windfall was the sticks, and she loved it. No city bustle like Williamsport. No random horns or sirens like Salt Springs. Just the birds chirping and the occasional moo from a heifer down the road.

But this was different. This wasn't silence. This was lifeless. There was no vibration of human life or even the touch of another soul. It was dead, still air. The only noise was the slush shuffling and the snow crunching beneath them.

A clump of snow plopped to the ground from the limb of an evergreen. A stray 2x4 clapped against the side of an abandoned barn alongside the road. Kate slowed the Outback to nothing more than a roll. She knew she was close.

"Umm, sweetheart." Colby croaked as he pointed ahead. There was a large patch of bare road. No snow or ice. Hell, it wasn't even wet. 100 feet of bone dry gravel was before them, but it didn't matter. They knew that they had to turn up the adjacent road, but that was even uncovered.

Kate squinted, she remembered that she left her contact lenses in the container on her bathroom sink. "What's that sign say, Colby?"

He leaned over, "Steam Hollow Road."

"That's it." Kate said dryly. She turned the wheel and started up the road. Her face remained ahead but Colby's didn't. His eyes wandered out of the passenger's side window. Poking above the snow was a large hunk of concrete, but his eyes widened larger with every hunk he saw.

Trees started to thin out and he could see the large, white ominous structure looking over the hunks of concrete. He wasn't fully familiar with the stories and rumors, but he could put 2-and-2 together.

"Is that a graveyard?" he gulped. His Adam's apple fluttered as he scratched the stubble on his chin.

"Yep." Kate said disgustedly. Her eyes remained forward and she turned the wheel right. The Subaru rolled into the vacated parking spot. Still no tracks anywhere and she was pleased by it. Nay, she was fucking ecstatic about it.

She beat that son of a bitch there. Him and his dumbass fucking friends were going to get theirs.

Those motherfuckers... Their faces are going to be AMAZING! Fucking Zack... I can't WAAIIITTTT for him to come here and see me... Getting all pissed and depressed in front of Jade... that stupid bitch. Fucking poser. Out here acting like she's some goodie-goodie but she's just a dumb whore. I hope someone says something to me... and then Sasha's ass comes and tries me.. Get that bitch kicked off

the team... Probably get her kicked out of school.
Send that bitch back where she came from...

"Soooo...." Colby uttered, "What now?"

Kate turned off the ignition, "we go in."

"Huh?" Colby cackled and Kate ignored him. She got out and slammed the car door shut. Colby watched her walk in front of the car, lifting her legs obnoxiously as she lumbered through the calf high snow. A white mitten held onto the hood for support, but she finally released it as she angled toward the "NO TRESPASSING" sign.

Colby opened the passenger's side door and plopped one foot into the snow. He admired the light on the door, shining on both his pant leg and the snow. Droplets of water gleamed on the four inches of accumulation, and some moisture developed on his forehead despite the freezing temperature. The sweat trickled along his hairline and dropped to the snow. He felt his heart beat harder and harder—

"Yuh coming?" Kate turned around and asked condescendingly. Colby was surprised at how far in she was. She was far passed the sign and was already standing next to the first of the long line of tombstones. A small red, white and blue cloth fluttered in the breeze next to the large hunk of cranked concrete.

"A Civil War vet?" Colby thought. *"Must be for the time..."*

"Yes, sweetheart." Colby started to waddle through the snow. He offered his best effort to trace Kate's steps but this footprints were much larger than hers. It made no difference. Melted snow had leaked through his shoes and his socks completely absorbed the residue. They felt like sponges on his feet. Freezing cold sponges, at that. By the time he reached the "NO TRESPASSING" sign, his feet were tingling and had a bizarre itching sensation.
Kate began walking again once he entered the cemetery. She kept a three stone lead on him but Colby barely noticed. He kept his head down, and his eyes further below. His heartrate continued to rise, but now it wasn't pounding in his chest. He could feel it in his throat.

Snow continued to crunch under their feet and out of the corner of their eye, they could both see that they were now walking alongside the church. They could smell the musk float in the atmosphere with the brisk air. Somehow, the church's paint was even whiter than the powder below them. Colby started to calm. Kate was slowing, allowing him to reach her as they neared the porch. Her green eyes glowed in the darkness and her hair swayed in the wind like a model's during a photo shoot. But it was the smell that eased his mind the most. A familiar smell. His mind wandered back to when he was a kid.

Man, we sat on that futon for HOURS... just me, Nick, Brandon and hours of Donkey Kong on the Nintendo. Ha! Those graphics were terrible. Diddy was just a bunch of brown squares... Nick's favorite character though... Man, I miss him. If they would have jus—just waited. Five minutes. That's all. Heck, they shouldn't have even gone... that concert wasn't worth it...

Jeez... look at her... So beautiful. Dark blonde hair, big beautiful green eyes AND loves the Lord.. she too perfect. That Zack guy is an idiot. Who would let that go? I wonder how that moron feels. She's all mine... and I'm all hers... Where on Earth would I be without her? Probably depressed, thinking about that dang car accident all the time. Stupid towel head, taking my brothers away from me because he couldn't figure out his stupid radio. Rot in hell, sand ni—

An airy ball of white crossed their path and shot in front of the porch. Colby's fear didn't fully return, but he was uneasy. "Umm, Kate. Did you see that?"

"It was snow, Colby." Kate was annoyed, "It's also windy... Quit being a pussy. This place isn't anything special."

Kate reached the steps and stopped one Ugg boot on the platform. She raised the other, and stood alone on the rickety porch. But she didn't take another step, she was uneasily surprised at what she saw. The entrance to the church was wide open. It was just a gaping doorway. That musky smell released from the building like a yawn from someone that hasn't brushed in weeks, but it was accompanied by something much more foul. It's only comparison was rotten eggs.

Someone's been here... that's all...

Kate turned her head and looked up the path. There were footprints from only two people. Her and Colby. She glanced down at Colby, who stood still about 10 feet from the steps. His face was as white at the powder at his feet and he tugged frantically on the collar of the sweatshirt underneath his winter jacket. Kate turned back toward the yawning doorway, her lips puckered angrily and her mind started to wander.

Oh for the love of God, what a pussy. It's fucking snowing... Why is he so fucking scared? This is literally...just...a...place...in...the...woods!

The door slammed shut forcefully. Echoes bounced off of the mountains in the valley. Dust flew from the doorframe and the casing splintered. Kate fell back, busting her ass on the steps until she landed in the snow. Her left pant leg tore in the back from a loosened nail.

Blood leaked from the back of her calf but the pain wasn't eminent there. Her buttocks pounded in agony and she started to sit up with a grimace. She leaned to one side and rubbed her back pocket, she could feel a large lump.

"OH MY GOSH, SWEETHEART! ARE YOU ALRIGHT?!?!?!" Colby's scream was accompanied by the crunching of snow under his feet. He wasn't sprinting, but that was impossible given the conditions. It was an accelerated lumber.

"Yeah..." Kate winced. "I'm fiiii--... neee..."

The crunching behind her stopped abruptly. "Colby?" she asked, but received no reply. Kate craned her neck back and saw him, standing with a blank expression on his face. His jaw dropped and his mouth gaped open. A droplet, presumably from melted snow, dripped from his goatee and onto the sweatshirt that now sagged from his neck. His large brown eyes were fixed forward over Kate and she turned into the direction of his stare.

A woman in white stood three feet from Kate. She was beautiful, but somehow so ominous. The woman's skin was milky white and as smooth as a baby's buttocks. A long train followed her ghostly gown.. Kate tried to stand up but couldn't, she was mesmerized and was in the same hypnotic state as Colby.

The woman took a step forward, leaving no tracks from beyond. She leaned in, closer and closer.

Her gray eyes stared into Kate's and her long, transparent hair hung off of her shoulders. Kate felt her stomach become more nauseous with each inch that the woman approached, vomit built up in her throat. Kate was about to spew when the woman grabbed her shoulders and smiled. Dimples and impeccable teeth appeared through her complete smile, but her mouth exposed a familiar smell. Musk and rotten eggs.

Her voice wasn't nearly as attractive, screeching accompanied the foul odor like a car that hasn't been started in years. But when her larynx finally warmed, her voice started out soft, "Don't..." she said. But it progressively got lower, and changed its tone. Her face turned to Colby, "ruin his life". Her face returned and stared at Kate dead in the eyes, the ending voice was oh so familiar, "like you did mine, Kate. *Don't ruin his life like you did mine...*"

Kate jolted up and ran up the hill toward the car with Colby joining her. Their jaunt was clumsy but quick. Half way up the hill, Colby grabbed onto Kate's jacket for support but he fell to a knee anyways.

Colby got up without dusting off, he could feel the woman close behind but she wasn't. Kate turned around to check but there was nothing. Not a soul was in the cemetery, including them.

They were beyond the "NO TRESPASSING" sign and were off of the church grounds, but that didn't stop their accelerated pace. Kate jogged around the hatchback. A dusting of snow had covered the vehicle, she unconsciously wiped the snow off of the back and the windows, but Colby barged into the passenger's side door.

Snow fell from the roof in one giant log as he opened the door. Inside Kate's outback were Colby's mutilated brothers. A hunk of windshield lodged through Nick's eye socket and was nailed to the leather seat behind him. Stuffing from the seat sprinkled his shoulders in bloody clumps and teeth spread over his lap. A car engine sank through Brandon's stomach, completely impaling him. Blood poured out of his broken mouth and onto the engine. It evaporated on impact from the heat.

Colby fell back and screamed. Kate had yet to open the driver's door, "Colby! What happened?!?!"

"The c—Nick...Brando—'

A middle eastern man walked out of the woods, swinging something in front of him. His long, jet-black beard waved in the cold breeze, but somehow, his turban was unaffected. Just like the woman, he was leaving no tracks behind him.

As he got closer, Kate and Colby noticed that his half buttoned, white long-sleeved shirt was slowly but surely fastening. With each five steps, one button hooked.

He was only 20 feet away, and a light clicked on the device that he was holding. A lime green sliver that read "88.3FM" in digitized letters. It was a car radio, detached from the console but it wasn't playing music. It was playing conversations.

What the fuck was he doing here!?
Zack, I broke up with him last night. He was picking up some things I had of his.

Colby furrowed a brow at Kate. She returned a look of confusion but the man quickly took back control of their attention. His shirt was now all of the way buttoned.

*Is that why he went the other way? He turned
around when he saw me.
I told him I wanted you back, okay?*

His turban was disappearing, and was being
replaced by black hair. Touches of silver emerged
on the sides.

Static released from the radio's speaker, but a new
conversation began.

*So, my father has to go to some conference this
weekend. My mom is taking Tommy and Anna to
our grandparents, soooo--
You have the house to yourself.*

The man's beard was gone and he had a full head
of black and silver hair.

*Zackary Bristol: Jeopardy Champ.
When they coming back?
Sunday.*

Blotches of white skin appeared on the man's
forehead and spread down to his face. "STOP!"
Kate screamed, holding out her hands. "We'll
leave! Whatever you want!." She opened the car
door but no dice, the driver's side door was
occupied with a grotesquely butchered Nick Baker.
She puked. Vomit splattered on the side of her car
and on Nick Baker's bloody shoes.

Shit, babe. I'm tied down tonight but tomorrow I am all yours.
I want you tonight though.
Well, I'll want you tomorrow, too. You win. What are you doing tonight though?

Kate started to cry, "Please... what do you want?!" His brown eyes turned green, and his face was now completely white.

I don't know if I should tell you. Dave and Mrs. B jumped up my ass about it.
Why the hell would they do that?

White blotches reached his hands. Colby started to plead, he could see that the man was walking more toward Kate. "Please... we'll do anything... Just let us go..."

You ever hear of the Lequin Church? Well, we're going to, ya know, break into it tonight.
Seriously, Zack. Where are you guys going tonight? Please don't do it.
Oh Jesus, babe not you t—

"IS THIS BECAUSE OF FUCKING ZACK?!?!" Kate wailed. A smile slowly generated on his face, but they could see the rotten enamel in the night. He was only three feet away and stopped.

Seriously! Mr. Stonehammer locked it up, you probably can't even go in there.

"DO YOU WANT ME TO TAKE HIM BACK?!?! I WILL! I THINK I...
It was 84, I think and how do you know any of that even happened?... I didn't mean it that way, I'm sorry. But really, how does anyone know? Urban legend.

"Kate please don't!" Colby screamed as the man looked down, sneering at Kate. Musk and rotten eggs stunk the air out of his mouth also. She looked up at him, his black dress pants and white button-down were unwrinkled. But blood splatter decorated some of his shirt. No doubt the blood was from his mouth. Some dripped from one of his black stubs onto her forehead.

Except there is actual stuff about it. It's not like Ulster where the plague killed a whole town. Evil-ass people killed innocent ones in there, Zack. It's true. I don't believe it's haunted or anything but still...

"So..." the man grumbled, "You think we're evil?"

Kate's wail became helpless, "...is this because of Zack..."

"No." the man dropped the radio into the snow. "It's because of you."

Both of the car doors opened. Nick and Brandon Baker got out of the car in their abused state and walked toward their brother. Colby swung at them, trying to beat them away but his left arm was caught.

And then his right.

His brother's warped his arms, breaking them at the elbow. It sounded like a deer, prancing on branches in the woods. Bones protruded through his skin. Jagged fragments tore his bloody forearms. Colby screamed in agony and his brothers dragged him back down the hill. Blood trailed them, leaking from the wounds of the two compound fractures.

Kate started to run after them, but the man grabbed her by the back of the jacket. Her zipper dug into her throat, making her bleed even more as she watched Nick and Brandon pull Colby through the graveyard. The further they took him, the smaller they got.

And younger.

Their Toby Keith t-shirts were white button-downs and dress pants by the time they reached the porch. Two boys no older than 10 took Colby in the church and his screaming stopped.

"Where'd they take him?!?!?!" Kate cried.

"I think you have a good idea, whore."

Kate turned to him and scowled. Her lips puckered with aggression. She puffed out her chest and squeezed her hands to fists.

"Well?" he asked. "You must be a *stupid* whore."

Kate took a swing but her punch went straight through him. "Maybe she knows where they're going.." the man pointed down the hill and toward the front of the church. Standing by two large monument-like gravestones was the woman. Still dressed in her elegant gown.

"If I turn away from you... what're you going to do...?"

The man laughed heartily, "Kate..." he snorted, "*I'm* not going to do anything."

He had a point, Kate thought. She had no reason to believe him, but she did. Kate walked back down the hill, and in no way was her waltz perky or graceful. It was laboring.

Kate reached the woman, and she leaned up against the large gravestone. Blood was starting to dry on her calf but the ache in her ass didn't cease. She was emotionally drained, this was just a ploy to get back at an ex and now... she truly didn't know what was going on. It was the most frightening of dreams but she was lax.

"Hi Kate." The woman said softly.

Kate sniffled, "I don't know what you want from me... Why are you doing this?"

"Kate," the woman got closer to her. Her eyes sparkled, "Do you know who I am?"

Kate shook her head. Mascara ran down her face in long, black streaks. "No..." Kate managed, "I don't."

The woman grabbed Kate by the shoulders and pulled her tight. She whispered in Kate's ear, "I'm everything you could have been."

The long, beautiful, white gown. The train that followed. She was all prepared for a beautiful wedding ceremony.

"I can still." Kate pleaded. "I... I still can."

The woman's thumbs caressed Kate's shoulders, "I know you can. But you won't... Even if I tell you to. You won't obey."

"YES I WI—"

"No..." she looked at Kate reluctantly, "You won't." The woman pushed Kate back into the stone. Kate's head bashed into it and she fell to the ground. Her vision went black momentarily, but it returned in a haze. Her ears rang as she pawed the snow, trying to gain traction but she was pulled back. Her blood splattered the snow, mostly from her leg but some was from the back of her head.

The woman picked Kate back up. Her face never changed. She was beautiful, but had such an evil look, much like Kate's scowl. She turned Kate toward her, and bashed her head against the gravestone again. A chunk of hairy flesh flew from the back of her head and plopped into the snow.

Another bash. Blood spewed over the stone and snow surrounding it. A chunk of flesh and brain stuck to the edge of the stone.

Another one. Blood glued hair to the gravestone of Titus McLaughlin in streaks and the woman disappeared into the night.

Blood continued to pour out of the back of her head. Kate's body laid in the snow, still and lifeless.

CHAPTER 41: The Church (Again)

Route 6 had turned into a complete disaster. The further we penetrated the forest, the deeper the snow, even on the roads. We were surprised to see that we weren't the only fools to make the trek out on this frozen tundra, though. Tire tracks from a smaller vehicle helped pave our way, but it was certainly no easy task.

Flakes speckled the windshield like dandruff on a black shirt. The heat in the car was optimal but we knew all too well that when we got out, our skin would rival the ice at First Arena in Elmira.

The tracks ahead were lightly covered. Whoever decided to come out this far, came out here recently. We rounded the turn and they were still there, never veering off and turning around. They weren't lost, they knew exactly where they were going.

We were almost there, just as we passed the old abandoned barn, TI played over the SUV's stereo.

Oh! Hey! I've been travelin' on this road too long...

Matt slammed the brakes.

Just tryna find my way back home...

He gripped the wheel even tighter, his knuckles looked like they were going to pop out of his skin. We could hear Gordy's stomach rumble but other than that, a dropping pin would have sounded like an amplifier on 11.

A solid path of road was bare ahead of us. No snow. No tracks. No nothing. But it continued about 100 feet up the road. It was like if someone placed a tarp over that part of the road, but the perpendicular avenue was just as bare. Steam Hollow Road didn't feature a flake.

Matt inched the SUV onto the barren pavement and his headlights illuminated the entire stretch, even some of the road where the snow began again.

No tracks... They must have turned up the hill...

"We sure we wanna go?" Sasha asked.

I saw Matt glance into his rearview, looking for cars... or something... behind us. "Vote on it." He said. "All for yes?"

Each one of us raised our hands and Matt slowly turned the wheel up Steam Hollow Road.

The tree line thinned and the church was as visible as ever. Snow flew through the graveyard, adding to the already significant accumulation. Neat piles topped each gravestone like a stylish fedora and the powder looked unscathed.

If we didn't know what we did, this would be an absolutely picturesque scene. Especially this close to Christmas.

Matt pulled in behind the church. I could see his eyes squint with confusion in the rearview mirror. Crowfeet embedded in their corners, "What?" he mumbled rhetorically.

The tracks reappeared, but there was no car. Nor were there turnaround tracks. It was as if the car drove in and disappeared...

Or caught on fire...

But we were equally as intrigued to see that there were footprints in the graveyard. It looked like two sets but one of them definitely fell down the hill. Neither were all that big. Probably a couple of girls looking for a scare, but again, it looked like it was earlier. Not super early, but probably about a half an hour to an hour ago. The two of them were probably long gone.

Gordy opened his door and planted his own feet into the beaten tracks. Matt was next. His boots crunched the snow beneath him. His feet were much larger than whoever stood in that spot earlier.

I followed thereafter. My winter boots lodged into the snow without the support of a prior print. My tracks were fresh, and Jade's quickly joined them. She plopped into the snow with little grace. She was expecting the powder to have a thicker consistency and her knees buckled. I grasped her waist and pulled her close to me. One of her arms went around my shoulder and the other rested on my chest. We stood there for a moment, "You good?" I asked.

"Yeah." She smiled and her blue eyes sparkled like sapphire. Snow fell and glistened in her dark eyelashes.

Pears barged over the seat. He drew the short stick of having to sit alone in the "way back" seat. He got out on Jade and I's side and bumped us, breaking our embrace.

Jade started walking toward the cemetery before us. Pears grabbed me by the arm and he looked up at me. His eyes widened with regret, "I'm so sorry, bro..." he whispered.

"Dude, you're good." I smiled and started to walk toward the cemetery. His head drooped, feeling like he screwed up a perfect moment between two lovers to be.

Matt and Gordy's flashlight beamed in two long streaks through the graveyard. The light swayed back and forth like airport signals. Sasha waded her legs through the snow behind them until she reached the second stone that donned an American Flag. The flag waved gently in the freezing breeze. Its dowel was covered but the cloth still flew freely. Sasha kept her eyes on the flag. Jade placed her hand on the small of Sasha's jacket, the rubbing created a shy swiping sound.

"Come on, girl." Jade said softly. "Let's go." Sasha followed, but her eyes remained fixed on the gravestone. Her eyes moved forward just in time to see Matt and Gordy climb the steps. They both stomped their boots clean of snow on the wooden deck, not even noticing the two graves directly in front of them.

Jade and Sasha were shortly behind them. They reached the steps a mere 30 seconds later and finally, Pears and I mounted the porch.

It was a much easier trek to the porch than before. Old Glory was well behaved and Jed McLaughlin didn't greet me through the window. But it didn't make us feel any better. That porch had too much room. There were three other people that should have been there with us, and because of that fucking church, they weren't.

Maybe it wasn't the church. Was it the land? Was this place cursed or something? Is it really the evil spirits of Titus, Jed and Gabriel McLaughlin? Whatever it was, it had to stop and making it stop was our only goal. We'd do whatever it took.

We stood in a circle on the edge of the porch. I turned to my right, Jade. To my left, Pears. Across from me was Matt and he asked, "So… should we like… pray or something?"

None of us were all that familiar with the Lord, but I felt that might have been appropriate. Sasha apparently thought so too, "Yeah." she said sincerely. "But before we go in there…" she glanced at the closed door and continued, "No matter what happens tonight. I fucking love you guys."

"I love you too, Sash." I said. Pears wrapped his arm around her should her pulled her in for a hug, "Love you too, sis." he said.

Gordy reached across the circle and rubbed her shoulder, "On God, Sasha. Same here, man." A tear welled in Jade's eye, and she bolted to Pears and Sasha and joined their embrace. "Come on, woman. Let's get these fuckers."

Matt stood back and uttered a monotone voice, "I actually hate all of you. You cost me so much gas money a—" Jade pulled him by the jacket, forcing him into their group hug.

Sasha's head hung in the middle of the pack. I heard her start to sniffle, she was crying. Her head eased up, tears rolled down her brown face and onto her jacket. Her arms remained around the shoulder of Pears and Jade, and she began, "Guys... I've only ever told Zack this..." she snorted. "I... I watched my..."

"Sasha, it's oka—"

"No! It's not!" she screamed at me. "Anything can happen in there! I have to tell *all* of you guys..."

"Nothing will happen to any of u—"

"I watched my parents die..." she cried wistfully, "I was *fucking* six years old! And I couldn't do anything..."

"Sash..." Pears hesitated, "It's okay..."

"And I *barely* remember them..." Sasha croaked. She struggled to speak through the tears, "and... and... you guys... and... Brooke, Ryan... and Kara...

are the only family that I know... I can't lose any more of you guys..."

"You won't." Pears said lowly, "We're ending this shit."

"Okay..." Sasha sniffled and stood up, releasing her arms from Jade and Pears' shoulders, "Let's get these fuckers."

"Well.. on the 'fuckers' note, let's pray." I joked.

"Nigga, you even know a prayer?" Sasha still sniffed some leftover mucus, but she laughed through it. We all joined her. How on Earth could we be standing on that porch laughing? Our bond was so unique. We really did love each other.

"All those years he wasted on Kate, eh Bristol? You have to know one..." Jade nudged me with an elbow and smiled. I noticed Pears and Sasha sharing eye contact. It's wild how friends can speak without talking. Their eyes and smirk told the story, they thought something was going on between Jade and I, and this interaction was proving it.

"Well..." I said, "I know the Our Father who art in heaven one. Everyone know that one?"

"Kind o—"

The front door creaked open slowly, sounding like a crying baby and the knock on the wall when it was fully opened sounded like a brick falling on concrete.

I noticed that the string was off of the door the entire time. Breeze probably pried the door open. No one spewed out of the entrance and upon first glare, it looked completely empty inside. All we could see was the one end of pews with mountains of books stacked on top of them.

"Sk... skip the prayer?" Pears peeked in. His upper lip curled back with uncertainty.

"Might be best..." Matt agreed. "Let's just get this over with..."

Matt didn't really just want to 'get this over with', though. We needed to finish this, because this torture that we were suffering was self-inflicted. *We* broke in. *We* opened this portal. *We* "let out the McLaughlin's." But most importantly, we felt like we were responsible for the death and/or disappearances of our friends. It was up to us, and *only* us to end it.

And this time, we were let in.

We admired the yawning entrance. Although we weren't all staring inside the vacated church, we glared in the general vicinity. The doorway was large, not quite the size of a barn door but only a foot shy of that diameter. It was a large, toothless mouth leading to the most vile of insides with the flames of Hell in the pit of its stomach.

Those are the flames that torched one of my best friends and his girl. I thought of the Salt Springs High School Baseball hat that he always wore with the number 23 on the back and there I imagined it, sitting atop the pile of books in the first row of pews. Forest green with the letters "SS" in white fancy script, a gentlemanly touch for a player that was in no way a gentleman.

He was a damn good guy though and would do anything for a friend, but especially Kara. The goddamn abuse he took over the years from her father would make most run away. It was something we started to bond over, as if our natural connection wasn't enough.

It was only four days at the time, but fuck, I missed the hell out of him. I missed the way he'd slap you on the back instead of saying "hello." I missed the phone calls, begging me to come over and play Xbox and I even missed that dirty ass ball cap that was rested atop the stack of hymnals.

The bill was turning a shade of orange and started to peel back. Ashes started to flake and blow into the church's atmosphere like a paper plate in a campfire. The "SS" started to fray and the embroidery charred in an instant.

I blinked and the hat was gone. Another figment, another trance, but it wouldn't distract me from the task at hand. I moved toward the entrance and infiltrated the hellish domain. The musky aroma hit me like Mike Tyson as my boot planted on the church's hardwood floor. I glanced to the left and saw the stairs to the balcony but my feet kept moving, feeling as involuntary as a heartbeat. The pulpit quickly arrived to my right and I stood alone in the empty sanctuary.

Jade entered immediately thereafter, followed by the rest who infiltrated in a cluster of four. We idled in silence in the same exact spot that we split up in two months before but this felt different. No, it *was* different. We were alone. Heat didn't rise from the pews, windows weren't going to shatter, blood wasn't going to fall from the ceiling and green powder wasn't going to paint my crotch like Picasso. Tonight, it felt like the Lequin Church was just an abandoned building miles away from civilization with no history. This bitch was a fort. Just a pile of wood nailed together to make something you could walk into. Fuck, use the leftover 2x4's to make some long-ass chairs. Got enough for 10? That'll do.

We all felt the nothingness. Only a few moments were filled with anxiety, but once we felt the lightness of the air inside, all of that vanished. Before, the air was heavy. So much that walking felt like the most strenuous of labor, both physically and emotionally. Tonight it was so thin that Pears looked like he flew into the first pew to sit down.

"Well…" Pears thumped on the wooden seat, boots clapped against the hardwood floor and his hands smacked his thighs, "Not much going on tonight here, eh?"

"Just wait…" I said, "They'll be here."

Sasha leaned up against the outer frame of the pulpit. She folded her arms in front of her, "These muhfuckas told Matt K to 'come back soon' and they gonna fuckin' play us like this…" Sasha said disgustedly and sighed, "bunch of fuckin' shit, man. Fuck with our friends and a nigga gonna hide…"

"Sash, they aren't people…" Matt explained, "It's not like they can just show up when they want… or at least I don't think they ca—"

"Wait." Jade said sternly. "Do you guys want them to be here?"

"That's why we came here, right?" Matt asked with some confusion. "That's the only way we can stop them."

"Yeah, but…" Jade answered. She started to paw at her hair. Long black nails served as a brush for her long blonde locks, "do we really think that if we talk to them or whatever, they'll just stop?"

"That's why we have to obey them." I walked toward the center of the group. They looked at me puzzled, but I felt that I knew the answer to our dilemma. We had to obey. "They wanted us to 'come back soon', like on the mat at Kara's. Well, it's soon. Fuck, it was a couple of days ago… We're staying for however long they need. We do what they want."

"I can tell you this much, Zack." Matt said with a smirk, "I'm not going back up in that balcony. And I'd prefer to stay away from any window."

"No worries, brother." I chuckled. "You just want to stay in the pews?"

"We splittin' up again?" Pears perked up in his seat. Going from a slouch to an erect posture.

"I mean, there's six of us." I answered nonchalantly. "We could go by two's."

"I'll stay down here with Matt." Gordy said frankly.

Sasha released from the pulpit's barrier. She arched her back with a relaxed stretch and glanced at Pears, "Who's goin' upstairs with m—"

"I'll go." Pears shot up out of his seat before Sasha could even get out the phrase. He peered in my direction with a contagious smile. Sasha grinned as they both trotted toward the stairs.

"Welp." Jade's voice was charismatic, but not energetic. "Guess it's to the pulpit for us again, Bristol."

"Wouldn't want it any other way." I replied and offered a sly smile. *"Damn, was that me? A fuckin' true players move right there. Thata baby, Bristol!"* I thought as I followed Jade up the winding steps. Her perfume was at a perfect potency, not smelling like the inside of the goddamn bottle but I'd be damned if she didn't smell like the store. I could see the definition of her leg flex as she mounted the steps. She had slight tone even through the extra pair of leggings but that ass. Holy Jesus. So perfectly round and firm, like two fully inflated balloons connected by static.

I watched the subtle jiggling as she reached the final two stairs. There wasn't much under those leggings. A g-string, tops, but commando was more realistic. I had the urge. No, the need. Each cheek would fit perfectly in my hand with some of that cushion seeping between my fingers. I reached my hands out, only three inches away. My thumbs lined up with the indentation of her asscrack and my pinkies could wrap around the outside of her waist.

I could feel her warmth, and surprisingly, a detached blonde hair from her scalp that connected onto the fabric on her ass. It cramped my style. I couldn't, but was I really going to anyways? Hell no, that wasn't me. Not the time or place, but damn. Maybe that day was coming.

Jade sat down on the bench in the pulpit. She looked determined. Determined to finish what we accidentally started. I remained standing, but only long enough to see that the rest of us were still okay.

CHAPTER 42: Matt and Gordy

The first pew was freezing cold. Gordy felt as if he were sitting on the solid sheet of ice like he used to do up at Lake Nephawin when he was a sprout. He used to go up with his dad and brothers on the weekend. Old Cliff White used to tie a snowtube to the snowmobile and drive it over the lake when it froze. Gordy always fell off and onto his ass, but it was fun. The chill from the wood brought back fond memories.

It was old hat to Matt, though. He didn't even think of the frigidity. Matt compared it to sitting on an empty feed bucket in January. Like when the son of a bitchin' auto milker broke and he had to get down there to do it by hand. By that afternoon his forearms cramped from squeezing the teats of all 84 heifers, and he felt like the frostbite was starting to settle in on his denim covered ass. Crazy to think that these were so warm a few months ago.

Burnt the burnt pockets right off Ryan's jeans...

"Gord-O" Matt whispered as he tapped Gordy's outer knee. "You remember what row they were in?"

Without hesitation, Gordy remembered and he needed no clarification as to who 'they' were. "This one." He said quietly.

"You sure?"

"Yeah, brother."

Matt's face turned forward and he glared aimlessly toward the pulpit. He was thinking. The idea of the increasing pew temperature concerned him and he had no intention of staying seated. He arose and walked further back in the church, patting each pew as he penetrated deeper and deeper into the sanctuary.

He reached the eighth row and a foul aroma streamlined into his nasal cavity. Smelled like a bad fart. His old man always said that was a sulfury smell, but truthfully it just smelled like eggs that have gone bad. It reached its smelly peak when he reached the final row of pews.

What the fuck is th—

Matt needed a closer look. He saw something...strange, but it might have been an illusion. Splinters of wood shot up from the bench in a series of odd shapes. His heart beat faster and harder. Matt felt like the whole damn thing was going to shoot out of his chest and on to the pew beside him.

Gordy was much more relaxed. So relaxed that his ass slouched so far in his seat that he would have taken a shit on the floor. His long brown hair kept the scalp warm, and surprisingly, his whole body was too. No meat on his bones and he only donned a hoodie and sweatpants, but his mind was somewhere else. Magnum 5 had a gig at the Warrior Lounge in a few weeks. Pretty big gig. All of the Canton Mafia would be there for a night of hard rock covers. "Beast and the Harlot" by Avenged Sevenfold was giving Gordy a hell of a time. He held his hand out, palm up and started to fiddle his fingers, imitating or as he'd prefer to call it, practicing on the air guitar.

Gordy flipped his hair to the side and plucked the imaginary strings. *"Damn tabs are crazy on this solo..."* he thought, he added his other hand to mimic the strumming, *"17-17-13-down-17-up-13... Jesus Christ what the fuck... why is this shit so hard?"*

Gordy mimicked one more time. He leaned in and furrowed his brow on B string's 17th fret just as Matt ran his index finger over a carving in the final pew.

They heard three clear knocks coming from the balcony. Gordy's strumming hand dropped to the pew. He leaned on the free hand as he turned toward the sound. Matt yanked his hand back from the carving with fear. A splinter implanted into his index finger. Blood leaked lightly from the small wound.

Matt could feel his spine freeze with terror. He knew it was the thrower of the welcome mat at the Murphy's, whether it was one of the boys or the man. He knew it for sure. It felt as if ice was shattering in his neck when he looked up at the balcony.

CHAPTER 43: Pears and Sasha

Sasha covered her mouth, keeping her laughter in.
She placed her other hand on Pears' forearm and
continued to seize with muted cackles.

Pears' knuckles were a shade of red and still felt
the slight pressure from rapping a wooden bench
that aligned the back wall of the balcony.

Sasha changed course and walked toward a stack
of hymnals at the end of the pew. She held it to her
side and waved it in Pears' direction, gaining his
attention.

"Should I drop it?" Sasha mouthed while making a
dropping motion with the book. The smile still
resonated from Pears' prank but he wasn't all that
impressed with himself anymore and it showed.

"Not yet." Pears shook his head with mild chagrin.
He could feel the tension rising from downstairs.
After all they've been through, he did that? He was
appalled at himself.

*This is the fucking place that this whole goddamn
nightmare started... and I did that. What the fuck
did I even do that for? Like... Brooke, Kara and
fucking Ryan died because of this place and I'm
making fucking jokes...*

Pears stepped down to the ledge, planting his hands on the barrier. He looked all around the church from the best seat in the house. Pears could see everything.

The main entrance remained ajar directly across from him. Wind was heavy and he could see flakes of snow making their way in to the church. The back of Gordy's hair waved gently in the breeze that entered the open doorway and he looked like he was watching the entrance intently from the first pew in the sanctuary, but playing the air guitar in the process. It reminded Pears of back when Gordy sweat profusely at his shows. He used to place a box fan behind a speaker, blowing cold air on Gordy during the entire show. Pears thought of an occasion two years ago when Magnum 5 played a show at the Rialto Theatre in Canton.

Pears stood in the standing area by the stage, looking up at Gordy start the opening riff to "Enter Sandman." *Fucking 16 years old and this dude can do THIS….*

The beat dropped and the rhythm guitar joined him. Pears felt a tap on his shoulder and he turned around. There was Samuel Bedford, the president of the Salt Springs school board, at a rock concert with a button-down, tie and slacks on.

Pears thought back to his expulsion for gang-related activity and death threats toward Salt Springs' faculty, students and administration. Pears was there that night, at the school board meeting where all allegations were addressed and of course, the verdict on what to do with the students involved.

Samuel Bedford had the final say and even with no evidence or concrete allegation, Samuel Bedford banned Franklin Perez from Salt Springs High.

"What do you want?" Pears asked.

"There are just a few people that feel threatened that you are here, Mr. Perez."

"Like who?" Pears asked respectfully, but he was stern.

"There are a few." Samuel said, "Just can't say."

Pears saw Luke Larson making his way through a crowd of people over Samuel's shoulder. "What's he doing?" Pears asked.

"Who me?" Larson asked, "I'm getting your peanut butter looking ass out of here. You're causing a scene."

"Causing a scene?!" Pears yelled, "I'm just fucking standing here! I'm watching Gordy!"

"Just fucking cooperate this time, spick." Larson demanded. He grabbed ahold of Pears' wrist and the back of his blue South Pole t-shirt. Larson pulled and shoved Pears' through the mass of people, all still rocking to *"EXIIIIITTTT LIGHT... ENTER NIIIIIGGHHHTTT."*

"Fucking blue South Pole shirt." Larson grunted as he continued finagling himself and Pears through the crowd . "Go down to fucking Philly and see what kind of crip you are, ya fuckin' beaner."

TAAAAAKKKKE MY HANNNNDDDD... WERE OFF TO NEVER NEVER LAND..

They heard the music take a strange turn. The lead guitar was no longer playing and the entire band eventually stopped. Buzzing from the crowd muted. Pears and Larson involuntarily turned around.

Gordy White took the place of Kirby Lewis at the microphone. The Les Paul still draped over Gordy's bony shoulder and sweat dripped the tips of his long brown locks. He flipped his hair to the side, revealing his foggy glasses.

"He wasn't doing anything, officer." Gordy said and he pointed into the small mosh pit at the front of the theatre, "He's been standing there the entire show."

"Doesn't matter." Larson yelled.

"How doesn't it matter?" Gordy returned calmly.

A stray voice in the crowd yelled, *"Luke Larson is a dirty fucking pig!"*

Larson looked in that direction, but continued, "He isn't allowed to be in here."

"Why?" Gordy asked. "We're the ones putting on a show. We want him here."

"Kill yourself, Larson! You fucking piece of shit." Another stray voice hollered.

"Bet you do..." Larson turned back around and started heading for the door in the back with Pears still in his grasp. He then mumbled, "you fucking faggots."

Larson escorted Pears out of the door and out of the theatre. Pears loaded into the back of Luke Larson's police cruiser and was forced to stay at the Salt Springs Police Station until his parents picked him up. Meanwhile, Magnum 5 wrapped up their concert early. They didn't even finish "Enter Sandman."

Pears noticed his grip on the bannister was much more firm than it was before. Thinking about that story still pisses him off, but it now gives him a bittersweet feeling. The kid that only talks about music and video games went completely out of his comfort realm and told a dirty cop to fuck off.

Every damn person in that church did that for him. Pears' reputation wasn't even remotely good but there was no reason for it. (Well... there was that one thing... the fact that he wasn't white.) He always felt upset that all of his friends had to keep justifying him and their friendship. Only Miss Shelly and Miss Linda brought him in with open arms from day one. It never ceased through all of the bullshit that entailed a few years ago.

Sasha came up next to him and rested her elbows on the barrier next to him. They watched Gordy continue playing the air guitar, Matt scan the sanctuary carefully and of course, their attention was fixed solidly on the pulpit.

CHAPTER 44: Jade and Zack

Everything seemed cordial, but I was uneasy nonetheless. Despite his concentrated scowl, Gordy was at peace. His eyebrows furrowed with determination as he went over tablature in his mind. His fingers were quick, mirroring their motion on the neck of his imaginary Les Paul.

Matt continued to scan the pews but he was more leery than before. Pears and Sasha's antics in the balcony forced him to slow. His flashlight moved from side-to-side quickly as he maneuvered through the pews. I saw him wince, his girth pinched against the side of the wood when he turned the corner to the next row. But he adjusted his Philadelphia Eagles ballcap and continued into the next row.

Sasha and Pears returned lowered to a knee in the front of the balcony. They sat directly across from the pulpit in silence but they continued to pan the entire sanctuary from above.

We were all somewhat affected by the cold breeze as it continued to blow in the main entrance but luckily, for Jade and I, we were mostly protected from the direct gusts by the large wooden cylinder that we were in. Regardless, the building was still chilly. Jade's arms folded across her and she buried her chin in her chest. I could hear her teeth clank slightly as she looked up at me. Her large, baby blue eyes pierced through the darkness.

My stomach dropped. I didn't know if it were the nerves or the stunning girl that accompanied me in the pulpit, but my anxiety ran high. I started to gnaw on my fingernails and my other hand tapped against my thigh before Jade grabbed it. Her hands were cold, but soft as they cradled mine. Baby blues widened as she pulled me in.

My heart beat like a drum in my chest. As a matter of fact, I could feel the pulse all the way in my throat. *What is she doing? Why is she grabbing me?*

It felt like an eternity. Her touch was welcoming but she only led me to the seat next to her. It was a small bench so we were close. Our legs pressed next to each other like strangers in a crowded stadium.

Or like they did in the booth at the Pump.

I looked at my hands that rested in my lap and the idea resurfaced. *The way you look at her, man... she looks at you the same way...*

Maybe she did, maybe she didn't. There were times that I thought she might be interested, even when Kate was in the picture and there were times that I thought that we were just... bros. I wanted to make the move at the Pump, but this was the perfect opportunity. It was just her and I alone in the pulpit. No one could see in and if she wasn't for it, I could blame the powers of the church or... something.

I wanted her. Badly. Without any hesitation, I craned my arm around her waist and pulled her in tight. She didn't back away. Actually, she moved forward with a move of her own. She leaned in and rested her head on my shoulder.

My hand rubbed her back and she started to breathe deeper. I pressed my mouth and nose against the top of her head. Her hair smelled impeccable, it was a dull fruity smell, a lot like her natural aroma.

I relaxed. The butterflies were gone. It was just like a big football game. Pregame brought the most anxiety, but once you stepped on that field, it was all over. Making the first move was nerve-racking, but now, I was on autopilot. My hand rested over her ribcage, before I started to stroke up and down to the swell of her buttocks.

It felt right. But even more so, it was fun. Her warmth was welcoming, especially in the freezing elements. But the passing caress of her ass and her firm breast pressing against my chest had me slightly aroused. My hand clutched her waist and I snuck a cold thumb under her shirt, gently swaying it back and forth. Her skin was soft and smooth like silk. It made Jade moan ever so lightly and she adjusted body tighter on me. Blonde hair tickled my neck and the top of her head rested just under my chin. She finally placed her hand on the middle of my thigh.

There was obviously something. This wasn't an *I'm scared, comfort me* or *I'm sad, comfort me* thing like it was at Brooke's funeral. This was something different. This was attraction. This was interest. I could feel the blood gush in my loins and the butterflies start the engine for their wings in my gut. It was time.

I removed my mouth from the top of her head, ignoring the strands of blonde hair that tangled in stubbly chin. "Jade." I whispered and she looked up. Her blue eyes widened, looking just smaller than two golf balls. They were stunning. Somehow, even in the darkness, they glowed like jewels in a museum and her mouth revealed a sparking smile as she said, "Yes, Zack?"

I moved in. Her lips were perfect, not a single crack or crater to be seen. My eyes closed and I could feel her breath on my face. She reached a hand around my back and gripped my baggy sweat pants with the other.

Her warmth was stronger now. I could feel the slightest touch of her lips on mine and she pressed in, wrapping her lips around my bottom lip. Her grip became firmer on my back. I brought my hand to her face, blonde hair streamed through my fingers. She retreated, but for only a second. Jade came back in, her mouth slightly open this time. Our open mouths met. Her tongue had infiltrated my mouth. My thumb had separated her shirt a little further from her skin, allowing my hand to caress her bare side. It reached around to the small of her back and I pulled her in closer.

A light appeared through my sealed eye lids, like when you have your eyes closed next to an open window.

I pulled back and opened my eyes. "Everything okay?" Jade asked.

"Yeah, couldn't be better." I smiled, but it wasn't. The church was light, almost as if the sun was rising but that was impossible. We had only been in the church for what felt like 30 minutes. I pulled out my cell phone. It read 1:24 a.m.

Jade noticed the glow, as well. We both stood up, the bench creaked from the release of our weight and I gained a whiff of a familiar smell.

"Night Blooming Jasmine," I thought.

Gordy and Matt were looking toward a window as well. Light started to shine through it.

"Fuck!" Sasha yelled from the balcony, she ran over to the other side, "Nahhh fuckin' way, is that the cops?"

"No." Matt said from beneath her. "I... I think the fucking sun is rising."

I looked at the other windows. Pitch black accompanied flakes of snow. Only a single window was brightening.

The light was now eminent enough to glisten morning dew on the window, looking like the beginning of a bright September day.

"Zack..." I heard. I looked around but I knew that it didn't come from one my friends.

You can't be fucking serious.

"Zack. I'm so sorry."

It was Kate, sitting in the last pew the entire time. She stood up and walked in front of the illuminated window. Guilt poured through me like a bottle of Hennessy. I still loved her, and there was no doubt about it. Jade was a pawn, or something to distract me from my true feelings and I needed to explain that to her.

Kate stood in front of the window. She looked so perfect, light glistened through her long hair like an aura as she donned a navy blue cardigan over a lighter colored cami with jeans on the bottom. Her green eyes glistened and were traced with the most miniscule amount of eyeliner and mascara. Kate Ford once again glowed like an eclipse. She was even more beautiful than the first day I met her. I was almost magnetized to her. All of the pain and suffering extinguished. I turned toward the pulpit exit and started to step down the stairs.

Kate batted her eyes toward me, "Zack.. I am so sorry... For everything." She was sincere, "Really." Kate continued. "If they come first, it doesn't matter to me."

Both of my feet dismounted the last step of the pulpit. I walked slowly in front of the pews and turned up the side aisle toward her.

"I just want you back." she said with her arms dangling with desperation at her sides. She seemed physically weak, like she was fading with exhaustion. "I need you back..."

I could now see the whites of her eyes. Those big, beautiful green eyes. Looking like emeralds resting on a white pillow. Her aroma gained potency with each step I took. It was Night Blooming Jasmine. The scent that she fell in love with on our first Valentine's Day together. It was fresh, but somehow, I knew that it was out of an almost three year old bottle.

"Kate..." I hesitated as I passed the third row of pews, "I... I'm the one that should be sorry."

"No." Kate said, "You shouldn't. I need you. I can't live without you, Zack."

I bashed my thigh on the fifth pew, but I paid no mind. It was right this time. This was it. Finally, the last hurdle. Kate was mine again, but this time, it was once and for all. It only took the powers of the Lequin Church.

"You can be friends with Jade... and I love Sasha. She makes me look a lot better at basketball than I am." Kate explained with a light laugh. "I just need this. It will work this time. I promise."

I placed a hand on each of Kate's shoulders and caressed her arms on the way down to her hands. Her hands were cold, but I grabbed them anyways. Our fingers laced and I pulled her in, "Go to Duquesne. I can wait. It's only a year and I'll join you. We can move in together and we can do whatever you wa—"

I unlaced my hands from hers and slipped them under her cardigan. She placed both of her hands on my chest but I soon pulled her entire body into my grasp. There was no atmosphere between us, it was just her and I, as it always should be.

"Kate." I said as I heard a sniffle come from several feet behind me, "I love you."

Kate smiled, revealing the slightly crooked canine, "I love you too, Zack." I moved in and I kissed her. Her lips were chilly, but so incredibly smooth and moist. I sucked on her lower lip and released, then she took mine but added a nibble.

My hands moved up and cradled her face. She pulled back and looked deep into my eyes. Nothing was said, it was a glance to reassure the moment. It was all too serendipitous. My thumbs stroked her jawline once and she flashed a sexy crooked smile. I couldn't take it and I pulled her in again. Fingers laced around the rear of her neck.

But the back of her head was damp. Very damp. But it wasn't the consistency of water. It felt syrupy.

I heard the faint smack from the release of our kiss and I looked at my hand that cradled the side of her head. "Kate!" I said sharply. "You're bleeding... badly..."

Kate's eyes sparkled and her angelic smilereturned, "I know."

"What do you mean you kn—"

"They got me." Her smile grew wider and her eyes darkened to a forest green. "Be with me, Zack. Be with us."

Both my hands dropped and I jolted a step backward. My ass rammed into a pew, knocking down a stack of books that sat atop it. "Who's us, Kate?"

Kate took a step forward, her eyes were now pitch black. I could hear shuffling come from the balcony, pulpit and the other side of the sanctuary, but my sole focus was on Kate, "All of us." she said. "We're all here, Zack. You can be too."

"Kate..." I shuffled back another three steps, "Who are you talking about?"

"Brooke," Kate took a step forward and out of the light. Her eyes turned to solid white discs, "Ryan." Kate's skin started to crack and crater like the

Sahara as she took another firm step on the hardwood floor. "And Kara."

I retreated again, my back plastered against the outside of the pulpit. "We're all here. Even Mrs. Stonehammer." Kate said, and she lumbered closer clumsily. Blood dripped from the back of her scalp in syrupy globs. A long clot plopped to the floor out of the void in her head. The clot wriggled in a small pool of maroon and inched away from the bloody puddle. It continued inching but it was losing its brick-colored tint the further it crawled until it returned to its natural color. It was never a clot. It was a worm.

"Listen to her, Zack." A low voice grumbled from the balcony with a coarse dissertation, "We aren't done." It was the man. He leaned his elbows on the bannister across from Pears and Sasha. Purple wrinkles swayed under his eyes as he spoke and moss crumbled from his forehead. "They're all here."

"No... you didn't..." I stumbled, "You didn't get *her* too.."

"We did." The man said as he stood up and one of the boys appeared from behind a pew in the balcony. I heard frantic footsteps pound the balcony toward the stairs.

"Please…" I begged. A tear rolled down my face and splattered on the floor. "No more. Whatever we did, I'm sorry. Whatever you wa—"

"Whatever we want?" the man said and walked toward the balcony stairs, "That's what all of you say." He rubbed his dry and callused hands together, sounding like sandpaper, "You *never* get what you want," the man continued, the silver streaks of hair on the side of his head illuminated in the darkness. He pointed at Kate from the balcony, "You wanted Katelyn Sally Ford back and that's what you got."

I looked at Kate. She had fallen to her hands and knees. Blood continued to ooze from her scalp like rivers of maroon. Her skin was pallid and scaled like a gator before she fell face down to the hardwood floor. A lake of blood progressively formed over her shoulder.

"But I don't want her ba—"

Pears grabbed me by the jacket and pulled me with him as the group ran for the exit. Sasha hesitated at the door, expecting it to close abruptly but it didn't.

"Sure you do." I heard the man say from behind me, "After *allllllll* you've been through. Her father, Colby, Carter Winthrop…"

I pulled away from Pears' grasp just as we hit the doorway, "How the fuck do you know about Carter?"

Kate's body moved. She still laid lifelessly face down, but it was only five feet behind us. The man was still in the balcony. There was no way he could have moved it there but there she lay, blood continued to stream out of the back of her head. Her arms spread out like an eagle's wings.

She started to twitch and her face jolted up instantly. But it was the face of Carter Winthrop. His beady brown eyes looked glazed over and he sported his normal babyface beneath his John Lennon haircut, "I'm hopping in the shower. Wanna Join?" he said in his nasal tone.

Kate's head seized and shuffled into her normal 16-year old face, "Give me a minute."

"Zack!" Pears yelled, as he grabbed my arm again. But this time he had help and Sasha grabbed the other. We ran, but I noticed something immediately that I didn't on the way in. A bloody clump of hair nestled on top of one of the gravestones in front of the porch.

I looked around as we ran up the snow-covered hill and through the cemetery. There were only five of us, Jade was missing.

"Where the fuck is Jade?!" I screamed.

"Already in the car!" Matt yelled noticing that the man and two boys were walking up the hill behind us. "Hurry up! Let's go!"

I could see Jade's silhouette in the "way back" seat of the Knickerbocker SUV. Gordy piled in the front and Matt mounted the driver's seat, starting the vehicle before his ass even touched the leather. Pears and Sasha dove in the back and before I could join them, I heard someone call my name behind me.

It was the man, with his boys at both his side. They stood beside the church about 50 feet back.

A moment later, Kate and Colby joined them. The back of her skull was missing, showing the goo and grey of her brain. His arms completely dismantled. Bones protruded out of his skin in three places up both of his arms. I turned back around and started to trek back to the car.

"Zack!"

"Zacky!"

"Zackary!"

"Zachariah!"

"ZACKARY GEORGE BRISTOL!"

"ZACKARY BRISTOL: JEOPARDY CHAMP."

No. Fucking. Way.

I turned around with a rebuking glare.

"Say good-bye." He said.

I entered the car without saying a word.

CHAPTER 45: Aftermath

We barely spoke for the rest of that weekend. Pears and I went to the Chatterbox for Saturday brunch, but we didn't speak of the night before. Not even about Jade or bowling, the conversation was solely about the upcoming Penn State bowl game with a side helping of the Steelers and Giants. Well, there was some comic relief. His waffles had too many blueberries, so blue waffle jokes were pretty potent once Tracy Wilson brought us our food.

Tracy wasn't doing well and it was noticeable. It was Day 6 of Ryan's disappearance, and the thoughts of losing her only child were even more eminent. He was gone and she knew it. Tracy was clearly at her breaking point. Her eyes were glazed over when she took our order and her forearms looked like a topographic map of the Alps when she placed the pancakes in front of me.

Monday morning came. Sasha and I's morning ritual finally broke. We didn't go to the Chatterbox, but she still picked me up. She claimed that she was running late but her demeanor said otherwise. She was pissed. The bass was significantly less potent that morning.

The old me is dead and gone... Dead and gone...

"You talk to Jade?" I asked as he rolled slowly over a speed bump.

"Fuck do you care?"

"Okay."

Jade wasn't in school for the next three days. Sara O'Sullivan told me that she came down with a stomach virus. She had to make up all of her final and mid-term exams in the final two days, so there was little time to talk. I needed to explain everything. Whatever that was in the church was not Kate. Even if what happened in the pulpit was a one-time thing, I wanted her to know that my feelings for Kate were really gone. Not that it really mattered now. Kate was gone and most likely, my friendship with Jade was too.

Police were once again called to investigate two missing teenagers that were last seen in Bradford County, PA. This time they searched every square foot around Windfall and Alba, but naturally found nothing.

Four missing teenagers in a week caused an uproar. Salt Springs was no longer looked at as the small, quaint, lower-middle class town. WNEP's top story the following Wednesday was about Salt Springs. Four teens vanish and a disturbing suicide two months prior was the topic of conversation. Some thought there was something serious happening, a serial killer perhaps, and others believed it was just the nature of the town. Salt Springs High School students died in packs and it occurred about every five years. It was due to happen again.

It was only a matter of two weeks before people forgot all about it, though. No talk of the missing students, except in their family circles, plus it was Christmas break.

I came home on the evening of December 23rd to a package on the back (front, sorry mom) porch. It was wrapped in green holiday paper with a black ribbon. Snow had melted on top of it, making the paper wilt.

To Zack, it read in bleeding ink. That was all.

I dropped my gym bag in the house and returned to the porch. I picked up the package.

Clothes

Funny thing is that 10 years before that, I hated the idea of getting clothes on Christmas. Everyone did. But now, that's really the only thing I wanted. I opened the package vigorously and couldn't believe that someone had just given me an authentic Troy Polamalu jersey. The son of a bitch must've been 125 bucks.

Things really went back to normal after that. Kate was gone but honestly, it felt like she was gone a long time before that night at Lequin. Our Thursday night bowling league resumed and the crew all met at the bowling alley on Friday nights for a few hours. It even continued until school started again in January. Only thing was that Jade never attended. She didn't release herself from the loop, but she excused herself from anything that involved me.

It sucked, but I didn't blame her. If I would have watched her do the same thing that I did, I would have had the same reaction. There were only a few months to make up with her which added to all of it. It would have been different if I had time, but I didn't.

Another page of the calendar flipped. February started off great. The fucking Pittsburgh Steelers won the fucking Super Bowl! It was literally one of the best nights of my life. Super Bowl XL was different because the game was shitty, but man... When Arizona took the lead that late I thought it was a wrap, but Ben pulled it off in the end just like he did all season. It was unreal.

Sasha came over after the game and celebrated with my mother and I. Mom and I didn't have people over for the Super Bowl that year because the Steelers turned us into maniacs, especially in a game of that magnitude. Sasha was equally elated. We finished off the chips, pizza and Pepsi in our diminutive living room, still twirling our Terrible Towels.

The next morning came all too quickly, but damn, I had my new Troy Polamalu jersey on and I was ready to have the best and most obnoxious school day of all time. I came downstairs to a plate full of eggs and wheat toast. Mom held the newspaper close to her nose, and looked to read an article over the top of her glasses.

The front page of the Towanda Times read, "Steelers Win Their Sixth", but mom didn't look like she was reading anything about football. Mom looked intent, and also very disturbed. She grabbed her glass of Pepsi and took a sip. The glass clanked on the table top, "Another kid, Zack." She shook her head.

"What?" I replied with a mouthful of eggs.

"Another three." She dropped the newspaper to the table. The picture of Santonio Holmes on the front page splat into my breakfast as mom pointed to the headline of an article inside the cover.

Troy High School Students Slain in Accident.

"So sad." Mom shook her head and took another gulp.

I flung the paper off of my plate and continued eating, "Where'd they crash?" I mumbled through chewed toast.

"Says Route 6."

Say good-bye.

I choked. Chunks of chicken embryo splattered the large photograph of crime scene tape surrounding the old Jennings Barn. It was happening again, and I was sure of it.

Part 3:
Live Your Life

You're gonna be, a shinin' star

In fancy clothes, and fancy cars

And then you'll see, you're gonna go far

Cause everyone knows, just who ya are-are

So live your life (AYY! Ayyy ayyy ayyy)

You steady chasin' that paper

Just live your life (OHH! Ayyy ayyy ayyy)

Ain't got no time for no haters

Just live your life (AYY! Ayyy ayyy ayyy)

No tellin' where it'll take ya

Just live your life (OHH! Ayyy ayyy ayyy)

-T.I. and Rihanna (2008)

CHAPTER 46: The Accident

On the morning of February 1, 2009, Nolan Seeley, Dean Vermilya and Eric Foster died in a severe car accident on Route 6 near Lequin Township. Bradford County Coroner, Thomas Carney, pronounced their death at 3:16 a.m. It is presumed that the individuals died on impact.

Nolan Seeley's mother, Faith, told police officers and reporters that her son had taken his new vehicle to a semi-pro hockey game in Elmira, New York earlier that evening. She thought it was odd that he and his friends didn't come home immediately, but she was not overly concerned at the time since it was a Saturday night/Sunday morning.

Although it is unknown why the three young men took an alternative route, it is assumed that they were on their way home since the car rammed through the old Jennings Barn on Route 6 between Lequin and Troy.

Thomas Carney declared this to be only an accident. Drugs, nor alcohol played a factor in the one car MVA, but Carney did mention in inner circles some items that did not make it to the press. There were elements of the crash that he wasn't necessarily disturbed by, but he was certainly uneasy about.

There were no skid marks. Almost as if Nolan
Seeley didn't even try to stop or maneuver the
vehicle before crashing into the barn. Under that
assumption, Carney had officers investigate if the
brake lines had been tampered with. But they
weren't.

Word surfaced quickly three weeks later that Dean
Vermilya and Alexandra Maddox, Nolan Seeley's
girlfriend, had a moment of weakness at an
O'Sullivan banger in Salt Springs.

Eric Foster and Ellie Reynolds were playing some
tonsil hockey on the O'Sullivan's living room sofa
that night. Eric was a few beers in and his seal
quickly broke. He could feel some piss leak out of
him, but his hormones had other plans. It was a
classic heavyweight battle between the bladder
and a boner, who would pull through? Hint for the
ladies at home: the piss always wins, and it is
fucking bullshit.

Eric's hands were under Ellie's shirt. His fingertips
had just reached the smoothness of her bra. Silk or
satin, it didn't matter. He made it over the wire
that supported her bust. Ellie thrust her hips in. She
wanted—no—she needed the friction between her
legs. Ellie thrust back and forth on his bulge,
making Eric leak a little more.

The pressure finally broke the seal and he had to excuse himself. Eric made his way up the shag carpeted stairs. He could feel his feet indent into the rug slightly, but it never felt like a full stomp. He was light on his feet, trying to take as little time as possible during this piss so he could get back downstairs and give Ellie Reynolds a good Foster fucking.

Eric reached the bathroom. His toes pranced over a dark, but faded stain on the white carpeting in front of the bathroom entrance. The door was sealed shut and the light was on, but there was no time. He could feel more urine leak out of his tip. Ten more seconds and it would be leaking all over the stained carpet.

He clutched the doorknob and twisted. The door shot back like a cannon and in front of him was one of his best friends giving it to his other best friends' girlfriend. Dean had Alexandra bent over the bathroom sink. Her bare breasts bounced and her nipples tickled the edge of the bathroom sink. Dean flipped his long, brown hair back with one hand but clutched Alexandra's waist with the other. Dean turned in Eric's direction and smiled. His hair hung back in front of his face from the continuous forceful thrusts into Alexandra's vagina. Neither of them stopped.

Eric felt a slight caress on his back only seconds later. It was Ellie. She reached around him and unbuttoned his jeans. Her hands were smooth and she stroked him gently. She pressed her body in and forced him into the bathroom toward the toilet.

Dean and Alexandra still didn't stop. Actually, they did momentarily to switch positions. She sat on the bathroom sink now and faced Dean. Her legs wrapped around him, giving her a bit more leverage to control him.

Eric finally emptied the tank. He was amazed that he could piss under the circumstances. Eric was the kind of cat to get gun shy at the urinal line, but somehow he could drain the main vein with a hot chick rubbing his balls while standing next to his buddy nailing his friend's girlfriend.

He started to zip up. Ellie grabbed his hand and interrupted the act. She took over on the zipper and his pants. Ellie pulled them down around his knees and led him to turn around. Eric's manhood poked out in front of Ellie's face and just like Mortal Kombat, Ellie Reynolds finished him.

Once that story came out a month after the accident, it was pretty well understood that Nolan wrecked the car on purpose. A murder-suicide. His

friends were traitors and Nolan couldn't take it. It made sense.

Yet another story of a group of young folk dying within the confines of Bradford County, but this added a grisly, potent fuel to an overwhelming inferno. Brooke Beckett, Ryan Wilson, Kara Murphy, Kate Ford, Colby Baker and now these three. When the fuck would it stop?

Nobody knew, not even us and we were the ones responsible.

CHAPTER 47: Ice

With one smooth glide, ice scraped off of the windshield of mom's new Chevy Impala. I use the term "new" loosely. It was an '02. Used. About 90,000 miles on her, but it was a step up from that old piece of shit Regal that rivaled Arnie Cunningham's purchase from Roland LeBay.

Another stroke. This one sounding more harsh. Like a fart after you've eaten too much popcorn. I flicked the ice scraper, knocking it clean of the snow. It was probably one of the last times that I would have to do this for a while. It was mid-March, but we were always good for a good ass-fucking from the abominable snowman around St. Patty's Day.

Scraping the ice wasn't an issue. As a matter of fact, I kind of enjoyed it. Shit, I liked shoveling it too. But it all became rewarding once mom got hired at the dentist's office. Sure, she had her virtual freelance gigs of watching over people's houses and walking their dogs for the weekend but this was something. This was steady income. Not a half-assed donation from the town's elite.

Say Shell, can yuh take Ol' Red for a walk and do the dishes and mow the lawn for us this week'n? Might need yuh to do the gardenin' and fix the

upstairs bathroom sink, too. Whaddya say, Shell?
25 bucks and a thing a' Moon Pies sound good?

More ice cracked off the windshield. I was down to the wipers when a car horn started to wail.

"Almost ready, my nigga?" I hear from the street. Who else could it be?

"One second, sis." I yelled back.

The residual powder from an earlier shoveling packed under Sasha's tires as she pulled in the driveway behind the Impala. Her engine hummed and let off that sweet smell of exhaust that is only eminent when the car is working like hell to heat up. The aroma still existed in the garage. I placed the ice scraper next to the snow shovel and hustled up the stairs to the front (Damn it, mom. Sorry. *Side) door.

Mom was sitting at the kitchen table. Her usual perch. She didn't like the new job all that well, thus she milked the morning for all its worth.

Sometimes the excuse was, "just let me finish this glass of Pepsi" or "let me finish this article."

"Honey, did you see the Penguins won in the shootout last night?" she said as I entered the door. "That's five in a row. Bylsma has done great."

"Yes, mother. I watched it." I offered with snark, knowing what she was up to. It was 20 minutes to 8 and she hadn't even brushed her teeth yet. "Geno got the closer in the shoo—"

"How the hell did you watch it?" Her surprise wasn't angry, but curious. "I didn't get it up at Pete's."

"That's because we have Dish and they have— something else, I don't know. Are you leaving soon? Sash is here."

She took a long drag of Pepsi and clanked the glass down on the wooden table. Her eyes peered toward the microwave clock.

"Yeah…" She sighed, "I am in a second."

The chair creaked from under her as she stood up. It took her a moment to stand completely erect but she made it. Her hand supported her lower back, almost looking as if she were pressing it in.

"Have a good day, sweetie. Love you." She limped over and pecked my forehead. "Tell Sasha the same and that I love her too."

"Sure thing, Mama." I said. "Love you too."

CHAPTER 48: Sasha and Zack

Artificial heat was more than welcoming in Sasha's PT Cruiser, but the leather seat still obtained a chill. Untouched and dull was the passenger's seat, much like those first few minutes in Lequin. But surely, it would heat up. It always did.

My body adjusted as Sasha California Rolled through the stop sign from Fassett to Main Street. The Chatterbox was only a mere quarter of a mile away.

"So... Uhhh... Bruddah..." Sasha said as she reached toward the CD player under the dashboard. "You uhhh... talk to Jade recently?"

I looked toward with curiosity, but with almost as much suspicion. *Girls, man. She knows if I've talked to Jade... and she knows God damn well that I haven't... since December.*

"No. Not for a while." I said, doing my best to ignore the collateral on the floor from Temple University.

The PT started to merge unintentionally over the double lines in the middle of the road. Sasha regained attention and maneuvered back into the lane, but only after she turned to Track 4.

"Oh." Sasha returned nonchalantly. Her lower lip bulged as she cranked the volume knob up two notches.

Miya-hee! Miya-haw! Miya-hee! Miya-hawhaw!

"Why?" I asked. The red and blue cloth awning started to appear beyond the red light. An old beat up Chevy Silverado's turn signal started to flash through the fog ahead.

"Just askin'." Sasha replied. "We were kinda talkin' 'bout you the other day."

I perked in my seat. Posture turned from a 'C' to and 'I' in an instant. "Really?!" I asked excitedly but I eased quickly, "Wha... what about?" I stuttered.

"Fuck do you care?" Sasha sarcasm was as thick as the fog. Tires squealed when Sasha slammed on the brakes. They skid under us until her front bumper was two inches from the back of the Silverado that halted at the red light.

"Well?" Sasha continued with no recognition of her questionable driving sequence. "Why do you care?"

"I don't." It was a lie. "If you guys were talking about me I just want to know what the hell it was about."

"Nigga we were talkin' 'bout everyone don't fuckin' feel special." Sasha said. "'Bout graduation 'n shit."

"Oh…" my disappointment must have appeared in my tone.

"Psssttt…" Sasha snickered as the light turned green and we followed the Silverado onto Lycoming Street and into the Chatterbox Diner parking lot. Sasha shook her head, "I don't get you, bro. You've been like my fuckin' brother since we were 8 and I still don't fuckin' get you."

"The fuck are you being so real for?" I asked defensively.

Sasha flipped the visor down and batted her eyelashes with her index finger, "You fuckin' care about her man. You have for months."

I sat back in the seat and rubbed my hand over my face, "She was one of my best friends, Sash… and I lost her."

Sasha's finger lowered from her face and onto her lap. Her face slowly turned in my direction. One eyebrow furrowed like Dwayne "The Rock" Johnson and her glare could have burned a hole right through my forehead. Not a look of hatred or anger, but one that was so annoyed that it was amused. I admired it for a split second until she offered one word:

"Nigga..."

I chuckled. Actually, I guess it was a singular chuckle. Sasha wasn't an idiot. I did miss Jade as a friend but I had to face it. Out of all of us, even Kara, Ryan and Brooke. I was the least close to Jade up until Kate and I broke up. Was it *really* that? Was it *really* because *that* friendship ended? Or was it because she was the hot one? The hot one that was actually *single*?

Or was it more? To tell you the truth, I didn't know.

What I did know was that it ended because of Kate, but did I dare bring that up? We hadn't spoke about Lequin since December and other than the fact that a couple of kids from Troy died in a car accident 500 feet away from it, we had no reason to.

But I needed to be transparent with Sasha. She deserved it and quite frankly, Jade did too. I took the chance and told the truth, "That wasn't Kate that night, man."

Sasha bit her lower lip, "I know, bro." She said seriously, "I kn—"

"HOLY SHIT IT'S HALL AND OATES!" It was Butch Slocum, yelling from two parking spots over. Butch's brown Carhartt was unzipped, exposing the patented all-too short grease stained gray t-shirt. Alas, the old rusty Silverado must've been his. Probably bumming it from Curt Updegraff.

"Haulin' oates?" Sasha turned to me confused.

"Hall and Oates." I stated clearly. Enunciating consonants. "Black and white singers. Racially charged comment, but not racist. Actually, it's kind of funny."

"Ya still want to go in?" she asked.

"Hmm... eh why not?" I agreed. "Either way, if we don't I'll be fuckin' starving by lunch."

We got out, but remained 20 feet behind Butch. I could see Dave Wilson sitting at the bar through the window.

CHAPTER 49: Beckfist

Butch Slocum kicked the unlatched entrance to the diner lazily. The door swung back before he could get all the way in, but he barreled through like Jerome Bettis on the goalline. The smell of fryer oil and Marlboro Reds traveled back to Sasha and I. We entered shortly after Butch. The bar was full but we were able to find a vacant booth.

"David! Yah dirty cock sucker! Fuck you doing in here!" Butch hollered as the door deflected off of his girth. Patrons of the diner looked coldly in his direction until they realized who it was. His vulgarity was brushed off.

"Christ Almighty, Slocum. Pipe down." Dave replied. "They're people in here, yuh know."

"Well, what the fuck yuh doin' in here so early!" Butch's voice went from an 11 to an eight. "It ain't nine yet!"

"Had to take sis back to the hospital." Dave pointed toward the kitchen and his voice lowered. "'nother OD."

Butch's face sobered, "Oh. Sorry to hear that bub."

Dave seemed unphased by it. It was just old hat by now. It was an issue even back when Ryan was alive, but now Tracy's ship was sunk and it crashed quickly to rock bottom since December 8th.

"Kids!" Dave's voice elevated toward Sasha and I at a corner booth. "Gonne come in here and not say hi, eh?"

"We were comin'!" I shouted back. "Just wanted to put the order in first."

"Mmmmmuh huh…" Dave uttered sarcastically. "Grab yer stuff 'n come on over." He poked his thumb in the direction of the couple at the bar next to him, "The Vermilya's are headed out."

…Vermilya…

The couple sitting next to Dave were a pair of attractive older folk. Early 70's probably. The man fished in his pocket. Took out a set of keys and clanked them on the countertop. Immediately after, he dug into the same pocket and pulled out a thick brown wallet. He pinched two five dollar bills between his index and middle fingers like a cigarette. Only moving the knuckles, he flicked the bills onto the counter next to his keys.

"Ready, dear?" he asked as he retrieved the keys and crammed them back into his jeans pocket.

"Yessiree." his wife answered cheerfully.

"David." The man said while stroking his wavy brown hair behind his ear. "A pleasure, as always."

"Blessings to yuh, Russell." Dave paused from stirring Splenda into his coffee. He reached out his hand and shook the man's. "And Sharon, keep this man outta trouble."

"I'll do my best, Dave." She said in a sweet and soft voice. "We're thinkin' of ya."

"'preciate it." Dave said and he started to stir the coffee once again. The spoon clanked lightly against the inside of the mug and he continued lowly, "same to you, as always." The woman patted Dave's beefy forearm lightly, her husband squeezed Dave's shoulder by his trapezius passionately and then moved toward the exit.

I began walking toward the bar with Sasha directly behind me. We passed the couple. I offered a faux, but friendly smile and nod to them. They returned it.

"Who were they?" I asked as I mounted the stool next to Dave.

"Russ and Sheron Vermilya." Dave said before taking a sip of coffee. He flexed his cheeks. His jowls moved from side to side. The coffee was strong, so he added another packet of Splenda and one shot of half and half. "They're from out Troy way."

"Related to Dean?" Sasha asked as she got on the stool beside me.

"The boy that was in the accident last month?" Dave asked and Sasha confirmed. "Yeah... grandparents. You kids knew him?"

"...*of* him." I answered.

Dave took another sip. This one without a wince. The mug clanked back onto the counter, "Your mother and I used to hang out with his Uncle Denny. Good family. It's a damn shame."

"They takin' it okay?" I asked before I saw Tina Mitchell come out of the kitchen with a sausage, egg and cheese on a bagel. She placed the breakfast sandwich in front of me.

"As good as they can." Dave's eyes followed the sandwich down to the counter, but they returned to me once Tina returned to the kitchen. "Didn't at first. Got ugly with the situation. But really, I don't think any of them buy it. Really, I don't either."

"Buy what?" Sasha asked. Tina was on her way out of the kitchen with her bacon and egg on English muffin.

"You really think the Seeley kid did that?"

"I... I don't know..." I replied. But what I *did* know, or at least think was that it was the church. Or Lequin, at least. They probably made the plan at the Jackals game. *Say fellas, wanna head down through Route 6 to get home? Drop by that church in Lequin to see what the fuck is up?*

Hell yeah, Seeley. Let's do it.

"So apparently Nolan just bought the car. Mitsubishi Eclipse, I think." Dave said through another gulp of Maxwell House. "Doesn't matter. Guess where he got the car from."

"Don't know." Sasha's voice made its way through a chewed up hunk of sandwich.

"Don Fox Auto." Dave stated stoically. "Carney's brother-in-law's dealership. *HE* buys the car and runs it through a barn on purpose? Nah."

"But the cops would be the ones with the call on that, right?" I asked.

"Doesn't matter who has it, son." Dave finished the last gulp. "Carney's been the county coroner for 35 years. That's just how it is around here."

I disagreed. "Ehhhh, Tom's a good guy, Da—"

"Oh, he's always been damn good to me, Zack." Dave defensed. "But it really depends on who ya ask if he's a good fella or not. No way in hell *he's* the one covering that up though. Tommy wouldn't do that..."

I definitely agreed with that. Tom wasn't a villain. A little strange, sure. But aren't we all? Either way, I knew what I believed, but no one in their right mind would ever think the same. Not even Dave or Mrs. Bishop.

"You kids playin' hookie today, or what?" Dave's demeanor transitioned from gloom to jolly in a breath.

"Nah, we're about to get outta here. Ready Sash?" Sasha choked down her last bite of sandwich and nodded. She stood up and reached out to hug Dave.

"Where's mine?!" Butch Slocum yelled from the other side of Dave. Sasha said nothing in return but Butch took no offense. He was used to it. He wiped ketchup on the front of his grease laden t-shirt.

I grabbed my wallet out of my jeans pocket only to have Dave knock it out of my hand and on the floor.

"I got ya's." he said.

"Da—"

"Nope. I got it." Dave stated gently. "Won't be able to when you move to the 'burgh, so take it and shut up."

We both laughed. Sasha and I gathered our jackets and prepared to leave. But before we left I had to asked Dave, "Tracy okay?"

Dave nodded unconsciously before he answered, "Just wish they'd keep her there, son."

"Yeah, me too. See ya, Dave."

"Say hello to your mother for me."

"Always do."

Sasha and I moved toward the door. The wallpaper seemed to darken more and more every day. The smell of cigarette smoke eased when I opened the door.

"Hey Zack." It was Dave with one final question. "What're ya kids doing with weekend?"

Sasha and I exchanged a look. We hadn't discussed it.

"Not sure. Probably Williamsport or something on Saturday." I answered.

"Good."

Chapter 50: Still in Psych

2009 was the first year without block scheduling. Before, we would have five classes, each around an hour and 20 minutes, but that only lasted half the year. Then, we'd do the same in the second half of the school year, only with different classes that time.

But in '09, we had periods. Nine classes a day for 45 minutes. Depending on the class, they did change from the first half of that school year. But that wasn't the case with P6. Psych didn't stop. The love I had for my classmates was unparalleled but in December, I wished for the class to be over.

First there was Brooke. The girl that I met at Salt Springs Lanes, 14 years before. A girl that suffered a life of verbal abuse from her father, but never complained. It only made her kinder. I still think of the times when our family cat, Miss Olly would approach her when she entered my mother and I's apartment.

Olly would waddle with her short wheelbase and reach both of her paws to Brooke's leg. Brooke would pick her up, and not let her go until it was time to leave. Animals know a good person. Brooke was one of the best.

But for so long, all I could think of was the stub that I saw in the casket. A stub that was the result of an absolute butchering. A butchering that was believed to be of her own doing. But it wasn't.

Then Ryan. Not my oldest friend, but maybe my best at the time. We had everything in common. We were virtually the same exact person, but we only realized it four years before his death. I still think of those four years as the best ones of my entire life. We loved sports. Playing and watching. Both of us had our females, too. Kate and Kara. We loved them, nay, we were obsessed. Our feelings for them was so strong it was to a fault, but we bonded over it.

I learned a lot from my friendship with Ryan. However, the thing that I realized the most is that stereotypes with teenage boys are false. Hormones are raging, yes. Sex drive is through the roof, yes. But there are some goddamn good kids out there that find a girl that they are nuts about. Youth limits them, whether it be parents or school but it is love that they have. A fucking strong one. So strong that it is unique or strange. So strange that they will never have one quite like it again.

And finally, Kara. The girl that my best friend was obsessed with and really, I couldn't blame him. She was beautiful. Long brown hair and chocolate brown eyes. She was a stone cold fox, but even more so, she was strong. An entire life of beatdowns from her father, Jim. For almost 14 years, she wasn't even allowed to speak to a boy. For almost 14 years, she wasn't allowed to show any skin except for that on her face.

On the day that Jim hit her in the back of the head with a shoe horn for watching MTV's Real World, all of that changed.

Enough was enough. Fuck that guy. She lived her life, albeit in hiding. But she knew the chances she was taking. It was a small town. Everyone knows everything about everyone, remember? Jeans and t-shirt out of the front door then she changes to the sundress at school.

"You little fucking cunt!" He would say later that night, only to then beat her in the kidneys with the barstool, making his daughter piss blood for a week.

It didn't matter. She was strong. She'd keep doing it. Jim Murphy knew that there would be a day that he wouldn't be able to control her. Turns out, that day came long before he realized.

The nine people in that class were some of the best friends I ever had. Hell, they are THE best friends I have ever had. And in that first half of the school year, when that class dropped from nine to six. You better bet your fucking ass that I wanted that class over with. But by March 16th, through time and college preparation, things were going as well as possible.

Except with one classmate, in particular.

Even on the 100-somethingth day of the school year, we all sat in the same spots as Day 1. Sasha, Pears and I in the front. Gordy and Matt K. in the middle, but in the back, next to three consecutive vacant seats was Jade Davidson. The only one in the class that I hadn't talked to since our second trip to Lequin all the way back in December.

And for good reason.

Mrs. Bishop, once again, had *"What About Bob?"* playing on the projector and once again, we weren't paying the slightest attention. Nor was she, as she fed her Spider Solitaire fixation.

"Bro... I still can't believe Hollinshead caught Jimmy with chewin' tobacco." Pears said, recalling his experience of Jimmy Ellsworth getting busted in P4. "He really said it was gum. Then I'm here like, dude. It's black and leaking out your damn lip."

"Honestly, what's the problem if he's chewing?" Matt K. said. "It's not bothering anyone. It's not like he's smoking or something."

"Fuck that." Jade interjected.

"Ms. Davidson!"

"Sorry, Mrs. B." Jade replied. "It's disgusting. He *literally* has a Mountain Dew bottle in his backpack that he spits in. It's fu--... It's freaking gross."

"I agree." I said, not even realizing who I openly said that I agreed with. It was my first verbal interaction or reply to her in over three months.

She acknowledged my response. Her eyes shot toward me with content, but the remainer of the class looked surprised. Matt actually looked anxious, as if he were expecting her to come unglued.

But she didn't. "Yeah, it's disgusting. Like, why even do it?" She said in my direction.

"Yeah, obviously, I never saw the appeal." I replied.

The rest of the class was silent, and it remained that way until the bell. Whether it was from shock, or awkwardness, no one spoke. That is until I heard a voice come from behind me as I exited Mrs. Bishop's classroom.

"Hey, umm..." I heard a soft voice, "Zack."

It was Jade.

I turned around slowly with caution. "Hey." I replied and let her catch up to me. I was three feet into the hallway by that time.

She was finally at my side. It was time for a conversation three months in the making.

"What, uhh, are you doing later?" she asked.

"Baseball practice tonight..." I said disappointedly, "But that's not until 6. We're in the gym tonight. Weather sucks and coach wants us to at least take some BP in the cage."

"Oh..." she said. We were approaching my locker, I started to veer off toward it but she remained beside me. "Umm... I just want to talk to you about something."

"Sure what's up?"

"Not here." She demanded. "Meet me at my locker at the end of the day. Walk me to my car."

"Done." I replied. "See ya then."

Jade responded with a short, "Yep."

Chapter 51: Much Less Animated Dialogue

Students flooded the hallways in unison with the final bell of the school day on March 16th. They flowed a bit more cantankerously than usual. Bellicosity from the Monday jaunt was usual, but these days had a bit more fervor with the dog days of the school year present.

My stroll at the end of the day was anxious, but I calmed when I saw Jade's smile as I approached her locker by Mr. Bowman's Chemistry Lab.

"Hey." She said when I reached her. My reply was generic. I returned a "Hey."

Small talk ensued as we headed down the steps and toward the main hallway of the first floor. It was a barren hallway, despite it only being three minutes after the bell. Salt Springs's faithful were the fuck out of dodge.

"So, Zack…" she said wistfully, halting her speech. She looked as though she was trying to find the words. One eye scrunched as if she were thinking about what to say, or how to say what was coming next.

She stroked her blonde hair behind her ear, "You know that jersey that you have… the Polamalu one?" she asked.

"Yeah...?" I asked hesitantly.

"That was from me."

I was shocked. The authentic Troy Polamalu jersey that I wore for every playoff game all the way to the Superbowl was from Jade. I couldn't believe that she spent 125 on that motherfucker.

I stopped dead in my tracks, "What?" I asked. "Why?"

"I got it on your mom's birthday. When we got the candle." She said sadly. "Even with everything that happened, I had to give it to you."

"Well... thank you. " I said, still surprised. "You didn't have to though. Those things aren't cheap."

"Ehh..." she said and smiled in my direction. Her blue eyes weren't dull, but didn't glisten like they did in the pulpit that night in December. "I worked my magic."

I laughed, "of course you did." My head turned toward her. Her smile was still there, but she looked down at the floor bashfully. "Why'd you buy it?" I asked.

We reached the main lobby and her walk stopped abruptly. She took a large deep breath in and looked up at me, looking like she was ready to recite a novella of animosity.

But she didn't. Jade regained composure and we walked out of the door. Our conversation continued outside on the path to the parking lot.

"Well?" I asked, hunching my shoulders to protect the back of my neck from the freezing rain. "Why'd you buy it, Jade?"

"Come on, Zack." She answered, continuing to look forward. "Don't be fucking dumb."

We had reached the parking lot. Rain started to spit harder, but still nothing more than a light drizzle. Jade's hair was noticeably damp, and the shoulders of her North Face jacket were covered with condensation.

"What do you me--?"

"Zack, I was into you." She interrupted sternly. "And I thought something was there. But, you know, clearly there wasn't."

Oh, yes. The proverbial "elephant in the room" has been addressed. Kate, or whatever it was in the church, seemed like a dream by this point. And truly, making out with Jade in the pulpit did too. However, one thing that I knew was Jade was really there that night. Kate wasn't.

"Jade..." I said sincerely. "That wasn't Kate."

"I know." She admitted. "At least I do now. Then, I didn't. But I do now."

We stared at each other blankly momentarily through the rain. Rain drops perched on her long, dark eyelashes. Her arms folded under her bust but it wasn't in disgust. She was disappointed, but also clearly freezing her ass off.

"And Jade, there was something." I assured her. "I was in to you too. Honestly, I probably still am. That night is all I've thought about for the last three months. Not just what we did, you know? But how I know we both felt after."

"Well," she offered a cocked smile and continued, "I'm glad you can admit you fucked up."

I returned a chuckle.

"But it doesn't really matter anymore." She said. The rain started to pick up, "Probably shouldn't have mattered that much at the time, either."

I looked down and nodded.

"Zack, I'm moving to Laramie a week after graduation." She proclaimed.

My head straightened in disbelief. I knew she was headed to the University of Wyoming, but I didn't expect her to leave in less than three months.

"Wha—… Why?"

"If I told you it was because I'm taking courses in the summer, would you believe me?" she asked.

I knew Jade too well. Courses in the summer? Fuck no.

"Not a chance, Davidson." I smiled and she returned one.

But she became serious a second after. Her hands reached up and touched my forearms. She stroked them gently and a tear rolled down her cheek. I wiped it for her. Her skin was incredibly smooth, just like I remembered it.

Another tear rolled. This time down the other cheek as she said, "Zack, I have to get out."

Tears continued, but her voice remained unphased. "We all have to get out. As soon as possible, Zack. Because how long will it be before another one of us go, huh? How long?"

"Jade..." I said calmly, "We're done. We aren't going back. It can't get us."

"What about Brooke?" Her voice started to flutter. "That wasn't at the church, Zack. It wasn't."

"No, but it was the same nigh—"

"We were out of there for two fucking months and it got Kara and Ryan, Zack." She said, "Two fucking months."

I said nothing. I just looked into her beautiful blue eyes blankly. She was right.

"Nolan, Eric and Dean..." she said again. "Them too."

"Jade, that was just a car accide—"

"How do you know that, Zack?" her question didn't come across rude, but she was certainly upset and maybe a touch frustrated. "How do you know it was *just* a car accident? They wrecked through that goddamn barn! Right next to the fucking church!"

"I...I don't know, Ja—"

"People our age die here *all the time, Zack.*" Her voice now reflected the tears fully, "It's like this place is fucking cursed or something."

She continued, "Dylan Liberati. Jared Hunt. *Fucking Ashley O'Donnell! Car accidents...* Kelly Kitchen fucking drowned! What if they are all because of that fucking place? It's a curse, Zack... or something."

I continued my blank stare into her eyes.

"Please..." she begged. "See if you can move in with your aunt or something before you start at Duquesne. *Get. Out. Of. Here.* I love you too much to lose you. I love all of you guys too much to lose you. I can't lose another."

"Jade, you won't." I promised. "It's over."

"I hope so, Zack..." her cry was slowing. "I'm sorry I came at you like this."

I wrapped my arms around her and said, "Don't be sorry, Jade. I hear you. Everything is going to be okay."

Her head released from my chest and she looked up at me, "Okay..."

"Friends again?" I said and smiled down to her.

"Of course." She answered.

Our embrace broke, and we both went home.

Chapter 52: The Next Week

The following Monday, March 23rd marked game one of our 2009 high school baseball campaign. It was the only sport that I played my senior year and I was content with it. We were set to be a decent team, even without our starting shortstop.

That season we had an embroidered '23' on the left side of our hats in generic lettering to honor the life and baseball career of our own, Ryan Wilson.

During the pregame festivities of the opener, both us and the members of the Towanda Knights baseball squad lined up on each baseline for a moment of silence.

Our baseline was anything but silent though. Sobbing was all too obvious. Dave Ramsey's sob heaved through the silence, so much that my mother and my friends heard it in the stands.

For the first time in five years, I would be playing in a baseball game without Ryan to the left of me. I knew it wouldn't be easy, but I had no idea that it would be like this.

We returned to the dugout to acquire our gloves and to pop last minute sunflower seeds before we took the field in the top of the 1st. Dave Ramsey was taking a last minute grope of the rosin bag when I clapped him on the back, "Let's fuck 'em up, Ram."

His chewing gum snapped, "Hell yeah, Bristol. Let's fucking go."

We jogged out of the dugout together in unison, leaping over the baseline chalk. Ramsey slowed to a walk when he reached the mound and halted on the rubber. He bent over, kissed his middle and forefinger, and tapped the rubber plate that he would be dealing from for the next seven innings.

I continued toward third base, glancing over to the sophomore Lincoln Montgomery who now occupied shortstop. He fielded a two-hop toss from our first baseman Dominic Vermetti, and returned the ball with a nice sidearm chuck.

I stared him down, pounded my chest once with a closed fist and he returned the gesture.

Game fucking time.

Dave Ramsey was dealing. Nine up, nine down over the first three innings and he made it easy on his defense too. Only three Knights found contact in the early going. Two fly balls to left and I was able to field an easy ground ball for the third out to end the top of the third inning.

Dave Ramsey led off the bottom half of the third inning and we were certainly hopeful. He was pitching well and we had the middle of the order due up. The three, four and five hitters in the lineup. My spot in the order was, "in the hole" or, for the non-baseball people, I was due up third in the bottom of the third inning.

That's how it is in baseball. Your best hitter is normally third in the lineup, and that was the case with us, Ramsey wasn't just our best hitter, but he was our best player in general, big Dom Vermetti was the slugging clean-up hitter and then there was I, the five-hole hitter who hit for average and an impressive one RBI per contest.

Ramsey took some warm-up cuts in the on-deck circle between innings while Mason Vanderpool prepared on the mound for the bottom of the third. The front of his green button down jersey was smeared with diamond dirt tan and the cursive "Spartans" font was hardly legible from the mud.

The umpire tapped the catcher's shoulder.

"Coming down!" The catcher yelled, indicating the pitcher's final warmup pitch of the inning.

Dave turned his back to us from outside the tall, chain-link fence that separated our dugout from

the field and approached the batter's box. The back
of his jersey showed a crisp and clean '12' and
spotless white baseball pants. He tapped the bat to
hit cleats, knocking caked mud from the metal
spikes and took his pre-stance cadence.

Mason Vanderpool delivered a fastball right down
Broadway. Ramsey didn't even flinch from his open
batting stance. He was taking the first pitch all the
way.

"Strike one!"

Dave took a step out of the box and took a mock
swing.

"Come on, Ram!" I yelled but my voice trailed as I
turned my attention to the parking lot. A white
Dodge Ram pickup was pulling into the outfield
parking area.

It's chrome grill sparkled from the mist the flew
through the atmosphere. Tires protruded on the
sides from the lift kit. The outer end on each tire
was moist from the light rain, but the inner half
was dry.

It stopped in an open spot just beyond the
centerfield fence.

Dave entered the box to face the second pitch of
the at-bat. Again, he would hold off on a swing and
for good reason. Vanderpool's curveball broke
about three feet too early and bounced twice
before the catcher could even corral it.

"Ball! 1 and 1!"

"Good eye, Ram!" I said, still with focus on the
white pickup truck in center. It bothered me. On
the day we recognized the life and baseball career
of Ryan Wilson, a carbon copy of his vehicle arrives
in the parking lot. But then again, how many
people in Salt Springs drove a Dodge Ram? Luke
Larson did. He drove a lot of things, actually.
Particularly Sara O'Sullivan in the aforementioned
vehicle's bed.

Jesus Christ, Dave Wilson did too. And so did Mark
Davidson.

Ryan Wilson wasn't the only motherfucker to ever
hear of a Dodge Ram.

But he was the only one that had a white one. On a
lift kit, at that.

Vanderpool delivered another pitch. This one with
little movement. Fastball all the way but Dave was
just a little too early on it. He made contact near

the hands and roped it down the third base line but in foul territory.

"Foul! One and two!"

I said nothing. My focus was solely on the pickup. I heard, "Good cut, kid!" in the distance, presumably a teammate complimenting Dave's swing.

The truck's driver's side door opened. From under the door, I could see two sneakers plant into the mud. Mud splashed all the way up to the knees of the driver's blue jeans, but the rest of the body was barren of filth as I could tell when the driver closed the door. He walked in the direction of left field.

Dave waited on the next offering, and made contact with the off speed pitch. Roping a hard single down the third baseline.

If it weren't for a fence in left (and, of course, the left fielder cutting off the ball's travel), the ball would have rolled right into the feet the tall and skinny driver of the lifted Dodge Ram who was now about 20 feet from the left field foul pole.

Dave Ramsey took a hard turn at first but held up. He returned to first base and pounded his chest toward the dugout. As we say in sports journalism, we had "a turkey on the table" for Dom Vermetti.

Dom had the natural build of a slugger. Had a neck as thick as a 12-point buck's. His forearms were at least 16 inches in diameter and had just a slight gut. But, if you were to punch that gut, you'd better be expecting some broken knuckles.

Left-handed batter, his back turned to us, exposing the large number 48 on his back.

However, the driver of the pickup *was* now facing us. He turned the curve of the left field fence and walked toward the Knights' dugout on the third baseline.

The driver donned a ball cap under a pulled-up hood of his forest green Salt Springs Spartans hoodie, but I couldn't make out a face. He looked as if he was staring down toward the ground for the duration of the trek. Not that I could have seen his face anyways from the distance, but I figured I would try. My attention remained on him as I entered the on-deck circle. I took a swing and he kept walking. Immediately after my warm-up cut, I adjusted my batting gloves, but I still couldn't see his face.

Dom Vermetti had the most open stance on our entire team. His back leg grazed the white chalk on the front of the box and his front foot's heel grazed the back of the box.

He took up the entire area, making him look even larger than he was.

Dom was first-pitch swinging and roped a single to right field. As he trotted down the first baseline, the driver halted and leaned up on the fence right next to third base. His elbows rested on the chain-link fence, still not acknowledging the game.

Two on, no outs and I was due up. I walked to the plate and took my spot in the batter's box. My pre-pitch cadence was simple. I took the end of the bat, tapped in directly in the middle of home plate, took one pull on my crotch, twirled the bat in an even circle that was perpendicular to the ground and then finally settled with the bat over my right shoulder, parallel with the Earth's surface.

I was aggressive at the plate and took a giant swing at the first-pitch fastball, missing by a mile.

"Oh and one!" the umpire yelled and I took a step out of the batter's box for a practice swing. But during that time I looked toward the spectator by third base. For the first time, he wasn't looking down. He was looking directly at me, but the ball cap over his pulled-up hood made it impossible to see his face. It was eerie, like in a horror movie when you can see the outline of a person in the dark, but then they take a step forward into the light.

I got back in the box for the second pitch of the at-bat, only this time, I didn't miss. Vanderpool's fastball got the inner half of the strike zone. I pulled in my hands and made contact with the barrel. The ball popped off my bat forcefully. It was a no-doubter. No sprint was needed out of the box, that son-of-a-bitch was out of here.

"Fuck yeah, Zack!" I heard from the stands on the first baseline. I knew the voice, it was Pears. He was standing on top of his seat.

"Let's go, baby!" I heard from the other ear. That cheer was out of the mouth of Dave Ramsey, as he began his trot toward home.

My eyes continued to follow the ball, slicing through the atmosphere and into the parking lot. It struck the concrete and hopped into the side of a white Ford Taurus. There was aloud thud, and I saw the field umpire twirling his finger above his head.

Baseball's universal sign for "homerun."

I rounded first base, hearing even more of a roar from the Spartan faithful. Screams and the old, "BRIST-OLE! BRIST-OLE!" chant filled the air. Some voices I could recognize, like my mother and the rest of my psychology class, but there were many that I didn't.

It felt good. And that was welcoming. Good feelings weren't all that common anymore.

I heard clapping as well. Almost everyone in attendance was doing so, except those wearing black and orange Towanda garb.

In my peripheral, I saw Ramsey cross home. My head started to turn toward him, but it was interrupted when my line of sight crossed the driver of the pickup.

He was clapping in his Salt Springs garb. When I rounded second base, I could see the brim of his flat bill. It blended in perfectly with the forest green hoodie.

As I approached him, his clapping slowed, and his head started to rise.

"Nice rope, Bristol." the Towanda shortstop said but I didn't hear at the time. My focus was on the driver.

I could see his chin, but something was off about it. It looked marked. With each step I could see more of his face.

Scars streaked with black polluted his chin and mouth. His lower lip was busted open but not bleeding. Like when you leave a hot dog on the grill too long.

I was three steps away from third and he looked up. Directly into my eyes.

It was Ryan.

His left eye drooped to his cheek, even with his imploded nostrils. Charred skin hung on the left side of his face. Black and crusty. The other side was scarred, looking Freddy Krugeresque.

"Ryan?" I said.

His face perked, despite the mutilation. The hood pulled backward slightly, exposing what I feared most.

That god damn hat. Fabric frayed on the bill.

He smiled, showing broken teeth and eroded gums. A foul, but familiar odor struck me as soon as my foot touched third base. Sulphur.

"Come back." He hissed. "Fucking come back, Zack! EVERY FUCKING ONE OF YOU!"

I wasn't surprised, saddened, or angry. Deep down, I knew who (or what) the driver was the whole time. I rounded third normally and said, "good bye" as I passed him.

I met Dave Ramsey and Dom Vermetti at the plate. We exchanged fist bumps, along with as ass slap from Ramsey. Teammates congratulated me when I got in the dugout. The environment was electric and the celebration was rowdy. Someone poured a cup of water on my head. It trickled down my neck and under my jersey in freezing cold streams. In May, I'd welcome it. But the climate in the mountains of northeast, PA, in late March. No, thanks.

The celebration eased after what felt like an hour, but meanwhile it was only about 30 seconds. When I returned to my spot on the bench and watched the 6-hole hitter, Kyle Reynolds enter the box, Ryan was gone. The truck was too.

An hour later, we finished off Towanda by a final score of 8-4.

Chapter 53: A Short Explanation

I didn't tell the crew about what happened. Hell, I didn't tell a goddamn soul. Because, honestly, why would I? It would have only brought more hostility, but most of all, more disappointment.

"Guys, I saw Ryan." I would have said, presumably at the bowling alley or in Psychology class. "He was at the baseball game against Towanda, but it wasn't *really* him. If you know what I mean..."

I would have told him about the chars and scars. I would have told them about the hat and his eyes. And then I would have finished this outrageous story by telling them about his voice and the foul stench that released from his gaping mouth.

We'd all feel terrible, but there would also be a feeling of anger. Potentially a feeling of revenge, as well. Lequin was a predator on the hunt for its prey. It was a game of cat and mouse. They wanted us back, and this was their stunt to lure us in.

But that was just me. Who knows how the rest would feel. Especially since they were at the game, too.

They didn't say anything about the truck after the game, nor did they say anything the next day.

Could it be possible that the whole thing was my imagination?

Sure. Absolutely it could have been. At least, that is what I thought at the time. It was a rainy and cold afternoon, my seasonal depression was rearing its ugly head the entire day. Changing of seasons does that and from winter to spring in northeast, Pennsylvania, it hits hard.

Add that to the obvious. It was the day that we were celebrating the life and baseball career of my best friend, Ryan Wilson. Funny how that is always said. *Celebrating the life of...*

No, you are celebrating 'what was' the life of. They're gone, and will never come back. There is only one feeling in the world that is worse than that realization.

That one feeling is when you know they aren't coming back, and it is *your* fault.

Going into that church was a mistake and for whatever reason, the Lequin Church wanted us finished. But why?

We weren't the only ones to go in. Ellsworth's crew had gone in. Dunlap and all of his fellow junkies went in. Fuck, Hank Stonehammer opened it up for the public a few years ago. They had *fucking* church services.

But for whatever reason, they wanted us. And they were picking us apart, one by one.

It is our fault that Ryan, Kara and Brooke passed. No matter what anyone says, even to this day, no one can tell me any different.

But I started to doubt that day and started to blame the guilt. We all donned the '23' decals on the side of our caps and held a long moment of silence for our fallen friend.

It was on my mind. Ryan was on my mind. The entire goddamn situation with the church was on my mind. Why would Lequin make a statement three months after our last visit?

Because they didn't. It wasn't real.

Or, at least, that's what I thought.

Chapter 54: Sasha and Marco

Sasha gripped Marco's shoulders. Her nails dug into skin drawing blood. Marco didn't care, his thrusts were strong and he could feel her ass jiggle in his hands as she rode him.

She leaned over and kissed him. Her tongue intertwined with his. One of Marco's hands made its way to her chest and he ran his thumb over her nipple.

"You fuckin' like that?" Sasha asked, riding him with more vigor now. Marco spanked her and she let out a moan. "You like it rough, don't ya?" His thrusts started to take over. Both of his hands were back on her ass and he squeezed.

"Oh, fuck me!" Sasha moaned, "Harder, Marco." He obliged. He took over from underneath her, their skin slapped together in harmony.

Her boobs bounced in his face and he took a nibble of her left tit, still thrusting hard. "Harder! Harder! Fuck me harder!" Sasha screamed.

His grip tightened on her and he released her nipple. Marco's thrusts were at his hardest now, but not as fast as they were. He was about to lose it.

"Oh baby!" Sasha said, blood caked under her fingernails from Marco's broken skin. She could see his face start to grimace. It wasn't a mystery of what was soon to come... literally.

Sasha hopped off of him. She still wanted some, though. Her fingers were a decent enough substitution for Marco's cock. She ran them through and over her. With her other hand, she stroked Marco. His veins protruded, and his head was firm.

He did a damn good job of fighting it off, until Sasha wrapped her lips around him. After three stokes, he gave her a mouthful.

She didn't mind, she liked Marco. A lot. But at only 18 to his early 20's, she knew what it was. They were casual. Not even that. They were fuck-buddies. There were feelings, yes. At the end of the day, though, she knew that in four months, when she headed to Temple University, the fucking would cease.

But for tonight, Bill and Bev thought their adopted daughter was hanging out with Jade Davidson. After all, when midnight hit on April 4th, her best friend, Jade would be 18. Instead, Sasha was emptying out Marco Martucci's nuts.

"Ahhhh, fuck!" Marco sighed after his final pump. Sasha came up and rested her head on his chest. "That was fucking wonderful."

"Not bad." Sasha said sarcastically. Her tone wasn't even generically sarcastic. She just had her world rocked. Actually, halfway through she thought she'd have to tap out. He was too good. Easily the best she's ever had.

Hell of a lot better than Jimmy Ellsworth

"Fucked up ya shoulders a bit." Sasha came back to reality as she was dabbing at the wounds that she created with her fingers, "Sorry 'bout that."

Marco replied, "Sash, I came in your mouth. I should be sorry."

"Don't fuckin' bother me none." She answered.

"You're a fucking gem, Sasha." Marco said tiredly. She could see his eyes start to flutter and not the way they were a few minutes prior. His eyes quickly shut and a faint snore came out of his mouth. It was about 11:30 p.m. and it was his day to work both the lunch and dinner shifts. Whatever energy he had left, he put it into fucking the hell out of Sasha. He had none left over.

Sasha wasn't about the cuddling bullshit. When she heard him cast off to sleep, she rolled over to the open side of the bed.

She laid in bed, thinking about her post-graduation plans. There was no contemplation about what she was going to do, but there was about how she would reveal it.

Sasha played it over and over in her head. *I'll tell each separately. Zack on our way to school... Jade on our way to Williamsport or something... Matt... hmmm...*

There wasn't a good way to tell them, because she couldn't even believe it herself. 13 years ago, Sasha's parents were murdered right in front of her. Somehow, through three different living situations, she ended up here, in Salt Springs, Pennsylvania. Somehow, through it all, she became a NCAA Division 1-caliber basketball player at a high school that would only graduate 60 students.

She couldn't believe it. Actually, she didn't believe it. There was no way that she, Sasha Jacobs, could do it. Even though she did. Sasha was doing something that was nearly impossible.

The papers were signed. She was heading to Temple to play basketball.

It made sense, but at the same time it didn't. She rolled over, with her face looking off of the bed and through the window of Marco Martucci's Troy Street apartment, still thinking about the next four years of her life. Only four more years of playing the sports she loved so much and then she'd head to the police academy. It sounded so simple, but she knew it wasn't.

Sasha's first family, her biological family, was broken up and under different circumstances, it was happening again. And again, there was nothing she could do about it.

"They were all so nice..." Sasha thought back on her first day at Salt Springs Elementary. Sasha never saw a pine tree before that day. It was like she was on another planet, but a very good smelling one. She entered the door and told the secretary who she was. Miss Walters looked at her strangely, as if she were surprised. It took Sasha a long time before she realized why Miss Walters had that look on her face on her first day.

She theory was confirmed in January of her senior year, when she found out that she was going to be the first ever African American alumna of Salt Springs High School.

All students were accounted for in the lobby, they headed to class. The classroom was filled with the aroma of eraser shavings and packed lunches. An abundance of bologna and cheese sandwich packed in their respective bags in each of the students' cubbies.

Mr. Vannoy divided them in groups. She was scared. It was her first interaction with classmates at this new school where nobody looked like her. Nobody talked like her. And she was certain that nobody felt like her.

"Yellow is my favorite color." One of the boys in her group asked her and pointed at her shirt. Sasha was so nervous that she forgot what she was even wearing that day until she looked down. Curious George t-shirt and a pair of jeans.

"I like it too." She replied to the boy. His glasses were thick and he was missing one of his two front teeth. He said back to her, "I'm Zack. What's your name?"

"Sasha." She responded and pointed to his (or I guess it would be to *my* shirt), "I like the Steelers too."

"Booo..." the husky boy to 'Zack's' left said. "Go Eagles!" he continued as he pumped both fists above his head. His shirt raised too and some of his belly peeked out from underneath.

"Matt! Gosh! Your belly's showing!" the boy with the mullet said and he tugged at the bottom of the husky boy's shirt to conceal the gut. The boy with the hair quit tugging once the husky one's hands lowered, "I'm Matt." The husky one said, "He's Gordy."

A few days later, some pretty girls introduced themselves to her. They were the same ones that made her first group of friends googly-eyed. Their names were Jade and Kara. The three of them were best friends within a matter of minutes after they bonded over how cute Dave Ramsey was.

Brooke Beckett came into her life in fourth grade when they sat next to each other in Mrs. Leonard's class. That class rearranged seats with a month left in the school year, and then her neighbor became Ryan Wilson. At age 10, it's tough for boys and girls to make friends sometimes, but that wasn't the case with them. Ryan was wearing a Tim Duncan San Antonio Spurs jersey they day they met and from there it was a breeze. He never talked to a girl that knew that much about sports before.

That classroom was laid out with three rows of five desks. Ryan's seat was to Sasha's left but tonight, Marco Martucci was on her left.

She looked over at him, admiring his tan, unblemished skin. His face featured a perfectly groomed beard that was just long enough to tickle her when intimate. The blanket only covered his bottom half. Sasha panned him his naked chest. Defined, but not bulky. A small patch of jet-black hair grew on his sternum. It nestled in the crease of his pecs.

His stomach was bare, making his abs look even more distinguished. She could see an outline of his obliques. One of her favorite tricks was to trace the outlines of his defined body with her tongue on her way down. She liked it, he loved it.

Under the sheets she could see his bulge. She wanted it again and was sure that he could deliver. Her hand started to reach toward it.

Until she heard a crash come from the kitchen.

She took a hollow breath in, upset that his god damn cat killed the moment. Sasha was more of a dog person, but Ms. Olly Bristol was different. Fucking Jimbo Martucci, though. Fuck that cat.

Her hands ran through her hair and grabbed the pillow behind her. She looked back over at Marco, the broken glass in the kitchen didn't wake him. He still lay there, tan and peaceful. But she was about set to interrupt that. His bulge looked even more desirable then before.

Sasha moved her hand toward him again, and she leaned in to kiss his neck.

But there was Jimbo curled up in slumber on the other side of his head.

She looked through the open bedroom door casing with surprise, but even more than that, she looked with caution. *Did we leave the light on?*

Sasha couldn't remember. It got hot quickly as soon as they entered his apartment. But either way, she knew they hadn't gone into the kitchen and it's light was shining brightly from down the hall.

There was no way Jimbo could have knocked over a glass on the kitchen counter and hopped into bed in that amount of time. *Would have heard him, the fat fuck.*

Something else knocked onto the floor, but this didn't shatter. It was a thud. Marco and Jimbo remained unphased.

Sasha threw her legs over the side of the bed and her feet planted on the floor. She put on the first shirt she found and given its size, it was undoubtedly Marco's. It hung to the middle of her naked thighs so there was no need to look for underwear, let alone pants.

She entered the hallway, feeling the cold linoleum underneath her toes. Her feet pried off of the material, sounding sticky. Sasha was now passed the apartment's front door, close enough to the kitchen to see the green glass shards on the floor by the counter.

An aroma came from the kitchen's opening that was only three feet away now. Marco wasn't the best housekeeper, but what man in his mid-20's is? This was unacceptable though, she couldn't believe that he would let eggs rot to the point of stinking his entire kitchen.

When she entered the kitchen she saw a man sitting at the kitchen table. His head rested on the wooden surface.

"Hello?" she took a step forward. Blood soaked the wooden table and the man laid face down in a pool of it.

She ran toward him "Oh my fucking God are you oka—" the back of his head was bashed in. Chunks of pale flesh littered the floor around him, accompanied by curly black hair. The man was babbling and gurgling on his own blood. Sasha reached the table.

It was her father.

A woman ran through the kitchen door. "Sam!" the woman cried. "*Saaaaaaaaaa—*". A gunshot went off and she collapsed onto the kitchen floor. Her blood shot from a wound on the back of her head. Sasha ran to help her. She slipped on the blood soaked floor and fell on her ass.

Sasha crawled toward the woman, blood painted her hands and knees. The woman started to seize on the floor, blood continued to gush out of the back of her head. Her face moved toward Sasha, but Sasha wasn't looking.

Sasha was staring through the kitchen entrance and into the hallway. A Rugrats backpack hung on the coat hook.

"Sa—" she heard the woman gurgle, "Sa—". Sasha's neck craned slowly toward the woman, by the time Sasha's attention turned to her, the woman's eyes went dull. It was the first time that she saw the woman's face clearly.

It was her mother.

Another crack came from the table and Sasha turned around. More blood flew across the room, some of it splattered all over Sasha's shirt.

She followed the streaks of blood through the atmosphere. When she looked down, she saw Angelica Pickles screen-printed on her t-shirt.

"What would they think?" she heard a husky voice ask. Sasha looked up, and next to the man at the table was a police officer holding a bloody nightstick. More of her father's head was missing at the kitchen table and he laid face down in even more blood.

"Sasha?" the officer asked, "Well?" His face was one that she recognized. Silver streaks of gray hair loomed on his temples. His skin was pale, so much that it looked clear.

She continued to stare blankly at him in disbelief.

"Sasha?" he asked. "Yoo-hoo!" he continued, snapping his fingers in front of her face. "You fucking there!?!"

Her chest puffed out and she nodded her head. Sasha's lips puckered with anger and a tear rolled out of her eye.

"Answer the fucking question." The police officer said. "What. Would. They. Think?"

"Of what?" Sasha hissed.

"Of your mouthful of cum." The officer sneered. He pointed the nightstick to both of her parents and said, "How would they feel that their daughter is nothing but a little fucking whore!"

Sasha said nothing, but her lower lip started to quiver. More tears welled in her eyes until they gave in and poured down her cheeks.

"You really are a whore, aren't you?" he taunted. "And... you know it!"

"No..." Sasha uttered. "I'm not..."

"Really?" he asked sarcastically and he pointed the nightstick to her parents again, "They'd disagree. First there was Duncan Lee. Then there was Harper Lewis... and then his brother Hayden, of course. Really went through that family."

She continued her stare.

"Nolan Seeley. You're favorite... Jimmy Ellsworth. You sucked off Kyle Reynolds nice and then there's that one." He turned his nightstick toward the bedroom.
Sasha didn't address the man's list of Sasha's lays. Instead she asked, "What are you doing?"

"What?" he asked. "I'm just showing you who you really are, you stupid *nigger!*"

"Why?" Sasha started to cry. "Why?"

"Because you need to come back."

Her crying halted and she stared into his black eyes. That's where she knew that face. The scar on her forehead started to throb.

"No. We don't."

Yes. You do." He replied. "All of you.

"No." Sasha's voice started to raise.

"Yes!"

NO!" She screamed.

"COME BACK!" the officer yelled.

"NOOOOO!!!!"

Marco ran in urgently and wrapped his arms around her. Sasha turned and smothered her head into his bare shoulder. She heaved in his arms from sobbing.

"Sasha, what is it?" he asked calmly. "What happened?"

"I—, I—, It's here..." she bawled.

"What's here?" he asked.

Sasha released her head from his skin. There was nothing. No parents, no police officer. The kitchen table was free of blood and so was the floor. She was no longer wearing a t-shirt with Angelica Pickles on it and there was no backpack on the hook in the hallway. It was a dream. A nightmare. A goddamn night terror.

That's what she thought until she saw what brought her into the kitchen in the first place.

Green shards of glass still littered the floor by the kitchen counter.

Chapter 55: Jade's Birthday

On Saturday, April 4th, 2009, Jade Davidson became an adult. Well, an adult in the eyes of the law. For what she had been though in her short time on Earth thus far, she was an adult. Jade was grown beyond her years. Little did we know, we were too.

As each day passed during our senior year, Jade changed. Back in September, Jade would encourage an absolute fiesta at the O'Sullivan's *on* her 18th birthday. Bottles on bottles. Attention on attention. Even though she's always been a genuinely good person, she still would have wanted that. And she would have gotten it, because she was Jade *fucking* Davidson.

But in April? No, she didn't want that on her birthday. She wanted something relaxed and that is exactly what she got.

Jade tagged along to Williamsport in the afternoon with Ellie Reynolds, Sara O'Sullivan and Alexandra Maddox. When it came time for the weekly O'Sullivan banger, Jade felt tired. But, "that's okay!" Sara said. "Better rest up before three weeks from now..." she said tantalizingly.

"What's in three weeks?" Jade asked, ignoring Sara's blatant disregard for grammar.

"My and your birthday parties!" Sara replied in her cliché preppy teenage girl voice. "It's going to be wild!"

"We're combining them?" Jade asked.

"Uh huhhhhh!" Sara said perkily.

"Oh, okay. That works." Jade reluctantly agreed that it was fine to go about that way. Even though she didn't want to.

"Two more months" she thought. *"Two more months."*

At least on the 4th, we all went to Gordy White's instead.

Linda White always had the place prepared. Gordy's was, at least, the domestic hang out spot for Pears, Matt and I for years. It was a good sized house, unlike mom and I's apartment. It was also just out of town toward Minnequa, unlike my house, in the heart of Salt Springs. We could go outside at night, No cars, no people. Just coyotes and black bear and they weren't going to fuck with us. (That thought present in our teenage stupor). Plus it wasn't a far walk from Kate's. There were a good bit of occasions that I would give the fellas a "be right back". Only to come back with hickeys on every square inch of my skin.

Gord-O never had girls over though and neither did any of his brothers. But Linda didn't disappoint. Her hospitality appealed to both sexes.

The night was relaxed. It was just a group of six friends hanging out. It didn't seem too special at the time, but thinking back, it was one of the best nights that I had in Salt Springs.

Gordy and Matt picked up two guitars. They strummed up and down, following the guitar controller's direction on the 32 inch television until they found a song they could agree on. Most of us felt that Guitar Hero 2 had the best setlist, but each of us had our different reasons. Matt and Gordy felt it was the case because of Beast and the Harlot by Avenged Sevenfold.

Matt pressed the green fret button and the loading screen appeared on the television. Pears, Sasha, Jade and I watched the two battle it out over the five-plus minute tune. We sat still on the couch behind them, in awe of Gordy's talent. He was unreal at the game, even though he said it was much different than playing in real life. He played through all of Beast and the Harlot without missing a single note.

"Jesus Christ, Gordy..." Matt said as he let the guitar hang from its strap over his shoulder. "That's like the hardest fucking song."

"Free Bird's harder." He said with a touch of arrogance. "Lot of experience, that's all."

"You shouldn't be too cocky about being good at a video game, Gordon." Jade said sarcastically.

"Uh oh!" Gordy matched her sarcasm. "Birthday girl over here thinking she's a bad ass!"

She brushed her shoulders off with sass. Her cocked smiled showed a little bit of the glow from her pearly whites.

"Let's see what you got there, Goldilocks." Gordy said back to Jade as he dismounted the guitar controller's strap from his shoulder. "Get up here." He continued and she lifted herself from the couch.

"Bristol." She demanded and pointed her finger to the ground next to her. "Come."

"You don't want any of this smoke, Davidson." I said.

"Sure, I do..." she replied.

I looked her perfect body up and down. Leggings snug on her legs, revealing the gap between her upper thighs, just under her crease of her legs. My eyes wandered up to the V of her mid-section. Jade's shirt was just short enough to reveal some of her stomach as she pulled the guitar strap of her shoulder. A sapphire bellybutton ring peeked out to say "hello" but it immediately vanished.

When I finally looked up at her face, it was like she knew what I was thinking, *"Oh God, I'd love to give you all of the smoke."* She batted her baby blue's at me and smiled flirtatiously.
"Come on." She demanded with a smirk. "Get up here."

Jade turned around, knowing that I would soon be next to her. I pried myself off of the couch and took the other controller from Matt. It's strap was short, while adjusting it, Jade whispered, "Loser has to eat those anchovies in the kitchen out there."

"You're on, Davidson." I whispered back.

Jade didn't even make it halfway through "Cherry Pie" by Cheap Trick. When the song cut out, she let out a groan and craned her neck back in disgust.

"Ayyyyyeeeeeee!" I yelled. "Thata girl, Davidson!"

"Wow, you fuckin' suck, Jade!" Pears howled. He threw his head back and laughed hysterically.

"Ooooohhhh... fuck." Sasha added. She stated laughing also and said "Bitch, you 'bout weak as fuck."

Jade was frustrated, but it was all in fun. "How 'bout you fucking guys try it then?" she asked.

"Yeah, we will and we'll mop the floor with your weak-ass score!" Pears taunted.

"While you guys do that, we're running into the studio real quick. Runnin' low on these Dew's" Gordy said and Matt followed him through the door that separates the game room and Gordy's music studio.

Jade and I took the seats of Sasha and Pears when they got up. They put on the guitars in unison and then their disagreeing commenced.

Pears controlled the screen. He hit the strum bar until it got to "Carry on Wayward Son" by Kansas.

"Nah, nigga not that one!" Sasha exclaimed.

"Why the fuck not?" Pears responded, "You don't like that *duhnuhnuh-nuhhhhhhhh-nuhnuhnuh-nuhhhhhh-danananana-na-na-na...*"

"Noooo... nigga, fuck that..." Sasha's voice raised an octave. She started to control the screen now against Pears' will and directed it to "Killing in the Name" by Rage Against the Machine.

"Oh why am I surprised?" Pears said with overwhelming sarcasm. "The song about killing off the KKK, alright we get it, Sasha..."

"You tryna kill off niggas too!?!?!" Sasha leaned back and asked rhetorically.

"Bitch, I'm Mexican!" he responded and the both cracked up laughing uncontrollably.

Jade and I both started laughing at them, too. It was humorous, and those two's delivery was bar-none the funniest part. Sasha was super tall and lanky. Pears was short and his teeth pointed every which way. Both charming kids and their own right. Actually, both pretty attractive kids, at that. But in their "hang out" Saturday night attire, they would have won no beauty contest.

Even with Jade's heaving laughter and her own Saturday "hang out" attire, she could have won a beauty contest. Her head rested on the best support of the couch with her face toward the ceiling. A gleaming smile spread across her face with her dimples accompanying each cheek. Her skin was smooth and a hand made its way up to touch her forehead.

I could see she was coming off of her laughter but the way the bouncing on her chest slowed. My 18-year old libido was off and running a full marathon. I could feel the blood rush in my loins.

"Jade..." I whispered and poked an elbow into her side. I could feel the side of her boob against my skin. Truthfully, it was my plan all along. "You still have to eat those anchovies."

"Zack. God damnit." She threw her head back again in disgust but it was only for a second. Jade turned to me and stuck out her lower lip. She asked bashfully, "Do I have to?"

We were only inches apart on the couch and it was everything in my power to not pounce on her right then. I wanted that full, pouty lip in my mouth. I wanted my hands all over the full chest and most of all, I wanted her hands all over the chub that I had between my legs.

I fought off the erotic urge enough to spit out, "Yeeeeeeessssss". She rolled her eyes at me and smiled. The back of her hand slapped the outer part of my thigh, and she said, "Come on." I followed her to the kitchen.

It was dark. My hand searched the wall blindly for the light switch until it was ultimately found. I flipped it up but no light shone. Flipped down. Nothing. Up and down, I kept flipping it, until I heard Jade say sarcastically, "I think it's burnt out, pal."

Her blonde hair illuminated in the dark. My eyes followed her as she made her way to the refrigerator.

"You just gonna stand there?" she asked. Her teeth were visible in the dark too, but by this time, my eyes were adjusting to the lack of light. They wouldn't have to adjust too much more after Jade opened the refrigerator. The light gleamed from the inside of it.

She bent over to peruse the lower cabinets and cubbies for the anchovies. I was magnetized to her ass. I made the walk across the kitchen. My eyes never left her, even through the toe stubbing on the leg of the kitchen table.

I slid in next to her, trapping her between my body and the refrigerator door. Her shirt rode up on her lower back. Smooth, tan skin revealed between her shirt and her yoga pants.

"Find them?" I asked, still looking at the bare gap.

"Right here." She answered and stood up. Her t-shirt snug to her bust. Jade pried the lid off the can of anchovies and asked. "Which one you want me to eat?"

I gazed into her eyes intently. They were such a bright shade of blue that they were even visible as she faced me, away from the light. After a moment I looked down into the tin can and pointed at the anchovy that lay at the top of the heap.

"That one." I said. Then I hesitated and pointed to one that poked out at the bottom of the container. "Wait, actually that one." I smiled at her.

Her face was disgusted. "Ugh. Are you fucking serious?" she asked, still showing a facial expression the looked like she saw someone be decapitated.

"Dead fucking serious." I laughed and watched her fingers pinch at the head of a slimy fish. It slid through her fingers twice, until she could finally grasp it on the third. The goo on her fingers twinkled from the refrigerator light as the anchovy dangled. Jade held it in front of her face, looking as if she was going to puke.

"Do it, Davidson." I urged.

She tipped her head back and dropped it into her mouth. *So hot... Well...* If it weren't a slimy and salt covered anchovy, it would have been sexy. Jade's gnaw was laboring, and she gave it a hard swallow. A droplet of oil from the can sparkled below her lips.

"Well?" I asked.

"Well..." she responded, smacking her lips together. "It actually wasn't all that bad."

"Really?" I asked surprised.

"Yeah." She said. "Take one."

I refused. I put my hands up to indicate I was holding back and said, "Hell no."

"Why?" she asked slyly. "You a pussy?"

I raised my eyebrows and glanced down at the anchovy juice that still nestled below her lips. "Me?"

"Welllllllll...." She exaggerated. "We *are* the only ones in here... and I'm definitely not talking about myself."

"Oh is that fucking right?" I asked playfully.

"Yeah." She also said playfully and she nodded in agreement.

I didn't have any words after that. There was nothing to say. I was struck by her sexiness and I sure as fuck wasn't going to eat an anchovy. Sexual tension rose to new highs. When have anchovies ever helped to people break ice?

Ice broke months ago, but everything froze back over. Until now. Now it was just Jade and I in an empty kitchen with only a tin can of anchovies separating us.

Her eyes looked into mine and I could see her start to relax. She smiled confidently, yet seductively.

I took my hand and touched her cheek. Jade closed her eyes and rested her face as I caressed with my thumb. With one stroke, I was able to wipe the anchovy juice from her lip.

She took a step closer and rested her hands on my chest. Her chin started to point up and I leaned in. I could smell the spearmint gum mix with anchovy on her breath. It was a putrid smell but I didn't care. She was so sexy. Our lips continued to move closer until she turned away and buried her face into my sternum.

Her muffled voice said, "I'm sorry."

At first I was disappointed, but then I understood. I wrapped my arms around her neck and hugged her, "Don't be sorry, Jade. It's my fault."

"No, it's not." Her voice was still muffled and I heard a light sniff. "I just… I just can't…"

"Can't what?" I asked and rested my chin on her forehead.

"I like you, Zack. A lot." She said. "But I can't do this. Our timing never worked out…"

She was right. Our timing never worked out. We were close to becoming more than friends a few years prior, but then out of nowhere, Kate Ford came into the picture. After Kate, we ran into Lequin and now, it was just too late.

Jade pried her face away from my chest. Black streaks of makeup marked up my shirt and she looked up at me, I could see why. Mascara and tears bled down her smooth cheeks like the Susquehanna.

"I wish it could have but it can't." she cried, "Not now."

"I know…" I responded.

Jade took one last drawn out sniff. Snot bubbled in her nostrils. It is normally a disgusting sound but it wasn't under this circumstance.

"I have to go home." She said.

"Jade…" I said, "Why?"

"I just have to." She released herself from my grip.

"Jade, I'm so sor—"

"Zack." She said and grabbed her purse from the kitchen counter. "You have nothing to be sorry about."

"Don't g—"

"I have to, Zack."

She started to exit the dark kitchen, but when she met the door casing between the kitchen and the living room she turned back to me and said, "Zack. I love you."

"I love you too."

"See you Monday."

Jade got home that night and immediately sent a text to all of those who still filled the White's game room. "Home!" it said. It set my mind at ease that she was able to make it home safely.

She climbed the stairs, turned the landing and trekked the remainder to the stairs to the second floor hallway. Outside of her door were three boxes, all wrapped in colorful gift paper. Two boxes were long and skinny. The other was flat, but the surface area covered about one foot in each direction.

Jade collected them, stacking the two skinny boxes on top of the flat. Quietly, Jade opened her bedroom door. It squeaked. Surely loud enough to awaken her parents, but she didn't hear any stirring from the bedroom next to hers. Once again, she snuck in late successfully.

She placed the boxes on her bed. A pouch of wet wipes was on her nightstand. She took one, stared into the mirror on her dresser and wiped her makeup from her face. In the reflection she saw the boxes staring back at her.

Her heart started to beat harder as she approached the bed, curious to see what was on the inside of that paper. She sat down and placed the long box on her lap.

It was wrapped in purple paper. She unfolded the paper that was taped together in triangles on the side of the box. Paper released from the surface of the cardboard and she ran her index finger through the flap on the base of the box, breaking the tape from the paper.

Jade flung the wrapping paper to the side, revealing a black box with the word, "CONVERSE" written on the top. Admittedly, she did appreciate a nice pair of Chuck Taylor's but never thought she could pull off a pair.

When she opened the top flap of the box, she was surprised. There were no shoes inside of this box, it was a bottle of Tropicana orange juice. She held the bottle up and looked at it confusingly.

What the fuck kind of gift is this?

Jade placed the bottle next to her on the bed and grabbed the other long box. Same wrapping paper and same unwrapping sequence. It was another original home to a pair of Converse sneakers, but again, no shoes on the inside. It was a half full bottle of Grey Goose.

"I'll shove this whole fuckin' bottle up your ass if you don't get out of this kitchen."

...

"Finish it up, girl. Let's go try to have fun."

...

"Brooke, are you okay?"

"It was Shawn! It was Shawn! He's gone! He's dead!"

"Brooke... Shawn isn't here."

"I fucking know that! He isn't now! But he was! He was just here..."

...

"No fucking way..."

To Jade's left were shreds of wrapping paper, to her right, the ingredients to what was once her favorite mixed beverage. Again, once her favorite beverage. That ship sailed back in October.

By the ingredients was one last box. Flat and wrapped in black paper. There was no rhyme or reason to this unraveling. Jade tore back the paper frantically until she revealed one final cardboard box. This one plain which no lettering. She pried open the flaps forcefully, ripping it at their folds. Inside was a lime green binder. Inside the clear sleeve on the front was the name "Brooke" written in pink Sharpie.

A tear rolled out of Jade's eye and landed on the plastic. She removed the binder from the box, and threw the cardboard across the room. Jade flipped over the outer shell, revealing the front page inside.

Each page were two photographs. Horizontal 4x6's, stacked on top of one another. Resting on top of the stack was a photograph of her on her cellphone, underneath it was her getting in her car.

The following page showed her screaming at Alex Giroux at the Salt Springs vs. Muncy football game, and then at the bottom was her arriving at the bowling alley.

She turned the page to see herself in the pulpit and her rushing out of the Lequin church.

Another flip. Her drinking directly out of a bottle of Grey Goose. Her looking at Brooke Beckett laying on the bathroom floor.

One more page turn. The picture at the top of the next page was the little boy, gripping the bottle of Grey Goose. At the bottom was an image of him screaming at Brooke, while she sliced her wrist with a shard of the broken bottle.

Jade dropped the binder to the floor. It still lay open to the page she left off.

"What do you want?"

The binder started to flip pages by itself. It showed in Williamsport, holding up a Troy Polamalu jersey. It showed her being intimate in the pulpit. There was a photo of Kate Ford walking toward the pulpit. Another flip. There was Jade sitting in Psychology class. Another flip. She saw herself dropping an anchovy down her gullet.

The binder snapped shut and inside the back sleeve was a sheet of paper. In the same pink lettering, it said "Come Back."

Chapter 56: The Farm

Six days later, Magnum 5 was set to have another show at the Rialto Theatre in Canton. It was Gordy's favorite venue to play. Out of all of the places that his uberly-successful band (for the area, at least) played, it easily held the most people.

We all loved watching Gordy play there, except Matt K. Minnequa's theatre was much closer to Stoney Corners, so it gave him a bit more time. Going all the way to Canton, though. Not too popular to Matt. But, he would support Gordy until death. Even if it meant waking up at 3:30 a.m. to get all of the farm chores and deliveries done before school.

It was an easy morning. Temperature stood in the high 40's. Matt completed the milking of all 84 heifers quickly and headed into the barn's office area to gather the abundance of milk and eggs that were set to be delivered.

On the desk next to the door was a sheet of paper that Matt's dad left for him. Normally, Matt was greeted in the morning with a text from his old man but on this morning, it was only a sheet of paper.

The composition page was filled until just over halfway down. Matt went in order of the 18 names on the sheet.

It began local. He dropped off milk and eggs to those in Stoney Corners, then to those in LeRoy, and then to Windfall. Normally, the deliveries turned the opposite direction. The run of the mill route was Windfall, Alba and then to Salt Springs but not today.

Matt placed two glass jugs of milk next to Russ Vermilya's doormat and he collected the five dollars in cash from inside of their mailbox.

He hitched up his pants, and placed the folded five dollar bill into his back pocket. Daylight started to peek through the trees just enough that he could see inside of his Jeep.

It was welcoming. Chores were a hell of a lot easier when you could see for over half of the time. Unfortunately, in northeast, PA, it was only daylight and warm for a short amount of time. Three months tops. But those months were coming soon.

He opened the door. The dome light illuminated the passenger's seat. Donut crumbs sprinkled the chair and the piece of paper that nestled on it.

Matt passively reversed out of the Vermilya's driveway and turned toward Alba.

Only the paper showed that he was going in a different direction. Fred and Marcia Jennings's place in Lequin.

Matt pulled over and took a stronger glance at the paper.
Russ and Sheron Vermilya. 44 Kindling Road. Windfall. 2 gals. (Lola)
Fred and Marcia Jennings. 84 Burlington Road. Lequin. By the old barn on Rt. 6. 2 gals. 1 doz.

He let out a long and drawn-out sign, "Fuck." He said.

Matt made a U-turn and headed in the opposite direction. Three minutes later, he passed Machmer Taxidermy and turned onto Route 6.

It felt different this time. Obviously. He was alone. He was listening to 106.1's morning talk show. It was humorous. On Friday's they had an hour-long segment called "Friday Funnies". The subject of this week's show was an evening news skit, but with the most bizarre stories.

Head anchor Nigel B. said on the microphone "Elmira man arrested for stealing laptop and bag of grapes" as soon as Route 6's surface changed from paved to dirt.

That was the final phrase the Matt could hear on his way to Fred Jennings's. Immediately as the road changed, the radio lost signal. No matter what direction, or many times Matt jimmied the tune knob, he heard nothing but static. He finally pressed the knob inward to turn off the audio completely.

The old barn started to appear on his left. Further down the road he could see Steam Hollow Road. Luckily, he wasn't going that far. Burlington Road veered to the right directly across the street from the old barn.

He made the right turn. 84 Burlington Road was the first house on the left and parked the car on the curb. A mailbox was held up on a post that stabbed the Earth with the letters "J-E-N-N-I-N-G-S" spread across the box.

"Jennings...where have I heard that name before?" he thought. *"Jennings"*

Matt took the two jugs and carton of dozen eggs out of the hatchback. The jugs clanked at his side and he carried the eggs like Brian Westbrook. Edges to the carton protected by his inner elbow and palm.

He reached the small sidewalk path that led to their porch. Their property looked unattended to. Grass stuck up even with his waist and the uneven and cracked cement almost tripped him over. Green fabric frayed on the edges of the Jennings's front porch. Large blots looked charred on the surface by the door.

"Jennings..."

Matt placed the eggs and milk by the Jennings's front entrance. He dismounted the cracked steps. His head turned toward Route 6 involuntarily, and then it came to him.

"Jennings Barn. The pigs. The buckets. The blood."

His vision returned to his Jeep. The front passenger's seat was occupied and the window was rolled completely down. It was an old man. A very old man. The top of his head was bald and littered with liver spots. Grey hair decorated the side of his head and face in twirling cords. Wrinkles were so potent on his face that Matt couldn't tell where his mouth was.

One of his overalls were fastened, the other strap hung and rested on his tattered red undershirt. Matt was frozen and watched the old man turn his head to look at him.

Matt could now tell where his mouth was, because he began to open it. The old man's eye sockets were deep, but the whites of his eyes started to become clearer once he started to speak.

"Ohhhhh, deliverin' milk to my great grandson, are yeh boy?" his voice screeched and squealed. Matt responded with only noises. Subtle ones like a series of "uhh's."

"I remember doing that when I was your age, son." The old man continued to squeak and his eyes started to widen. "Nice of yuh to help out yer old man, iddn' it?"

"Yuh." Matt uttered dryly.

The only man placed his long, bony and spotted hand on the open car door window frame. "Christine and I never had a whole lotta help up there." With his other hand, he pointed a long and twisted finger in the direction of the old barn. His eyes widened even more and his face started to show a mostly toothless smile, "that is until the McLaughlin's came to town!"

"No... No..."

"Oh yes!" the old man exclaimed, "Titus would come down with his boys every day and 'Oh Abe! Oh Abraham! How can we help?'"

Matt could feel his donuts boiling in his gut and working its way up. "Nuh... Nuh... Ssss..."

"You need some help, don't you Matt?" the old man asked heartily. Both hands gripped the door. His knuckles looked like they were about to pop right out of his skin. "Sure, you need help! That barn will be FUCKED without you! Tommy Ford? No... Duncan Lee? What do you think, Matt? Huh?" His head started to poke out of the open window.

"I... I..." he said. The old man in the Jeep was taunting him, nodding his head back and forth. His blackened tongue hung lazily out of the corner of his mouth, swinging with his movements until he abruptly returned to his normal sitting position.

"No... you don't need any help." He squeaked and turned his face back toward Matt. "Not until you go back."

"Where?" Matt asked.

The old man pointed his long, bony finger toward the barn and then moved it to the right. Matt followed the path. His finger was pointed at the Lequin Church.

"Go back."

"No..."

"Go back!"

Matt had no rebuttals, but after a few seconds he asked the old man, "Why do you keep doing this? Just leave us alone.. Please. We're all so sorry."

"Just go back", the old man said and he smiled. His grin was sinister. Three sharp teeth poked out from beyond his lips. "One more time."

He disappeared. After a minute Matt returned to his car and then had to finish the rest of the deliveries. He brushed more crumbs off of the paper and was directed to Tom and Sally Ford's in Alba.

Chapter 57: Before the Show

While Matt was completing deliveries, Magnum 5's lead guitarist, Gordy White realized that they needed some extra help setting up the stage prior to the big show at the Rialto later that evening. He sent out a text to all of his male friends, inquiring about their interest to assist later that night. They only needed one extra pair of hands so it was a first come, first serve basis. Or, in this case, a first come, first help serve basis.

The first to respond was Pears.

At 3:16 the end of the school day bell rang. Pears stopped at his locker to grab his windbreaker, taking him only two minutes off schedule. He told Gordy that he would be at the Rialto at 3:30 p.m. to help set up and Gordy was thankful, even though he would be the only one on set at the time. The band wouldn't be arriving until nearly five, but Pears was meeting the rest of us before the 8 o'clock start.

Pears pulled up in front of the Rialto Theatre in the neighboring town of Canton. Canton was about the same size as Salt Springs. Most people didn't quite understand why they just never merged as neighborhoods and made one good-sized town. That day was coming though, eventually the schools, at least were going to merge together, but that is still about 20 years down the road.

The theatre was rustic looking. Not poor or run-down like most of the town. It was nice. Quaint, if you will. Two large showcases big enough to contain movie posters flanked the main entrance that consisted of four doors side-by-side. Inside the showcases were large photographs of Magnum 5 with text above it that said, "Magnum 5. Tonight! 8pm!"

Pears got out of the car and walked toward the entrance. He noticed something new on the sidewalk just before the entrance. It was a large and discolored block. It had more of a reddish tint and engraved in the cement was "In loving memory of David B. Morris."

David Morris was the proprietor of the Rialto Theatre for years and a staple in the community of Canton, PA. He was also the minister at their only non-denominational clergy and was the one who officiated Brooke's funeral. When Reverend Morris came on as the minister of the Canton Church of Christ, it was a small congregation and was in danger of losing the property as a whole.

But David was ever persistent and he made that church into a place that people wanted to go. They had trips to Broadway shows and professional baseball games up to three times a year. He also founded, "Stained Glass", a theatre group of high school students. Each year starting in January they would practice weekly until June, when they would perform the musical that they worked relentlessly on.

Over time, the group received national recognition and even went on tour throughout the United States. The Canton Church of Christ was the place to be and the congregation to join. It was solely because of David Morris.

Pears heard of David Morris many times, but his only true interaction with him was at Brooke's funeral. He stood in front of the memorial block of David Morris. Pears looked down on it with affection and compassion until David's replacement, Craig Coffey, opened the theatre doors.

"You Frank Perez?" he asked dryly.

"Yes, sir." Pears responded. Craig waved him in.

Pears entered the theatre. Saw the bathrooms to his left and the ticket stand in front of him. Both were vacant and dark. Beyond the ticket booth was the concession stand, barren and dead. That was sure to change in about three hours.

Next to the concession stand was one door on each side leading into the large auditorium.

"You're good to go in." Craig said. "I'll grab the light" he continued as he entered the ticket booth. He reached under a counter inside of it, reaching for what must have been a control panel.

"Perfect." Pears said indifferently. "Thanks." Pears waiting for a response but never received one. He entered the auditorium.

It was dark and empty. His footsteps alone created echoes as his feet slapped the marble floor. The light snapped on when he was halfway to the stage. Eight foot speakers were placed on each side of the stage. More speakers outlined the front of the platform with small lights accompanying them. There was an elevated platform at the back of the stage for the drum set, but the band was taking care of that. Pears' job was to plug in the speakers but more importantly, set up mic and guitar stands.

Pears maneuvered through the obstacles, weaving around the speakers and stepping over the cords. The final cord before he reached the backstage area almost got him. The black wire made its way over his black Nike and wrapped around his ankle. Pears wriggled his leg, knocking the wire off of him.

As soon as he entered the small backstage area, he saw the bundle of microphone and guitar stands in the corner. He walked over the hardwood floor, hearing nothing but his footsteps. The clunking of his shoes on the floor made him truly comprehend the loneliness.

It was a strange and eerie feeling in the soulless theatre. Goosebumps spread on his back and arms. He felt frozen, but managed to collect all five microphone stands in his hands like cornstalks in front of his body.

Pears returned to the stage and placed them by the drum set platform in a heap. He took one and placed it where Gordy was set to perform from. Pears returned and grabbed one for the front man, Kirby Lewis.

Kirby was a shorter dude. Maybe 5'5. Pears took the liberty of adjusting the stand for his height. He measured it for himself and then dropped it another three inches. It was a guestimate, but he thought it looked accurate.

Pears turned around to acquire another stand but he was interrupted. He heard the door separating the lobby and auditorium open. Dim light made it impossible to see all the way up the aisle but he could tell there were two people that walked into the auditorium.

The duo were walking down the aisle toward the stage.

"Must be 5 o'clock" Pears thought.

"What's up guys?" Pears asked.

"Need help, Pears?" one of the people said in a low, gravelly voice. With each step they became more visible. One was wearing a baggy blue "South Pole" t-shirt with a Yankee cap. His jeans hung low and frayed at the hems by his feet. The other walked a step behind him. His shirt was also blue, but more of a navy color. Orange cursive lettering spread across the front of his shirt that said, "Mets". An orange knit cap rested on his dome.

Their faces started to show. Yankee cap had a thin, post pubescent mustache and the other had a patchy beard. Pears knew who it was and his stomach dropped.

It was Freddy Turner and Cal Thomas.

"Wha— What are yo— you guys doing here?" Pears said and swallowed hard.

"Juss wanna help ya out, ol' boy." Yankee cap aka Freddy Turner said.

"Oh." Pears replied shyly. "It's good. I got it."

"Oh. Ite." Freddy said. "What you been doin', Frankie?"

Freddy and Cal turned and stood directly in front of the stage. Cal stuffed his hands in his large pants pockets while Freddy held onto the collar of his shirt, like an NFL player on a sideline. "Huh? What you been doin', Frankie?" Freddy asked again, starting to lose patience.

Pears was fearful, yet confused. Freddy and Cal were sent away to a halfway home in Nebraska. Maybe they let them back? Maybe they've changed. But they left on bad terms.

"Just chillin', bro." Pears said.

"Got some new friends, I hurrrrr." Cal chimed in.

"Always friends with them, Cal." Pears' voice started to quiver. "Just a little closer now, prob."

"Oh." Freddy said. He started to walk closer to the stage. "You motherfuckers got in a lil trouble too, right?"

"No, man." Pears replied honestly, "No trouble. Or at least I don't think."

Freddy reached the stage and placed his fists on it. The light shining down on the stage hit him differently than before. Bags hung under his eyes, wrinkled and puffy. Freddy looked like he hadn't slept in weeks. Dirt caked under his fingernails and as he spoke, Pears noticed that his teeth were rotten.

"You broke in." Freddy sneered. "All of you. You broke in."

"Where?"

"Lequin." Cal answered. He also walked toward to the stage and leaned on it with his elbows. Scars decorated his forearms and all of his teeth were missing. His New York Mets t-shirt was filthy and he smelled as if he hadn't washed in months.

"How do you know about Lequin?"

Cal laughed. The sharp smell of rotten eggs came from his mouth, "Everyone knows about Lequin, Frankie." He said.

"Really?"

"Yeah." Freddy said. "Now when you guys get busted for it. You gonna take any of the blame this time? Or are you gonna say you didn't do shit?"

"Is that what this is about?" Pears asked calmly. He continued to say genuinely, "Guys, I didn't have anything to do with that. I'm really sorry everything happened to you bu—"

"Nah. You're right." Freddy said and backed off the stage. "All ya fucks are getting what you deserve anyways.

Pears took a step forward, "What the fuck does that mean?"

Freddy tapped Cal and they started to walk away. They reached the second row of seats in the auditorium when Pears yelled, "Huh, Freddy? Cal? What the fuck is that supposed to mean?"

They were at the fifth row.

"What the fuck does it mean?!?!"

Freddy turned around. His face clear even through the darkness. He gained more wrinkles and his eyes sharpened. The whites of his eyes looked bleached and his pupils dilated to black balls. Freddy's rotten smile spread across his mouth.

"You're friends, Frankie." He hissed. Bloody spit shot out of his mouth with each word. "Brooke. Kara. Ryan."

Pears fell back on his ass. His back bumped into the drum set platform. "Fuck..." Pears uttered and held his back.

Cal and Freddy both laughed. "Hurt?" Freddy asked. "You know who was hurt? Brooke." Freddy mocked a wrist cutting gesture with his hands. "Kara and Ryan?" He made an exploding gesture with his hands.

Pears was speechless. They knew, but how? Were they there? Were they stalking him this whole time? How the fuck did they get out of the halfway house?

It's not even them...

"It's your fault, Frankie." Freddy's rotten face grinned again. His skin cratered and cracked, "It's all of your fault. Zack. Sasha. Jade. Matt. Gordy. Every *fucking* one of you!"

"No it fucking isn't." Pears replied angrily. Freddy and Cal returned an infuriated face. "It fucking isn't you little fucking bitches. Fuck outta here."

Freddy lifted his shirt, revealing a 9 millimeter. "Say that again, cuh! Say that again! Pop your bitch ass like we shoulda that whole fuckin school that day, nigga."

"You ain't gon' do shit, fam!" Pears replied. "Ain't shit. Bitch-ass mothafucka…"

Freddy lowered the shirt and a smile returned to his face. A tooth fell to the ground. Pears heard it shatter and spread over the marble floor.

"Just go back." Freddy said frankly. "You can make it all right if you just come back."

"Go back where?" Pears asked shortly.

"Lequin." Freddy answered.

"We ain't going back." Pears said. "Done with that shit."

"Shouldn't be." Freddy replied. "Come back. You need to."

"Fuck outta here."

Freddy and Cal took their final steps to the exit, but before they pushed the door open, Freddy said, "Come back" one last time.

Pears didn't answer. He continued to place stands in their rightful location and finished plugging in all amplifiers.

Chapter 58: The Show

Doors opened at 7 p.m. for Magnum 5's concert at the Rialto Theatre. Butterflies fluttered in Gordy White's stomach two hours before hand but once folks started filing in, the butterflies seized. He stood in the back, watching folks file in for an hour through a crack in the curtain barrier separating backstage from the auditorium.

Gordy heard the news from Kirby Lewis earlier that day. The concert was sold out and based on the theatre being half full by 7:15, it was settling in.

This was the biggest show to date. Larger than any other show at the Rialto and certainly bigger than any performance at the Spartan Lounge, Canton Grill or the Park Street Brewery. With still about a half hour to go until they would perform their opener, a cover of Coheed and Cambria's "Welcome Home", there were already close to 500 people in attendance.

When Gordy walked on stage with his Les Paul draped over his shoulder a half hour later, attendance doubled.

He plucked the opening note. The fan at his feet blew his long hair like he was in a scene from Baywatch. A spotlight illuminated him from above as he played the opening guitar riff. 1,000 people were screaming for Gordy White. The tall, skinny, nerdy kid from Minnequa was rocking an opening guitar riff like he was Tom fucking Morello. It was his dream come true.

Gordy didn't just look the part up there that night. He *was* the part. Long brown hair flowed below his shoulder blades. The tint on his glasses were dark, almost to the point that they looked like sunglasses. His guitar hung down below his waist, over his Megadeth t-shirt and ripped Wranglers.

The bassist strummed and another spotlight shined upon him. Drums joined as well, attracting another spotlight. They fucking killed it. They were un-fucking-believable. Those of us in the front started to jump up and down to the beat of the music. Almost in unison with Gordy's bopping head. Finally, the last spotlight hit Kirby Lewis and he started to sing.

"You could have been all I wanted. But you weren't honest. Now get in the ground"

It was amazing. The spotlights went away when Kirby began singing, but flashes of green, blue and red lit up the stage. Strobe lights flashed suddenly and a fog machine released enough mist to just cover the band's feet.

"You choked off the sorriest of favors. But if you really loved me. You would've endured my will"

Magnum 5 kept crushing it, but as everyone that enjoys rock music knows, the band is only as good as their lead guitarist. And he was fucking unstoppable. Gordy's fingers massaged the guitar's neck frantically through the entire song. He knew the audience wasn't that familiar with the song, and he knew the best was yet to come.

When Gordy told me earlier that day what song they were opening with I knew what the reaction would be too. The intro would make the audience wet, but the end would give them the unexpected orgasm.

"One last kiss for you. One more wish 'til you. Please make up your mind girl, before I hope you die!!!! GORDY FUCKING WHITE, EVERYONE!!!"

Gordy walked slowly to center stage, ripping the two minute long guitar solo. His fingers pranced gracefully over the strings during his drawn out strut.

Kirby Lewis moved to the switched places with him. Gordy stopped directly in the middle of the stage with the spotlight directed at only him. Those green, blue and red lights flashed the entire stage but he was the focal point. Gordy White, the quiet nerd that only spoke to five kids in the entire school on the regular was in his element. He banged his head to the beat. Sweat flung to the floor from his long, brown mop with each bop of his head.

The crowd was silent. There was no jumping or moshing in front of the seating section. Those in the rows of seats stood in amazement of what they were seeing. I looked to my left and saw Jade. Her mouth dropped and her stare at Gordy was blank. She wasn't the only one that looked that way. I panned the entire auditorium, everyone looked star struck. No one said a word. Even Kirby Lewis watched Gordy wail on the guitar in awe.

Toward the end of the tune, the lead singer is supposed to let out a series of "ooohs" but Kirby didn't sing a word. It was like he forgot. He still held the microphone at his side as the sound of Gordy's guitar started to fade out.

Gordy strummed the last cord and held his hand in the air. He made a fist with the index and pinky fingers raised. As soon as the auditorium was completely silent, the entire crowd erupted in cheers.

I heard, "FUCK YEAH, GORDY!" come from my right. It was Pears. Matt grabbed Jimmy Ellsworth's shoulders in front of him and shook him with excitement. Both Jade and Sasha screamed in approval.

As for me, I just stood there. Still in awe of Gordy. I was proud of him. But even more so, I was happy for him. Music was his thing. He was a quiet kid and never promoted himself. Everyone knew he played, but no one knew how he played. That is unless you were a regular at one of the shows. But about 80% of the folks in attendance that night popped their Magnum 5 cherry. A thousand people were screaming his name. It was his night and he deserved every minute of it.

Mid-cheer, Gordy began the opening riff of the next song, "I Write Sins Not Tragedies" by Panic! At the Disco. It was an easier song for Gordy. He needed the break after that "Welcome Home" performance.

They'd complete "I Write Sins Not Tragedies" and move on to a pretty diverse setlist. They played "Bring Me to Life" by Evanescence and then went into "Eleanor Rigby" by The Beatles. Toward the middle of the show, Gordy broke out the acoustic and they performed "Time of Your Life" by Green Day, only to be followed up by a rock version of "No Diggity" by Blackstreet.

They fucking killed it. Every song was performed perfectly but after nearly an hour and a half, it was about the time that they wrap it up.

I knew the setlist. Next to last was "Smells Like Teen Spirit" by Nirvana and the final song, "Beast and the Harlot" by Avenged Sevenfold.

Gordy had been practicing the A7X tune for months. Even as far back as December, when he mimicked the tablature in a pew within the confines of the Lequin Church.

He struck the first cord of the finale and looked toward his lead singer. Kirby started the opening scream of the song to complement the guitar intro.

Beyond Kirby, Gordy could see the open door to get backstage. Standing in the doorway was a man in a sweatshirt with the hood pulled up. It was a plain black hoodie with dark pants on the bottom.

"Stage crew" he thought.

He plucked the last note before the big beat drop. His attention returned to the man who stood motionless in the doorway.

Each time Gordy looked in his direction, he became more uncomfortable. The man never moved and never showed his face.

"Pears was the stage crew..." Gordy thought again, growing more suspicious of the man. He looked out in the crowd and saw Pears banging his head to the hard rock music. Next to him was Jade. Matt was there too behind Jimmy Ellsworth.

"She's a dwelling place for demons, she's a cage for every unclean spirit, every filthy bird. And makes us drink the poisoned wine to fornicate with our kings. Fallen now is Babylon the Great"

Gordy ripped off the final cords to the finale with ease and the crowd went insane. People jumped up and down, screaming that they wanted more. Someone even lost their popcorn bag after getting ran into. It was a circus and the cheering continued after all of the lights went out.

There was only one light on and it was backstage. It was bright enough to still show the outline of the man in the doorway. Gordy looked in his direction. He stuck out two fingers and curled them, nonverbally telling Gordy to come.

All of Magnum 5 stayed on the stage for the final bows except Gordy. He followed the direction of the man in black.

Gordy placed his guitar on the stand and the man walked behind the curtain. He still followed him.

"Gord, where you goin'? Kirby asked him as he trotted by.

"Be right back." He replied.

Gordy reached the doorway and went behind the curtain. The man in black was thrusting into a female who was bent over a large black box dedicated to moving sound equipment. Her hands were tied together with rope and so were her ankles. Purple bare feet laid between the man's knees as he humped forcefully.

"Heeeeelllllp!" she cried as she tried to crawl away. "STOOOOOOOPPPPPPPPPPP!"

"Shut the fuck up, cunt!" the man yelled at her and cracked her ass with his bare hand. The box moved across the hardwood floor from the force of his thrusts until it was stopped by a concrete wall. The girl continued to squirm. Blood oozed from large scratch wounds on her side from his fingernails. Droplets fell to the floor.

The girl started to fight him off harder. She let out another cry for help, "MAKE HIM STOPPPPPPPPPP!! GORDY MAKE HIM STOOOOOOOPPPPPP!!!!!"

Gordy ran toward them just as the man reached around her and shoved his fist in her mouth. The girl bit down. He removed his blood soaked hand and clubbed her in the back of the head, still fucking her from behind. It knocked her out. Gordy reached his hands out to stop him, but the man took a handful of the girl's hair and smashed her face into the box. Blood flew across the room. Chunks of bone and teeth scattered across the box and onto the floor.

"What the fuck are you doing to her?!?!" Gordy yelled and grabbed him. "Stop i—"

The man removed his hood and smiled at Gordy. Blackened enamel spread across his sinister grin. His skin was so pale that Gordy could see his veins, arteries and capillaries. Streaks of silver populated the hair on his temples.

Gordy took a step back and his jaw dropped. He started to dry heave and finally he puked on the hardwood floor.

"What's wrong, Gordy?" He sneered. His blue tongue licked his rotten teeth. "You never seen a pussy before?"

"Wha—... why did you do this?" Gordy asked and pointed at the girl. Blood continued to rush over the box, still leaking out of the girls face.

"Do what?" the man asked. The girl started to move. Her head raised from the box. Skin tore away from her cheek, revealing her orbital bone. Her lower lip was torn to the chin. She turned her head in Gordy's direction, through the blood he knew who it was.

It was Kara Murphy.

"Hi Gordy" she said and he puked again. "Didn't believe any of it, did you?"

"Kara…" Gordy stuttered in disbelief. "K…K…Kara… what is go… going on?"

"Nothing." She said nonchalantly. "Hell of a show…"

Gordy looked at her naked body. He didn't understand how he didn't notice the burn marks before he got close to them. Black streaks of charred skin marked her back and arms.

The man started to thrust into her again but this time she was unphased. She continued to speak, "Answer the question, Gordy. You didn't believe any of it, did you?" her head moved back and forth from the force of the man shoving himself inside of her. "You didn't think anything about the church was true…"

Gordy stood in shock. She stared into his eyes, "Well it *is*. It *is* true, Gordy." She sneered through the blood. With each of the man's humps, more blood dropped from her face. "All of it."

He was finally able to utter a word, "Okay... I beli—"

"Yeah! You fucking better believe it!" Kara's voice started to deepen and became hoarse. "You know what fucking else you need to believe Gordy?!"

"Wha...wha...ttt..."

"That you did this." She hissed. "You all *fucking* did this. You *fucking* killed me you *fucking* cocksuckers!!!!"

A tear rolled from Gordy's eye.

"But you're too fucking stupid to know that." Kara heaved harder than ever. The box beat the concrete wall in a consistent pattern with force. Her neck whipped back and forth. "You weird fucking twat! You're nothing! You never fucking will be!"

Gordy scowled at her. "Really?" he asked.

"Yes!" more blood flung from her scalp. "You're all too fucking stupid!"

Gordy remained calm. "When did we go to the church, Kara?"

"OCTOBER FUCKING 3RD!" she screamed. The man's fingers sunk into the open scratch wounds on her sides. Kara was unphased.

"When did Brooke die?" Gordy asked. "And when did *you* die?"

"What the fuck does that have to do with anything?!?!" she screamed.

"We didn't kill anyone." Gordy said. "You died months after we went in."

Kara started to scream. She wasn't saying anything particular, it was just nonsense. Her extremities started to seize in anger, but the man went on fucking her anyways. Gordy knew that she wasn't refusing the man anymore. Actually, he knew the whole thing was a ploy to get his attention anyways.

He stared at her angrily. Blood still dripped from her face. Her lip started to dangle off of her face and bounced with each thrust inside of her.

Gordy was filled with hate. Hate for the man. Hate for the Lequin Church and somehow, hate for what used to be one of his best friends.

Until he saw her ankles. On her 17th birthday, Kara got a tattoo. It was small. Maybe one inch by one inch and only the outline of a heart. She got it on the inside of her right ankle so her father wouldn't see it. "Who the hell looks at the inside of someone's ankles, right?" he remembered her saying in Mr. Hollinshead's algebra class.

Tonight, there was no tattoo.

He heard, "GOR-DY! GOR-DY! GOR-DY!" from beyond the curtain. It was his turn to take a bow.

"What happened, Kara?" he asked and pointed to her feet. "Where's your tattoo?"

"WHAT TATTOO?!?!" she screamed.

"The heart." He said. "On your birthday. 17th. Where's the heart?"

Kara started to scream again and again, it was nothing in particular. "Stop it." The man said.

"Where's the tattoo, Kara?" Gordy asked. "I'm looking at the one place that you said no one looks. Where's the tattoo?"

"Stop it." The man stopped thrusting.

"Where is it, Kara!?" Gordy asked and she started to seize. Saliva accompanied blood on its way to the floor. Brown hair detached from her scalp in clumps.

"Stop it!" the man demanded.

GOR-DY! GOR-DY! GOR-DY!

Kara started to gurgle. Blood clots and mucus fell from her detached lip. One of her eye balls plopped into the lake of blood on the box.

"WHERE'S THE TATTOO, KARA?!?!"

Kara's seizing halted and she laid lifelessly on the box. Gordy turned to the man. They stared at each other angrily, like two drunks at a bar ready to scrap.

"You did it again." The man said.

GOR-DY! GOR-DY! GOR-DY!

"No." Gordy said. "I didn't."

"Make it right, faggot." the man demanded. "Come back. Make it right."

GOR-DY! GOR-DY! GOR-DY!

Gordy turned around without saying a word and returned to the stage. The crowd went ballistic when the spot light turned to him. Gordy raised both fists with the index and pinkies pointing up. His face panned the crowd and he mouthed, "thank you."

He then turned to our group directly in front on the floor and he mouthed another phrase.

"I love you."

Chapter 59: Two Weeks

It didn't take long for me to completely forget about that game against Towanda. Especially since it was accompanied by something so monumental.

That was my first homerun of the season. I'd smash two more over the next two weeks and my fellow Spartans were defying odds as well.

We were picked to finish 5th in the Northern Tier League, otherwise known as the NTL, during the preseason, but we were 14-1 with the playoffs looming at the end of April.

Dom Vermetti led the NTL in homers with 11 and also added 44 RBI's to the stat line. Dave Ramsey's ERA was under 2.00 and Lincoln Montgomery was the most sure-handed shortstop I'd ever seen. Even more so than Ryan.

It was fun to compete again. So fun that the day I rounded third was deep in my memory. Seeing Ryan was like a car accident. It hurt when it happened and there is some bullshit to deal with for the next few days. But time passes, and you almost can't even remember it happening.

That was the case with everyone, though. Sasha started offseason workouts and was working to get

in shape. Basketball shape. Motherfucking NCAA
Division 1 basketball shape.

Jade's move to Laramie was quickly approaching.
The night after she received her gifts, she told her
parents of her intentions. It's amazing that neither
she, nor they cared enough to discuss it earlier
than that.

Matt just continued his day-to-day grind. It was
something that literally never stopped. Work, then
school and then work again. It was a never-ending
cycle. The best way to deal with grief is to stay busy
or start a project. With Matt, that was his life.
Through deaths and disappointments, the show
always went on. There was no time to look in the
rear-view.

Pears did dwell on the incident at the Rialto, but it
wasn't over fear or anger with Lequin. It was
regret. He constantly thought back to the dark
place that he was in six years prior and how
different his life would have been if he didn't make
that one decision. It was the decision to help
Freddy and Cal break into Mark and Jen Reynolds's
house. They recruited Pears to help. Why not? He
was classmates with their sexy daughter, Ellie. He
knew where they lived. He knew how to get there.
But most importantly, he knew where their
valuable belongings were.

If he hadn't agreed to help, Pears may have been heading to college just like the rest of his friends. He didn't want to go to the service and without any guidance at home, Pears was set for the infantry by way of Fort Benning, Georgia. He became one with the thought that it is what he deserved.

And then there was Gordy. He changed after that concert. Whether it was confidence or realizing who he was as a person, he changed. He spoke. A lot. To more than just us.

Gordy always had a thing for Megan Birch. Megan was a cute little blonde girl. Quirky and nerdy, just what you'd expect Gordy to go for.

But Gordy never went for it. He crushed on her from Kindergarten until graduation, but never did a damn thing and certainly never dated or liked anyone else. Actually, the majority of the school was suspicious of Gordy's sexual orientation because of it. None of them had a clue that Gordy was actually helplessly in love.

Who knows if Megan would ever feel the same way. Honestly, she probably wouldn't. Gordy was kicking a little out of his field goal range and he knew it. That's why he never told a soul, except for Pears, Sasha, Matt, and myself. It only took him 10 years to do so. Over time, Jade, Ryan and Kara found out but it was always a topic we just didn't speak about. All you had to do was look at Gordy's face when she entered a room.

Megan came up to Gordy at his locker on Friday, April 17th. She had to look straight up at him as she was only half of his height. Gordy was replacing his American History book with his Geometry II hardcover. He slammed the steel cubby and turned around to walk to class until he was struck by Megan's presence in front of him. His jaw dropped and his olive skin turned to mayonnaise white.

"Gordy. Hi!" Megan said.

"H... Hello..." he said. Pears, Matt and I watched it unfold from the end of the hall. Old Gordy would have ran away or thrown up. Not this Gordy. He continued, "How.. How are you, Megan?"

"I'm great! How is your day going?"

Gordy smiled down at her and said softly, "Very, very good."

"Well that's good!" she responded with her usual pep. "Hey, I haven't seen you all week. I just wanted to let you know that you were amazing last week."

Gordy's skin tone went from rivaling mayo to Heinz 57. "Thanks." He said shyly, but with a wide smile.

"No problem!" she said. "I couldn't believe it. I never heard you play before. Like, I knew you did but... wow."

"Well, thank you so much, Megan." Gordy's blushing face got redder by the second. "That means so much."

"Of course!" she answered. "I have to get to class but let me know when your next show is. Please!"

"Will do."

"Nice." Megan said, "See you later!"

Gordy waved and she walked off to her fifth period class. He saw us at the end of the hallway. I had only ever seen him smile larger and look happier that that once in our 14 years of friendship. It was on the stage at the Rialto Theatre the week before.

Life went on. We smelled the finish line of the school year. It wasn't just the school year, it was the finish line of our high school career. A new chapter was opening. Hell, it was an entirely new book. We were all leaving everything we ever knew. In a town of only 2,000 folks, though, it wasn't a lot. But damn, we knew it well.

We'd cake down the final stretch and just enjoy it. Enjoy the time we had left together because God only knew when or if, we'd all ever be back together again.

The thought of leaving them almost killed me, but looked forward to one last ride. We only had another month together and I was sure to enjoy every moment.

Chapter 60: Last Call at the O'Sullivan's

I wasn't going to go to Jade's party. O'Sullivan bangers weren't the place that I wanted to be. You always heard of the term "guilty by association" and I wasn't going to be convicted of it. Girls could get off easy, especially since Luke Larson was consistently on duty for the Friday evening/Saturday morning shift but guys didn't stand a snowball's chance in Hell.

At the final bell of the school day that Friday, Jade came up to my locker. My Pittsburgh Pirate windbreaker hung on my shoulders loosely and Jade gave the back of it a tug, gaining my attention.

"Hey, what the fuck?" I said sarcastically.

"Alright, prick." She responded in a similar angry tone, but recognizing the sarcasm. "You coming tonight?"

"Ughhh..." I sighed. This bit of vocals were serious and Jade knew it. "Pirate game starts at 10 tonight. They're in San Diego."

"You're really going to watch the fucking Pirate game?" her eyes rolled up to me and he arms hung to her sides in disgust. She gripped her binder in her hand, "They have a million games and they suck. You're really gonna leave me alone with this?"

"Sash, Pears, Gordy and Matt are all going. Give you some relief." I said sincerely. I knew that she didn't want to go either and my voice reflected that. I was empathetic, but I didn't plan on doing anything to help beyond letting her know that the rest of the crew was going.

She didn't even look disgusted anymore. Jade was visibly upset. "You really aren't going to go?" she asked. "I'm leaving in a month and you really aren't going to go to this?"

"Jade, you know I hate the drinking and drugs and all that sh—"

"You don't have to drink, Zack." she said.

"I know..." I replied. "But you'll be drinking. Everyone else there will be drinking. I just don't want to be around that."

"But I won't even be drinking that much."

"Come on, Jade." I said, "We both know you're going to drink. It's your birthday, you should have fun."

"It was my birthday three weeks ago, Zack." She said dryly but she perked up a little to say, "I just really want you to go... Even if it's for a little bit. Fuck, I probably won't even be there that long."

"Then why are you going at all?"

"Sara..." she said.

"Well, then..." I replied. "Why do you even want me to go for a little bit?"

"Because..." she hesitated and crunched her eyebrows. Her hand rubbed her forehead quickly. Baby blue fingernails itched her cheek and she returned the hand to her side. "Because if you aren't there, the whole crew isn't there. It's like... incomplete or something."

Her eyes looked up at me and widened. They sparkled. Mascara darkened her eyelashes but they didn't need the help. Her burgundy turtleneck was modest but tight enough to accentuate her bosom. Whether it was intentional or not, her chest puffed out as her stance erected.

"I just really want you to go." she said. "Please."

I hesitated and sighed again. "When are people getting there?"

"10."

"First pitch is at 10:10."

"Fuck you…" she snickered.

"Alright, I'll go." I agreed. "But only for an hour."

"Good enough for me!" she smiled.

"Alright." I walked passed her and toward the main lobby. "I have to get to practice. See you at 10."

The time finally came for Matt to pick up Pears and I. This was uncharted waters for me. A party. Not like a family outing or something of that nature but a fucking party.

I used to see Ryan get ready for these sorts of things. He'd wear a nice t-shirt and jeans. Pretty simple sounding, yes. The t-shirt would have an American Eagle or Hollister logo on the front and the jeans would be fashionably ripped at the knee. He'd wear cologne that he slipped in his pocket while at the retail shop. If he would have ever gotten caught, he would just say, "Forgot I had it." or "Forgot to pay."

It wasn't that easy for me. I stood in front of the mirror that used to reside in my sister's room. The mirror was long and stood upright so you could see yourself from head to toe.

My closet consisted of t-shirts, but each supported a different sports team. My jeans were fine. Mom was the master of finding sales at the preppy retail joints like Aeropostale, but I hated their shirts. Too clingy. I liked my stiff, black pinstriped Orlando Magic Gildan t-shirt with "Howard" and the number 12 on the back.

That's what I decided to wear and I thought it looked pretty damn fresh. I threw on some Axe body spray to finish off the job.

I could hear a knock on the back (front) porch. "Who is it?!?!" my mom yelled.

I heard a mumbled, "Matt" in reply.

"Should I wear the Polamalu jersey instead?" I said, scoping each possible angle of myself. *"Maybe Jade would like it if I wore that instead..."*

"ZACK!" mom screamed. "Matt's here!" I heard the door creak open. She continued "Hey, honey! How are you?"

"Good, Ms. Shelly." He said. "How are you?"

"No. Too obvious." I thought. *"Just wear this, Zack. Fuck it. No, not fuck it she's sexy as fuck... No wear it... FUCK!"*

I came to the conclusion. I was out of time, the Dwight 'shersey', if you will, was the attire. But I looked in the direction of my dresser, just in case it would job my memory of having something better in there.

Nothing came to mind. The drawer next to where I kept my t-shirts was my socks but most importantly. I still had some old Trojans in there.

"Maybe..." I thought and looked away from it. *"Nahhh... she turned it down at Gordy's."*

"Coming, Zack?" Matt yelled from the bottom of the stairs.

"Yeah, bro!" I took one last glance at the sock drawer. *"Well, maybe just in case..."* I thought again. I walked to the drawer and fished to the bottom. There they were. Two remained in the damaged box, but the wrappers remained intact with an expiration date that was not of yore. I placed on in the money fold of my wallet and went downstairs.

Mom had the Pirate game on the television and Padres' pitcher, Kevin Correia was tossing his warm-up chucks. A graphic of his early season stat line covered a part of the screen.

"I'll tape it for you, hon." My mom said. "Be careful, okay?"

"Always am, Mom." I said and kissed her on the forehead. "Love you."

"Love you too, hon." She answered.

"Love you, Ms. Shelly!" Matt yelled as we exited the apartment.

Mom answered, "Love you too, Matt!" She blew both of us kisses and closed the door.

Rain spit lightly and dripped over the headlights on Matt's Jeep. Wipers remained on and through the precipitation, I saw Gordy sitting in the front. Pears rolled down the back window and stuck his head out, "Let's go, motherfuckers!" he yelled.

It didn't influence us in the slightest. Matt and I walked around the side of the garage at the normal pace until we got to the car.

Just live your life! Oh! Ay ay ay ay ay ay...

Matt reversed out of the driveway. Rain started to spit a little harder. A light flash of lightning filled the sky, followed by the faint sound of thunder, just loud enough that we could hear it over Rihanna and T.I. on the radio.

"You gonna finally have some alcohol tonight, boys?" Pears asked us. Neither Matt, Gordy or I ever had a drop of alcohol before, but they weren't adamant about maintaining the straight-edge lifestyle like I was.

"Might have a beer." Matt said. "But I'm driving you bastards so that's it."

"Same." Gordy agreed. "We have practice tomorrow so I want to be good for it."

"What time is your fuckin' practice, Gord?" Pears asked.

"Thre—"

"Oh fuck you'll be fine!" Pears interrupted. "Get fucked up with me because this little bitch won't do shit..." and he pointed at me.

"Yep." I said complacently. I saw from over Matt's shoulder and through the windshield that were turning onto the O'Sullivan's street. "You're absolutely right."

Cars of those in attendance started to line each curb. Half of each car crowded the road, making it one way. Further down the road was their house. It was the only illuminated house on the street. Red cups littered their large front yard and a group of about 10 teenagers stood congregated on the porch, all holding beers.

We strolled slowly passed the house. Through the large front window, we saw a bunch of our classmates and many additional people that we hadn't known. They danced to a beat that we couldn't quite hear yet, but we knew that we soon would. Each and every one of them looked inebriated. I hoped that Jade Davidson wasn't one of them.

Beyond the house and further down the street, the line of cars from the attendees stopped. Matt pulled into the space. Gravel crunched under his tires and before he could even turn off the ignition, Pears jumped out of the car.

His feet planted into the curb and then we all saw it. At the end of the road was a Ford Taurus with a decal on the side that said, "Salt Springs Police Department." It was at least Gordy, Matt and I's first encounter with a Friday night at the O'Sullivan's. We always said that we wouldn't be surprised if Luke Larson's antics were true. But seeing this first-hand was surprising.

"Come on, fags!" Pears urged. "Let's go!"

Gordy, Matt and I sat in the car in silence. I glanced at Matt in the rearview and our reflections met. We didn't say a word. We didn't have to. Just through the look we were trying to figure a way out of this.

But then the passenger's side door opened and Gordy joined Pears on the outside. Matt offered a nod in the reflection and I returned it.

We headed into the O'Sullivan's.

Empty beer cans scattered on the decorative end table in the long hallway that lead to the kitchen and immediately to our left was the living room. Thirty of our classmates danced on the suede carpeting. A dozen red Solo cups spread across their wooden coffee table and on the couch was the hostess with the mostest, Sara O'Sullivan with Mike Wilde. Her fingers ran through his hair as she pulled him toward her. One of his hands reached under the back of her denim skirt. Sara's bare ass cheek flashed the whole room, but we were the only one to notice. Mike stroked her ass cheek but stopped at her orange thong.

"Zack!" I heard from the living room and then I saw Jade. "Gordy! Matt! You're all here!"

Her words slurred slightly and she stumbled through the mass of people dancing on the floor to Ciara and Missy Elliott's "1, 2 Step". She wore a tight black dress with the skirt stopping at the middle of her thigh. You could climb those tall, tanned and defined legs. Her feet were bare. A true power move going barefoot at a party. Baby blue paint on her toes matched that on her fingers.

"Where's Pears?" she asked.

We looked around. Pears was nowhere to be seen, but he was somewhere to be heard. He was in the kitchen. I heard him say, "Where's the beers?" from the end of the hallway.

"Come on!" Jade pulled on the sleeve of my shirt, "I need another drink, anyways!"

"I don't think you do…" I said dryly, but still let her pull me in the direction of the kitchen. Matt and Gordy followed behind. A glass shattered behind them. We heard the crash and the scatter of the glass over the marble floor.

"FUCK!" we heard and turned around. It was Sara. She bent over to pick up the pieces until the front door opened. Dave Ramsey arrived at the party with Dom Vermetti and Lincoln Montgomery.

"Saraaaaa..." Dave held his arms out. "What's up beautiful?"

Sara completely disregarded the broken glass now. She walked with force toward them. With one hand, she grabbed a fistful of Dave's black American Eagle t-shirt. And with the other, she grabbed a handful of his package.

"Upstairs. Now." she tugged on his cock through his jeans and released. But she never let go of his shirt. She dragged him through the opening that led to the living room and to the steps upstairs.

"I'll be right back, boys." he muttered to Lincoln and Dom, who were both smiling with pride for their homie.

"What. In. The. Fuck?" Matt said.

"That's Sara..." Jade said disgustedly.

Matt replied, "Dude, she was just making out with that Wilde kid like two seconds ago..."

"Yep..." Sara said with even more disgust. "That's Sara..."

Jade finally let go of my shirt and we all entered the kitchen. The kitchen was beautiful. Marble floors accompanied marble countertops. A large oak kitchen table sat to our right, but for the time being, it wasn't holding any dinner. It served as a beer pong table. Ellie and Kyle Reynolds teamed up and were destroying the team of Duncan Lee and Megan Birch.

For the second time in a week, Gordy's tanned skin lost all color. It may have even a tint of green. He looked sick.

"Zack..." he said.

"Don't worry about it, Gordy." I whispered. "There's nothing going on between them. One just needed a partner."

One cup remained in front of Megan and Duncan. "Ballgame, bitches!" Ellie yelled and tossed the ping pong ball into the cup.

"Game. Blouses." Kyle said as he walked toward Megan and Duncan. He gave them both a fist bump and talked toward the refrigerator once he was finished.

"Bristol!" He yelled when he saw me from the other side of the room. I waved, but nothing more.

I panned the room. One eye caught Jade, pouring Belvedere into a red cup filled with orange juice. The glass bottle wavered in her hand. I wanted to think that it wasn't because she was drunk, but because it was heavy. The bottle was mostly full but she got some help pouring it from Alexandra Maddox. Alexandra held the bottom of the bottle while Jade held the neck.

"Megan, thanks for partnering up with me." I heard Duncan say.

"Yeah!" Megan said with her usual perk, but from there the slurring commenced. "No prowl-belem!"

Color returned to Gordy's face and he smiled. Almost involuntarily. But it was interrupted by Pears, who yelled from the refrigerator. "You boys want a beer?!"

"Sure." Gordy said without looking at him. His eyes were still on Megan.

"Why not?" Matt added.

"Zack?" he asked. My eyes were still on Jade. It wasn't just because she looked unbearably sexy in that dress, but because her drink pouring process was humorous.

"No." I said, giving Pears a quick glance.

Pears returned with the beers for Matt and Gordy at the same time as Jade returned. Matt and Gordy snapped open their cans. Bud Light spewed from the top of Gordy's, spilling all over his hands. He shook them off. Beer splattered off of his hands and onto the marble floor. Gordy took his foot and swiped from left to right. He thought it would wipe up the liquid, but it only streaked on the floor.

"Where's yours?" Jade asked me.

"Fuck out of here, Davidson." I said and she offered a lazy smile. The dress was tight to her chest, but only liberal enough to reveal only an inch of her cleavage. I could feel myself start to swell but I fought it off. Her look was a familiar one. The same one I saw while she was eating anchovies at Gordy's and it was the same one that I saw that night in the pulpit at Lequin.

But I knew she wouldn't, or as she said, she "couldn't". It made me disappointed. No, I believe "sexually frustrated" is the right term. I wanted her. Badly. Jade was my top fap. The most common deposit at "The Crank Bank", if you will. She was so fucking sexy and that night was the worst case of lust that I have ever had.

I grabbed her by the neck. My thumb wrapped around the front of her throat. With the other hand, I grabbed her ass. I sucked on her neck forcefully and slipped my fingers under her skirt. My four fingers meandered between her legs and through the lace of her thong. I massaged her and my index finger entered. It was tight. She let out a moan, but I wanted her to scream.

"Where's Sasha?" Pears asked.

"Oh no..." I thought.

"Marco's here..." Jade said slyly. "You know what that means..."

Pears made a circle with his thumb and index finger with one hand, forming a circle. With his other index finger, he penetrated the circle. Matt, Gordy and I howled with laughter, but Jade let out a disgusted "ugh!" She then continued, "But you're right..."

Kyle and Ellie Reynolds passed us once again on their way to the beer pong table. Their cups were filled and the looked intent on dominating another poor duo that couldn't handle Salt Springs' most provocative set of twins. Megan Birch remained at the other side of the table, drinking out of a plastic cup. She leaned on the table, looking for her partner, Duncan Lee.

"Where'd he go, Meg?" Ellie asked.

Megan started to look around the room. "I down't knowwww..." Megan slurred. Her head continued to swivel, until she saw the long, brown hair. "Gordy!"

His eyes widened and you could see his gut fall into his lap. He turned toward her. "Hi, Me..Megan…" he stuttered and pushed his glassed up with his forefinger.

"I need a parrrrrrtnurrrrrr…." she said. "Come play!"

"Get it done, Rockstar." Jade looked at him and smiled. "Go get her."

He looked at Jade and took an exaggerated deep breath. A large smile flashed on his face and he flipped his hair, "Wish me luck."

Gordy walked toward the beer pong table. His strut was confident but we weren't overly optimistic about his chances. Gordy's wardrobe consisted of t-shirts with heavy metal band's logos on the front and the baggiest jeans known to man.

And that is exactly what he was wearing. Baggy blue jeans that were tattered at the hem and an extra-large Led Zepplin t-shirt that draped over his 160 pound frame.

"I'd pay a lot of money to see that work out for him." Pears said. Megan handed Gordy a ping pong ball. We couldn't hear them but it looked as if she were telling him the rules. She acted like she was shooting it, but explaining *how* to shoot it at the same time. Her mouth moved with the motions of her hands and Gordy just stared at her blankly.

"Same here, brother." Matt replied. "They don't get a whole lot better than him."

We watched them from the other side of the kitchen. Megan missed her first shot badly, but Gordy drained his. Nothing but the bottom of the cup, like he was some seasoned frat boy from James Madison University.

"Allie..." I heard behind us.

"Hey, Mike..." it was Alexandra Maddox's voice. Gordy, Pears, Matt and I knew of her for years. She was one of the famous hot chicks from our rival school. Every small high school has them. Dudes always want to go over and tame the strange from the rival. Pisses all of the guys off. They're their territory, right? No, fuck that.

Jade and Sasha knew her well, though. Well enough to know that she does by Allie.

Our attention split between the beer pong contest and the conversation behind us. Kyle and Ellie both missed, so there was Gordy and Megan. Up a cup.

"Didn't know that you were gonna be here." Mike said.

"Mmhmmm.." Alexandra hummed flirtatiously. "I'm sure…"

"Naw, really…" Mike replied. His voice was low and cool. Like a douche. He sounded like a fucking asshole, because he was. Crusty ass, motherfucker. Dude's nutsack was like the Bi-Lo Deli: crabs everywhere. His arrogant voice continued, "Had no clue."

"Oh, yeah?" Alexandra said and took a sip out of her cup. Her eyes rolled up at him seductively. Alexandra tugged on her cami, making sure that even a little more of her titties popped. "So, when am I going to pay you back on that deal?"

He walked over to her and started to caress her side. "You want to do that now?" he asked.

Gordy sank another one. He and Megan were up three cups.

"Can't really do it in school." Alexandra took a finger and traced an outline on Mike's pecs. She looked up at him and undressed him with her eyes. "Fuck me right here." she whispered in his ear.

Mike grabbed her by the waist with both hands and started to suck on her neck.

Alexandra didn't have a clue that Mike was just finger blasting Sara O'Sullivan on the couch. Maybe if she would have known that, she wouldn't have been so promiscuous and desperate to cash in on this deal.

"Jade…" I said. "What the fuck is going on back there?"

"Mike's dad is Troy's softball coach. Allie plays." Jade said. "And Allie got caught at a party two weeks ago and Mike's dad was gonna kick her off the team. But Mike talked his dad off of it."

"Oh…" I said.

"Yeah…" Jade said coldly, "The old, 'I did this so you fuck me' routine."

I'd love to…

Jade continued, "Allie's wanted to fuck him forever, though.. Don't get it. He's a fucking asshole."

"Wait a minute!" Pears said and took another long chug of beer. "You mean to tell me that chicks want to fuck guys just as bad as guys want to fuck chicks?"

"Yeah." Jade said. "We just don't talk about it all the time like you clowns."

I could feel the blood rush. To think that Jade had lustful thoughts too was fucking sexy, but Pears yelled, "WHOA WAIT ANOTHER FUCKIN' MINUTE! Who do you want to fuck Jade?"

Now I was nervous. What was she going to say? Me? Someone else? But, fuck, what did I care? I just wanted to have sex with her. Nothing more. But what sucked is that she was like a sister… almost. No, she wasn't like my sister, she was a really good friend. You can't be into your friends.

Actually, you can. I was still so conflicted.

"No one!" she yelled.

"Nahhhh! Nahhhhh!" Pears drunkenly disagreed. "You just said chicks want to fuck as bad as guys…"

"Franklin." Jade demanded jokingly. "Shut the fuck up."

We heard cheering from the kitchen table. Megan wrapped her arms around Gordy and jumped up and down. His face was a Christmas Tree and Megan was the gifts underneath.

"Nice fucking game, Gordy." Kyle said proudly. "Fucking Rookie of the Year over here."

"Holy shit, they won." Jade laughed.

Glasses clinked from behind us. Mike Wilde kissed Alexandra's neck from shoulder blade to ear. He leveraged her ass with his hand, and thrust his clothed midsection into hers. Alexandra spread her legs, letting the friction between her and Mike get deeper. She moaned loudly.

Mike unlatched his mouth from her neck and move to her mouth. His tongue entered her mouth first and he grabbed her boob. He groped it and she enjoyed it. A lot. Her dry-humping was just as forceful as his. "Fuck me." she moaned. "Take me upstairs. Fuck me."

"No rooms." he said and made his way back to her neck. He wasn't wrong. From the sounds of things, every room was occupied. Even the bathrooms. Sasha and Marco. Sara and Dave. I saw Dom Vermetti and Molly Grant go into one of the bathrooms.

"Fuck me in your car." Alexandra demanded.

"No room, baby." Both hands groped her boobs now. He pressed them together and shoved his face between them.

"Fucking take me somewhere then." Alexandra moaned and started to rub between her legs under her skirt. "I fucking need you."

"Mmmm..." he released his face from her chest. "I know where to go."

Mike and Alexandra left the kitchen, walked down the hallway and out the door.

"Jesus Christ." Pears said. "Thank God that's over..."

"You aren't fucking kidding." Jade said.

"Rematch!" I heard Ellie say from the beer pong table.

"Bring it on!" Gordy yelled. Megan finished off her drink and agreed. But after a moment though, she needed a refill.

A congregation circled the table, watching Gordy with amazement. This motherfucker could ball, man. It was like Charlie Murphy watching Prince play basketball in that episode of Chappelle's Show.

Gordy was an enigma. The quiet, nerdy kid was finally coming out of his shell. Last week everyone discovered he can fucking rip on the guitar, and now he is some drinking game hero.

He made four shots in a row. All four were before the Reynolds's could even make one.

Pears looked at me and said, "Bro, what the fuck is going on with him?"

"No clue, bro."

Gordy sunk three more consecutively, with Megan adding one make to the mix by some miracle. Megan leaned up against the table. Without it, she'd be on her face. Blonde strands of hair hung in front of her face like electrical wires. Her eyes were dead and her neck was the consistency of a Ramen Noodle.

One cup left for Gordy and Megan to knock out. "Come on, Gord-O!" Jade yelled.

He sunk it and the crowd went wild. Megan couldn't even get off a shot but it didn't matter. Kyle and Ellie missed their redemption shots. Gordy and Megan were victorious once again.

Gordy didn't have time to celebrate. A second after Kyle missed his final shot, Gordy heard Megan mumble, "Gordy, can you help me to the bathroom?"

Megan's face was green and she couldn't stand up on her own. I helped him drape one of her arms over him. It wasn't a comfortable looking situation for Gordy. He had to bend over to a right angle to support her being he was double her height.

"Good luck, buddy." I slapped him on the back as he began helping Megan to the bathroom.

"This is all I ever wanted, Zack." He smiled at me.

"You're a sick bastard, Gordy."

CHAPTER 61: A Wet Drive

Alexandra's forearm began to cramp. She had stroked him off for the last ten minutes as he swerved on the back roads of Bradford County.

She had no clue where they were going, but she knew that she was on her way to climax. And she didn't even need his dick. Her grip tightened when she could feel herself coming. Mike's fingers caressed gently between her legs.

Alexandra grabbed his wrist with her free hand and pulled him away. Her mouth moved to his neck, she whispered, "You're turn." And her lips strayed away to his lap.

Her head bobbed front to back. She swirled her tongue around his head and then continued fellatio.

They hit a bump in the road. Mike's dick stabbed her uvula and she choked.

"Oh, fuck…" Mike said. "Sorry."

Alexandra stopped to catch her breath, and to make sure that she wasn't going to vomit all over his member and blue jeans. She looked up and offered a seductive grin, "No problem…"

Mike pulled her dirty blonde hair back and she continued to suck. She knew they were long out of town. Streetlights had ceased and the road was rough, but not bumpy. Alexandra wondered where they were going, but wherever it was, they'd be alone and she was for sure going to be railed by the Wilde one.

He reached his arm around her and played with her ass. His fingers made their way under her skirt and they were once again penetrating her. She liked it. Loved it. It didn't take long for her to climax again.

She lifted her head and rested it on his stomach. Her hand returned to his shaft and she stroked. She could see out of the rain soaked windshield. Pine trees lined each side of the road.

"Where we going?" she asked.

"Somewhere I know no body will be." He said lowly to her and slapped her bubble butt. She let out a moan and he did it again. "You like that, baby?"

"Mmmmm.." she moaned. "I fucking love it."

She saw now that the tree line ended up the road on the left side. A an old barn with siding torn off of it sat in the void of trees. Passed that barn was a road that led up a hill.

Alexandra's mouth returned to Mike's lap when she heard the clicking on the turn signal on the dashboard.

Chapter 62: Gordy and Megan

Chunks of angel hair and ground beef plopped into the toilet. Water splattered over the top of the toilet bowl. Another heave. This one was mostly liquid. A reddish brown smelling of stale Coca-Cola.

Gordy held her hair back with one hand and rubbed her back with the other. "You're okay…" Gordy assured her. "All good."

Megan limply laid with her arm extended around the toilet bowl. Her forehead rested on the seat. Gordy couldn't see any more come out but he heard it.

Five minutes passed after Gordy heard the last plop. He released her hair, but kept rubbing her back.

"Megan?" he asked. "Megan, you awake?"

She grunted.

"I'm going to take you to bed, alright?" Gordy asked.

Megan nodded her head and turned toward him. She was still beautiful, even in her semi-conscious state. Her eyes remained closed and she reached for Gordy like a child wanted to be held. He picked her up. One of her arms dangled over his shoulder loosely and his hand supported her around her waist.

He was able to turn the knob and he leaned into the door to open it. Gordy struggled as he carried her dead weight down the hall. He heard the squeak from her Converse sneakers dragging on the marble floor. Megan had accidentally trapped some of his locks between her body and his. With each stride, it pulled on his scalp painfully.

"Gordy!" Jade yelled as she ran down the long hallway. "There is a couch in the basement. That'll be way better for her.

"I'm not going to put her in the basement, Jade." Gordy said sternly.

"Gordy…" Jade replied sympathetically. "Trust me. It's just as nice down there as it is upstairs. Whole thing is redone."

Jade grabbed Megan's other arm and draped it over her shoulder. They carried her down the hall to the staircase to the basement like a pair of trainers carrying a player off the field who just tore their ACL.

She was right. It was just as nice. The O'Sullivan's basement was just like their upstairs. There was a kitchen, complete with a bar. A game room. Gordy thought about going upstairs and challenging Pears to some billiards.

But directly at the bottom of the stairs was a room that looked just like their large communal area upstairs, without the chandelier. Gordy and Jade laid Megan down and turned her on her side. In the associating bathroom downstairs was a mop bucket. They placed it next to the couch.

"You're a good fucking guy, Gordy." Jade said and rubbed his shoulder.

"Thanks..." he replied. "Jade, maybe it is because I've been drinking—"

"Gord, you've had two beers..."

"Yeah, I know but they were Yuengling..." Gordy refuted.

"Those are only like five perc—" Jade cut herself off. He wasn't seasoned to the drink and she adored him. He had something to say, so she held off. "Never mind. Continue?"

"I love her." Gordy pointed at Megan. "I've had a crush on her since Kindergarten. She's so pretty and nice. I've known it since 10th grade, Jade. I love her..."

Jade wrapped her arm around his shoulder and squeezed him toward her. She rested her head on his upper arm, not shoulder. Gordy had about nine inches in height on Jade.

"I know you do." Jade answered sincerely. "I don't blame you. She's great."

"I just don't know how to ask her out, you know?" Gordy said. "Fuck... I don't stand a chance anyways..."

It made Jade upset, but he was probably right. But she knew that Megan was too nice to shoot him down. She was sure to let him down easy.

Jade looked at Megan on the couch. She only stood about 5'2. Cute and blonde. Had emerald-green eyes. Her personality was fantastic. One of those kids that was always happy. She was modest too. Jade always admired it. *"Bitch has some features..."* Jade always thought. Megan had an ass and one hell of a rack. But guys didn't seem to pay attention because she would never flaunt it. Except for Gordy.

Jade then turned her head toward Gordy. Gordy wasn't ugly. Hell, he was actually pretty damn good-looking. Tall but a little too skinny. Actually, he was way too skinny. His skin was flawless and stayed tan even in the dead of winter. And then there were his dark brown eyes and darker hair. She always thought that Gordy just needed some fixing up. Get contacts. Lose the glasses and cut the hair short.

But then what would Gordy be? Would he take on a different role? If he did those things, would he still have been in their friend group? Fuck, he might not have even been in her Psych class.

While standing in that basement she realized that she was wrong all along. Gordy was perfect the way he was. She couldn't have asked for a better friend.

"Come back upstairs, Gordy." Jade said. "She's going to be fine."

"Jade…" Gordy said. "I think I might stay down here with her."

She knew that is what he wanted. "No problem, kid. I'll let you know if we leave or anything."

"Thanks." he said and sat down on the end of the couch by Megan's feet.

Jade returned upstairs.

Chapter 63: The Driveway

Mike reached under his seat, looking for the lever
to push it back. With his other hand, he held
Alexandra's hair back and she massaged him with
her lips.

She felt his seat slide back to its point of no return
and she lifted her head for the first time since they
reached a complete stop. Rain splattered onto the
windshield at the heaviest pace of the night. Mike's
Mazda Miata was off but the headlights were still
on. They brightened the cemetery. White
gravestones sprinkled the yard next to the large
white church that loomed over the hillside.

Alexandra had never been inside, nor had she ever
been on the property before but she knew where
she was. She knelt on the passenger's seat, facing
Mike. "I'm *not* going in there..." she said.

"Don't have to." He replied and motioned for her
to get on top of him. She obliged. Alexandra
straddled him. Her hands gripped his shoulders as
he led himself into her.

He thrusted lightly and she rode. But with each
hump, the top of her head smacked against the
roof. She cocked her head to the side, burying her
ear in his shoulder.

It didn't help. Her temple smacked the roof of the car. Mike wasn't altered though. He kept plunging into her.

"Mike…" she said. "I'm hitting my head."

"Shit…" Mike said and pulled himself out of her. Alexandra leaned back onto the steering wheel while they pondered what positions would work in the two-seater.

"Can we take the top down?" Alexandra asked.

"Can't." Mike said, staring right at her large bust.

Mike felt her stomach and then reached around to give her ass a grab. He kissed her neck. One of his hands made its way up to her chest, a finger on his other hand entered her.

"Ohhhh fuckkkkk." she moaned. Both of his hands were on her chest now. He squeezed her large breasts together and released. Mike lifted her shirt, exposing her pink bra. He squeezed them together again and nestled his face between them.

Alexandra's back began to cramp, but the friction she felt between her legs made her spine tingle. She could feel her underwear getting wetter by the second.

She needed him.

"Fuck it..." she moaned. She looked down at Mike, who had a mouthful of the inside of her boob.

He released abruptly. She felt her breast jiggle. It felt wonderful.

"What?" Mike asked.

"Take me inside." Alexandra replied.

"Inside where?"

Alexandra pointed her finger in the direction of the graveyard. "Take me in the church."

Chapter 64: Pong

"Well guys, we lost him…" Jade said as she approached Pears, Matt and I.

"Gord?" I asked.

"Yep." Jade replied. "Said he wanted to stay down there with her."

"Oh Gordy…" Matt said as he took another sip of the same beer he'd been nursing for three hours.

The kitchen was much less congested than it was earlier. Mike and Alexandra had thankfully left. Gordy took Megan away, which led to much less entertaining beer pong matchups. But Kyle and Ellie Reynolds still manned the table.

"Jade!" Ellie yelled from the table. Ping pong ball in one hand and a beer in the other. "Get a partner!"

"Pears." Jade demanded. "Let's go."

"Why not me?" Matt asked curiously.

Jade didn't say a word. She looked at him stupidly and pointed at his can of Bud Light. He understood. Matt nodded his head in agreement as Jade pulled Pears toward the table.

"Looks like it's just you and me, brother." I said.

"Yes, sir." Matt replied. "Not going to lie, man. I'm not having that great of a time."

"Oh no..." I responded. "This shit fucking sucks."

We both laughed. "Want to go out to the fucking porch or something?" I asked.

"Hell yes." Matt answered. We walked out of the kitchen and down the marble hall. The living room was still infested with drunken juveniles. Dave Ramsey and Sara O'Sullivan were making their way down the steps. Several hooted at them. They looked like a homeless couple. Their hair was a mess and their clothes were stretched. Half of Dave's shirt was tucked in and Sara's shirt hung off of her shoulder. There was no doubt where they were coming from. Literally.

Matt and I took one last glance in the living room. Danny McBride was on the couch trying to swoon Courtney Winthrop. *Good luck with the one, fella. Fighting a losing battle on that one...* Lincoln Montgomery met Dave Ramsey at the base of the stairs with a beer. They clashed them together like Stone Cold Steve Austin and they both chugged. Hannah Seeley stood with Kristen Leonard, Miley Machmer and a group of other girls who attended Troy High School. They were really nice to look at, but the Troy Herem didn't quite look right without Alexandra Maddox.

I wondered where they went. I'd like to avoid that place at all fucking costs. Wherever it was, it definitely wasn't the O'Sullivan's front porch.

Matt opened the door and I joined him outside.

Chapter 65: Mike and Alexandra

Mike wrapped his arms around her and kissed her neck from behind. Alexandra's back arched, her ass grinded into his groin as she untied the baler twine from the nail. She let go of the string and the door creaked open. The smell of musk lingered around them but their lust helped them fight through the smell. Alexandra grabbed his bulge and turned around. She wrapped her arms around his neck and led him into the church.

Their kiss broke at the front of the sanctuary. They looked around. Small, wooden pews filled the room from both the first floor from wall to wall. Dirt covered the hardwood floor in sheets of brownish gray.

But directly next to them was the large cylindrical structure that was accompanied by a staircase. It stood at the front of the sanctuary, looking over the pews.

"Up there." Alexandra demanded. She led Mike up the stairs.

This was better. The pulpit was roomy. Two benches sat on the inside. Alexandra leaned on the wall, facing Mike and rested her elbows on the ledge. Mike looked her over like a lion would a gazelle. She flipped her dirty blonde hair over her shoulder her puffed out her d-cups.

Mike walked to her and grabbed them. He feasted on her neck as he took her shirt off. She unzipped her pants and jerked him off.

He strayed one of his hands from her chest and worked on her panties. He got them down to the middle of her thighs before she helped take them down the rest of the way.

Mike lifted one of her legs and placed her foot on the bench inside the pulpit. He entered her and she moaned. She was tight and he was large. He swayed into her slowly but his speed increased.

It was one of the best he'd had, and that's saying something. She was the sexiest he'd had, and that's saying something too. Even Mike Wilde himself was having a hard time controlling himself.

He fucked her hard. Alexandra tits bounced with grace as he entered her rapidly. Her fingernails punctured his back in streaks. Blood leaks slowly out of the scratches but it didn't matter. Her ass started to bruise already from Mike's grip.

"Oooooohhhhh fuckkkk!" she cried. His humps were harder and faster than she ever had. He also filled her the best. She was climaxing. Her nails dug into his back harder and she screamed. "Oh fuck me!! Harder, daddy. Harder!"

It was hot. He fucked as hard as he could when her back arched. Mike grabbed her long hair and pulled, trying to hold himself from coming. He could feel himself start to fill, but he didn't want to be done.

He called the "college timeout". Mike pulled out and kissed her for a minute so he could cool off. If he were to swim right now, the water would sizzle around his groin. Alexandra felt for him, "You aren't done yet, are you?"

"Fuck no." Mike said and turned her around. Her elbows rested on the pulpit's ledge and she faced out toward the sanctuary. Alexandra's ass was flawless. Pear shaped with smooth skin. Mike caressed her cheeks and gave one a slap. He was about to enter her.

"Nolan?" Alexandra said and stood up.

In the third pew was her ex-boyfriend, Nolan Seeley.

"Seeley?" Mike's member went limp and his skin turned white. As if he saw a ghost.

Nolan said nothing. He sat silently with a face full
of anger. Both brows scowled over puckered lips.
His shoulders looked tense, even covered by a
bulky Elmira Jackals jersey.

"Nolan!" Alexandra's voice raised. "What the fuck?
I thought you were dead!"

Nolan's sharp brown eyes darted to her. A
deformed hand brushed his wavy black hair to the
side. "Yeah?" he asked.

"Yes!" Alexandra picked up her shirt from the
bench and put it on. "Where the fuck have you
been? Where's Eric? Where's De—"

"I have a question, Allie." Nolan interrupted. He
was monotone. His voice didn't sway. "Did you
think I was dead when you fucked Dean?"

Alexandra looked down guiltily, "Nolan, I was
drunk." She said with sorrow. "I'm sorry."

"Hmm." A dark liquid spewed out of his mouth
when he grunted. It fell onto the white jersey and
without moving his head, his eyes turned to Mike.

"You tell her?" he asked.

"Nolan." Mike said sharply. "What the fuck are you doing, man? Let's all go home. Forget about this shit. Okay?"

"Did you *fucking* tell her?" Nolan's scowl was filled with rage. More liquid shot out of his mouth and fell in red drops to his jersey. It started to leak out of the corners in streaks of maroon.

"Tell her about what, Nolan?" Mike asked impatiently.

"Chlamydia." Nolan said angrily.

"Nolan..." Mike's tone was defensive. "You don't want to go down this road, bro."

"What you gonna do, fight me?" Nolan asked sarcastically. More blood leaked from the corners. He gripped the pew in front of him. One hand was deformed. Fingers pointed in different directions. Broken bones shot out of his skin and blood poured from the wounds. "Alright. Great. I'm in for that. You tell her about that bitch down at Lycoming that gave you Chlamydia? Fuckin' gave it to Sara O'Sullivan and never told her either. You fucking piece of shit."

"Alright, Seeley." Mike said and dismounted the steps of the pulpit. "How about you come right fucking here and say something to me." He said and walked to the front of the sanctuary.

Alexandra's face was disgusted, "Alright, Mike. Enou—"

"Shut it, bitch." Nolan said and stood up. His midsection was a bloody, gaping hole. Threads from his jersey hung in bloody strands. He turned and started to walk down the alley. His intestine dangled from the void in his stomach. Blood marked his trail on the dirty floor as he walked toward Mike.

"Oh my fucking God!" Alexandra screamed.

"Shut the fuck up, whore!" Nolan screamed as he continued to lumber toward a frozen Mike. He was stunned. Mike started to offer words but none were regurgitated. "You a big shit now, huh? *HUH?"*

Nolan reached the first row of pews in the front, *"YOU GONNA FUCKIN' ANSWER, WILDE? YOU A BIG SHIT NOW?!?!?!"*

Mike turned and sprinted toward the front door. His shoulder rammed against the wall on the way out before it slammed in his face. Mike pulled on it, but it didn't give an inch.

Nolan took another step. His skin was paling. A vein popped out of his forehead, "Wilde! Get the fuck over here!"

Mike grabbed the broom that sat in the corner by the door. He held it in front of him defensively. Mike's strides back in to the sanctuary were slow and conservative. His heart pulsed rapidly and he could feel vomit creep into his esophagus. Alcohol boiled in his gut and he flashed memories in his mind.

He thought about how poorly he treated his mother over the years. Especially the last three. He loved her but he hadn't acted as if he did recently. His parents divorced five years ago, and he never had a great relationship with his father. It was even worse now. He hated him. The lying and the cheating tore his family apart.

Mike felt like that is what he was doing; tearing people apart. He's given Sara O'Sullivan an STD and God only knows how many more. Alexandra Maddox was sure to have it too.

It only took him four years to realize what a piece of shit he was. He walked slowly toward Nolan's tattered and torn body. Blood gushed out of his stomach profusely. Within the void, Mike saw something shiny. When he got closer, he saw what it was.

A spark plug.

Nolan smiled at Mike. His teeth were black and caked with blood clots. Blood poured out of his lips like fondue machine.

Mike swung the broom and nailed Nolan in the temple. Splinters of wood flew through the room. The top half of the handle traveled through the atmosphere and landed by Alexandra in the pulpit.

Nolan was unphased. His smile widened even larger. Blood bubbled in the void of his torso and the spark plug dropped to the floor. It rolled over the wood. Clinking and clanking it's way to Mike's feet. He looked at the bloodied hunk of metal. Three strands of hair wrapped around it along with a shred of blue fabric.

Mike looked up. Nolan reached his hands to Mike's face. His thumbs pressed in on Mike's eyes.

"Nolan, stop it!" Alexandra said but he didn't stop. Nolan dug into Mike's eye sockets. Mike struggled to swipe at Nolan's arms. It only made him stronger. One of Mike's eyeballs split open and oozed down his face. Nolan's deformed thumb was fully into Mike's skull.

Mike started to faint. He fell to his knees and Nolan supported him on the way down.

Mike other eyeball shot out and plopped to the floor. Nolan laid Mike down onto the filthy floor and mounted him. Mike's hand flailed limply, holding on to the little bit of life that he had.

"Nolan..." Alexandra cried from the pulpit. "Please... Please... Please stop..."

Nolan smiled at her. Two teeth dropped out of his gums and clanked on the floor. Blood rolled from his mouth like a waterfall. His eyes were now solid white discs.

He returned his attention to Mike underneath him. Nolan grabbed his head and smashed it into the hardwood floor. Blood flew from the back of Mike's head.

Nolan grabbed Mike's head and smashed it into the floor again. Shards of bone projected through the sanctuary.

Another crushing blow. Fluid and brains catapulted throughout the room. Alexandra saw that the floor boards under Mike were broken too.

One more hard smash. The front of Mike's face began to cave in. Nolan grabbed Mike's head and continued to bang it against the floor.

Alexandra sobbed and fell to the bench, but underneath the bench was Mike's keys. She heard more banging, but these ones were quicker and didn't sound as forceful. Alexandra reached underneath the bench and grabbed the keys.

She stood up carefully and looked over at Nolan. He continued to smash Mike's head into the floor but now, Mike only had his face. The rest of Mike's head was a fleshy casserole.

Alexandra went down a step, never moving her eyes from Nolan and Mike. Nolan continued to beat on Mike.

Another step and another. Alexandra was only one step away from being able to sprint out. She dismounted the final step and stood on the floor. Nolan was turning Mike around onto his stomach as she creeped to the door.

Nolan grabbed Mike's ears and smashed his face to the floor. Teeth scattered the floor as she reached for the door and opened it. Alexandra snuck out of the door and closed it quietly behind her. She was out. Alone on the front porch of the Lequin Church.

She heard the stories, the rumors and the legend, but never knew it to be true.

It was.

She tiptoed over the wooden porch and walked down the stone steps. When she met the welcoming moisture of the grass and the evening rain, she sprinted up the hill. Dodging the gravestones in her path. Mud flung up to her shins, splattering all over her bare legs.

Still running, she turned her head back and saw Nolan stepping off of the porch. One bloody shoe planted on the stone, the other squished into the muddy grass.

She moved faster toward Mike's car. Her shoulder smashed into the No Trespassing sign. It hurt, but it didn't break her fall. Blood started to soak through her shirt.

Nolan was completely off of the porch when she reached Mike's Miata. He left it unlocked. She got into the driver's side, expecting the engine to not start.

But it did. Against all rules of a horror movie, the car started.

"ALLIE!" she heard Nolan shout. "GET THE FUCK BACK HERE!"

Alexandra reversed the car out of the barren path off of Steam Hollow Road. The front end fishtailed through the mud and onto Steam Hollow Road. She didn't look back as she flew down the hill.

The RPM's redlined, and the speedometer's needle pointed at 60 around the right turn onto Route 6. She hit the straight stretch and hit 70 passed the old Jennings Barn.

She reached for her purse that was still on the floor in front of the passenger's seat. Gravel no longer crunched under the tires, she was on pavement and inching closer to civilization.

3:16 a.m. spread across the home screen. Over the background photo of her with her friends Kristen Leonard and Miley Machmer was a text message preview.

Mom: When will you be home?

Above it in the right hand corner of the screen, she saw that gained a bar of service. She clicked the home button and dialed...

9-1-...

A text appeared.

Mike Wilde: Don't text and drive

She dropped the phone. It bounced off of the seat and onto the floor. Her eyes returned to the road. Standing in the middle of the road was Nolan Seeley. Blood dripped from his hands and body. His bowels hung to the pavement. Abdominal muscle dangled out of the void in his stomach like a frayed hem.

He held up one of his hands and waved. A sinister grin spread across his face, almost from ear to ear.

She swerved to avoid him. A loud pop filled the atmosphere. The steering wheel wouldn't give. Alexandra heard grinding. Metal punctured through the rubber tire, exposing the wheel to the pavement.

The Miata's speedometer read 60 as it veered off of the road, crashing through guardrail and into a pine tree. Alexandra's face smashed through the windshield. Her jawbone unhinged downward. Broken teeth embedded into her gums, spraying blood over the broken glass. Her skull split open and brains projected all over the pine's branches. Alexandra's body was pinned to the seat by the car's engine that heaved through the dash and into the cab. Blood squirted out of her stomach like a geyser. Her liver released out of the void and sizzled on the steaming engine.

Doug Machmer heard the pop from the blown tire. He muted the Pirates broadcast and listened to the screeching from the main road. Doug jolted up and hustled to the living room window.

He saw oil spewing through the demolished windshield, soaking the hair of the crushed head the poked through the glass. The phone was on the end table by the door. He dialed 9-1-1.

Chapter 66: The Porch

"...and then Mr. Romanski came out and there was Pears eating that fucking cinnamon roll with the toilet paper in his hand." Matt said and burst out laughing.

I joined him in hearty laughter. "Yeah, brother... that night was fucking wonderful!" We recalled the night we toilet papered the house of our Biology teacher, Bill Romanski. Big, bald guy with a huge beard. The cat had three huge dogs, but they were nothing but lumbering oafs. He was an easy target. Super nice guy and little to no protection for his house.

The Psychology class littered his yard with toilet paper, until he came out on the porch to catch us. Directly in front of his house was Pears, about to heave a roll of toilet paper into the tree in his front yard.

"Frank!" he yelled. Pears looked at him, with a roll of Scott in one hand, and a cinnamon roll in the other.

Matt took a sip of his beer. It was still the same can he nursed all night, "Man... have you ever wondered..." he burped. "If we would have just gone toilet papering that night?"

I looked down at the brick laden porch sadly. The smell of rain filled the air and all I could hear was the downpour pelting the Earth with Rihanna and T.I.'s "Live Your Life" in the background.

"Yeah." I said reluctantly. "I have."

"You think they'd still be here?" he asked.

I could feel a knot tying in my throat. Thunder rolled and lightning cracked the sky. "I do."

"Me too." Matt replied with a sniffle. "What do you think the reason is, Zack?"

"What reason?"

"Everything happens for a reason, right?" Matt asked. "What's the reason?"

"I have no clue, brother." I said and rubbed my forehead. "Just like, how would our lives be different if we didn't go in? Do we *know* if they'd still be alive? Would Sasha be playing ball in college? Would Jade be going all the fucking way to Wyoming?"

"Butterfly effect." Matt said.

"You're goddamn right."

"Like…" Matt halted, and then continued. "Brooke helped out so much with the farm… it would all be so different. Would something have happened to her anyways, you know? Would something have happened to me? Would I have…?"

"Would you have what?" I asked.

"Nothing." Matt replied and looked down to the ground. He made fists and lightly tapped them together. His toes wriggled through his shoes and he sighed, "Never mind."

"No, Matt." I demanded and looked at him. "What were you going to say?"

"You're going to think I'm crazy…" he shook his head.

"Brother." I patted him on the shoulder, "After the last few months. I'll never think *anyone* is crazy."

"Fuck. Alright." Matt's back erected in his seat. He took another deep breath in and out. Matt pulled down his shirt that rode up over his swelling gut, "I was on a delivery the other day. Couple weeks ago, actually. I got the list. Went through and… and…"

"And…?" I asked.

"It was like the ninth or 10th stop... Fred Jennings in Lequin..." Matt's eyes turned to me. They looked tired and uncomfortable.

My eyes stared back at his. I didn't know what happened but I already believed it. "What happened, Matt?"

"Went to his house. Right by that barn." He swallowed hard, "Dropped the eggs and milk on the porch and there was an old guy in the car."

My brow furrowed with curiosity. Matt saw it. "He said that Fred was his great grandson. Fred's in his 60's. He told me it was nice that I was helping out my dad and that he and his wife never had any help... until Titus McLaughlin."

"Abraham Jennings." I said softly.

"He knew that I was thinking about hiring Duncan and Tommy, Zack. He knew!" Matt's voice raised and quivered. "And his eyes... his teeth... his—"

"Matt, buddy." I put my arm around him and he cried into my shoulder, "It's okay... I don't need to know anymore."

"He told me to go back." Matt whimpered. "He told me that we all needed to go back."

"Matt, it's okay, buddy..."

"No, man." He cried into my shoulder. "It's not. I shouldn't have said anything..."

Lightning flashed, illuminating Salt Springs as I looked over it from the O'Sullivan's front porch. "No, man..." I said. "I'm glad you did."

Matt sat back up, wiping his eyes. "You believe it?"

I actually chuckled lightly, "Yeah, of course I do." I said. "Now I have to tell you something..."

"What?"

"Remember the baseball game against Towanda?" I asked. "Where we had the ceremony for Ryan and all that?"

"Yeah..."

"Well, Ryan showed up." I said dryly. "He was there."

"...but it wasn't him, right?..." Matt asked.

"Yeah..." I replied. "It wasn't him. White truck pulled into the parking lot. Guy in a Salt Springs hoodie got out of it and went to the fence by 3rd base. I hit the dinger. Rounded third and saw him.

Face was all fuckin burnt. Lip was busted open like a hot dog."

"No fucking wa—"

"That's not it." I interrupted. "When I rounded third, all I could smell was rotten eggs. It was coming from him. I know it. Teeth were all fucked up. Tongue was black and... Matt..."

"Yeah?" he asked and looked at me intently.

"He told me to come back too."

Matt sighed and his face returned to the ground, "So what do we do?"

"You've always been the one with the answers, bro..." I replied.

Matt chuckled briefly, but then answered, "I think we need to talk to the crew..."

He pulled out his cell phone and flipped it open. The screen lit his tear soaked, but determined face. I could feel my phone vibrate in my pocket.

When I saw my phone's screen, I wasn't surprised at the text. Matt was already orchestrating. His text message read: "Breakfast at Chatterbox tomorrow."

By the time I was done reading it, he got a confirmation from Sasha and Gordy.

It was happening.

Chapter 67: Another Breakfast

I took a sip of coffee when I heard the bell jingle on the front door of the Chatterbox. It was Butch Slocum. Grease smeared all over his plain gray t-shirt and blue jeans. A handkerchief hung out of his pocket, he wiped his hands with it and yelled, "Mornin' Nora!"

Nora Kelly was the new server. She took over in February after Tracy Wilson's substance abuse issues landed her in rehabilitation. "Hi Butch." She replied coldly.

"Zackary! Matthew!" He yelled and took his seat at the bar. "Haven't seen you cock suckers for a while! How the fuck ya's been?"

"Been good, Butch…" Matt said quietly and seemingly embarrassed to be interacting with him in front of the half full diner.

"Zackary!" Butch yelled again. People at the tables casted devious stares in his direction, "Ya not even gonna fuckin' answer or what?"

"Solid, Butch." I uttered. "Been solid."

"Your dick better be solid, I'll tell yuh that! Here come's that cute lil Davidson girl of yours…" Butch yelled and people scoffed under their breath. I looked out of the diner's large front window. Jade was on her way in. "Nora! Coffee! Black! Just like how I like my women!" Butch said and whispered to me, "Black and bold, son."

The door swung open and the bell jingled again. Jade's brown University of Wyoming hoodie was loose and so were her gray sweatpants. Somehow, she still looked stunning. Her smile at Matt and I brightened the room.

"Hey guys!" she said perkily as she walked toward us with her swinging ponytail.

Jade plopped down into the chair next to me and rubbed her forehead.

"You good?" I asked her.

"Just trying to fight it off, you know..." she replied as she leaned back in her chair. She looked out of the window and pointed. "The rest are here."

Sasha's PT Cruiser rolled into the parking lot across the street. It ran over the curb and the bottom scraped on the yellow painted concrete. Through the back window you could also see Gordy's mop. The rest of the crew was arriving.

One more time, we heard the jingling of the bell.

Sasha entered first. Her wardrobe rivaled that of Jade's. Gray sweatpants hung off of her thin waist and a forest green Salt Springs Basketball hoodie on top. Gordy and Pears wore the same exact thing that they did at the party. The neck of Gordy's black Metallica t-shirt stretched, exposing his bony clavicle. A baggy navy blue sweatshirt with the Yankees logo draped over Pears' torso. They waddled on their way in, looking as if movement was a chore.

"You guys look fucking wonderful..." Matt said sarcastically.

Sasha held up a middle finger and plopped in the chair next to him. The vacant chairs on the end of the table were soon occupied by Pears and Gordy, who sat down across from each other simultaneously.

"How was you guys' night?" Jade asked.

"Ugh... fuck..." Sasha said and rubbed her head with a grimace.

"Bruh, fuck outta here..." Pears said. "You were laid up all night, you weren't even drinking..."

"Fuck you, fam!" Sasha's grimace exited her face and she looked at Pears sharply.

Nora flipped over the mugs that laid upside down on each of our placemats and filled them with coffee. A drop of Folgers fell off of its path and onto the Salt Springs Lanes advertisement on the paper placemat. I wiped it off. Smudging the ink.

"What can I get you guys?" Nora asked.

"Blueberry pancakes." Pears blurted out first. "Side of bacon... and sausage links."

"Same." Jade said. "No pork."

Matt raised a finger, "Belly buster, please."

I agreed and so did Gordy, but he demanded an extra helping of white toast. We didn't even question it anymore. Somehow this fucking kid could fit all of the food in the world somewhere in that scrawny body of his.

"French toast." Sasha concluded the order and Nora confirmed each of them. She was spot on.

"Nora!" Butch yelled from the bar. "Top me off!"

"Coming Butch..." she replied. Her voice was irritated.

"God..." Jade scoffed. She looked in Butch's direction and said, "What a fucking prick."

My spoon clinked against the inside of the coffee cup as I stirred the cream into it. The coffee became more blonde with each stir. I could hear and smell a cigarette lighting. I coughed and then caught my breath, "Definitely not the nicest."

Pears tapped Sasha with the back of his hand, gaining her attention. He pointed in the direction of the bar. Butch's asscrack caught Sasha's attention. It emerged from between his greasy blue jeans and the gray t-shirt that fit snug around his love handles.

The sight was repulsive to Sasha. She exaggerated a dry heave and Pears responded to it, "You want to stick your face between those cheeks. Don't you, Sash?"

"Ugh!" Sasha hurled and slapped Pears on the shoulder. He winced and she said, "God, fuck you!"

"Alright..." Matt said regretfully. "Zack and I were talking last night..."

"About?" Jade asked curiously.

I took another sip of coffee. I peered over the mug at my friends when I heard Matt ask, "Have... have you guys had any weird shit happen to you recently?"

"What do you mean?" Pears asked.

Nora came back with the pancakes. Two plates rested in her hand and on the inside of her forearm. In the other hand she had a plate of French toast and on that forearm she had Pears' sausage and bacon. She placed the plates in front of them after Pears, Jade and Sasha cleared their coffee cups out of her way.

"Nothing..." Matt said. "Nevermind..."

We heard a loud ping. Like a bell thatyou'd press at the deli when the butcher is in the back. There was another one. And then a third ping. It came from the bar.

"God damnit!" Butch yelled. "Fuckin' thing!"

Jade rolled her eyes and took a bite of pancakes. Pears nearly choked on his from laughing at the constant public cussing from the neighborhood buffoon.

"Zackary! Frank!" Butch yelled, but then added under his breath, "Ms. Davison, preferably."

His voice returned to a normal volume, "Can one of you kids help me with this fucking doohickey!?" he asked and held up his flip phone. "Stonehammer won't leave me the fuck alone."

"There's a button on the side, Butch." I responded. My voice was just loud enough to project 15 feet to the bar. "Click the minus until you see on the screen that it's muted."

He looked down at it and scowled, but then his face turned surprised when he found the plus and minus buttons. "Oh, well fuck me!" he said happily. "Thank yuh, Zackary."

"What's Hank got you doing, Butch?" Pears asked. Jade offered him daggers. The look you'd give someone when you just want them to shut up.

"Well, Frank." Butch said strongly. "Think the old bastard wants to open that church back up."

Each of us looked at him. I could feel vomit creep up into my throat. Jade dropped her fork with a bite of pancakes stabbed on it. It clanked on her plate and thumped on the ground at her feet. Matt spilled a stream of coffee on his girth. He didn't even feel the scald.

"Wha..." Pears stuttered. "What church?"

"That one out in Lequin." Butch said seriously. "I think the guys a fuckin' crackpot for it but fuck... his decision, ya know?"

Butch jolted up when his cellphone began vibrating in his hand. "Speakin' of the fucker..." he said and flipped the phone opened. He turned on the barstool and rested his elbow on the bar, "Hankie! The fuck ya up to?"

We sat in silence. Jade picked up her fork from the floor and placed it next to her plate. She looked down at it. Hair and fuzz glued to the pancakes. She would have been revolted, but not now. I soon saw her eyes turn to Sasha, who was slowly, but anxiously stabbing through the syrupy bread on her plate.

I heard the pitter-patter of Matt's fingers tapping on the table next to me.

"Yeah, Matt..." Gordy broke the period of silence. His voice sounded regretful, but he continued. "Something did happen to me."

"Really?" Matt asked gravely.

"Yeah." Gordy's response was strong. "At the show. I went backstage and..." Gordy started to stutter but fought through. "And... there was K... Kar... Kara. But..."

"It wasn't *really* her?" I asked confidently.

"Not even close... She was bad or something... and didn't have her tattoo." He replied. "She was being... raped... But, she wasn't? I don't even know. It was... I... I..."

"Cal and Freddy were there too" Pears replied and looked at Gordy. "They like... knew everything... Like about you guys... and Lequi—"

"I saw my parents." Sasha interrupted, still looking down and puncturing her French toast. "In Marco's kitchen. The cop that did it was there too."

Sasha looked up and stared directly at me. She twirled the fork with ease through the soggy bread. Maple syrup dripped from the fork, "My bookbag was even on the hook. It was the exact same. The same as that day..."

Jade reached her hand out and touched Sasha's forearm, "I got presents on my birthday." Jade said. She ran her tongue gently over her lips with angst, "I opened them. Some Goose, OJ and Brooke's binder. I opened the OJ and Goose first and thought it was a little fucked but the binder... there were pictures in it..."

"Pictures of what, Jade?" I asked and stared deep into her blue eyes. Dark bags hung under them and she bit her lip. She smiled through the bite and she tapped the table lightly with her closed fist.

She returned my stare, "Of us..." she said. "Of *all* of us. They weren't even just at Lequin. They were at the football game and at Gordy's."

Tears started to well in Jade's eyes, "There were pictures of Brooke in Sara's bathroom. They did it... Fucking Lequin did it..."

Her other hand cradled her forehead. Jade's lower lip quivered, "The back of it said 'come back.'"

I reached my hand out and caressed her arm. She didn't pull back and she started to cry. I looked at her and then panned the table, looking each of my best friends in the eye before I said, "I saw Ryan." I swallowed hard, feeling like my saliva was peanut butter. "At the Towanda game... I rounded third and there he was but—"

"It wasn't him." Gordy finished it for me and I nodded. My eyes returned to Jade, still stroking her arm, "He told me to come back too."

"I had a delivery out there." Matt's eyes darted around the table assuredly. "Fred Jennings. Got out my car. Dropped the stuff off on the porch.

Abraham Jennings was in my car when I got back to it. Looked like a leper. And he told me to come back."

"Who's Abraham Jennings?" Sasha asked.

"Jennings Barn." Matt responded sharply. "Right next to it."

Sasha nodded in response and then added. "Cop told me to go back…"

"Kara did too…" Gordy added and Pears was quick afterward. "So did Freddy and Cal…"

"So what do we do now?" Matt said and looked around the table to each of us. An ambulance sped by the front window of the Chatterbox with the sirens wailing. I could see out of the window that it blew the red light on Sullivan Street as Nora brought the Belly Busters to the table.

"Hey, do you kids know that Maddox girl from Troy?" she asked.

"Allie?" Jade responded. "A little."

"Oh jeez." Nora said sadly, "She died in a car accident last night."

It was all too convenient. We were with her less than 12 hours ago. We saw her. Watched her pound drink after drink and hook up with Mike Wilde in the kitchen. Too obvious to be wrong. We knew it. We didn't need any confirmation. All of us sat calmly in the wooden chairs. Jade looked into my eyes, without looking away she asked, "Where was the accident?"

"Back way from Elmira to Troy." Nora said. "Almost made it back to Troy. Someone said she must've been drunk or something. Guess it wasn't calmly... and supposedly she crashed Mikey Wilde's car? And no one knows where he is..."

Jade's eyes were still locked on mine. Her eyebrows raised and she nodded. "That's terrible." Jade's tone was glum. Her eyes left me and looked at Nora, "They're both good people."

"That it is..." Nora said and placed the Bully Busters in front of Matt, Gordy and I. "I'll be right back with the toast, Gordy."

"Thank you." Gordy responded and Nora returned to the kitchen.

"Well?" Jade asked the table, "Could that have been any more obvious?"

"I think they're back..." Gordy said.

"They never left." Matt amended. "So what do we do?"

"Well Zackary. Frank." We heard Butch's voice approach us. His gut nearly prodded the table, "Thanks for the help, fellas. I'm heading up the road. Gotta add some floorboards for Hankie."

"You're really headed up there?" Pears asked.

"Yeah, fuck it. Why not?" Butch said nonchalantly. "Not too fuckin' scary this time-a-day."

"It just gonna be you out there or...?" Pears asked again.

"Nah, Hankie's meetin' me up there." Butch said. "Said maybe a few others too."

"Alright. Well. Be safe." Pears told Butch.

"Course." Butch patted Pears and I on the back. We both looked at each other curiously and our eyes turned to Jade. She even looked confused. He never said a word to her.

It didn't seem right. Butch always had a crude comment to Jade and there was no talk about Hank reopening Lequin like there was when he took over it 2003. It wasn't popular then and it certainly wouldn't be popular now. I thought my mother would know if that was Hank's intention. My syrup laced fingers smudged the keys on my phone as I texted my mom.

"Is Hank opening Lequin back up?"

I could see Butch feeling around in the bed of his pickup through the window. He tossed ratchet straps to the side. Flinging off one of the straps was a beer can. He labored to get something out of the bed. Butch worked on it until the handle of his toolbox appeared. He held it up over the side of the truck and supported the bottom of it with his other hand.

"Not a chance, hon. Just talked to him the other day when he got home from the Poconos. Moving down to Florida. Why?"

I nudged Matt with my elbow and showed him the text message. He passed it to Gordy. Gordy to Jade. Jade to Sasha. And Sasha to Pears.

Pears and I stood up. We scurried toward the door. Pears' hip checked the side of a table, knocking the glass bottle of Heinz onto the floor. I pulled the door open vigorously. The bells jingled hard and fell off of the knob.

His pickup rolled down Sullivan Street. "Butch!" I yelled, but he never stopped.

Butch Slocum was off to Lequin.

Chapter 68: Butch

Muggy air swarmed through the open windows of Butch Slocum's Chevy Silverado. It was a humid, late spring morning. Sweat seeped through Butch's gray t-shirt and moistened the back of his leather seat.

Butch looked out the window, admiring the scenery. A peaceful graveyard surrounded the Lequin Church. Wet grass stood ankle-high. In a few months, with a few more showers, Butch was sure old Hank Stonehammer would ask him to mow the lawn.

"That's gon' be a sum bitch." Butch thought. A mosquito landed on his forearm that hung out of the driver's side window. He felt it's bite and he slapped it. The mosquito's carcass smashed and divvied into three pieces.

He left it. Over the landscape, Butch could see several hordes of mosquitos. There was a collection by the road and several over a number of graves.

But none by the church, nor did they congregate the path to get in.

Butch opened the door and sunk his feet into the mud. One of his ankles rolled. A deep tire track sunk even deeper into the Earth.

He caught himself. His hand gripped the side mirror on the truck so he wouldn't fall. Pain elevated in his ankle before he started his trek to the church. He wiggled his ankle to work out the kink. Mud flung from the tread under his boots.

Butch reached over the side of the truck's flatbed. The toolbox was heavy. He picked it up by the handle, but supported the bottom with the other hand. Once he got it out of the bed, it was easy to carry with the handle.

Butch lumbered passed the *No Trespassing* sign without anxiety. He wasn't trespassing. The proprietor specifically asked him to fix some floorboards. Specifically by the pulpit. Even though Hank wouldn't be there, he'd know which ones needed some English.

Out of the corner of his right eye, Butch could see a gravestone accompanied by a small craft of an American Flag. It waved lightly in the still air. It's peculiarity evaded Butch. He stopped and admired it without a concern.

"Thank you for yer service, soldier." Butch whispered. "Obama don't give a fuck but I do."

He continued. Muck squished under his feet. The tread of his boots sucked on the mud. He looked to the left, and could see in the window.

Barren. Empty.

He walked passed the next window, toward the front of the church. The cylindrical pulpit was void and so were the pews dedicated to those who wanted a close up and personal seat to listen to Titus McLaughlin's sermon.

His foot smacked the stone step. Caked mud released from his boot. Butch's other foot landed on the porch. Grass was included on these chunks of torn environment.

Butch stood alone on the porch, catching his breath. His chest heaved over his protruding gut. Wheezes released from his mouth while his hands rested on his hips.

He looked over the countryside. A cloudless, blue sky oversaw layers of trees and vegetation covered the land in the valley. A small barn with an associating silo parked five miles away in the distance. It looked like the only life within the radius.

Not a car engine, nor person talking. All he heard were the birds, chirping gracefully. The smell of pine filled the atmosphere.

Sweat rolled down his temple and onto his cheek slowly. He wiped it and could feel that his breathing had calmed. Butch picked up his toolbox from the porch and turned around. He was surprised to see that the front door was ajar.

He looked through the yawning doorcase. Butch could feel the emptiness of the church. A musky aroma spewed out of the open door. Ten rows of pews sat empty on the floor. Fifteen feet passed the entrance, Butch could see a shapeless void in the floor. Wood splintered each way like a bad case of bedhead on the hole's perimeter.

"Looks like Rosie O'donnell was riding a fuckin pogo stick in there." Butch thought as he entered the church. His steps sounded no different from the porch. The density of the floor on inside was the same as it was out. His boots continued to clunk as he passed the staircase to the balcony.

Leaning up against the pulpit was a large piece of plywood. A Post-It note stuck to the board.

This will do for now, Butch
Thanks
Hank

Butch put his toolbox on the floor and grabbed the both sides of the board with each hand. Small splinters jagged on the edge of the wood, busting into his skin. He felt pinches throughout both of his hands. The board wobbled in his hands, bouncing off of his gut with each step.

He plopped the board on the floor and slid it to completely cover the void. The scratching from the plywood's friction on the floorboards filled the sanctuary, echoing off of each cement wall. Butch knocked on it, to make sure no side was elevated.

None were. The board laid flat over the hole in the floor and Butch returned to the pulpit to grab the toolbox.

He clasped the cold, metal handle in his hand. Butch's back was aching, and he waddled gingerly back toward the plywood.

Lower back muscles spazzed harder with each step. He was thankful that the trot wasn't far.

Butch planted one knee on the hardwood floor and opened the tool box. A collection of nails, both large and small, laid in a side compartment.

He grabbed four. One for each corner of the board. He figured that he'd need more, but that was the start. The head and claw of a rusty hammer poked out from under screwdrivers and wrenches. He grabbed it.

It was cold, and the rusty residue sprinkled over his hand. He grabbed a nail and pinched it between his thumb and index finger. The prod of the nail poked the wood and he brought the head down on top of the nail.

Another smack to the head of the nail. He could feel the top of the nail push halfway to the floor.

Butch had to stop. The ache in his back was fierce and pulsed painfully. He bit his lip, trying to hold in a cry. A sharp pain shot into the middle of his back and into his shoulder blades.

He let out a yelp. The hammer dropped to the floor and banged on the plywood.

"Fuckin' cock sucker!!!" Butch hissed and reached his hand to his back. He massaged the area above his tailbone with his forefingers. *"God damnit!"*

"Butch!" he heard from the church's entrance. He turned around. Standing in the doorway was Hank Stonehammer wearing his patented khakis and checkered flannel. He always looked like he was about to cut down some trees. Except the old bastard looked like he could barely pick up an axe.

"What kinda way is that to talk in the Lord's house?"

"Sorry, Hankie!." Butch pivoted on his knee so he could face him. "Back's killin' me!"

"Ya know, Butchie..." Hank said and he entered the church. His loafer patted on the ground softly, reflecting the weight, or lack thereof, that came down onto the floor. "Gotta get in better shape."

Butch rubbed on his beer gut and replied, "You want some of this Hankie? Got plenty for ya." Hank took another step toward him. His defined cheekbones supported his wrinkled skin. Hank hung his old Canton Warrior ballcap on a nail that stabbed into the bannister on the staircase to the balcony. "You could use some of this, Hankie. Ain't got an ounce of it or an ass to shit it out of."

Hank rolled up the sleeves and smiled. His old voice quaked, "Why dontcha let me take care of it, Butchie. I'm just happy you thought enough to come all the way out here."

"Hankie, stay the hell back. Would ya?" Butch encouraged. Despite Butch being overweight, he would still certainly be more able to fix the floor that Hank who fought the mid-70's monster.

But Hank continued to walk, now beyond the pulpit. His smile was kind and empathetic. Despite his age, dental work was never an issue for him. In 75 years, never a cavity or any kind of oral surgery. Just the light yellow stain from coffee. Crow's feet indented by his eyes, looking like they were drawn on. The long wrinkles on his neck jiggled as he said, "Butch…" he said and took a knee next to him on the plywood. "Just go home. It's okay. I'll get the tools back to ya. Just take care of yourself."

Hank crawled on his hands and knees to finish penetrating the nail that Butch started. He took two hard whacks with the hammer and grabbed another nail. Hank pinched the nail between his index finger and thumb. He lined it even with the floor. In three whacks, Hank had the nail fastened into the wood. Connecting the board to the floor.

Butch sat on his ass next to Hank and admired his work. His gut rested in his lap. Butch's chin rested on his heaving chest. Hank was making short work of the repair, already onto the third nail. The outline of his spine was visible under the flannel. His medium-length gray hair swayed with each knock of the hammer.

"Fuck, Hankie…" Butch uttered impressed, "Got some strong bones cuz there ain't no muscle in there."

"Just gotta give it a little English, Butch." Hank gave another whack. Pressing the nail in a quarter of the way down. The tendons in his forearms flexed from supporting his body. The other arm seized again on the head of the nail. "Gotta have good aim, too." He said as he planted the hammer's head down again.

Butch was impressed. "I hope to be workin' the way you are when I'm you're a—"

The room went black. Pain arose in his side. He saw stars and felt himself weaken. His torso started to feel empty.

Colors started to emerge, but the outlines of shapes were fuzzy. He could see the outline of someone staring directly at him, but then he looked down.

His vision quickly came to. The claw of the hammer was lodged into his side. Blood spewed from the wound under his ribcage and dripped off of the head.

An old hand clutched the handle and Butch looked up. It was Hank Stonehammer. Staring directly into his face. A smile began to emerge through his winkled lips and his jowls began to expand.

Black, sharp teeth spread across his old face. His green eyes changed to plain white discs and his face paled. Streaks of blue appeared through his wrinkles.

Butch lifted his arm and he started to swing, but Butch yanked on the handle. The claw shredded through the front of his torso. Meat plopped to the ground.

"HANK!!!" Butch screamed. *"What the fuuuu—"*

Another yank. A deep gash spread across Butch's torso. Blood leaked over his grease stained t-shirt and splat on the ground in waves.

"You fat fuck!" Hank sneered through this blue lips. "I fucking fixed this floor! Not you!"

He sunk the hammer deeper into Butch's torso. Butch gurgled and hurled a mouthful of blood. It rolled down his chin and onto his chest. The front of his body was submerged with his own blood.

"The town pervert!" Hank hissed. A vein prodded out of his forehead, looking like it was about to rupture. "Not a GOD DAMN person can fucking stand you! You're nothing!"

Hank dug deeper into Butch's split open gut toward his belly button. "You. Your brother. Your mother! All of you! Fat. Fucking. Slobs!"

Butch's head was limp and dangled to his chest. Hank felt the claw on Butch's intestines. The hammer writhed and Hank pulled.

"Dave! Zack! Frank!" Hank yelled and pulled. Butch's bowels laced through the claw. "That little Davidson girl that you smash your fucking meat to... they all HATE you!"

Butch's intestines fell out like a fleshy snake. He sat lifelessly on the floor with only his weight to support him. Hank grabbed the intestine with his hands and yanked.

Over and over again.

Chapter 69: *Oh hell yeah, 69*

My mother called Hank Stonehammer immediately after I got home from the Chatterbox that Sunday morning. He had no intentions on reopening the church. Hell, every memory that he had from that church was erased. The man reopened it and held church services in there for three years, but couldn't remember a god damn minute of it. Even the time where he went back to his car for three minutes, only to come back to a churchful of bibles opened to Revelations.

Hank called the Pennsylvania State Police immediately after my mother and his conversation. Paul McBride, Canton boy, and a long-time state policeman, went out to Lequin with fellow officer and father of Salt Springs' baseball's gifted shortstop, Vick Montgomery.

On their arrival, they saw Butch Slocum, 62, of Salt Springs, Pennsylvania completely disemboweled. Coyotes were feasting on his carcass, damning most evidence.

After an autopsy, they found no DNA evidence that could have led them to a murderer.

Again, we knew. There would be no evidence. No sign of foul play. Nothing. Not a god damn thing.

Butch was dead and there would never be an explanation. Just like Alexandra's death would always be *just an accident*. Just like Nolan Seeley, Dean Vermilya and Eric Foster. Mike Wilde, Kara Murphy, Ryan Wilson, Kate Ford and Colby Baker would always *just be missing*. Brooke will always be the girl that killed herself.

But what about the others? All of the deaths in the valley over the years. Nick and Brandon Baker's accident. Kelly Kitchen's mysterious drowning. Dylan Liberati, Jared Hunt and Ashley O'Donnell's accidents too. Also there are those from more recently, with Emma Winters, Austin Pettit and Tyler Lucas.

Something was off about this one though. Yes, Butch was the town perv. Yes, there wasn't a god damn person that gave a fuck about him. And yes, *we* knew him. Just like we knew all of the people that the Lequin Church slain over the last eight months.

But he wasn't young. All the others were high schoolers. Kids. Or fucking punks most of the time.

Butch was older. Not ancient, but older. And who would be next?

Even before Butch passed, we came to the decision that we were going back for one final time. This upcoming Saturday. May 2nd.

It had to stop. The Lequin Church was destroying everything in its path and the only way that we would not be their next victims was to do one thing.

Obey. Like it told us so many times.

It told Jade to come back. It told Gordy, too. Same with Matt, Sasha, Pears and I. And even though we felt like we were immune to the pain, I thought about what it would be like to lose my mother. If somehow Lequin got to her.

I couldn't bear the thought. At all.

On Thursday, April 30th, I came to that realization. What if that happened to my mom? Or to Ms. Linda White? How would Gordy feel? How would *any* of us feel if it got to them, knowing it was our fault?

Obeying them wasn't enough. It needed to end it. Forever.

From Dylan Liberati in 2003 to Butch Slocum. It was all Lequin. No doubt. There couldn't be another victim. Another life couldn't be lost to the hands of it.

How do we end all of it? How can we kill Lequin forever?

I knew who had the answer.

Chapter 70: One Final Strike

Dave Wilson's bowling squad on Thursday nights slimmed recently with the unexpected success of Salt Springs baseball and the death of Butch Slocum. At five o'clock, Dave Ramsey threw the first pitch of the PIAA District 4 semi-finals, and at quarter after seven, we rushed the mound in celebration. Dave Ramsey pitched a gem, Dom Vermetti hit two dingers, Lincoln Montgomery and I added 3 RBI's. We beat the Sayre Redskins and advanced to the district championship baseball game for the first time ever.

At 9:00 p.m., I entered Salt Springs lanes.

"Congrats, Zack!" I heard someone say as they passed me through the doorway. It was Kirk Manson, maybe the greatest competitor in the history of the Salt Springs VFW.

"Thanks, Kirk. Appreciate it." I replied.

"Now go beat Wyalusing's ass!"

"We'll do our best."

The bowling alleys aroma was standard and once I was able to fully avoid the conversation with Kirk, I saw Dave Wilson sitting at the bar. He was the only patron left inside and he faced the television set that mounted on the wall.

His face was enlightened. The Yankees just pulled ahead of the Angels with a 3-run, 8th inning. "Mo's just gotta shut them down here, Denny!" Dave yelled to Dennis Kelly, who was flipping the large switches behind the bar. With each flip, the lighting on each lane turned off and you could hear the motor operating each lane shut off.

"Best closer of all time, Dave." Dennis replied as he wiped off the countertops of the bar. He spritzed the cleaner on the grill behind the bar and wiped that free of grease too. "I think we're in good shape here, Dave. Game's over."

I walked through the communal area of the bowling alley, weaving in and out of the tables. My hip struck one of the chairs, gaining Dennis's attention, "Well, son of a bitch! If it isn't David Wright himself!"

"Fellas..." I greeted.

"Zack!" Dave yelled happily. "Helluva game tonight, buddy! Sorry couldn't stick around after. Had to get my ass up here."

"No worries, Dave." I said and sat on the barstool next to him. "Yanks on?'

"Big inning in the 8th." Dave said and took a sip of his Diet Coke. "Bringing in Mo Rivera. Gotta shut em down."

"Sure they'll be fine."

They were fine. Rivera shut down the Angels offense and the Yankees won 7-4. Dave looked happy. Of course, he was. As a baseball fan, there are only two times of year that you get truly excited when your team wins. The first month and the last month. In between doesn't matter. Everyone goes 50-50. It is what you do with the remaining 62 games. For Dave, he's historically happy. For me, and the most pathetic organization in pro sports, the Pittsburgh Pirates, it's a little different.

But Dave looked tired. Dark sacks hung under his eyes. The bill of his Yankee cap pulled far enough over his face that it was tough to see them. When he looked at the light, he winced.

He'd been through a lot. He helped his sister, Tracy, relentlessly. A trip to her rehabilitation appointments in Sayre every other day took up two hours per. Plus his 9-5.

His exhaustion wasn't just physical, it was emotional. He saw the knot between his sister and her son untie, slowly but surely. And now, her son is gone. Ryan was as close to a son that Dave will ever have, and he missed him.

Similarly with Butch. Dave would always say, "Butch is Butch". He had his moments where he wished Butch would just 'shut the fuck up', but Dave loved Butch. Dave hated to admit it but he mourned Butch's death hard. He might have been the only one to do so.

"Alright, fellas." Dennis said, "I'm headed out. You guys too?"

"Damn, Dennis!" I joked, "I just got here and you're gonna lock up?"

Dennis laughed, "Need me at the garage in the morning, Zack. I ain't a fuckin' kid like you. Can't be up until the asshole of dawn anymore."

"Sounds like you're just a pussy to me." I responded sarcastically.

Dave joined us with laughter. He chuckled enough to jiggle his jowls, "Denny, if you wanna get outta here, I'll lock up." Dave adjusted his cap, revealing a little more of his face. "Leave the keys, get Zack a Coke and I'll put 'em in yer mailbox."

"Good enough for me." Dennis said. He placed a
set of keys and a Coke in front of us. "Congrats on
the win again, Zack. I'll definitely be in Williamsport
to watch you guys raise gold next Tuesday,"

"Thanks, Dennis." I said and he left.
"Hand me that, would ya, Zack?" Dave asked and
pointed to the remote. He flipped the channel to
TNT which aired the Houston Rockets and the
Portland Trail Blazers. Wasn't much of a game.
Metta World Peace or the artist formerly known as
Ron Artest, dropped 27 for the Rockets who were
about to end the Trail Blazers' season.

Dave took a sip of Diet Coke as the Rockets held
onto the rock to run out the clock. He winced from
the strong carbonation and said, "See the Sixers
are done? Bet that makes ya happy."

"Sure does. Go Bulls." I replied. "Now that was a
hell of a game tonight. Game seven's gonna be
great."

I was pleased. The Chicago Bulls forced a Game 7
against the Celtics after winning Game 6 in triple-
OT. I was able to watch some of it. And was ecstatic
at triple zeros once the game was over, but I didn't
enjoy the game. It wasn't from nerves, but it was
from thinking. Thinking about how I would go
about the situation I was in right now.

"Ehhh…" Dave grunted. He turned to me and smiled. "Those boys don't stand a chance."

"Probably right, Dave." I said somberly. "You always are…"

"You're damn right, Zackary." He said while taking another sip of Diet Coke.

I uttered a single chuckle. My hand craned up to my scalp and I ran my fingers through my hair, "How you holdin' up, Dave?"

Dave ran his finger around the rim of the can. He looked down and followed the tracing with his eyes, "As well as I can, buddy." He turned his face away from the can and toward me, "What about you?"

"About the same, Dave." I responded sadly. "Not gonna lie, this one's pretty disturbing."

Dave's hand stroked his chin, combing his imaginary goatee. "Yeah…" Dave paused. His eyes returned to the can and he traced again, "Pretty brutal."

"What do you think it was?" I asked.

Dave continued to run his index finger over the rim of the can, never moving his eyes this time. "Don't know." He said.

I looked at him sympathetically. False, I looked at him empathetically. I wanted him to feel better and I was going to try to make this all right. But in order to, we both had to face harsh reality.

I sighed and then said, "Yeah, you do, Dave. We both do."

Dave stopped circling the rim of the can instantly and slowly turned his head in my direction. His scowl wasn't an angry one, but it was exhausted. Like he was fighting to stay awake. His eyes drooped, black circles tattooed them underneath, "What are you talking about, Zack?"

"You told me that place was bad, Dave." I said seriously. "You were right."

"Zack, stop." Dave put up his hand, "I'm not talking about that place, buddy. I'm not gonna do i—"

"Dave, you know it was Lequin." I said. "You know it killed Butch…"

"Yes, Zack." Dave said sternly. He rested his head in his hand, "I know it was, alright?"

"How do we end it, Dave?" I asked. "Forever."

Dave looked down at the bar. He gripped the can of Diet Coke in his hand, "I don't know, Zack."

"Dave…" I said, "No one knows this town… this area… better than you. If you don't know for sure, I know you have an idea. We started it. We have to end it."

"You don't have to do shit!" Dave shouted in frustration. His voice then lowered quickly, but his tone was still sharp. "I'm not going to tell you anything, Zack. If I tell you anything, you kids will go back there and God only knows what will happen. I can't do it. Enough is enough."

"Dave, it's not just kids anymore." I said calmly. "This isn't Brooke or Nolan Seeley. He was a 62 year old man!"

"What the fuck does that have to do with anything, Zack?" Dave flexed his jaw, moving his jowls.

"Come on, Dave…" I said. "All the deaths… The 'accidents'… They were always kids. Just last week, Allie Maddox from Troy was impaled by her fucking car engine. Her head crushed through her windshield. Pretty much the same god damn thing happened to Nick and Brandon Baker. That's just three, Dave… and now a 62 year old man is fucking disemboweled by what? An animal?"

"Enough, Zack." Dave grabbed the bowling alley keys and dismounted the barstool. He began walking toward the door, evading the tables on his way to it. "Go. Get out. I'm closing up."

"Brooke Beckett had a countdown in her binder. It was the days until her mom got out of prison. You think she really killed herself?"

Dave grabbed his bowling bag off of the table, completely ignoring the question. "I'll lock you in here, Zack. Let's go."

"Oh yeah…" My voice elevated as Dave got closer to the door. He continued to disregard what I said. I watched his back turn around the final table that separated him from the door. "I guess all of those kids just 'ran away'… Kara… Kate… Mike Wilde… Colby Baker…"

"God damnit, Zack…" Dave hissed as he clutched the door handle. "Let's g—"

"It got Ryan." I shouted sharply and Dave froze. His head dropped, staring at the floor like a weight was taken off of him. Dave bit his lip and squeezed his eyes closed, looking like he was fighting off an intense sob.

"What did you say?" Dave's voice cracked.

"Dave, Matt saw it..." I croaked. A knot began to tie in my throat thinking about the Murphy's television. A tear rolled down my face, "It's a long story, Dave... But Matt saw the whole thing but... but... It was on the Murphy's television."

"The television..." Dave confirmed. He bit his lip to stop it from quivering.

"Yeah." I muttered. "I believe it. Especially after everything that has happened."

Dave took his hand off of the handle and turned to face me from the door. His hands hung to his sides limply, even with one hand gripping the bag that held his size 12 shoes and 16 pound bowling ball. The Yankees cap cocked on his head slightly to the side, covering most of his gray hair. I could see his thick lips start to quiver, jostling his flabby jowls, "What day did Ryan die, Zack?"

I looked into his eyes from across the room. My voice fought my cry, "December 8th."

"Of course he did..." Dave said sadly and he took a step back toward the bar. He placed his bag back on the same table as he picked it up from, "My nephew died on your mother's birthday."

I nodded. He continued to lumber back toward me. Dave was close enough that I could see the tears start to well in his eyes. The moisture made them sparkle intensely from the shine of the lights on the ceiling, "Zack..." his voice trembled, "I've been in love with your mother since I was 14."

I nodded.

Dave took more steps forward. Only one table separated us now, "Do you know why?" he asked.

I shook my head. I understood how someone could love that woman so much, but I had no idea about the roots of his infatuation. Dave returned to the barstool that he initially sat in, "Because your mother and I went in."

I wiped the tears from my face, "You guys went in to Lequin?"

"Yeah, Zack." Dave said regretfully. "We did."

"H...How?"

"We knew the stories. Old man McLaughlin, the wife, the kids. Sebastien Adams... Isaac McKean... all 'em. Russ Vermilya stole his old man's car, picked us up..."

"Vermilya…" I said lowly.

"Yep." Dave uttered, "Dean's grandpa."

"Jesus Christ…" I said under my breath.

"Back then it was Clete O'Brien, Toby and Miles Walker that went 'missing' and it was Rodney Young, Darlene Murphy and Randy Bishop who were in car accidents."

I sighed, and chuckled from the irony, "Bishop and Murphy…"

"Would have been Kara's great-aunt and your teacher's brother."

"…What in the fuck?…" I groaned.

"Yep." Dave said. He let out a slight sigh when he parked his ass onto the barstool. Dave arched his back and continued to say, "Toby and Miles supposedly gang banged Diana McBride. She was Miles's girlfriend. Town kinda turned on 'em. Clete was a popular kid, but never had a really close friend and his parents weren't around a lick. Ya went to his house to booze and that's it."

"Okay…" I replied, letting him know verbally that he still had my attention.

"Randy had a boat load of friends, but after he got the football scholarship from Joe Pa, he became the world's biggest asshole. Same thing with Rodney. Darlene was always a stuck up bitch. Next thing you know her Plymouth Fury is wrapped around a light pole."

Dave paused. His tired eyes looked into mine as he touched my forearm with sincerity. "What does that remind you of, Zack? Turning on friends, being a dick to those you love, or fuck, just not having any feelings toward nobody."

I got it. The dim lightbulb in my head flickered as much as it could, "Butch Slocum... not a care for anyone. Mike Wilde... a fucking asshole."

Dave nodded and I continued, "Alexandra Maddox... Kate Ford... Cheaters. Dean Vermilya and Eric Foster turned on someone they loved."

"You got it, buddy." Dave replied confidently.

"But what about ours, Dave? What about Ryan, Kara and Brooke?" The knot in my throat started to untie, but the tears still rolled.

"I could see it in her eyes the night she died, Zack. Brooke was empty. She was numb. She loved you guys but had nothing left." Dave said, "And, honestly, I love the kid like he is my own, but...

Butch's brother was awful to my sister, Zack. Just terrible. It killed me to see it and as Ryan got older, he strayed further away from her. Never had anything to do with that asshole Scott."

"And you know about Jim Murphy." Dave continued, "Mean son of a whore. Kara's mom just dealt with it because of his money. All Kara and Ryan had at the end of the day was each other, and was that even all that strong? I mean, Kara was headed to college in upstate New York while he was gonna stay here."

He was right. I hated every thought of it, but he was right. Ryan was shitty to his mother, who needed him more than ever. Kara's life at home was a disaster. Now combine both of them and their relationship. The flirting. The sexual tension. The urges and the acts were a high-speed thrill ride. But they wouldn't ever last and they put their losing battle of a relationship in front of all.

"I never thought of it that way, Dave." I said and the sobbing was almost eliminated.

"I don't know what you kids are planning. I don't know if you're going back up there or what." Dave said. "But what I do know is that you guys have probably made up your mind. And no matter what I say, you're going to do what you've already determined."

I looked down regretfully. He patted my forearm to regain my attention. I lifted my head and looked back into his eyes.

"The reason I am alive is because I love your mother and I never lost that love. The reason she is alive is that she never let go of our friendship. And *THAT* is the reason that those we love haven't been taken away by it..." Dave paused and stared deeper into my eyes, "until now."

His hand moved from my forearm and to my shoulder. He squeezed gently with care and moved it to the back of my neck. Dave pulled me in, our foreheads pressed together. His eyes rolled up and met mine, like two NFL players praying before a big game.

"Listen to me, Zack." Dave said carefully. "Please, listen to me."

I started to cry again but I nodded anyways. A tear rolled down my cheek and dropped to the floor. It splashed on the white tile. "Yeah. Dave, I will. I'll do anything..."

He poked my chest, "Whatever you do. Where ever you go in life. Don't ever lose that love. *NEVER* lose that love." Dave demanded. His voice started to waver, "And if you guys ever go back. Stay together. That's how you kill it. There aren't many people that can do it, but you guys can. You love each other, you stay together, and no matter what happens, the six of you need to remain as one."

His gripped lightened and we released our embrace. My tears soaked my face and the floor at my feet. Dave continued to stare into my eyes, "If you think you guys can do that, go back and end that fucking place forever."

We knew we could do that and two nights later, we went to end it.

Chapter 71: The Last Time

Sasha picked me up that Saturday at 11:30 p.m. Rain sprinkled on her windshield. The streetlights shined on the wet pavement on Main Street.

We took a right at Salt Springs's only red light and turned onto Troy Street. Salt Springs Lanes was one block up. Sasha saw the small alley that led to its parking lot.

She cranked the wheel and entered the alley. Her PT-Cruiser bottomed out and scraped over the crumbling concrete. She ran over a hunk of cement. T.I's voice skipped through the speakers. My ass jumped off of the seat and slammed back to it. Sasha's elbow cracked against the driver's side door.

That chunk of elevated cement marked the end of the rough road. We glided over the smooth pavement that led to the bowling alley's parking lot.

The parking lot was completed vacant, except for Gordy's Buick and the Knickerbocker's Ford Explorer.

Matt leaned up against the driver's side door wearing his green Carhart jacket. Raindrops fell on him. His hair was damp and the droplets darkened the shoulders on his jacket.

Gordy, Pears and Jade stood around him. The hood of Gordy's sweatshirt pulled up over his head. Brown hair hung in front of his shoulders through the hood. His hands plunged into the pocket on the front of his hoodie. His shoulders were raised, bracing the chilly air and Pears was doing the same. Droplets of rain fell from the brim of his Yankee flat-bill. Jade's arms folded in front of her. Raindrops deflected off of her North Face jacket as she shivered. Her teeth clanked together like a smiling wind-up toy.

We pulled up next to them. Quietly, we exited the car and walked to them. None of us said a word. Rain continued to sprinkle. Steam from our breath flew out of our mouths in the cold air.

Matt crackled a knuckle, "Ready?"

"Yep." I replied. Gordy opened the passenger's side door and sat down. Pears and Sasha got into the back seat first. They went straight to the third row of seats. Jade and I followed and sat in the middle.

Matt drove down the alley and onto Troy Street. The light at the intersection of Troy and Main was green. Matt turned left through it. The streetlights illuminated the street until Bi-Lo Grocery and then we were reliant on headlights. Matt continued by the Pump. We could see Seth Dunlap smoking a cigarette while leaning on the convenience store entrance.

The rain strengthened when we drove through LeRoy. Small streams lined the road and flowed into the storm drains. Further out of the village, the stream widened on the curb. Tires ran through it, splashing and spraying the water into a house's front yard.

We turned onto Stoney Corners Road. Rain lightened by the time we reached the T-intersection. We stopped at the stop sign. Matt looked both ways. No traffic. But the car remained still regardless. This was the point of no return. Across the street was Machmer Taxidery, the last sign of civilization on Route 6 until Elmira, New York. A wooden cross, planted into the Earth passed the taxidermist. We couldn't see specifics on it, but we knew it commemorated the life of one of Lequin's most recent victims, Alexandra Maddox.

I could see Matt take a deep breath in the rear-view. His chest heaved. He took the turn right, passing Machmer Taxidermy and the small wooden cross. The rain kept slowing. Droplets splashed on the pavement sporadically until the surface changed. Fog lingered in the middle of Route 6. It spread all over the surface from pine tree to pine tree. A fawn stood peacefully on the left side of the road, but we couldn't see it until we passed it.

Fog thickened in the mist. The drizzle added to the visual impairment. Matt drove 15 miles per hour down the muddy straightaway, until he saw the abandoned barn on the left side of the road. He knew at the end of the barn, he would need to turn left.

And he did.

The steady incline of Steam Hollow Road was also sloppy, but the Explorer made it up fine. The tree line thinned. Gravestones started to appear between the trees. Fog surrounded them on the surface.

I looked out the window, through the drops of rain that laid on the glass. There was the Lequin Church. Fog surrounded the white building, looking like Magnum 5 on the stage at the Rialto Theatre a few weeks ago.

Matt turned the car around the back of the church and into the lone parking spot. Tires sunk deeply into the mud. Mist swirled in the air. A light breeze blew around the car when Matt turned off the ignition.

We remained in the car, overseeing the ominous structure before us. It all came down to this. For the last time, we'd walk through the graveyard, pass the stones of the entire McLaughlin family, and enter the evil structure that has wreaked so much havoc in Bradford County over the last 150 years.

But we had the answer. We knew how to end it.

To get there though we'd have to infiltrate through the thick, white fog. It was so thick that it looked like you'd need to cut through it with a knife. It surrounded the church, like it was protecting it. A moat, of sorts, surrounding the castle. Instead of Gators and Crocs, it was evil personas of God only knows who.

"Alright…" Pears said regretfully. "You guys ready?"

"No other choice, right?" Matt responded, looking into the rear view mirror.

"Let's go." Gordy said and opened the passenger's side door. His Etnies sunk into the mud. With each step, a sucking noise ensued. On his fourth stride toward the church, his shoe stuck into the mud. He returned his foot to it and continued.

Matt got out, he had no issues striding through the goopy terrace in his work boots. He led the charge down the hill, toward the entrance.

Jade was next. She had few issues getting through the slop. Her boots squished into the turf and mud flung up to her ripped Hollister blue jeans. Somehow, mud flung all the way up to the back of her jacket also.

I followed behind her, waddling through to find the solid parts of the Earth. It was a failure. My Nike lost its grip on the grass and slid until my legs split. My hands plunged to the slop and I caught myself before my scrotum tore open like a Thanksgiving turkey.

Pears and Sasha fought through the middle row of seating in the Explorer and exited the car.

"Damn, nigga… what the fuck?" Sasha said as he looked at the tread of her boots. "Lucky I don't got my J's on…"

"Jesus Christ, Sash." Pears chuckled and looked down to the ground. "This is fucking terrible."

Pears and Sasha reached us. He grabbed my shoulder and massaged it with one hand, "Ready brother?"

I nodded.

"Let's fucking end this." Pears said. He and Sasha passed us. Two by two, we trekked down the sloppy side yard of the Lequin Church. Matt and Gordy sliced through the fog first and passed the No Trespassing sign. Next up was Pears and Sasha. Pears walked with his hands shoved into his pockets up to passed his wrists. Sasha's hands swayed at her sides. She snapped her fingers with each step.

Lastly was Jade and I. No tension. No speaking. Just looking to the ground. Our ears pinned back, preparing for the war we were sure we were about to encounter.

I could see the church to my left as I heard Matt's boots slap onto the stone steps. Soon Jedidiah McLaughlin's grave was immediately to my left. Matt stomped his boots on the wooden porch and Gordy did the same. Mud fell rapidly around their shoes. Soon after, Pears and Sasha climbed the steps. They ignored the mud and grass that caked to the sides and the tread of their shoes.

Jade and I reached the bottom step. We looked up at the rest of the crew who waited for us on the porch. They backed up and made room. My right foot stomped down of the first stone and then my left. Jade's feet followed exactly. Another step.

With this one I could see the goop fall from my shoes. The ledge of the wooden porch was littered with excess Earth. Jade and I pranced over it. We joined the circle of friends that stood by the shut entrance.

"Well…" Matt paused, "What do we do this time? Pray or no?"

"I don't know how much that'll do, Matt…" Jade responded.

"I agree." I said while looking at the tied baler twine behind Matt. It wrapped around the nail loosely. My eyes moved from the half-assed latch and continued, "I think we know everything we need, guys."

I looked around and saw each of them confirm in their own way. Matt and Pears nodded in response. Sasha bit her lip. Gordy lightly tapped his fists together and Jade remained silent. She looked forward with a protruded jaw. Her cheekbones flexed and she licked her lips, "Let's end this…"

Matt turned around and untied the string. The door creaked open, sounding like a hungry baby in the middle of the night until it clanked on the wall behind it.

We could see the left side of vacated pews and we could smell the musk. It smelled wet, old and dreary. The aroma poured out of the church's entrance like vomit, but it didn't repel any of us. Matt took the first step in.

"GORDY!" we heard someone scream from inside the church.

"Jesus Christ it's started already..." I thought.

Jade and I prepared to run. We shuffled toward the porch steps until we heard it again.

"GORDYYYY... JADE... *PLEASEEEEEEE...THEY LEFT MEEEE!"*

"Holy shit, Megan!" I heard Gordy yell from inside the church. Matt, Pears and Sasha stormed into the church. Jade and I's confused faces met as we were about to sprint back up the hill and into the Explorer. "Birch?" I mouthed to her and she nodded. We ran inside the church. The sleeve of my Penguins hoodie caught on the nail as we entered through the doorway and Jade was able to pass me.

"Oh my fuck!" I heard her yell from the sanctuary. I yanked on the shirt and it ripped a large streak on the upper arm. It paled in comparison to what happened to Megan Birch.

When I finally made it into the church, I was greeted by seeing Gordy next to Megan on a pew. His arm craned around her as they held his hooded sweatshirt on her face. Jade was on the other side of her, rubbing her back. Sasha, Matt and Pears stood in front of them, pondering what we should do.

Megan was crying but fading at the same time. Blood soaked through the sweatshirt and leaked between she and Gordy's fingers. It fell to the floor. Between her feet was a puddle of maroon. The musky aroma was quickly replaced by the smell of pennies when I reached Pears.

"What happened?" I whispered to Pears.

He turned his head to me and mouthed sadly, "It's bad..." Matt leaned down and put a hand on her knee. Blood dripped from Megan's face and onto his hand.

"Megan..." Matt said softly. "Let me see..." His hand reached up to her face and grabbed Gordy's bloody sweatshirt. Megan's blood seeped all of the through the cloth and onto Matt's hand as he released it from Megan's cheek.

Megan's cheek ripped from the corner of her mouth to her ear. Tendons hung out of the gap like a windchime. Broken teeth crushed back into her gums, others stabbed into her inner cheek.

My stomach turned at the sight of her obliterated face. Blood continued to pour from the gash. "What the fuck happened Megan?" I asked.

"They left me..." Megan slurred. "Emma and Danny left me... Th... Th... The m...man chased them out b...b...but they left me..."

Titus McLaughlin. Lequin found an opportunity to feast again. Emma Green and Danny McBride evaded it. We were going to make sure that Megan Birch did too.

"Doesn't matter." Gordy said started to stand. He grabbed Megan under the armpit and continued, "We need to get her to the hospital. Now."

Gordy put one of Megan's arms and placed it behind his neck. Pears did the same with the other. Her head bounced with each step that they carried her. A path of blood followed tracked their path. Gordy stumbled on the raised plywood, but he caught his footing.

Gordy and Pears eased their way toward the door with Megan between them.

"Zack, can you get the door?" Pears asked. I went ahead of them and pulled the door open. Wind swirled through the open door. Mist sprinkled through the tear on the arm of my hoodie. I felt the rain while I watched Gordy and Pears drag Megan's limp body. Jade held Gordy's balled-up, blood-soaked sweatshirt to Megan's face but it did little. Blood continued to drip out of Megan's sliced cheek. Droplets of maroon painted the front of her green Aeropostale t-shirt. Red streaks flowed down her chin like liquid in an overfilled cup.

Megan's head flopped to the side. Her eyes lifeless. Wind blew back the Columbia jacket over her t-shirt.

They stood next to me. Pears and Gordy studied the door, pondering how they'd finagle Megan out of it. All three wouldn't fit through the door at the same time. Pears shifted to the side and faced away from me.

"Alright, Megan…" Pears said and took a step toward the open door casing. "We're getting you out of here…"

"We aren't going anywhere, motherfucker!" Megan hissed and sunk her rotten teeth into Pears' neck. Pears fell to his knees and grabbed his neck. Blood spouted out of the four punctures.

Megan pounced on him. Her plain, white eyes filled with hate. The blood from her face fell on him, painting his cheeks. He spit out her blood, but his continued to flow out his neck.

"Pears!" Gordy yelled and I threw a punch to the back of Megan's head. It did nothing. Her pale hands wrapped around his throat. Veins popped below her skin. Her forearms flexed as she tightened her grip.

I brought another hammer fist down on the back of Megan's head. This time she turned to me, her rotten enamel gnashed. Bloody saliva dripped from her torn mouth like a drooling dog. Her white eyes steamed, "You should have done it, you worthless fuck!"

"Do what, Megan?" I asked harshly. Her grip lightened on Pears' throat. "Do fucking what?"

"Jump..." she hissed. "You should have jumped in front of that fucking truck!"

Pears reached up, and punched her in the sliced cheek with an open fist. Tendons flew from the impact. Blood and teeth splashed to the floor, one chunk of rotten bone dropped into Pears' eye. "Tell him, Pears..." Megan yelled. Jade and Sasha grabbed her shoulders, trying to pry her off of him. She had otherworldly strength. Her shoulders felt like cinderblocks underneath her blood soaked jacket. *"FUCKING TELL HIM PEARS!"*

"T...te...tell hi..m what?" Pears choked.

"YOU TRIED FUCKING ME!" Megan screamed. Her hands lifted Gordy's head off of the ground and she pounded him back to the hardwood floor, splashing the lake of blood beneath him. Pears' eyes became googly and his neck became limp. Blood still gushed out of the punctures, seeping through Megan's fingers. "At Emma's! You tried fucking me! *You knew Gordy loved me and you still tried you stupid fucking spick!"*

"No..." Pears coughed through the gurgling blood in his throat. "I wa... wante—"

"He wanted to!" Sasha screamed as she pulled on Megan's shoulder. Her nails punctured her shoulder, blood leaked from the wounds. "He told me! He wanted to!"

More teeth fell out of Megan's bleeding mouth, "He didn't try!" Sasha screamed, still pulling with all of her strength. "Because of Gordy! Because he knew about Gordy!!!"

Jade dropped an elbow on Megan's back and took a knee to her kidney. More teeth fell onto Pears and the floor. Blood soaked Megan up to the forearms. None of us knew how much of it was from Pears' gushing neck.

"Gordy fucking loves you, Megan!" Jade yelled. "And Pears loves Gordy! He didn't fucking try!"

"I don't love her." Gordy said, watching over Jade and Sasha attempt to pry Megan off of Pears. Matt dove in to bring in another pair of hands, but Gordy pulled him back. His stare was blank through his foggy glasses. Dark circles hung below his eyes. They were the centerpiece of his stoic glare. "Because that's not Megan."

Megan head turned almost entirely around. Her eyes turned back to their beautiful emerald green. The gash still resided on the side of her face, but the blood didn't drip and her face was unblemished. Megan's smile was back to perfect. Her eyes looked up at him softly, just like the day she came to his locker after the concert at the Rialto.

"Why don't you think it's me Gordy?" Her normal voice returned. It was soft and innocent. "Why Gordy?"

"Why are you doing this?" Gordy asked calmly. 'We're your friends, why are you doing this?"

"Because everyone's here, Gordy." she said. "We're all here."

"No it's not. That's not why. You're alive. You're home right now." Gordy said. Megan flashed a confused look at him. One eyebrow furrowed and one hand let go of Pears' neck. I grabbed Pears' hand and started to lightly pry him out from underneath Megan.

"How is he doing, Megan?" Gordy asked, not pointing at anyone. He just looked at her.

"How is who doing?" Megan said. Gordy could see her front teeth wiggle slightly with her speech.

"Your cat." Gordy said sternly. "He's sick and old. You guys might have to put him down."

Megan's eye started to twitch. Blood leaked from her pink gums.

We looked at Gordy. He was doing it. My jaw dropped as I continued to try to pry Pears from underneath her. Jade took her hands off of Megan. She took Gordy's blood soaked hoodie and placed it on Pears' oozing neck. "You only told a few people about it." Gordy continued. "One of them got you flowers. They were on your homeroom desk."

Her skin started to wrinkle. Strands of her blonde hair fell gracefully to the floor.

"You know who did that, Megan?" Gordy asked. "You know who got you those flowers?"

Megan's head shook rapidly. Falling strands turned to plopping, bloody clumps. They uprooted from her scalp.

"Me." Gordy said. "I got them for you."

Megan's teeth sprinkled the ground. Her body started to seize. Her loose skin hung from her face and jiggled from the heaving. Her head twisted, globs of hair pelted into the bloody pond below her.

"What's your cat's name, Megan?" Pears said and then his voice elevated to a holler, *"WHAT'S HIS NAME?!?!?!"*

Megan fell off of Pears and onto the floor. She laid on her side, blocking the entrance. I dragged Pears back into the sanctuary, but still watched Megan seize. Her eyes rolled back into her bald head. It smacked on the hardwood floor with each heave. The remainder of her teeth splattered to the floor. An eyeball plopped into the bloody pool.

"Chester." Gordy said. "His name is Chester."

Megan stopped seizing and laid still. We admired
her for a moment, making sure she wouldn't get
back up.

She didn't.

Pears laid lifelessly in the sanctuary. He had lost a
lot of blood, but his steady stream of blood slowed
to an ooze. Jade tossed Gordy's hoodie to the side
and cradled his neck. Blood covered her entire
jacket and her face was spotted with dried dots of
maroon. A tear rolled down her face. I reached
over Pears and wiped it off of her cheek.

"He gonna be okay?" Jade asked.

"Yes." I said confidently. Like a duck, I was calm
above the surface, but fluttering underneath. I
wasn't sold. Pears was cold and stiff. His breathing
was slow and deep. "He's gonna be fine. We just
have to get him out of here."

"Is he good?" Sasha asked. She walked into the
sanctuary and knelt next to us. Her face was calm
until she looked down at Pears' lifeless body. He
was fading. She knew it. Jade knew it. And I knew
it. Sasha looked to the floor sadly and winced,
trying to hold in her tears. She gripped Pears' knee
and a tear rolled out of her sealed eyelids.

Matt and Gordy entered the sanctuary. Their walk was slow. Matt took a knee next to Sasha. His arm rested around her. He pulled her head in and kissed the top of her head. Gordy sat on the floor next to Jade. His hand stroked Pears' arm.

Pears' head flopped onto my forearm. My arms cradled his limp head. I ran my fingers through his short hair gently. His breathing slowed even more. Pears' chest only heaved once in 10 seconds. His tan skin paled and his body chilled through his jeans and sweatshirt.

"Frankie!" we heard from the pulpit. The voice was husky and certainly familiar. Butch Slocum was standing in the pulpit. He looked out over the pews and then down to us in front of the first row. All of our faces turned to him. His asserting and dominant face stared us down. A sinister grin spread across his chubby face.

His black eyes looked between us and deep into Pears' pale face. "Fraaaaannnnkkkkiiiiiieeeeeeee..... Fraaaaaaaannnnnkkkkiiiiiieeeeee..."

"Pears, don't listen to him, buddy." I whispered to him. "We're here. Don't listen to him."

"FRAAAAAAAANNNNNNNNNNKKKKKIIIIIIEEEEEEEE" Butch's voice raised. He took a step toward the steps of the pulpit.

"Pears..." Jade said. "Listen to me..."

"Jade!" We heard from the back of the church. Heavy steps slammed on the hardwood floor. They were getting closer. "Jade! What the fuck is this?!"

It was her dad, Mark. His eyes were bulging white discs. They matched his button-down dress shirt. Sleeves rolled up to the middle of his forearms. He turned the front row of pews.

She ignored him. "Pears... I thought you were in on it... I thought you were in on it with Freddy and Cal..."

"FUCKING LOOK AT ME JADE!!!" Mark screamed through his rotting teeth and he stomped closer to us. She didn't look but I did. He was holding a sheet of paper with a large "B-" on it. "YOU DUMB FUCKING BITCH! A FUCKING B MINUS ARE YOU RETARDED?!"

"FRAAAAAAANNNNNKKKKKIIIIIEEEEEE...."

"I did. I was wrong." Jade's voice started to quiver. "I thought you had a gun in your locker that day. I thought you were going to shoot up the whole school for three years. You know why?"

"Bitch." Mark stated sharply, losing energy. He heaved with each breath. "Fucking look at me!" Jade still ignored him. She continued to look down at Pears.

"Because my dad told me you did." A tear fell from Jade's face and onto Pears' sleeve. Mark fell to a knee. His black slacks tore on the hard wood.

"He's the mayor. He's my dad. What was I supposed to fucking think?" Jade cried. Her forehead dropped to Pears' shoulder. "I'm so sorry... I'm so sorry..."

Mark tried to stand but he couldn't. He tripped and fell flat on his face. Bone fragments plunged from his face in bloody splats.

"*FRANKIIIIIEEE*" we heard again in Butch's voice. It was a little further away now. He was out of the pulpit and walking down the steps. The steps were staggered, almost clumsy but they continued to the floor.

"Matt! You fat piece of shit!" Brooke Beckett's ex-boyfriend, Shawn Pratt lumbered through the doorway. His brown hair stood up in crooked directions. Drool hung from the side of his mouth, it fell to the floor when he started speaking again, "What you taking my girl out for, huh?!?!"

Matt's face turned in his direction, "She was helping me with a del—"

I grabbed Matt's arm, interrupting him. *"Stay with us."* I mouthed to him and he nodded. Matt looked down at Pears, watching him hold onto his life. Pears' skin was whiter than the chipping paint that covered the wooden church. "Guys..." Matt said. "I loved Brooke. As more than a friend."

"I FUCKING KNEW IT!" Shawn yelled. His orange polo hung loosely on his neck and swayed with each step. "You fat fuck! Fucking delivery, my ass!"

"I never said anything because I didn't want it to separate us." Matt said. He looked into each of our eyes, "But I should have said something. I shouldn't have lived in secret."

Shawn yelled, "You would have tried fucking her if you could find your shit under that fat fucking gut!" "I should have never kept anything from you guys." One of Sasha's tears fell to Matt's Carhart jacket as he said. "Because I love you guys... and I was fucking stupid to think anything could separate us."

Shawn tripped once he passed the pulpit, falling to the plywood square that Butch Slocum placed there. His elbow drove into it, splitting the board in the middle. Wood scratched up his forearm, making him bleed from long wounds.

"Because nothing can separate us. Nothing."

"Frankiee.." we heard again, but it evolved to a different voice. A soft and husky one. Limping around the end of the pulpit was Titus McLaughlin. Moss crumbled off of his wrinkled forehead. "Frankie." He continued. His mouth was vacant.

Pears' breathing stopped. "Pears!" Jade said and slapped his leg, "Pears!"

"He's… one of…" Titus stuttered and pointed to the back wall of the balcony, "us… now…"

Our heads craned around in that direction. In the balcony was Ryan Wilson, Kara Murphy and Brooke Beckett. Ryan and Kara were completely charred and Brooke's arm was mutilated. Kate Ford and Colby Baker arose from behind them. I could see some of Kate's bashed in head. Blood and brains dripped on her shoulders. Colby's arms hung to his sides in zig zags.

Allie Maddox joined them, and so did Mike Wilde. Beyond them we saw Kelly Kitchen, her skin completely blue. Nick and Colby Baker were next to her, beaten and battered. Finally, Jared Hunt, Ashley O'donnell and Dylan Liberati walked over to join them.

We turned around and held each other tight. This was the end. Matt hugged Sasha around the neck with one arm, and clutched Pears' leg with the other. Sasha heaved her head into Pears' torso and sobbed, soaking his hoodie. Gordy looked down, tears rolled from under his steamy glasses. He grabbed Pears' cold hand and rubbed Jade's shoulder with the other. Jade's hand rested on Gordy's thigh. She rubbed back and forth gently. Her tears rolled off of her face and landed on Pears' arm. Her other hand cradled Pears' neck. I grabbed it when I checked Pears' pulse.

His heart was beating. Not strongly, but Pears was still alive somehow. Thuds came seconds apart, after I felt three, I said, "He's still here, guys. It's beating."

Each of them looked down at my hand on his neck and I nodded back at them, confirming that it was still there.

"Frankie..." Titus said and took a clumsy stride forward. "Frankie... come with me..."

"FUCK YOU!" Sasha screamed.

"Sasha..." I said, regaining her attention. Her clutch returned to Pears arm, hugging it like a child would a Teddy Bear.

"FRANKIE!" the volume of Titus's voice increased.

Sasha tightened her grip and so did Matt's. His hand squeezed his shoulder like Jade squeezed the back of Pears' neck, willing him back to life. I stroked my fingers through Pears' hair with one hand and still checking his pulse with the other. The beats were faster now and in front of me, Pears' chest started to heave.

"FRANNNKKKIIIEEEEEEE!!!!!" Fire released from Titus's ears. It spread rapidly down to his white button-down shirt. His whole torso was aflame.

He fell to the floor and seized. Titus rolled across the floor and onto the plywood, igniting the board and Shawn Pratt. Flames spread across the floor to Mark Davidson. One quarter of the sanctuary was ablaze, but the inferno spread quickly like a forest fire. Flames rolled up the pulpit. The hymnal on the ledge caught fire and blew charred paper into the atmosphere.

"Come on..." I said, wrapping an arm underneath Pears. "Let's go."

Matt hustled around our huddling group. He put an arm under Pears' back and helped me stand him up. Jade and Sasha stood behind us. They held out their hands, supporting Pears' back as we carried him toward the door.

A burning bible flew in front of us and crashed against the wall. We avoided it and continued the trek.

Flames arose through the pews and they engulfed the pulpit, shooting all of the way up to the ceiling. They closed in. The only thing separating us from the exit was Megan Birch. Her Lequin ego lay lifelessly on the floor.

"Come on!" Jade yelled! She glanced behind her, the flames closed in on her. Jade could feel the intense heat on her back. She pushed.

We pulled Pears over Megan's body. His limp feet dragged over her carcass. One got caught in the crease of her elbow, making us lose grip.

Matt, Pears and I all fell to the floor and rolled out of the church. I rolled through the excess mud that released from the boots upon our entrance. Matt's hands scraped on the wood. A brush burn developed. Blood bubbled on the torn skin.

We both looked over to Pears. His eyes blinked.

"Pears!" Gordy yelled and rushed to him.

Jade and Sasha were quick behind him. The flames followed them to the doorway, but the inferno went no further. It stayed in the church.

"Pears!" Jade cried, "P...P... Pears...!"

"Wha..." Pears grunted. "Wha..."

Matt started to stand, "No time, guys." He bent over to help Pears up. Matt threw one of Pears' hands over his shoulder. I went to help. I wrapped my arm around Pears' waist to support him.

Jade, Sasha and Gordy followed behind again, spotting Matt and I as we dragged Pears down the stone steps.

Rain continued to fall, dropping from the sky and through the thick fog. Matt and I's feet sunk into the slop of the graveyard. We fought it and carried Pears up the hill.

He started to sag between us. Jade grabbed his waist and Sasha supported under his armpits.

Beside us we could see through the church windows. Flames continued to blaze, shooting to the ceiling like fireworks. The blaze shot through the pews. One of the windows shattered, flames spewed out of the void.

In the rear window, I saw Kate Ford. She pounded on the window casing desperately. Kate was sobbing. Streaks of mascara flowed down her cheeks like a stream. She was screaming with desperation. She was trapped.

I watched her struggle. Her blue cardigan started to ignite. It shot up from her waist to her shoulders. The flames reached her hair and engulfed her face. Fire closed in on her crooked canine last.

We hustled up the hill. The American Flags stood limply next to the stones. Cloth draped lazily on the dowel. Sasha looked to it and smiled.

We did it. It was over. We dragged Pears passed the No Trespassing sign with Gordy, Sasha and Jade behind us.

Mud was thick at the top of the hill. I could feel Pears squirm in my grasp, "I'm good." He muttered. "I'm good."

He released himself from our support. Pears stood at the top of the hill, off of the church grounds. He bent over and put his hands on his knees. His back heaved three times, taking in deep breaths.

Pears stood back up. He put his arms around Matt and I, and we walked back to the Explorer. Matt crossed the front end and entered the driver's side door, Gordy entered the passenger's. Sasha, Jade, Pears and I infiltrated the back seats.

Matt turned the ignition and reversed the car. He turned down Steam Hollow Road. Flames engulfed the inside of the Lequin Church, all six windows shattered. Fire shot out each one.

But we were out. Unscathed.

But more importantly, we beat it. We ended it. Forever.

"We fucking did it." Pears said.

"Yeah..." I said. "It's over."

Matt rolled the Explorer to the stop sign at the bottom of Steam Hollow Road.

He turned right on Route 6 toward Salt Springs for the last time.

Chapter 72: Last Legs

Life, as we knew it, was over. And that was a good thing.

Two days after our last night at Lequin, we dropped the District IV baseball championship game to the Wyalusing Rams, 5-1. It wasn't even *that* competitive. Those mountain boys could have beat us by 10.

Not all stories can end perfectly, right?

I didn't even care. I walked off that field not giving a shit. Sure, I felt bad for the likes of Dave Ramsey. A kid who pitched his ass off for four years and never got to advance to the state tournament.

He cried in the on-deck circle as Danny McBride swung and missed for the third out of the game and season. I came out of the dugout and embraced him. That was the limit of my emotion.

Four and a half weeks later, we walked across the Nelle Black Auditorium stage. Emma Green, Ellie Reynolds and (the real) Megan Birch were the first on the stage. They were the class Valedictorian, Salutatorian and third-honor, respectively for the Salt Springs' Class of 2009. Sasha got recognized at graduation for her on-court accolades. Craig Bunner, our high school principal, went on for five minutes about her accomplishments. First 50 point scorer in school history... First 1,000 point scorer in school history. Later in his speech he dropped her career point total: 1,844. He also let everyone know that she was the first player in school history to record 500 rebounds. 761 to be exact.

He stood up there and said she was the best athlete in school history. He was right.

After graduation, there were two options. A banger at the O'Sullivan's or a school orchestrated all-night trip to Williamsport. Started with late-night bowling and ended with a boat ride down the Susquehanna on the Hiawatha.

We all chose the latter.

A week later Jade left for Cheyenne, Wyoming. There was no pomp and circumstance. No going away party. She drove to each of our houses to say goodbye to each of us personally.

My house was the last one she came to. We sat on the back (sorry, mom) front porch for an hour. Neither of us mentioned Lequin. We only reminisced on our last five years of friendship. There wasn't an urge. There wasn't any sexual tension. Over the last couple months, I thought I liked her, but wasn't entirely sure. I am certain that she felt the same.

She left that day and drove to Pittsburgh International Airport. Her flight departed at 3:11 p.m.

That was the last time she sat foot in Salt Springs.

Three weeks after Jade left, Pears headed to Fort Benning, Georgia. His family held a small get-together before he departed and he was excited about it. For 16 weeks, he'd bust his ass and then leave for Afghanistan.

Sasha left for Temple the first Monday of August. I knew I'd see her again soon. When she left, I hugged her and said, "See you in a month." That turned out to be untrue. Temple's schedule didn't align with Duquesne's for fall break, and after that, her basketball season ensued. It was almost a full calendar year before I saw Sasha again.

That wasn't the case with Gordy. We moved in to college the same day. Duquesne and the Art Institute of Pittsburgh's dormitories were right next door. On move in day, our families went to Hard Rock Café over the Smithfield Street Bridge in the Station Square area of Pittsburgh.

Matt stayed behind to take care of the farm. His class schedule at Lycoming College was optimal. His classes were all on Tuesday's and Thursday's.

Thanks to the glory of the social media age, we could all keep in touch... a little bit.

It wasn't easy, but I managed. We managed.

Over time it got easier and it actually got to the point that you think that you forget. New friends come and so do new relationships. But I never forgot what Dave Wilson told me at Salt Springs Lanes on April 30, 2009...

Whatever I did. Wherever I went in life, I never lost that love. I loved them and no matter how many miles separated us, we stayed together. We remained as one.

Epilogue:

I keep looking at this newspaper, thinking of the impossible. A newspaper alone is the epitome of impossible in 2019. As a journalist, it brings me a great deal of joy to feel the texture between my fingers again. I was always a hard copy kind of guy. Whether it be novels or reading the news. There's a sense of accomplishment there with each turn of the page. I don't feel that when I see the page number turn on my Kindle.

Each page turn is a clean slate. New content and context.

But when you turn enough pages, you get a new chapter. Did Emma Winters, Austin Pettit and Tyler Lucas start a new chapter?

Again, I keep looking down at this newspaper, thinking of the impossible.

But this headline is all too real:

Three Dead in Crash on Route 6
Emma Winters, 16, Austin Pettit, 17 and Tyler
Lucas, 17, all of Stoney Corners, died on impact.
Drugs, nor alcohol were a factor.

But we ended it. Lequin was engulfed in flame, but then I remember that it was only on the inside. Because it doesn't burn. It never has.

I want to think that it is impossible that it could be awakened, but then the entire idea of Lequin should be impossible to begin with.

But it wasn't impossible. It was all too real. Brooke's wrist, Kara and Ryan burning to death. The disappearance of Kate Ford, Colby Baker and Mike Wilde. Car accidents involving Alexandra Maddox, Nolan Seeley, Dean Vermilya and Eric Foster. But the most disturbing one of all, the disembowelment of Butch Slocum.

All of which were tossed to the side. Life just went on.

I hoped this wasn't the start of another chapter in Bradford County's sinister history.

Am I really supposed to head up Route 15 tomorrow to Salt Springs High School and tell the Class of 2019 how life is kittens, rainbows and ponies?

Am I supposed to just ignore the soiled ground 15 miles east of them? Am I supposed to ignore the fact that those looking over those students know the history?

And it's Alumni Weekend. The president of the Class of '99 and '89 are going to go up on stage and rant and rave about how great their lives are because of Salt Springs High. '79 and '69 would reminisce about the 'good ol' days' and maybe throw a zinger about how they better keep it clean or the millennials in attendance would be offended.

I have a good life, but I am convinced it is because I listened to Dave Wilson. I never lost that love for them. Again, they say that you make your best friends for life in college and that might be right. But the ones you grow up with are the ones who shaped you into what you grow to be.

Salt Springs High has nothing to do with the state of my life. But the people that filled those walls do. And at the Alumni Ceremony tonight, I'll think 'sorry, President of '69 and '79, I didn't have the good old days.'

But I did have people. Those people are the only reason that I didn't jump in front of that tractor trailer back in 2008. They are the reason that I developed into this person that I am today.

And they are the reason that I am alive today.

On that stage tonight, I will look over those students who just lost a classmate. I will talk to them and they will undoubtedly tune me out. They will have their iPhones out, texting and snapchatting God knows who about some old fuck that won't shut up.

I get it.

But many of them will be mourning the loss of Austin Pettit, Emma Winters and Tyler Lucas. I hope those three kids rest easy but I know they woke it back up. I know they brought Lequin back to life.

This can't happen again. Maybe there is a group at Salt Springs High that can end it. Maybe those three were in a Psychology class, and six of their classmates can go and avenge their loss.

But that isn't a guarantee.

I know of six folks that can do it and they'll all be in Bradford County in a few hours.